After what just hap **way she was staying at the farmhouse.**

"I didn't mean to overhear—"

"It's fine. Our father's missing." He rubbed the scruff on his chin and for the first time looked tired.

"I'm so sorry." She got to her feet. "You obviously have to go. Can you recommend a place for me and the baby to stay tonight? I don't want to be here after what happened, and I don't know the area."

"Pack up a few things. You can come home with me and stay at the guesthouse on my family's ranch."

Renee wasn't quite sure she'd heard Cash right. "I'm sorry. What did you just say?"

"You said yourself that it's not safe for you to sleep here. Where else are you going to go with a baby?" Those steel-gray eyes pierced her.

KIDNAPPED IN TEXAS

USA TODAY Bestselling Author

BARB HAN

Previously published as *Texas Kidnapping*
and *What She Knew*

 **HARLEQUIN**®

PLEASE RECYCLE
THIS PRODUCT IS RECYCLABLE

Recycling programs for this product may not exist in your area.

ISBN-13: 978-1-335-42723-6

Kidnapped in Texas

Copyright © 2022 by Harlequin Books S.A.

Texas Kidnapping
First published in 2020. This edition published in 2022.
Copyright © 2020 by Barb Han

What She Knew
First published in 2020. This edition published in 2022.
Copyright © 2020 by Barb Han

This edition published by arrangement with Harlequin Books S.A.

For questions and comments about the quality of this book, please contact us at CustomerService@Harlequin.com.

Harlequin Enterprises ULC
22 Adelaide St. West, 41st Floor
Toronto, Ontario M5H 4E3, Canada
www.Harlequin.com

Printed in U.S.A.

CONTENTS

USA TODAY bestselling author **Barb Han** lives in north Texas with her very own hero-worthy husband, three beautiful children, a spunky golden retriever/standard poodle mix and too many books in her to-read pile. In her downtime, she plays video games and spends much of her time on or around a basketball court. She loves interacting with readers and is grateful for their support. You can reach her at barbhan.com.

Books by Barb Han

Harlequin Intrigue

An O'Connor Family Mystery

Texas Kidnapping
Texas Target
Texas Law
Texas Baby Conspiracy
Texas Stalker

Rushing Creek Crime Spree

Cornered at Christmas
Ransom at Christmas
Ambushed at Christmas
What She Did
What She Knew
What She Saw

Visit the Author Profile page
at Harlequin.com for more titles.

TEXAS KIDNAPPING

All my love to Brandon, Jacob and Tori,
the three great loves of my life.

To Babe, my hero, for being my greatest love
and my place to call home.

Chapter One

The sound of floorboards creaking in the next room shocked Renee Smith out of a deep sleep. She forced her eyes to open, sat upright in bed and searched the unfamiliar dark room. It took a few seconds to get her bearings and for her to realize she was in her new house. She must've dozed off while working on her laptop, which was now tipped on its side. She straightened it, wishing righting her life could be so easy.

The first night in a new home and her new life hadn't exactly gone as planned. Unpacking while taking care of her six-month-old adopted daughter had proved almost comic. The day had been consumed by stumbling through feedings, diaper changings and figuring out parenting in general given this was her first go as a mother. Renee already realized the job was going to be far more difficult than she'd imagined. This had also been the most rewarding day in all of her thirty-two years of life.

That being said, Renee must've been crazy to think that after getting a few months of parenting under her belt it was a good time to change cities. She'd kept her job in order to prove stability to the adoption agency and had started working from home instead. A new life in the old apartment she'd shared with Jamison in Dallas had been out of the question. It was time to move on, figuratively, literally and in every other sense of the word.

The movers had packed up her belongings in a matter of hours. It was the unpacking while caring for a baby that was going to take forever. At this rate, the house might be unpacked by the time Abby went to college. And yet, the small Texas town was exactly the place Renee wanted to bring up her daughter.

She set aside her laptop and pushed to her feet, still half-groggy, and felt around for her glasses. Sleep and being a new mother weren't on speaking terms, let alone friends. The noise was probably just the old house settling but she wanted to check on the baby, whose room was across the hall. Since Renee wasn't completely blind and the glasses must've tumbled off her lap, she could find them in a minute.

A few steps into her walk across the room, another creak-like noise sounded. This time it registered that it might be more than just the wood flooring of her rented two-story farmhouse settling. In her half-asleep state, she realized that the floors shouldn't make a sound unless someone walked on them. A wave of panic shot through her, quickening her pace. The baby's room had paper-thin walls with only a linen closet in the hallway between them.

A couple of scenarios ran through Renee's mind, her imagination no doubt spiraling out of control. And then she remembered that the temperature had been so beautiful that she'd left the second-story window to her daughter's room open while Abby slept.

But, wait, hadn't she closed that window? Yes, she

distinctly remembered closing it, afraid she might nod off. A thump sound from the next room caused another wave of panic.

Was someone inside the house?

First nights in new places were always unsettling, but there was no way this was Renee's imagination running wild. Heart in her throat, she glanced around the small hallway, looking for something she could use to scare an intruder if there was one. An old shotgun that had been left inside the linen closet popped into her thoughts. She'd spotted it during the walk-through yesterday.

She opened the door and grabbed the weapon, checking for ammunition. The gun was ancient, and she seriously doubted it would work even with a shell. The only other weapons she could think of were her kitchen knives and those hadn't been unpacked yet. The shotgun was going to have to do.

Abby cried and that got Renee's feet moving. She ran into the room and then froze. A male figure stood between the crib and the window. He was bent over the crib. She lifted the barrel, aiming the business end at him.

"Stop or I'll shoot," she shouted at the blurry male figure who was picking up her daughter. In the dark it was impossible to see him clearly, even if she'd had her glasses on. Turning on the light could reveal the fact she didn't exactly have a real weapon.

Abby's cries fell silent and for a split second fear shot through Renee that the intruder had done something to her little girl. But Abby was winding up to release an ear-splitting wail.

Renee's heart clenched in her chest. "Put her down.

Now. Or my contractor will be picking parts of you off my wall when he brings his painter in tomorrow." Talk about making threats with no way to back them up. She could only pray that he wouldn't call her bluff. There was no painter and no contractor, but she sure as hell didn't want him to know it.

Abby was inconsolable. The man seemed to hesitate. Renee cocked the gun.

The next thing she knew, Abby was being set down inside her crib and the intruder was turning tail. She wished she could flip the light switch now so she could get a better look at the kidnapper—kidnapper!—but one look at that shotgun and she could lose all her bargaining power.

The thought of someone sneaking into her house to steal Abby caused Renee's stomach to clench and her hands to shake. Her heart pounded against her ribs so hard she feared he would hear it.

In a fluid motion, he took a couple of steps back and then was out the window a beat later. The second he disappeared, Renee moved toward the window. She withdrew her right foot the minute she planted it because of something sharp. Glass? Had the window been broken? It would explain how the man got in. She checked to make certain he was gone. A blurry figure darted across the lawn and into some kind of vehicle that was too far away for her to make out.

Now that she was safe, she set the shotgun down and moved to her daughter.

"Oh, baby. I'm so sorry. That scary man can't hurt you now." As Renee spoke the words, the weight of them struck. She cradled Abby to her chest and raced to her bedroom in order to check the lock there, needing to be certain that he couldn't surprise her from another room. He'd slipped in and out so easily. Was he familiar with the layout? Someone who'd lived here prior? One of her movers?

There weren't many people who knew she'd moved and there wasn't much to the upstairs. The layout was simple. Two bedrooms, a linen closet and a bathroom with an authentic claw-foot tub was the extent of the space. Renee second-guessed herself for putting the crib in the other bedroom instead of in hers where she could watch over the little girl constantly. A child taken from his or her own bedroom had to be every parent's worst nightmare.

While balancing the crying baby, Renee darted into her bedroom and felt around for her glasses. This time, she kept at it until she felt them. With one hand, she managed to put them on halfway straight. Next, she retrieved her cell phone from the nightstand and checked the lock on the window.

The need to check doors and windows on the first level overrode any other rational thought. She made her way downstairs and checked the front window. There were no other vehicles parked on her street.

Could someone have come through the back door? Renee ran there, too. She hadn't heard anything else. Of course, it would be next to impossible to hear anything over Abby's wails, the sound of which nearly broke Renee's heart.

She called 911 even though she doubted the dispatcher could hear her. At least the person on the other end of the line would know Renee needed help.

The minute someone answered, she immediately rattled off her name and address. "I'm new in town and someone just broke into my house and tried to kidnap my daughter. Please send someone immediately. He's out of the house but he could come back at any moment and bring friends." The thought made her shudder.

Renee listened for a response. If one came, she couldn't hear it. Abby was so worked up she was starting to choke.

The new life that was supposed to feel like a fresh start seemed to be collapsing around Renee. And she was hanging on by a thread.

US MARSHAL CASH O'CONNOR had had a night for the books. He gripped the steering wheel tighter as he navigated his rental onto the highway heading northbound, home. The felony warrant he'd forced himself out of bed at two o'clock in the morning after a whopping hour and a half of sleep to serve had gone downhill faster than an out-of-control skier on his last run.

Not only had the scumbag arms dealer Cash was trying to pick up in Houston gotten away, but the jerk had shot up Cash's service vehicle and nearly shot Cash. Traffic was bad on the I-45, making the drive back to Katy Gulch take twice as long as it should. Traffic on Texas highways was becoming as unreliable as spring thunderstorms. He never knew when they'd occur or how bad they'd get until the exact moment one struck.

It was late. Cash's stomach growled for the third time. He was in no mood to stop off for a bite. All he wanted was to get home to his log cabin–style house on the O'Connor family ranch, heat up some brisket to make a sandwich and have a cold beer. He'd skip the alcohol because he was on call, but that didn't stop him from wishing he could have one.

Instead, he'd made a pit stop for coffee. He took a sip. The cup of black coffee from the gas station that he desperately needed to keep him awake and alert tasted old and burned and a bit like what he imagined a sweaty foot might taste like. Cash figured he had no choice but to work with what he had, so he took another sip, willing the caffeine to kick in and boost his mood. To say he'd had a bad day was a lot like saying rattlesnake venom was poisonous.

A few more sips of coffee made it evident the caffeine would do little to combat his exhaustion.

It was early spring. The busiest season on the cattle ranch that his family owned and had operated for decades now. Four generations of O'Connors had worked or were working the Katy Bull Ranch, otherwise known as the KBR. And even though he and four of his brothers had other jobs, most of which were in law enforcement, everyone pitched in this time of year. Sleep was as rare as a unicorn sighting.

Finn O'Connor, the family's patriarch, had always been the epitome of strength and honor and everything good about ranching life. He was a staple in the community of Katy Gulch and used the considerable fortune the family had amassed to benefit others through charitable work mostly headed up by Cash's mother. Folks couldn't help but admire the man's generosity even if they did envy his life.

From an outsider's view, the O'Connors had it easy—easy meaning they were wealthy. But no amount of money could bring back the daughter Margaret O'Connor hadn't seen since the baby last slept in her crib at five months old. The heartache and loss Margaret and Finn endured had shaped the O'Connor family.

Tragedy had a way of doing that. It wrote a different history for those affected. One of his brothers, Riggs, worked the ranch full-time. Each brother had a home on the property in a location of his choosing. Each was expected to take his rightful place on the land at some point in the future. For now, their father and Riggs kept business under control. But Pops hadn't been himself lately. There'd been mention of him being ill but he'd reassured the family it was nothing he couldn't handle. Finn O'Connor was made of tough stock. He was a good man and the kind of father most wished they'd had. He'd been married to Cash's mother, Margaret Ann O'Connor, for the last forty-two years. Both sat on top of the O'Connor dynasty because of hard work, honesty and generosity.

Cash had noticed that Pops seemed more tired than usual. Cash chalked it up to springtime on a cattle ranch. He thought about the home that had been built for him as a gift for his twenty-first birthday that he had yet to claim. Most of his five brothers were in the same boat. Six boys. Six future inheritors of one of the largest fortunes in Texas. Not one who wanted either of their parents to die in order to fill a bank account. The O'Connor boys had all done fine in their own right. None were strangers to hard work.

There may have been six O'Connor boys but there'd been seven houses built. A lone home had been built for Cash's only sister, Caroline, a sister he'd never met. Caroline had been kidnapped at five months old and the case had long since gone cold. Even so, their mother had started planning the house on what would have been Caroline's birthday. Just like the others that would follow, the keys had been ready to be handed over exactly one year later. His mother had overseen every last detail, fretting over whether she'd picked out the right color rug for the main room or the perfect pillow sham for the bedroom. Hell, Cash wouldn't even know what a pillow sham was if his mother hadn't spoken about everything during the decorating process. The detailed planning for each home had commenced on each sibling's twentieth birthday. The keys were delivered exactly one year to the day later.

Cash's cell buzzed. With the way his day had gone he couldn't help but wonder *what now?*

As soon as he glanced at his phone and saw his brother's name, Cash pulled off the road and into a convenience store parking lot.

"What's up, bro?" Cash answered before the call rolled into voice mail.

"Where are you?" Colton asked after a perfunctory greeting. Colton was the county's sheriff. A call from him most likely didn't signal good news.

"Getting close to my exit on the highway. Why?" Cash didn't like where this conversation was headed.

"My office just got a call from our town's newest resident on Cherry Street. Seems there was an attempted kidnapping involving her six-month-old daughter. Sounds like you're closer to her street whereas I'm forty minutes away. There are no deputies in the area, either. Any chance you'd be willing to stop off and take the report?" Colton had no idea the day Cash had had.

"This bad guy still in the area?" Cash asked.

"It's a possibility. Dispatch said they could barely make out what Ms. Smith said for a baby's cries," Colton said.

"I got your back." Duty called and duty had always

taken a front seat to Cash's personal life. Besides, how much worse could his day get?

There was also something in Colton's voice that didn't sit right. Cash put the phone on Speaker and navigated back onto the highway.

"Everything good with you?" he asked Colton.

"It's Mother. She's probably worrying over nothing." Colton paused a beat. "Pops isn't answering his cell."

"Is he out on the property?"

"I keep reminding her about the dead spots on the property and he'd last been around Hunter's Rock," Colton supplied.

"That place is the worst. I never get service out there." The O'Connor ranch was vast and there were plenty of dead zones when it came to cell service. "Have you noticed that she's been acting weird ever since Pops's checkup last year?"

"I have." Static came through the line, making it sound like Colton was on the move. "She's been keeping Pops on what he jokes is a short leash."

"I had the same thought." Even so, Cash figured their father had gotten winded somewhere out on the property and was taking a minute to rest. It wasn't too surprising that their father hadn't answered any calls, considering all the patches of land with no cell service.

"This time, she's not letting it go. She begged me to put together a team to go out and search for him. That's the real reason for the call. She's worked herself into a panic and I don't think it's a good idea that I leave her alone right now even though she practically tried to shove me out the door."

"Did you call Gayle?" Their neighbor and Mother had been best friends for decades.

"She's on her way now," Colton admitted. "But if there is a kidnapper and he's in the vicinity, you know better than anyone that time is always the enemy when it comes to criminal cases."

"True," Cash agreed. "You stay put. I'll take the call. I'm almost there already. Keep me posted on Pops."

"I will," Colton promised. He supplied the basic details of the complaint.

The two ended the call as Cash pulled in front of 724 Cherry Street.

Cash walked up to the two-story farmhouse, surveying the quiet street for signs of anything out of the ordinary. The suspect might still be lurking, waiting for an opportunity for round two.

No two crime scenes were alike. No two calls the same. Variety was part of the reason Cash loved his job. But attempted kidnappings always made him think of his sister, Caroline.

He white-knuckled his cell phone as he cleared the porch steps, thinking about the impact the crime had had on his parents. It was strange how a ripple could affect so many lives after it was felt.

At least in this case, the kidnapper had failed. Even so, Cash knew firsthand just how much crime changed people, how much it had changed him.

Chapter Two

Cash performed a quick check around the perimeter of the farmhouse on Cherry Street to ensure no intruder lurked around. Dispatch hadn't classified the call as a domestic disturbance. Those could turn into the deadliest calls. He always dreaded domestic cases and traffic stops for his brother Colton, the sheriff.

Standing at the door of the two-story farmhouse with coastal-blue siding and white trim, he heard a baby wailing on the other side. He knocked hard, unsure if the mother could hear. He'd barely lifted his knuckle to tap again when the matching-color wooden door opened enough for him to stare into the palest, bluest eyes. A baby wailed in the overwrought woman's arms, and, although the mother looked frightened, her set jaw and piercing gaze dared him to take one step toward them without identifying himself.

"I'm Marshal O'Connor. You can call me Cash." He immediately produced his government-issued ID. "I was sent by the sheriff to take a report on an attempted kidnapping at this address. Are you Renee Smith?"

"I am." The beautiful redhead examined his badge before opening the door enough for him to enter.

Renee Smith stood at five feet seven inches at his

best guess. Her cheeks were flushed on otherwise creamy skin. She had on yoga pants and an oversized T-shirt, and somehow made them look sexy on her long legs and smooth curves. One look at the striking woman stirred an inappropriate attraction. Cash ignored it and refocused on why he was there in the first place.

"I'd offer coffee but—" she glanced down at the crying child in her arms that she gently rocked back and forth "—I can't seem to get her to calm down again let alone…" She flashed those desperate blues at him and his heart clenched. "You came here to take a statement, not hear about my problems."

"Looks like you're in the process of moving in." Cash's mind started running through possible suspects. In cases like these, it usually involved a family member. Based on the boxes, his first assumption was Ms. Smith's husband. He glanced at her ring finger and didn't see a gold band or a tan line. Relief he had no right to own washed over him and that annoying attraction surged.

"That's right. I'm…*we're* new in town." She sniffed and Cash realized she was trying to hide the fact that she'd been crying.

"I'm pretty good with a coffee machine if you point me in the right direction." He did his best not to shout so as not to startle the little one or upset her further. But he needed to get a description of the suspect from the child's mother as soon as possible and he figured making her a cup of brew while she calmed the baby would go a long way toward achieving that goal.

She shook her head like she was turning down his offer. Then she seemed to reconsider as she shot him another distressed look before waving him toward the back of the house. "This way."

Kitchens in farmhouses were reliably both in the back of the house and small. This one didn't disappoint. Even the stove looked like it was from the 1920s. Ms. Smith followed, repositioning the baby in her arms to cradle her up to her shoulder, bouncing the little girl whose cries were pitiful. The homeowner didn't need to tell him where the coffee maker was because it was the only appliance on the counter. He made quick work of fixing a pot while the stressed mother seemed to be pulling out all the stops to soothe the child.

"Does she take a pacifier?" Cash's brother Colton was a single father of twins who'd just turned one. This child was about half their age and Cash remembered his nephews having an awful time with teething.

The leggy redhead shot him an embarrassed look. "I'll be right back."

She disappeared out of the kitchen as Cash checked the opened box stacked on top of half a dozen others. He located a couple of mugs and rinsed them off in the sink.

The crying stopped in the other room. When Ms. Smith returned to the kitchen, she held a tight grip on her child whose eyes were finally closed as she sucked on the plastic miracle.

"I completely forgot about her pacifier." There was so much resignation in her voice. The scene unfolding appeared to be that she'd left her husband, taking their child with her, and he'd come back to claim the little girl and possibly his wife.

Cash filled the mugs with coffee. A small white table, the round kind with flaps, had been pushed up against the wall with two chairs tucked underneath. He set the fresh brew next to her where she'd taken a seat.

"Please, sit down, Mr…" She seemed to draw a blank when trying to remember his name.

"Call me Cash," he reminded her.

"I apologize for the way I answered the door." She motioned across the small table.

Cash thanked her and took a sip of black coffee. This was so much better than the burnt-tasting brew he'd picked up at the convenience store earlier. "Can you tell me exactly what happened tonight, Ms. Smith?"

"You can call me Renee and I'm not married," she said quickly, giving the impression there was a story behind those words. "I fell asleep working on my laptop upstairs. My bedroom is next door to hers. It's a beautiful night so I left the windows cracked. I woke to a sound. I wasn't sure what it was, at first, I mean, I thought I imagined it, or maybe I'd left the TV on. I was so groggy my next thought was the house settling. But then I heard it again and my heart felt like it might burst from my chest."

She stopped as though remembering made her feel like she was experiencing it all over again. A tear streamed down her cheek but she brushed it off with the back of her hand and took a sip of coffee.

Cash focused on the notebook he'd pulled from his front pocket, jotting a few pertinent details.

"What happened next?" He glanced up and realized what a mistake that was. Those sky blue eyes pierced him. They were the color of a perfect summer-morning sky. The kind with white puffy clouds against a blue so soft, so pale, so delicate. Damn if he wasn't waxing poetic.

"I saw him." She visibly shuddered at the memory. "He was standing over her crib. The window was wide open and he was bent over, picking her up." She paused a beat. "A noise scared me. I remembered there was a shotgun in the hall closet. It had no shells in or near it but that was all I had to use. So, when I saw the man standing over my daughter's crib, I pointed it at him and told him to get the hell out of my house."

"What did he look like?" Cash perked up.

"It was dark. I was confused and scared. I'm pretty sure my hands were shaking. I had a tight grip on that weapon. For a split second, I considered turning on the light but quickly thought against it because I didn't want him to see the gun was useless. Plus, honestly, I wasn't sure how it all worked, if he could somehow tell it wasn't loaded. The light from the full moon outside Abby's window made it easy enough to see but he was nothing more than a shadow."

"Can you give me a general idea of height and weight?" Cash asked.

"He was taller than me, so maybe five feet, nine inches." She looked up and to the right, recalling facts. "He was medium build from what I could tell. I mean, he wore a hoodie so that's all I could see clearly. I think he had something on his face, too. Maybe a mask. Whatever it was, it was dark and kind of fitted. Shades covered his eyes so I couldn't see the color. Not that I would've been able to anyway at that distance. I think he meant to creep in and out without ever being heard."

"Excuse me for one second. The sheriff is waiting for a description." Cash fished his cell out of his jacket pocket and held it up. He needed to relay the information as soon as possible, however little it was to go on.

Katy Gulch's population was fifty-three percent male. This guy had medium height and build which narrowed the field. He had to be young or in great shape in order to scale the fence. He might've known the layout in advance.

Cash texted the information to Colton so he could issue a BOLO to his deputies. He glanced up at Renee. "Who was in the house today?"

"No one except for movers early this morning." She rattled off the name of the moving company. Her gaze narrowed. "There were four of them, but they were pretty big guys. Except for one, he might be a possibility."

"Did he mention his name?"

She shook her head. "He hung toward the back of the group. The crew leader's name was Paul. He did most of the talking."

Checking out the names should be easy enough. After scribbling more notes, Cash needed to take another lap around the grounds in order to get a closer look. "Would you excuse me for one minute? I need to check the perimeter."

"Mind if I come with you?" That fearful look returned to her eyes and it was a gut punch.

"Not at all. Just keep some distance so you don't accidentally disturb evidence." For her sake, he hoped there'd be a clue outside, a footprint or some DNA would give him something to work with.

"I'm sorry. I'm not normally afraid of my own shadow, but I left everything familiar behind to move here and start a new life with my daughter—"

"No apology needed." Cash walked out the back

door and noticed she locked it behind them when she followed.

"I picked this town to live in because I believed it was safer than bringing up a child in downtown Dallas. Now, I'm not so sure. And in case you hadn't noticed, I'm new to motherhood," she admitted. "I adopted Abby a little more than a month ago. This is our first night in our new home."

"You said you aren't married. Is there an ex in the picture?" He had to ask the question even though it might come off as insensitive. His job was to investigate, not judge or worry about stepping on toes. Normally, he didn't feel the kick of betrayal in his gut when he asked standard questions.

"Yes, but he has nothing to do with the adoption." Her voice had a musical quality to it even when she was frustrated, like a breeze after a cleansing rain. She added quietly, "I don't need a man in my life to have a family."

"I've met plenty of people who had two parents but still weren't a family." He hoped those words reassured her. He'd made note of the fact that she seemed like she was still finding her way when it came to caring for her daughter. Most seasoned mothers he'd met would've remembered the pacifier first thing if it wasn't time to feed their baby again. The blush to her cheeks when she'd returned after finding her daughter's and then allowing it to soothe her had given her away as a novice.

But the fierceness in her eyes when she'd first opened the door to him also said this woman might be a new mother but she was already bonded to her child. He'd heard about it and seen it with his brother Colton. He'd been hit the day his twins had been born.

It was one of those beautiful Texas nights with a million stars in a sky that seemed to go on forever. And that's where the beauty stopped. As he rounded the corner, he saw that a ladder had been placed against the side of the home that he hadn't noticed when scanning the yard for movement.

"I'm guessing your daughter's room is at the top of the rungs." Cash pointed it out as she followed close behind him near the base.

Her gasp was audible and echoed in the chilly night air.

"That's mine. It was on its side, lying against the house. I should've moved it. All I could think was how handy it would be to have around to paint the shutters and then I promptly forgot it was there." The moon reflected in her wide blue eyes as she stood next to Cash.

He didn't want to notice how beautiful her eyes were in this light. Or how her curly hair was barely contained in the band around it. A few tendrils were loose and he had to clench his fist to stop himself from tucking strands away from her face.

Renee made a move toward it and he knew exactly what she wanted to do.

"Don't touch it. There might be fingerprints on the metal." Although, he knew that was a stretch. Metal wasn't the best when it came to lifting prints.

"Oh." She stopped cold. "I'm sorry."

"Also, there might be footprints near the base and we might get lucky with a shoe or boot print. You already said it was dark. Any chance you saw what he was wearing on his feet when he climbed out the window?" Cash figured it was worth asking.

"I'm guessing tennis shoes but I didn't get a good

look because I didn't have my glasses on." She stared at him blankly. "I'm sorry. It all happened so fast and all I could think about was my daughter. Once he set her down, I was determined to get him out of my house."

"You did a great job. Your daughter is safe with you." Her small smile caused warmth to spread in his chest. Using his phone's flashlight app, he lit the area. There was grass all around the foundation, so no dirt. That would make it more difficult to get an impression.

The glint of metal caught his eye. He moved over to the spot and took a knee. From his pocket, he pulled out a rolled-up plastic glove. He sheathed his right hand and picked up the object. It was a Zippo lighter. The design looked to be a custom job.

Again, a metal object wasn't ideal for picking up fingerprints, but this gave a direction. "Let's hope this gives us a clue as to who tried to take your daughter."

He walked to his rental and pulled out a paper bag. After depositing the evidence inside, he set it on the passenger seat. Next, he closed the door and locked his vehicle. "Mind if I take a look at the inside of your daughter's room?"

"Not at all. Follow me." Renee turned and started toward the house. She unlocked the front door and let them in only to twist the lock once he was inside.

Cash could understand her fear. Being in a new city and a new house with a baby must have Renee feeling vulnerable. The thought was another gut punch. They were racking up today.

He followed the witness up the stairs. The landing area was small. There were two bedrooms, side by side, with a closet in the hallway and a bathroom on the opposite wall, just as she'd described.

Forcing his gaze away from her sweet backside, Cash gave a mental head shake. It was his job to notice things, but he'd never had an issue with professionalism when dealing with a witness.

This wasn't the time to break form despite a draw he hadn't felt in far too long.

Chapter Three

Cash moved around inside the Smith home with a shadow. Renee stayed so close behind if he stopped too fast she'd most likely crash into him. He didn't mind. He was used to it when a witness or victim felt threatened. The closer the person stayed, the more frightened.

The glass in the upstairs window was broken in a U shape around the lock. The perp seemed to know exactly where to go, giving Cash the impression that the intruder might have known the layout of the house. Had the place been cased ahead of time? Cash definitely wanted to interview the movers. He'd worked similar cases where the moving company picked up a day laborer in order to stay on schedule and the person turned out to be a criminal.

"You said this was your first night here. Is that correct, ma'am?" Cash asked his shadow. He'd switched to being formal with her in order to keep himself in check. He shouldn't allow himself to get too comfortable with a witness.

"Yes. And, please, call me Renee. I hear ma'am and I look over my shoulder for my mother," she stated.

The wood flooring creaked underneath Cash's weight. He was considered tall even by Texan standards. He kept in shape. And he was probably one of, if not *the* best shot at the US Marshals office, and that included his brother Blake.

Based on the efficiency of this kidnapper, Cash guessed the person was familiar with the place.

"I've seen all I need to. We can finish up the interview downstairs." He turned to walk out of the bedroom and nearly crashed into Renee. He'd made a point of putting some distance between them to clear his head of her flowery clean scent.

She apologized and smiled. His chest betrayed him by tightening.

This close, Cash had to resist the urge to reach out to the redheaded beauty. He reminded himself why he was there in the first place. His role was investigator. She'd been through a traumatic event and that was most likely the reason he felt such a pull toward her. It was his protector mode kicking in, and nothing more.

He followed her this time, and she led him back to the kitchen.

"Do you mind if I pour another cup of coffee while we finish?" he asked.

"Not at all," she said quickly. Too quickly? Damn, the fear radiating from her. For a split second he mused that he wasn't sure how much of that had to do with the possibility of the perp returning for round two, or if she was scared to be left alone with the child again.

"What agency did you use to adopt your daughter?" Cash took a seat and sipped the fresh brew.

"I used an attorney's office. Branson and Michaels," she supplied. "My lawyer was Kipp McGee."

Cash didn't like hearing that. He jotted down the name. There'd been a lot of questions over the years of questionable adoptions coming out of that law office and with that lawyer in particular. "How'd you find them?"

"Online. Why?" Her brow arched.

"Some of the questions I have to ask might seem personal and I apologize in advance for that. I have to look at every angle and ask—"

She put her hand up as if to say it was okay.

"I understand. Someone broke into my house and tried to take—"

She paused long enough to take in a sharp breath.

"*My daughter.* Ask me whatever you need to in order to find the jerk who tried to take her away from me." There was so much determination in her voice. Her chin jutted out. Her blue eyes stared at him in a dare.

"You mentioned that you're not married. Are you divorced?" He figured he'd better get the biggest ones out of the way.

"No."

"Are you in a relationship?" Cash didn't want to admit how much he wanted to know the answer to this question.

"Not anymore." There was a sharp edge to those words.

"What happened?"

"Do we really have to go into this right…" She looked up at him. "Never mind. I can see that we do and you prepared me for this exact thing. It's just—I'm not really comfortable talking about the details of my personal life to a stranger."

"Again, I apologize," he said and he meant it. Cash never enjoyed this part of an investigation. Serving felony warrants and tracking some of the worst criminals society had to offer were more up his alley, not interviewing witnesses who'd just had their lives turned upside down and sense of safety shaken to the core.

"There's no need. I'm a big girl and you have a job to do." She held her baby close to her chest and he figured her arms must be tired by now. The look on her face said she had no plans to let go.

"You were in a relationship?" he continued.

"Yes. For too long." Her cheeks flushed.

"When did it end?" He took a sip of coffee.

"A couple of months ago. It ended with my partner of seven years getting one of his co-workers pregnant." She flashed angry eyes at Cash. "I know how that sounds and it's worse. He stayed with me in order to save money for the baby they're going to have in two months."

The man sounded like a real prize.

"What's his name?"

"Jamison King." She gasped when Cash wrote it down.

"You don't think…it's not possible that he…is it?"

"Does he fit the description?"

She shook her head. "It was hard to see, though. I'm practically blind without my glasses and he was across a dark room."

"Did you end your relationship in a fight, or did he threaten you in any way?" To Cash's thinking, the man had no clue if he let Renee Smith slip away.

She blew out a breath that almost sounded like a bark. "He said he didn't want the relationship to end this way. But how else could it? We weren't married. We weren't even engaged. He would never discuss having a family."

"What was your reaction when he told you about the other woman and child?" The rim of Cash's coffee mug became very interesting to him as he ran a thumb along it.

"Relief."

"THAT PROBABLY MAKES me sound like a jerk, but it's true." Talking about Renee's past wasn't as difficult as she thought it would be once she got over the initial shock. It was embarrassing more than anything. The word *relief* had come to her without thinking much about her response. It was weird because she wouldn't have used it at the time but that didn't make it any less true now.

"Not in my book." Cash O'Connor was six feet, four inches of solid muscle. The man practically towered over Renee. His size would be intimidating to most and she figured it came in handy in his line of work. He also had the most beautiful, intense steel-gray eyes and sandy-brown hair—a potent combination.

"I was hurt, too. But I also realized that my feelings for Jamison had changed. I'd wanted to end the relationship last year but then he told me about his mother's diagnosis. We'd been together six years at that point and I didn't feel like I could abandon him or her. Then we found out she was terminal, and I couldn't walk away in good conscience after that. So, I stuck around and played the fool instead. He was sleeping around at the office and I didn't see what was right in front of me."

"Excuse me for saying so but your ex sounds like a class A jerk. Being deceived doesn't make you a fool." His words were low, soothing and provided more comfort than Renee knew how to handle.

But then she was pretty sure anything the handsome marshal said would make her feel better. His voice was like amaretto over ice cream and she could imagine a trail of women a mile long waiting for a chance to hear it. His gorgeous steel-gray eyes were framed by thick black lashes that were masculine. He had that carved-from-granite jawline like the kind that melted resolves. There were so many hard planes and angles to his face. To make matters worse, one look from him sent her heart fluttering, like someone had released a thousand butterflies in her chest. Even though she knew her re-action to him was completely out of place and inappropriate, she couldn't deny it was there.

A guy as attractive as him most likely had some-one at home waiting for him. And she was in no place in her life to care how attractive any man was. With a new baby and a new town, Renee's hands were full. And even though she could admit that she hadn't been in love with Jamison in a long time, being burned still hurt. It would be a long time before she could allow herself to trust again.

"Back to your ex. Is it possible he's holding a grudge?" Cash asked.

"Why would he do that?" Jamison had been the one to break off the relationship, if not in words then in ac-tions.

"Jealousy, for one. You've moved on with your life," he pointed out.

"He has a baby on the way with a woman who isn't me." The argument seemed strong until she thought about the hurt look in his eyes when she'd told him there was no going back.

"Believe me when I say that I've seen bigger turnarounds in people. He has a baby on the way but that doesn't mean he wanted it. You said he never talked about having a family with you." His logic made sense.

"That's right. I just assumed he didn't want that with *me*."

"He might not want that at all. He could be planning to leave once the baby's born. You said he stayed with you because he was saving money, right?"

Where was he going with this?

"I did."

"Have you considered the possibility that he stayed because he wanted to?" That question struck a nerve.

"If he wanted to be with me he had a strange way of showing it," she said quickly.

"Did you tell him about the move?" Cash's soothing voice softened the intrusive questions. Even if it didn't, she would do anything to bring justice to a man who'd tried to kidnap Abby, even if it meant relaying personal details of her life to a complete stranger. Renee couldn't think about the kidnapping attempt without involuntarily shivering.

"Hell, no."

"You said the relationship had been over for you for a long time. Do you think it's possible he figured out that you were planning to leave him?" Another good question.

"I guess."

"That could've been the reason for the affair. He might've wanted to make you jealous with her," he said.

"I suppose it's possible." She couldn't imagine anyone doing that to another human being let alone someone she was supposed to love, but when she really thought about it, Jamison hadn't been himself in years.

She figured he was slowly losing interest but there could be more to the story.

"I can't rule him out—"

"He doesn't know about my daughter." Renee stared at Cash. "What I do with my life from the day we broke up is none of his business."

"When I speak to him, I'll do my best not to give him any unnecessary details of your current situation," Cash reassured with a look that said he meant every word. "Have you had a fight with anyone recently?"

"Aside from Jamison? There was a co-worker who thought I was trying to sabotage her career when I got promoted instead of her. Her name is Chasity Radar. Oh, and there was a creepy guy at work who cornered me in an elevator recently. His name is Darion Figg and he's a contractor. I told my boss, who immediately handled it."

"What's your boss's name and what's your profession?"

"Rikki Drake. I handle all the updates for my company's website." She supplied her contact number. Rikki needed a heads-up and she figured this wasn't a quick email or text. She owed her a call if a US marshal would be contacting her boss.

"What about your family? Do you have any family nearby?" he asked, and it was another painful question.

"No. That was part of the appeal in moving here," she admitted. "My parents used to live in Dallas."

He rocked his head as he took notes.

"We didn't see eye to eye on much, I'm afraid. But they've been gone a long time." Renee wished she'd been on better terms with her parents. "They fought a lot while I was growing up. They died in a car crash."

"Shame," he said almost under his breath. "I'm sorry for your loss and I'm sorry their relationship was strained."

"Why is that?" She cocked her head to one side, curious. He seemed genuinely sad for her and her nonexistent relationship with her folks. It was pretty much all she'd ever known, so it didn't seem as strange to her as it appeared it did to him.

"I grew up close to mine. My whole family is there for each other. Hard to imagine life any other way even though I see it every day in my line of work." There was a sincerity to his steel eyes that pierced her armor and hit straight in the chest where it exploded. Renee had no idea what it was like for someone else to have her back. It had just been her for longer than she cared to remember. She'd been the only child of parents who thought shouting at each other and being violent should be a professional sport.

"You have brothers and sisters?" she asked, curious about the mysterious marshal.

"Five brothers." An emotion flickered behind his eyes that she couldn't quite pinpoint. Then came, "We had a sister."

"I'm sorry for your loss." Without thinking, she reached across the table and touched his arm. It was intended to reassure him but contact sent a fire bolt of electricity shooting up her arm.

If he had the same reaction he didn't show it. Instead, he nodded his appreciation for the sentiment and took another sip of coffee.

"Any fights about money with your ex?" he continued.

"No. He mainly didn't seem thrilled that I kicked

him out or wouldn't take his calls, but I wouldn't exactly say we had a fight. I guess a breakup in and of itself is never pleasant," she said.

"None I've ever been part of ended without someone's feelings being hurt." One corner of his mouth lifted when he spoke. She liked his face even more when he relaxed. "You mentioned the movers before. Did any friends drop by?"

"A neighbor grabbed me to say hello, but I had my hands full with Abby so I didn't invite her inside." A shiver raced down her back at the thought that one of the people she'd hired could've been a criminal who was casing the place.

"We can start with the movers, then." He picked up his pen. "Do you have any documentation from the moving company?"

"I have the receipt right here." She sifted through a couple of papers on the table and located the pink slip for College Boy Movers. The slogan had been College Hunks Move Your Stuff. The guys who'd shown up wouldn't exactly fall into the category of good-looking. Three slightly overweight men and a slightly smaller one in their late twenties had turned up at her Dallas apartment to get the job done. "They put together Abby's crib, so one of the guys was in her room. It was part of the deal. They helped set the place up. They don't unpack necessarily, but they were handy with a screwdriver and got my bed put back together."

They might not have been a good-looking crew but they got the job done well enough. Renee was in her new home.

Cash took the slip and studied it.

"Have you heard of them?" she asked.

"No. And that's a good thing from my perspective." He glanced up. "Mind if I take a picture of this to file with my report?"

The question was most likely professional courtesy. She shook her head and suppressed a yawn. He asked a few more routine-sounding questions before snapping a pic. His cell buzzed while still in his hand.

He glanced at the screen. "Excuse me, I need to take this."

"Go right ahead." She glanced at the clock. It was getting late. Exhaustion wore her thin but she doubted she could go back to sleep, especially now that she realized the glass had been broken in her daughter's room and there was no way to lock the window. Maybe she could pack an overnight bag and stay in a motel until she could have her new home secured. She needed a temporary fix tonight.

Cash stood and walked over to the sink, looking out the window. "Hey, Colton. What's the word?"

She surmised the call must be from the sheriff. And then it dawned on her. Her neighbor had said the sheriff's name was Colton O'Connor. He had the same last name as Cash, who'd said he had five brothers.

Renee wouldn't normally listen to someone's conversation, but she figured this one had to do with her as she heard Cash update his brother on the case and tell him about the lighter he'd found.

After saying a few uh-huhs into the phone and promising to run the evidence to his brother's office, the conversation must've shifted to something more personal.

"And no one's seen him?" he asked, with concern in his voice.

Suddenly, she felt like she was intruding. She stared

down at her little girl and tried to block out the sound of his voice, which was difficult to do with the way it seemed to tickle her skin like the first cool breeze on a hot day.

"Where was it found?" His voice went silent. "I see." More silence.

"And how's Mother taking the news—don't answer that. Stupid question." He was silent for a couple of beats. "He wouldn't part from his cell phone. The entire area has been checked? And nothing? It's still dark outside. It'll be difficult to find him now. He knows the area like the back of his hand. There's no way he's lost." Cash gripped the sink with his free hand as though he was bracing himself. He bowed his head and closed his eyes. "I need to finish boarding up the window at the victim's home. Since you're sending a deputy here to collect evidence, I'll wait until he's finished. After that, I'm on my way home."

Renee's heart was in her throat. She was scared and too stubborn to admit her fears. Cash said goodbye before ending the call. Maybe strapping the baby in the car seat and getting a hotel room was a good idea after all. But where?

An idea popped. She should ask the lawman for a recommendation. He'd know the area, and until the window was fixed there was no way she was staying at the farmhouse.

"I didn't mean to overhear—"

"It's fine. Our father's missing." He rubbed the scruff on his chin and for the first time looked tired.

"I'm so sorry." She got to her feet. "You obviously have to go. Can you recommend a place for me and the baby to stay tonight? I don't want to be here after what happened and I don't know the area."

"Pack up a few things. You can come home with me and stay at the guesthouse on my family's ranch."

Renee wasn't quite sure she'd heard Cash right. "I'm sorry. What did you just say?"

"You said yourself that it's not safe for you to sleep here. Where else are you going to go with a baby?" Those steel-gray eyes pierced her.

Well, when he put it like that it didn't sound so crazy. But she didn't know the man. "Thanks for the offer—"

"This is a practical solution. Besides, I don't know how long we'll be searching for my father. Everyone around here and in town knows who he is and people will most likely storm the ranch to help find him until he comes home or is found. I can't leave you and your daughter unprotected. There's a motel about twenty miles from here on the highway, but I'm pretty certain they rent rooms by the hour."

She must've made an awful face because he said, "That's exactly right. So, I'd like you to come to my family's ranch. We're good people. Several of my brothers and I work in law enforcement. The ranch has everything you could possibly need and you'll be safe until we can arrest the jerk who broke into your house or get a permanent solution for your window and install an alarm. Think about it while I board up the window in the baby's room. My brother is sending a deputy to gather evidence."

He glanced around.

"Any chance you have supplies anywhere around?" he asked.

"There's a shed in back."

She followed him outside, locking the door behind

them. He found a few supplies in the shed and then brought them into the house.

Renee wouldn't normally agree to stay at a stranger's house. She glanced down at her now-sleeping angel and then back at Cash several times as he worked. Because of him, her daughter was calm and sleeping. His job was to enforce the law. His family owned a ranch with plenty of room and, apparently, a guesthouse.

A few warning flares fired when she looked at that man because she'd never felt an attraction this fast and hard, or this strong. But this was the best plan to keep her daughter safe for the night until Renee could get someone over to repair the window and put in an alarm.

Renee could scarcely believe she was about to accept an invitation to stay with a practical stranger. The "old" her might have dug her heels in and tried to stick it out for the night in the new house just to prove a point. There was never a doubt in her mind having a baby would change her. She figured this was just the tip of the iceberg. Abby would always come first. Renee's pride would gladly take a back seat to ensure her child's safety.

It didn't take him more than ten minutes to hammer in a few nails and secure the bedroom. The deputy arrived while Cash worked and dusted for prints. He took the evidence that had been collected so far before thanking Cash and expressing concern for his father.

Once they'd seen the deputy out, Cash put the hammer down in the hall closet before turning toward her and asking, "Have you made a decision?"

"Thank you for the invite," she said to Cash. "I accept."

Chapter Four

Renee's eyes widened as Cash pulled onto the paved driveway of a massive ranch after a forty-minute drive. Even this early in the morning, the place was well lit. It was huge and grand and completely unexpected.

After being waved in by a security guard, Cash continued onto a paved road toward a massive white house. Before they got anywhere close, Cash turned onto a smaller road.

"The guesthouse is this way. The opposite direction leads to the barns where Pops keeps his offices. There's a bunkhouse over that way." His tone was much more somber now, his concern for his father evident. The emotion hit Renee harder than she wanted it to. All she could think was how much she respected his family for being so close. "Stacy is my parents' right hand."

"Was she the person you called before we left my house?" The forty-minute drive to the ranch went by in a flash with a sleeping baby buckled in her carrier that doubled as a car seat. Conversation had been light and interrupted often by calls from Cash's brothers that came over the speaker.

Cash nodded. "She made sure you'll have all the supplies you need for your little one. Fridge is stocked."

"She did all that in forty minutes?" Renee had packed up bottles and formula along with an overnight bag for herself. Feeding time should hit soon.

Looking down, she realized she'd fisted her hands. She flexed her fingers, trying to release some of the tension of being in new territory and feeling ill-equipped to handle it. None of this felt great but every day spent figuring life out on her own was going to be better than the last few years with Jamison.

"This place runs like a well-oiled machine because of the team my parents put in place. I have a cabin—"

"Hold on a minute. You're not staying the night in the guesthouse with us?" Renee wasn't trying to be forward or take Cash for granted. He was the only person she knew in the whole town.

"I'd planned to join the search for my father."

"Oh, right. I'm sorry." She pinched the bridge of her nose to stave off the raging headache forming along with a very real dose of fear that this motherhood gig might be biting off more than she could chew. Renee took in a breath and mentally shook off the negativity. She'd figure this out with Abby. No one could possibly want to do a better job at being a mother than her.

"I can send someone over to help until I get back after we find him." Those last few spoken words faltered. He tried to hide his emotions by clearing his throat.

"Providing us with a safe roof over our heads for a day or two until we can get everything straightened out at home is more than enough." The idea of an extra set of hands and possibly someone with experience caring for a child was almost too good to pass up, but she didn't want to impose. He was doing more than enough for her makeshift family as it was. And he'd received unsettling news about his father.

"It's no trouble and you might be able to get a few hours of shut-eye."

She was already shaking her head before he finished his sentence. There was no way she would ask that of him, no matter how tempting the offer. Abby needed stability in her life and that came with having a consistent caregiver. Renee was more than ready for the job and had been getting by okay for the past month despite plenty of moments that might make her feel otherwise.

"I'll manage okay. I have to get used to lack of sleep and taking care of her on my own, right? It might be scary but it's also the best job I've ever had." Her half smile was rewarded with a chuckle that sounded like a deep rumble from his chest. "Thank you, though. Your hospitality is above and beyond. It's more than appreciated."

"Your 'welcome to town' up to this point hasn't exactly been stellar. I'm hoping you'll see we aren't all bad." His cell had been buzzing like crazy for the past twenty minutes or so. He parked in front of a cottage and palmed his cell. "It's a one-bedroom but the rooms are good size."

Before she could unbuckle her seat belt, he'd exited the vehicle and come around to her side. As she reached for the handle, the door opened. Turned out, chivalry wasn't dead. Jamison had never displayed this kind of southern charm despite being from a Dallas suburb. She thanked him again as she climbed out of the seat.

Cash was already liberating the car seat from the buckle in back. Did he have a family? He seemed to know his way around children. Of course, a man as intelligent and hot as him would have someone waiting at home. Was that the reason he'd taken her to the guesthouse instead of his place?

"I hope I don't get you in any trouble with your wife—"

"No wife." Those two words were spoken with a finiteness that came with careful contemplation and a decision. Maybe he wasn't the marrying type. Plenty of people staked a claim on being single.

"Oh. Okay. Just don't let me keep you." Renee had always known she wanted a family. Despite her parents' endless arguments, she'd convinced herself that she would somehow magically get marriage right. She'd worked briefly at a preschool while finishing her basics at community college and loved the energy of having lots of little kids around.

Jamison was no doubt the wrong person for her but her confidence in finding the "right" person took a huge hit after everything that happened with him. After learning about his betrayal, marriage didn't seem like the best requirement for starting a family. He'd been reaching out to her a lot recently and getting frustrated with her lack of response to his frequent texts. What could she say? She was done. He had a baby on the way. He might regret his choices but his actions had consequences.

"I've got her. You want to grab the diaper bag?" Cash asked. "I can come back for the suitcase once you're settled."

"Yeah, sure." She couldn't help but notice the ease with which he handled her daughter. Curiosity got the best of her. "You're not married, which doesn't necessarily mean you don't have kids."

He laughed as he balanced the carrier in one arm and slid the key in the lock with his free hand. The door opened and he flipped on a light. "I have nephews. A set of twin boys who just celebrated their first birthday. I've learned to pitch in to help my brother. He's raising them on his own." He shot her a warning look. It wasn't so much the words as the way he'd said them that told her more discussion of the topic was off limits.

Changing the subject seemed like a good idea as Abby stirred. She had to be hungry by now. "You can put her down anywhere. I need to get a bottle ready."

True to form, the fridge had all the basics of milk, eggs and a couple of what looked like precooked homemade meals in ready-to-heat containers. She was even more impressed. The interior of the cottage was beige and white with just enough Tiffany blue to be considered feminine. The place was decorated to perfection, looking like something out of a magazine. She should've expected this but for some reason was surprised by the level of detail.

"It's beautiful in here." She set the bottle of formula on the wooden coffee table on top of a coaster. "Do people stay here often?"

"No. You're the first."

She would feel special if she hadn't picked up on a note of sadness in his voice. Figuring it was another off-limits subject, she picked up her baby and then settled into the deep couch adjacent to the fireplace.

Cash excused himself before bringing back her suitcase and taking it into the bedroom. He fished out his cell from his front pocket and frowned when he got a good look at the screen. It took a few seconds to scroll through all the messages he'd received in the last hour.

Drawing his brows together, he shook his head before looking at her. When he did, he was distracted and she imagined there was more bad news about his father. Her heart went out to him. Cash O'Connor seemed like a decent man. One who didn't deserve what was happening.

"What's your cell number?" he asked.

She rattled off the digits. A second later, she heard a buzzing noise coming from her purse.

"Don't worry about it. I'm calling so you'll have my number in case you need anything." His buzzed again. He issued a sharp sigh after checking the screen and walking toward the door. "There's a spare set of keys hanging on a hook on the kitchen cabinet next to the garage door and a car should you need to use one. I texted you Stacy's number in case I'm not around or not getting cell coverage. It's spotty here on the ranch and especially in remote areas." He stopped short of crossing the threshold but his hand was on the knob. "I'll lock this on my way out. Not because it needs to be locked, but because it'll make you feel safer. I'll be back as soon as I can."

Renee smiled. It had been a very long time since anyone had had her back. Before she could thank Cash again, he darted out the door. The snick of the lock, as promised, allowed her to finally exhale.

THE FIRST LIGHT was rising against the night sky. Normally, Cash would stop long enough to appreciate the multicolored canopy that contained a mix of the most beautiful orange and blue hues. Texas had always felt like home and always had been. And yet there was something extra special about the land at KBR, something that fed Cash's soul.

Today, all he could think about was Pops.

Walking into the kitchen of the main house, Stacy made a beeline for him and nodded toward the back door. Cash turned and stepped onto the screened-in porch. He folded his arms across his chest as she joined him.

"Where is everyone?"

"I'm sorry, Cash." Those words dropped a lead anchor of dread in the pit of his stomach. "I thought it would be better to talk to you out here rather than have your mother be forced to rehash the details again."

"Has Pops turned up?" Even though Cash had a solid two inches of height on Finn O'Connor, the man would always stand eight feet tall in Cash's eyes. Not only was he a great father and husband, he was a great man. The thought of anything happening to Pops tightened the screws in his chest.

"Yes." Stacy studied the rug like her next words might be found there. When she looked back up at him, he could see water gathering in her eyes. Instead of speaking, she shook her head.

Cash knew exactly what she meant and yet his brain couldn't fathom anything happening to a strong man like Finn O'Connor. Since Stacy looked ready to crumble, Cash brought the older woman who'd been like an aunt to him into a hug. Sobs wracked her shoulders as disbelief cloaked Cash. There wasn't a world where it made sense his buck-strong and healthy sixty-eight-year-old father was suddenly gone.

Stacy pulled back and wiped her eyes, apologizing profusely.

"It's okay. You've been just as much a part of this family for the past thirty years as I have." His words seemed to strike a chord with Stacy. She managed a weak smile through her tears.

"I've been trying to hold it together for your mother. I didn't mean to unleash on you." Dark circles cradled her eyes, outlining her stress, and her rounded shoulders seemed even heavier now.

"You're doing all right." He was still trying to wrap his mind around the fact his father might be gone. He'd seen the same look of shock and disbelief more times than he could count on victims' faces. The brain seemed set on a delayed timer when it came to unfathomable news. Cash probably had that same look on his face now. He wanted to go inside to get more details, figure out how this could've happened and be a comfort to his mother. Stacy had been part of the family for as long as he could remember. There was no way he'd abandon her.

She twisted her fingers together. "It's all happening so fast. I mean, we knew he was sick but we just thought he'd magically pull through somehow. You know your father. The man was strong as an ox."

"Who knew he was sick?" Cash had been told about a couple of recent doctor's appointments. There'd been no serious illness news.

Stacy brought a hand up to cover her mouth. "I'm sorry. Your mother asked me not to say anything to any of the boys about his diagnosis."

Cash must've given her quite the look because she quickly added, "Aortic aneurysm."

"What is that exactly?"

"It's a bulge in a blood vessel that carries blood away from his heart. The doctors measured it and it fell within the guidelines. He was supposed to go back soon and have it rechecked." She shook her head and her voice was weary. "It must've grown faster than expected and ruptured. He collapsed on the property and Slim found him near Bridal Pass."

Slim Jenkins was ranch foreman. Cash bit his tongue. This shouldn't be the first time he was hearing about an issue with his father's health, but it wasn't Stacy's call to make. Pops would want to keep this information under the radar. Even though his children were all adults, he'd see the need to protect everyone. It was surprising that Pops had gone to the doctor in the first place. "Where's my mother?"

"She's inside in her bedroom." More tears spilled down Stacy's cheeks.

"And Pops?"

"An ambulance transported him..." A few more sobs wracked her as she tried to finish her sentence. She apologized again even though it was wholly unnecessary. There wasn't much Cash or his brothers wouldn't do for their family friend and ranch manager.

Reality started to sink in as Cash heard more details about his father's condition. His brain still rejected the fact that Finn O'Connor was anything but alive. Cash needed to see the rest of his family and yet his boots were rooted to the floor. He swiped a hand across his face, realized it had been a few days since he'd shaved. "Who's here?"

Stacy seemed to know exactly what he referred to when she started rattling off a few of his brothers' names. "Colton left with the ambulance and I haven't been able to reach Garrett."

"No surprises there." As sheriff, Colton would see it as his job to accompany the body and ensure there'd been no foul play. Garrett had a convenient habit of letting his phone run out of battery. He liked to disappear with no explanation, leaving their mother to worry. He'd always needed more space than the others. Between marriages, separations and divorces, the O'Connor men had been preoccupied lately. "How long did Pops know about his medical condition?"

"Since last year," she admitted.

"And no one told us?"

"He said it wasn't a big enough deal to worry the family over. Your mom fussed at him, told him the boys deserved to know what was going on. He wasn't having it. He told her that he'd speak up when there was something worth talking about." She blew out a breath. "I don't have to remind you how stubborn your father could be."

Tightness built in Cash's chest. "It's a wonder she got him to go to the doctor in the first place."

"Her cholesterol numbers were running up and she was afraid his were doing the same. He didn't go willingly but he did go." Stacy's chin quivered. Cash's heart was breaking because in all the years he'd known her this was the first he'd seen her cry.

"Sounds about right." Cash grinned.

"Your father had no patience for anything that took him off his land or away from his family for longer than thirty minutes." Pops lived for the family ranch and the legacy the family had built over four generations. "Which shows how much more stubborn your mother is."

Margaret Ann O'Connor had a quiet strength, grace and dignity rarely seen. "She rarely takes no for an answer." And rarely had to speak above a whisper to get her way with Pops. The man was head over heels for his wife even to this day.

Was, Cash had to remind himself. That one word nearly gutted him. Finn O'Connor gone?

"I better let you go inside now. Thank you for giving me a few minutes, Cash. It means a lot."

"Any time you need to talk, I'm here." The look of appreciation she shot him was better than any verbal recognition. Actions always spoke the loudest.

With Stacy on better emotional footing, it was time to steel his resolve and face the rest of his family.

Chapter Five

When Cash walked into his mother's bedroom, the air changed. Palpable grief hit him like a surprise thunderstorm, hard and sudden. His mother was seated in her favorite reading chair by the window overlooking the expansive meadow on the east side of the family home. Three of his brothers stood nearby. No one seemed sure what to say in times of grief.

Blake spotted Cash first. His brother broke up the trio by making a beeline toward Cash. He couldn't help but notice the dark circles under Blake's eyes from worry and shock.

"Is it true?" Cash knew it was and yet part of him held out hope Stacy had bad information. She would never intentionally lie. The part of Cash's brain that couldn't accept the reality of his father's death took momentary control.

"Yes." Blake could be counted on to keep a cool head. Being second born and only eighteen months younger than Cash, the two had grown up best friends.

"Were there any signs of foul play?" Cash couldn't think of a soul who'd want to hurt Finn O'Connor. Years of experience had taught him that everyone had enemies whether they knew them or not.

"No." Blake shook his head for emphasis. This whole scene was confirmation of news he didn't want to be true. "Pops had a medical condition."

"Stacy filled me in. I just didn't want to believe it." Cash's words were met with a nod as brothers Riggs and Dawson joined the conversation. Cash glanced at his mother who sat with a rigid back, clutching a handkerchief and staring outside. She was the kind of mother who would think she needed to be strong for her kids, forget the fact she had six grown men for children now.

This wasn't the first time he'd seen her at that exact window with a similar look on her face, holding on to a handkerchief as though her life depended on it. Later, he'd learned why. A cavern opened in Cash's chest, the pain felt so palpable that it threatened to drag him under. Margaret O'Connor had always been there for him and he wanted to do the same for her. Although, he doubted she'd want to lean on one of her children.

"Before twenty minutes ago, I had no idea about Pops's condition," Riggs said. He was the tallest O'Connor by a quarter of an inch and normally liked to remind everyone when all the brothers were together. This time, he wore his sadness in the heavy lines bracketing his mouth and deep slashes across his forehead.

"Same," Blake said as the others agreed. The air in the room felt heavy.

Slim held the position of ranch foreman after working his way up from cleaning out stables. He'd become as trusted as Stacy, and as integral to running the family business. Cash realized how little he knew about the family business. Few of the O'Connor men had gone into ranching, only Garrett and Riggs. Pops had made no secret of the fact he wanted his sons to take over the family empire one day. With careers ranging from law enforcement to rancher, Garrett and Riggs were the only sons who'd followed in the family business. To prove a point, and basically be his stubborn self, Garrett had gone to work for a rival ranch.

"What was he doing over there alone?" Bridal Pass was a spot where folks called in favors from the O'Connors just to have the opportunity to take pictures against the beautiful backdrop of Texas's rolling hills. A few of the requests came from parents wanting to take their son or daughter's high-school-graduation pictures but most often a bridal party wanted to take wedding photos there, earning the place its nickname. Springtime was especially beautiful with bluebonnets for acres, making it the perfect location for photos. "He'd been checking fences, working right up until he collapsed."

There was a small measure of comfort knowing Pops went exactly the way he would have wanted to: working on his beloved ranch. "No one called a family meeting last year when he and Mother found out about his condition."

"We didn't think it would get worse so suddenly." His mother's attempt at bravery as she lifted her chin and pushed to standing lodged a rock in his chest. Breathing hurt while he had to fight every instinct that he had to march toward her and offer an arm. The only reason he didn't was because he knew in his heart she wouldn't want it.

"The doctors wanted to keep an eye on him." She shrugged. "I guess on some level we knew this was a possibility. He was overdue for his appointment. I should've insisted he take the time to go."

"This didn't happen because of something you did

or didn't do." Cash beat his brothers to the punch. Any one of them would say the same thing. Their nods confirmed it. With him being eldest, the others usually showed him the respect of letting him speak first. Everyone except for Garrett. He challenged Cash and anyone else in authority for his own amusement.

Her weary steel-gray eyes pierced right through Cash. "You know how he gets this time of year."

Spring was the busiest time on a cattle ranch, with calving season. "Yes, ma'am."

"He seemed fine this morning." She paused. "But then your father wasn't the complaining type."

"No, ma'am." Cash spoke on behalf of his brothers.

A wistful smile upturned the corners of her lips and a little of the spark normally found in her eyes returned. "He was a mule when it came to doing anything he didn't want to do."

"Truer words have never been spoken, ma'am," Cash agreed and it seemed like everyone exhaled at the same time.

"He wouldn't want us to make a fuss about him," she quickly added, wagging a finger.

"No, he would not." Finn O'Connor was the most down-to-earth man. The term *salt-of-the-earth type* was tossed around a lot when people spoke of him even though he shied away from praise. His standards set the bar high. The man wore jeans and a button-down shirt no matter how hot it got outside. In Texas, that meant triple-digit summers. He always spoke about his wife, their mother, with the utmost love and respect. And, maybe more importantly, treated her that way.

"I miss him already." Mother wiped away a tear. "There'll be another huge hole in our lives now." The first she referred to was, of course, Cash's sister. The similarities between her kidnapping and Abby's near abduction brought an icy chill racing down Cash's back. Any time he came across a case involving a baby around the same age as his sister, he thought of her.

The hours-old kidnapping attempt hit a little too close to home. With literally decades between the crimes, the likelihood that the cases were related was next to none. Considering his mother was about to bury her husband, Cash didn't want to add to her sadness by dredging up old memories of Caroline. Their parents had launched several investigations over the years to find Cash's sister, none of which bore fruit. They'd been honest with their sons about what they were doing and why. Mother had brought out a small birthday cake every July 28 after supper for Caroline's birthday. The cake represented a mother's prayer that her child was alive and being well cared for. It was accompanied by a quick prayer and a few precious shared memories.

For Abby's attempted kidnapping, the perp couldn't possibly be the same person. Caroline's kidnapping happened more than thirty years ago. If the perp had been in his twenties back then, he would be in his fifties now. Not impossible but definitely not likely. There hadn't been another kidnapping or attempt involving a six-month-old girl in town for three decades.

Cash should know. He and his brothers who worked in law enforcement had searched cold cases for similar crimes. Deep down, he wanted to bring closure to his family.

Margaret O'Connor had enough to deal with at present.

"Has anyone been able to reach your brother?" Everyone knew who their mother was talking about. Garrett. The man changed cell phone numbers more often than some people changed shirts, or so it seemed.

"Not that I know of." Cash fished his cell out of his pocket and held it up. "Does anyone have his latest number?"

"I don't think so," Riggs said.

Being an investigator, it shouldn't be this difficult to keep tabs on his own brother. And yet, Garrett knew a thing or two about not being found when it suited him. It wasn't unlike him to disappear for weeks or months on end. Being busy with his own life, Cash didn't think much of it. It was always just Garrett's way. He'd show eventually. No one had really needed to find him until now. Outsider or not, Garrett needed to know about their father. "I'll make a few calls. See if I can come up with something."

Their mother smiled. "In the meantime, how about I put on a pot of fresh brew?"

From the looks of his brothers, everyone needed a drink a helluva lot stronger than coffee. That cold beer sounded better and better to Cash. He wiped a hand across the stubble on his face, figuring coffee was the most appropriate option at this hour despite being up most of the night.

"I'll take a cup." Riggs was the first to speak up. The others nodded. "I can make a pot if—"

"I'll do it." Their mother was petite and thin with a soft voice, but also stubborn. She was always well put together, kind and a gentle encourager. Still beautiful inside and out. She also had a full head of hair, something she joked that her sons would thank her for later in life since it was rumored boys inherited the bald gene from the mother's side.

Their mother loved her library and spent many a night there long after her usual bedtime reading one of her novels.

A few of his brothers exchanged glances as their mother walked out of the room. Margaret Ann O'Connor did a lot of things. However, making coffee wasn't one of them.

No matter what else was going on, she woke at four o'clock on the dot six days a week to be with their father to eat breakfast with him before he headed out for the day. No one would ever accuse her of being a morning person and yet she managed to smile through her yawns. A cup of coffee later, and she'd spend mornings working in their home office. Pops used to say that she was a whiz with numbers. A good day to Pops meant being on the land with the animals, working side by side with his foreman and ranch hands.

Cash excused himself to make a couple of calls so he could try to track down their missing brother. Garrett came off like he didn't care, but that couldn't be true. It seemed like he'd been born with a chip on his shoulder and Cash couldn't figure out why for the life of him.

Last Cash heard, his brother worked on another ranch as a hand. The guy was heir to one of the biggest cattle fortunes in the state of Texas and he worked for little better than minimum wage, a roof over his head and three square meals a day. There couldn't be a better way to thumb his nose at his upbringing or his family.

Owning mineral rights on the family land had made the family beyond wealthy and Pops wasn't afraid to share the wealth with the men who worked for him.

Speaking of whom, Cash needed to see who planned to tell the hands what was going on. The news should come from one of Finn's sons.

Garrett was the first priority. Cash used his phone to look up the website of his brother's last known employer. He found it easily enough and then located contact information. This situation necessitated a call rather than an impersonal text. He entered the number and hit the call button.

"Thank you for calling Bullman Ranch." The female voice was perky. The young person sounded barely out of high school. She had a drawl to her voice that was decidedly country.

"My name is Cash O'Connor. I'm looking for my brother, Garrett. Last I heard, he worked at your ranch." He didn't see the need to say her parents' ranch, that was obvious. He also decided against using his law-enforcement title. It might scare her into thinking Garrett was in some kind of legal trouble.

"Oh, sorry. He took off weeks ago. No notice. He just up and left after an argument with his foreman." She sounded genuinely sad to deliver the news.

"Any idea where he might have gone?" Cash could've figured as much. It sounded like something Garrett would do.

"No, sir. My dad wants me to tell anyone who asks about him not to hire him and that if Garrett wants to get paid he needs to see my dad for a check. My dad didn't okay the electronic deposit like usual."

"I'll pass along the message next time I see him."

"That would be awesome."

Cash thanked her and ended the call.

HOURS HAD PASSED since Cash had left and Renee realized Abby's pacifier must've fallen out of her mouth either back at home or in his vehicle. It was midafternoon and she couldn't find the darn thing anywhere near Abby. After walking around the guest cottage with a crying baby over her shoulder for close to half an hour, she needed to come up with a plan. Going back to the farmhouse wasn't an option until she knew who was behind the kidnapping attempt and the jerk was behind bars.

There wasn't much more terrifying than moving to a new place, not knowing a soul and having a baby to care for. All of which was trumped by the crime that had happened last night. Between work and Jamison's sick mother, Renee was beginning to realize how small her circle had become. People she'd believed to be friends at work started avoiding her once word got around that she was helping care for a terminal patient. No one was obvious about it. At least, not at first. Then the lunch invites had started to dwindle. The sadder and more miserable Renee became by staying in a relationship whose breakup was long overdue, the more often she declined invitations. She'd reasoned that no one wanted to be around a killjoy and nothing depressed a mood like her being honest about two major things in her life: the end of her relationship and his mother's condition.

Sadly, those two things quickly became her life. Waking up at five to go to the gym and get in a workout every morning had become her saving grace. Looking back, it was almost comical that Jamison had accused her of cheating on him with the spin class instructor. She should've realized he was just trying to throw her off his trail. But his jealous streak had only increased over the years. He'd become more and more possessive. He would've freaked out if he'd known what Darion had pulled at work.

Jamison dropped the cheating subject real fast when she'd invited him to start coming to class with her.

Abby almost quieted as Renee gently bounced her up and down. Just when Renee was ready to declare victory, the little girl pulled in a deep breath and belted out the most heart-wrenching cry. "I'm sorry, Abby. I promise I'll get better at this. I'll figure out what you want."

Renee patted the little girl's back. She wondered if she should sit around and wait for Cash to show back up. After a few more laps around the cottage, desperation was mounting. Renee had to do something besides pace and pat her daughter's back. Abby was fed and her diaper was clean. Renee needed that pacifier.

Didn't Cash mention there was a set of keys to a vehicle outside?

Without hesitation, Renee moved to the key that was hanging on a hook in the kitchen next to the garage door. She put her daughter in her carrier and buckled it into the car. Renee and daughter were on the paved road toward the exit inside of five minutes.

Using the navigation system on her phone, she programmed in the nearest grocery store, figuring it would have a pacifier, and then from memory made it to the security gate leading off the property. At least the sun was going strong on a cloudless spring day. Abby settled down by the time Renee turned onto the main road into town. She'd be lost without GPS and her phone. Cash had mentioned there were spots on the ranch with no service. The thought made her want to shudder.

There were only a few vehicles on the road for the longest time. The car ride had soothed Abby back to sleep. Renee reluctantly pulled into the parking lot of the Green Grocers and found a space. A dozen vehicles dotted the parking lot. It wasn't full by Dallas standards but she had a sneaking suspicion it might be busy for the small town of Katy Gulch. And it was good she was getting out and learning the area.

Busy unbuckling her daughter's carrier that doubled as a car seat, Renee barely noticed when a car pulled up near hers and parked. Out of the corner of her eye, she did see another block hers in. Palming her keys and placing one in between her first and second finger, she fisted her right hand. Shoulders back, she set the car seat in the back and figured she could slam her car door into anyone who got close. With the jagged side of the key ready, she scanned the area. Pressing the panic alarm on the key fob could scare the baby.

Heart in her throat, she steeled her breath as the driver of the car near hers exited his vehicle. Glancing around, she cursed the fact it seemed like everyone was inside the store. Of course, the perps would plan it that way, she reasoned.

In a split second, three men were coming at her. All of the men wore baggy clothes, hoodies and sunglasses. It was impossible to get a look at their faces, considering they'd wrapped scarves around them.

Renee's pulse jackhammered. This couldn't be happening. Who would want to take Abby? Because Renee was certain they came for the baby, just like last night. No place felt safe. Renee knew one thing was certain, no one was taking Abby away from her.

Despite the three-to-one odds, Renee had no intention of handing over her daughter. "I don't know what you want but you need to leave." The words came out shakier than she'd hoped.

One of the guys shook his head. She blocked the carrier with her body and the door. As two of the men came directly at her, another one slipped out of sight. She realized a little too late that he'd come around to the passenger side. He opened the door. It would be so easy for him to slip the carrier out.

Renee needed to draw attention if she was to have any hope these men would scatter. Fighting three off at one time wouldn't end well. At the top of her lungs, she screamed, "Fire."

It was a trick she'd learned a long time ago from a neighbor who'd been a fireman. He'd taught her never to yell for help, always fire. People rushed toward a fire. Help, they might ignore.

"Fire." She yelled with so much force that she startled the baby. She vowed not to let these jerks take off with Abby. Desperation mounted as one of the men got close enough for her to take a swipe at him. He ducked and pinned her using the door as leverage.

Again, she yelled the word she'd been taught. With the door trapping her against the vehicle, she reached back to grab the handle of the carrier. Pain shot through her but a shot of adrenaline kicked in. The guy wasn't taking her baby. The two struggled for control of the carrier as she screamed over and over again.

Just when she thought she might be holding her ground, her fingers were being peeled off the handle. A wave of panic shot through her. Panic and more anger as she struggled for purchase.

One of the guys sneered at her as he pressed his body

against the door, keeping her from moving or fighting back. Her last finger slipped from the carrier when she heard the sirens. Movement hurt, but she managed to use her elbow as a wedge to shove the door. The guy blew out a breath and dug his shoes into the concrete.

"Hey!" A man's voice shouted from the direction of the store. Help was on the way. Was it going to be too late?

Chapter Six

In a matter of seconds, sirens filled the air and a few men came running. A car squealed its tires, roaring into the parking lot. Suddenly the pressure from the door was gone and Abby's cries were right behind Renee.

Abby. Her daughter was in the back seat as the three men jumped in their respective vehicles and peeled out of the parking lot in the opposite direction. All Renee wanted to do was hold her baby. She climbed in the back seat as an older gentleman darted toward her.

"Are you okay, miss?" The middle-aged man with a slight build and jean jacket stopped at her vehicle.

"Yes, thank you." She would be when she got Abby out of that car seat. Everything had happened so fast that she didn't get a good look at the vehicles. "Did anyone get a picture of those creeps or their vehicles?"

"I really don't know. I can ask." Looking up, she saw that he wore an apron that read Green Grocers.

Before she could say anything else, a car rushed into the spot next to hers. The face of the driver sent another shock wave rippling through her. Cash O'Connor. He tore out of the driver's seat.

"Everybody take a deep breath and an even bigger

step away from the vehicle." His voice poured over her, soothing her fried nerves.

The small crowd complied as the man wearing the apron gave a quick explanation of what he'd witnessed.

"Hold tight. I'm going to get you and Abby out of here." Those words were the best thing she'd heard all day. She was grateful that Cash hadn't asked how she was doing. Now that he was there and the immediate threat had passed, her hands started shaking.

"I was trying to buy a pacifier." The words sounded a little hollow, even to her.

"It's okay. You're all right. Abby's good." There was something so calm about Cash as he stood there, taking statements and handling the nervous crowd. Except when he looked at her, she caught a storm brewing behind his steel gaze. "I'm taking you home. Colton can meet us there to take your statement."

Cash offered a hand and she took it. He helped her out of the back seat. One look at her iron grip on the car seat handle and he seemed to think better of asking if she wanted him to carry the baby. He walked her over to his SUV where she climbed in the back with the baby. Renee secured the buckle and scooted so close to the carrier that it was practically on her lap. He locked up the other vehicle before claiming the driver's seat.

"Tell me everything that just happened." He started the ignition and reversed out of the lot. She couldn't wait to put this whole experience in the rearview. Somehow, this seemed like the beginning of a nightmare.

She briefed him on the events and tried to calm her racing heart in the process as he made his way back toward his family's ranch. "It was three to one and I thought they had her for a minute there. Thank you for showing when you did."

"Security alerted me to the fact that you left. I heard the call come in." There was a weariness to his voice that wasn't there before.

"You left to check on your father. Did they find him all right?"

"He was found." The heaviness in those three words told her the news wasn't good.

"I'm so sorry. I mean it, Cash." Words seemed hollow compared to what he must be feeling right now.

"Thank you. It means a lot." He nodded and she caught his gaze through the rearview. A powerful jolt rocketed through her body the minute their eyes locked. The force was so strong, her cheeks flamed and she diverted her gaze to Abby.

The attraction between them was so powerful, Renee straightened her daughter's pajamas to give her something else to focus on besides the current rippling through the vehicle.

Trying to apply logic to an out-of-control emotional situation made her think the strong pull to Cash O'Connor had to do with how broken he seemed. She could relate on such a deep level to the loss she'd glimpsed in him during those few seconds of eye contact. Hers was so much more than a relationship gone sour. Granted, that didn't help matters.

The rest of the ride was spent in companionable silence. Once they were back on O'Connor property, Cash stopped at the turnoff to the guesthouse.

"I need to check on my family and I won't be able to think straight if I'm wondering if the two of you are okay."

"I'm sorry about—"

"That came out wrong." He put his hand on the seat in front of her and twisted around to face her. "I care about what happens to the two of you. Leaving you alone to fend for yourself in a stranger's house was a jerk move on my part. I apologize for putting you in a bad position. I'd like to make it up to you, if you'll allow it. Right now, though, I need to get back to my family. I need to know what you want me to do. I can take you back to the cottage or to the main house with me."

The thought of being alone again didn't sit well with Renee. She had no doubt she'd get her bearings as a mother, but a lot had been thrown at her considering she couldn't exactly go home. "The main house is fine with me, Cash. I appreciate everything you're doing for us. I don't want to take advantage of your hospitality, though."

He started to argue but she put a hand up to stop him.

"I'm serious. If you need to do your job, I don't want to be in the way."

"You couldn't be," was all he said. "And for the record, it's not putting me out to help you and your daughter. I'm a selfish jerk because I'll admit that it feels good to impact someone else's life. It's the whole reason I got into law enforcement in the first place. As cliché as it sounds, I wanted to put bad people behind bars and help deserving people."

When he put it like that, her shoulders deflated a little because a growing part of her wanted to be special in his eyes. The reminder that he was a lawman who was doing his job was just what she needed to hear in order to save her from some potential embarrassment later. To Renee, there was nothing ordinary about her feelings toward Cash. "There's a reason clichés are what they are. They always contain a grain of truth."

CASH PARKED HIS vehicle in the small lot at the main house. Bringing a victim into his family's home was a little unorthodox. The way he saw it, there was no other choice. He couldn't rightly leave Renee alone. She was still new at being a mother. Add to the fact that she'd moved to a new town and on her first night there had become a crime statistic. This wasn't the welcome most folks received in Katy Gulch. Considering there'd been very little crime in town, residents might see her presence as an omen. People could be superstitious. He saw it as his job to make certain she and Abby were safe. He told himself the reason he cared so much was because of the lost look in her eyes and the fire that followed. A crime might have occurred, but she seemed determined not to be a victim.

Based on their conversations so far, she was intelligent. Her beauty was a given. Fiery red hair and blue eyes on a heart-shaped face made for one seriously beautiful package. She had legs that went on for days and which most runners would envy. Her creamy skin and the flush to her cheeks added to her beauty. Looks alone had never been the biggest draw for Cash. Going on a date with someone who was pretty on the outside and empty on the inside was a lot like expecting cake and getting cornbread instead. He'd gone on a handful of dates based on physical attraction alone. Most could be rated by how many times he sneaked a peek at his watch. Those were generally sixes, meaning he checked his watch six times in a two-hour span.

He'd gotten good at predicting his number within

ten minutes of a date. He suspected a date with Renee would net a zero. And, since the attraction to her was inappropriate considering she was his witness, he'd stop himself right there.

"Who would come back for her?" Renee asked as she unbuckled her daughter from her carrier and then held the little girl against her chest. The fire had returned to her eyes, which was a helluva lot better than the fear he'd seen there back in the grocery lot.

"There's a long list of people I'd like to talk to before I can answer that question." The rock stirred underneath his breastbone.

"Starting where?"

"With your lawyer. I'll need to coordinate the investigation with my brother, considering he's the sheriff. But I'd like to interview everyone involved in the adoption process."

"I thought you'd start with my ex," she admitted.

"He's on the list, too. And so is the contractor from work. As is anyone else you've come into contact with who might've had a bone to pick with you. Including your ex's new girlfriend."

Renee gasped. She held on to her daughter protectively. It would be hard to imagine anyone could pry the little girl from her hands. Cash had never thought of himself as a family man. He thought that ship had sailed a long time ago, after his last broken heart.

"I hadn't thought of her before. What reason would she have to want to take my child away from me?"

"A few come to mind. She might've lost her baby. She could've lied about being pregnant in the first place. He might have left her because he was still in love with you."

She blew out a breath. "I know he still has feelings for me. He's made that clear on more than one occasion. But I've been very honest with him. I've moved on and he should, too."

"The man's a fool," came out low and under his breath. Even the most intelligent person could make a bad decision when it came to someone they were attracted to. Renee had said she'd been with her ex for seven years, which meant she would've been in her early twenties when they'd met. "I'll put my head together with my brother. He'll be able to offer more perspective on the case."

Cash had to admit his growing feelings for the mother and child would impact his judgment. As an investigator, he needed to maintain objectivity in a case. Jamison King was an idiot for losing Renee.

He quirked a smile. So much for being objective.

More immediately, he needed to prepare Renee for what she was about to walk into at his family's home.

"As a warning, my family can be overwhelming to someone not used to us. Normally, we're a loud and caring bunch. The caring part is still true but finding out about my father has put the mood in the house at a somber level."

"It's to be expected under the circumstances." She practically pinned him with her stare. "Again, I'm so sorry for your loss."

"Your kindness is appreciated when it comes to my family." The O'Connors might not be perfect but their love for each other ran deep. No matter how big a mistake any of them made in life, the others rallied. Garrett included, despite his noticeable absence in recent years.

"Are you sure it's a good idea for me to be here while your family is going through so much?"

He tilted his head to one side. "You wouldn't be here if I didn't think it was a good idea."

"Fair enough."

"The timing isn't ideal but then there's never a good time to lose someone you love."

The look she gave him said she completely understood the sentiment. Cash tried to tell himself that he wanted to get to know more about Renee because of the investigation. A voice in the back of his mind called him out on the lie. There was something magnetic about the beautiful redhead, that clap of thunder he hadn't felt in far too long.

"Ready?" he asked.

She nodded.

He placed his hand on her elbow as he led her inside the main house. Her eyes widened as she stepped into the foyer of the two-story mansion his parents had called home for longer than Cash was alive.

"Wow," she muttered and he realized how impressive the place could be. He'd honestly gotten so used to it he'd forgotten how grand it could be. Big homes and expensive cars had never really impressed him much. His family was as down-to-earth as they came.

"My grandfather had this home built. My parents moved in to help take care of him when he became sick and he asked them to stay on. Mother always said she never really needed a place this big but it seemed important to her father-in-law. He was a kind man and she saw no reason to offend him. She'd had the downstairs renovated to her taste once they inherited the home, careful to keep important original details."

"Like?"

"A library with handcrafted bookshelves. You rarely ever see those built in homes now."

"That's so true. I love modern plumbing, don't get me wrong, but I've never even thought about having a full-fledged library in my home." There was so much awe in Renee's voice it was impossible not to let it affect him a little bit.

"Mother is old-school. I can't remember a time when she turned on a TV. We had 'em. Well, one. It's in the game room where we spent plenty of Sunday afternoons shooting pool, throwing darts and watching football when it was in season and chores were done."

"Sounds pretty great to me." She nodded and smiled, a first break in the tension that had been blanketing her. Football and Texans generally went hand in hand. "And it seems like I could learn quite a few parenting pointers from your mother. Your parents have obviously done a wonderful job with their boys."

"We had a sister," he admitted. He should probably prep her for the reaction his mother might have to a six-month-old girl being in the house. "Remember the sister I mentioned? She was kidnapped when she was little." He left it at that for the time being.

"Oh?" Shocked blue eyes blinked at him.

"My mother is strong, but I'm not sure she ever completely recovered from losing her daughter." Because he felt the need to change the subject before she asked too many questions, he added, "I hope you're not allergic to animals. We have quite a few critters running around the property."

"Are you kidding? I love animals." Her face brightened in the way only an animal lover's would. She glanced around, hugging Abby tight to her chest.

"Do you want something to drink first?" It might be almost evening but he could do with another coffee. When security had called to alert him to the fact that Renee had left the property he'd acted on impulse, jumping into a vehicle and taking off toward town. He'd guessed she wouldn't go back to her house. It was an assumption that had paid off. He didn't want to think what might've happened to Abby if he hadn't shown up when he did.

Timing wasn't always this good to him. He'd take it where he could.

"Coffee sounds good. I didn't get much in the way of sleep last night." She glanced at the sleeping angel now. "She started crying right after you left and nothing I did helped. You seem to have some kind of magic with her."

He didn't point out the fact she'd probably worn herself out crying earlier. "Give it a little time. You're doing better than you probably think."

"What makes you so sure?"

"I know how much my brother second-guessed himself when it came to his twins, especially in those first few months."

"I can barely manage with one. How on earth does he do this with two?"

"He had his rough patches in the early days but he's in a good rhythm now." Cash led her into the kitchen and then fixed two cups of coffee, surprised that no one was hanging around. His mother had most likely retreated to her library with her friend and Stacy. He was pretty sure he'd seen Gayle's car still parked out front. His brothers were probably in the barn, having a conversation with Slim and the others. "I'm afraid self-doubt seems to come with the territory for new parents." He set a cup in front of her on the massive butcher-block island. "It's easy to see how much you care about doing right by her. No one who cares that much could possibly fail."

She took a seat on one of the barstools and repositioned the baby, cradling her with one arm. "Thank you for finding her pacifier in your car. And I sure hope you're right. I've always wanted to be a mother. Life wasn't exactly ideal for a long time so I didn't think much about it but then lately it's like everything in my life snapped into place and I just knew the timing was right. For her. For a change. For a new life."

"Can't say that I have personal experience with an epiphany like that one, but I have always felt like I was supposed to be in law enforcement from as early as I can remember." He paused long enough to take a sip. "Which brings me to my next action. Calling in my brother."

"Are you sure that's a good idea with what your family is going through?" she asked pensively.

"Work is good for grief and there's a kidnapper on the loose in Katy Gulch." He stopped short of saying words like *kidnapping ring*. "Besides, we'll be grieving my father for a long time to come." Cash could scarcely contemplate the hole their father's death was going to leave in the family. If sadness got hold of Cash, it might not let him go. So, he decided it was best to deal with his emotions in doses rather than try to take it all in at once. It would swallow him up otherwise.

"As long as you're sure I won't be in the way." Those big blue eyes searched his for confirmation.

Cash was one hundred percent in trouble when it came to the little family sitting in his mother's kitchen. Nothing was going to happen to either of them on his watch. It was a promise he knew he couldn't guarantee no matter how much his heart wanted to.

The buzz of his cell phone indicated a text had come in. Cash glanced at the screen and then looked up. "Colton is parking right now."

Chapter Seven

Colton walked into the kitchen where Cash greeted him. The two embraced in a bear hug that nearly melted Renee's heart. Having grown up an only child, she had learned early on in life to depend on herself.

"Renee, I'd like you to meet my brother Colton O'Connor, the sheriff." Cash practically beamed with pride when he introduced his brother.

Colton extended his hand. Renee accepted the offering with a solid shake.

"I'm really sorry about your father." She meant those words. Mr. O'Connor must have been a wonderful father and man to have raised such amazing sons. It was easy to see both Cash and Colton were honest, respectful and kind men.

"Thank you for your kindness. We can't begin to fill the void our father leaves behind." Colton nodded his appreciation.

"He gave us a lot to live up to, that's for sure," Cash added. The warmth Renee witnessed between the brothers drew out a surprise longing to be part of a big family. She had always wanted to be a mother. But she figured hers would be a *one-and-done* situation. The sudden picture of big family holidays with three or four kids running around sent warmth shooting through her. She chalked the sentiment up to overwrought nerves and the biology class that had taught her about ingrained primal needs when it came to protection. A large close-knit family would offer more defense during a dangerous time.

Having a baby made her feel more vulnerable than she'd expected. Renee was slowly realizing just how much motherhood would change her. Hearing Cash review details as he brought his brother up to speed made her realize she needed to add security measures if she ever wanted to sleep at night after this ordeal. Having a complete stranger come inside her home without permission made her feel violated and angry.

"It's too early to rule anything out but I'm not as worried about the general population of town being at risk now that I've been caught up." Colton's lips formed a thin line. "On the surface, this crime appears to be targeted at Ms. Smith and her daughter."

"Please, call me Renee." She'd suspected as much. However, hearing those words caused her to hold Abby just a little bit closer.

Colton conceded her request with a small smile and a nod. She also noticed that his gaze moved from her back to his brother where it lingered a few seconds too long. In her mind, the attraction happening between her and Cash had been mostly on her side until then. Watching his brother, she was thinking that maybe the feeling was mutual. No one had ever stirred her heart or made her stomach free-fall the way he did. As much as she wanted to run toward the feeling, it was best to leave well enough alone.

"Since this does appear to be a targeted crime,"

Colton continued, "I'd like to start interviewing those closest to the witness."

Cash nodded in agreement. It seemed both investigators were on the same track.

"We can interview suspects together, separately or split the list. However you want to get this done. You're the lead on this one." Cash rocked on his heels.

"Considering there have been two attempts in less than a day, it makes more sense to split the list so we can cover more ground, faster." Colton paused a few beats. "It might be a good idea for me to call and ask suspects to stop by my office so you can watch them give statements from behind the glass of the interview room. Hearing the statements might spark something and we'll hopefully get further." He made a good point. One that had his brother rocking his head in agreement one more time. Colton looked to Renee. "I'd like to start with your ex."

"Agreed," Cash stated. "With a family on the way, he shouldn't be a flight risk. Asking him to come and give a statement shouldn't raise any red flags. We're merely requesting that he make an appointment to stop by, which seems a lot less threatening than showing up at his home or job."

"Very true." Colton cocked his head to one side. "I don't like the lawyer on the adoption case. His name has come up far too often in questionable cases."

Renee gasped. "Does that mean my adoption could be illegal?" Fear gripped her, squeezing the air out of her lungs.

"It's too early to make any predictions in this case and I know he's had legal adoptions to his credit." Colton's reassurance fell short of comforting her.

"He's like oil," Cash said. He and his brother seemed to be on the same page when it came to Kipp McGee.

"Nothing sticks," Colton agreed.

"The unknown guy from the moving company tops my list, as well." Cash tapped his phone where he'd been keeping notes. "As does the contractor from her office, Darion."

Hearing the names of possible suspects—people who wanted to hurt her—sent a chill racing down her back. Discussing her life and people in it struck her as surreal. Then again, after being stagnant for so long, at least her life was moving forward again. This situation was awful and creepy but at least she was living again.

"Her ex's new girlfriend has my attention as well. Do you happen to know the name of her boss?" Colton asked Renee. "I want to be able to verify their whereabouts from an independent source. I also might need to call her during the day to ask her to come in."

"Yolanda Tran works for the same person Jamison does. The guy's name is Adam Sartre." She gently rocked Abby who was surprisingly still asleep. Bedtime wasn't that far off and Renee might pay dearly for letting her angel sleep this late in the day but she didn't want to disturb Abby.

"Do you work at the same place?" he asked.

"Yes, but different departments. They work in sales and I work behind the scenes keeping our company's website up-to-date with products. We sell tax software. The company name is TaxedUp."

"A quick call to their boss might help answer a few questions." Colton got up and poured a glass of water. "Considering the first attack happened in the middle of the night, no one with a nine-to-five office job would've been at work. So, we can't rule anyone out based on the timeline. However, today's attempt is a different story." He looked at Renee. "Can you provide a cell number to Adam Sartre?"

With her free hand, Renee fished her cell phone from her pocket and scrolled through the contacts. She stopped on Adam's number. "This is his number." She rattled it off.

Colton thanked her. "Let me give him a quick call and see if we can find out if they were at work during the second attempt."

He excused himself before walking back to the sink to refill his glass. "Good evening. Is this Mr. Sartre?"

He must've said it was because Colton continued after a beat. "My name is Sheriff Colton O'Connor and I'd like to ask a couple of questions about two of your employees if I could have a moment of your time." There was silence for a few beats. "Yes, sir. I'm calling about Jamison King and Yolanda Tran." There was another pause. "Did either one of them show up for work today?" Another pause. "Neither?"

Renee's heart dropped. As mad as she was at Jamison for everything he'd done during their relationship and especially the past year, the thought he could be involved with a kidnapping attempt on Abby nearly gutted her. Losing his mother had accelerated the changes in him. Could he actually be that cruel?

Hearing the lawyer that she'd used for the adoption was shady sent her mind in another direction. Was it possible Abby's birth parents wanted her back? Had Abby been taken from someone illegally? Granted, if that were true it seemed like the person would use regular channels to get their daughter back. The court system would be the first line of defense for Abby's parents if she'd been taken illegally. Plus, wouldn't there be an AMBER alert issued? Cell phones would have been blasted and her picture would be all over the news.

Unless whoever had given the baby up had changed his or her mind. The mother or father could have known Kipp McGee wasn't honest. He might even have paid them good money to stay quiet. The person might have followed him to Renee. In that case, Renee might have the upper hand legally. But then she could end up bankrupting herself fighting it out in court.

Her brain cramped thinking there might be some way she could lose her daughter.

Renee couldn't go there. Not even hypothetically. Her gaze searched Cash's for some kind of reassurance. It should be odd that a man she barely knew had become like a lifeline in a matter of hours. And yet, there was something different about Cash O'Connor that she couldn't quite put her finger on. No man before him made her feel comforted when her world was careening toward the wall. In all the years she'd been together with Jamison, she'd never once had a sense of belonging or of the world being right.

Again, she blamed biology. Cash was strong and intelligent. He wore a badge. The man was clearly capable of handling any situation that came his way. Having someone around who she could lean on for a change was foreign but nice. She could get used to being a team with someone like Cash.

The situation was temporary, a little voice in the back of her mind reminded her. After the investigation, he'd go back to his life and she'd go back to hers.

So, why did the thought make her sad?

They both lived in Katy Gulch. She planned to stick around. With a stubborn streak a mile long, she had no plans to repack her belongings and head back to Dallas. Security needed to be installed to make her environment safer. Katy Gulch was home now.

His brother ended the call and shot her a look of apology. "Neither Mr. King nor Ms. Tran made it in to work this morning. She wasn't feeling well so she called in sick. Mr. King told their boss she made a doctor's appointment and he wanted to be there since the pregnancy was progressing."

"Does that mean what I think it does? She is his alibi and vice versa?" Was that even allowed? Renee had no idea how the law worked or how a judge would view testimony from someone who had a vested interest in hiding the truth.

"I'm afraid so. I can have my assistant dig up information about her doctor, see if they made it to their appointment this morning." Colton drummed his fingers on the granite island as Cash's gaze intensified.

"It'll be interesting to hear what they have to say." Renee couldn't help but roll her eyes. Interesting wasn't exactly the word that usually came to mind when she thought of Jamison.

Cash grunted. "I definitely want to be behind the glass of the interview room to hear their excuses in person."

"I'm going to make some calls on my way in to my office. See how fast we can get meetings set up for tomorrow. I want to move on this quickly before this perp has a chance to regroup and strike again." Colton's words sent another icy chill down Renee's spine. He turned to her. "You'll be in good hands with my brother here. As a US marshal, protecting a witness is one of the many things he does well. Don't hesitate to reach out to me if you remember anything that might help with the case."

"We'll head out soon." Cash's jaw tightened and it looked like he clenched his back teeth.

She thanked Colton again for everything he was doing for her and Abby. It surprised Renee that she wanted to be more to Cash than just a work assignment.

THE BABY HAD been fed and was happily sleeping. The little thing barely had any hair but she made up for it with the biggest brown eyes—eyes that melted hearts. Cash had been cycling through a few thoughts while Renee took care of the baby's immediate needs.

He had a dozen thoughts running through his mind. It was possible Jamison and Yolanda had something against Renee. Revenge? Why? What would they have to gain by taking her child? The thought occurred to him that something might've happened to Yolanda's pregnancy to make her lose her baby. Then Abby would be a replacement. Still, why? It didn't quite add up that the two of them would be in league against her. What would Yolanda have to gain? Jamison didn't seem to want a child. Or, maybe he didn't want a child with Renee, in which case the man was an idiot.

Renee was an intelligent, beautiful woman. Any man would be lucky to have her in his life. Jamison must be a real piece of work.

It was altogether possible that Jamison had realized that he'd made a mistake walking away from Renee. It was worth considering the position Yolanda would be in should Jamison declare he was still in love with his ex. But why try to kidnap the baby? Why not go after Renee directly? Taking Abby to hurt Renee was a roundabout way to punish her. Yolanda dropped a few notches down the suspect list.

Since this was a targeted crime and he and his brother had been focused on someone looking to punish Renee, it was worth considering the birth mother or father simply wanted their child back. Kipp McGee wasn't exactly known for dealing aboveboard.

A young mother or father who'd changed their mind had motive. It might even make more sense. The mover, in Cash's opinion, was a pawn if he was involved. He was a tool meant to accomplish a goal. He could also lead them to the real perp. Figuring out his identity could be the lead they needed to crack the case open. Cash couldn't count the number of times a case had exploded after a small piece of information lit a fire, creating a domino effect.

Then there was the contractor from Renee's job. The guy was a creep and most definitely out of line. Was he the criminal they were looking for?

Cash's thoughts circled back to Kipp McGee. That was the interview Cash most wanted to listen in on. When he got the green light to take Renee to his brother's office, he needed to have a conversation with Colton about the lawyer, who moved up the suspect list based on his reputation in the law enforcement community.

"Any word from your brother?" Renee had kept Abby within arm's reach since they'd arrived at his family's home. She must need a break by now but she seemed determine not to let the little girl out of her sight and he couldn't blame her. If the shoe was on the other foot and it was *his* daughter, he wouldn't let her out of his sight until he taught her basic self-defense moves.

"Nothing yet." He wondered if he could convince her to eat something or go to sleep. "Are you hungry?"

Renee shook her head. "Not really."

"I can't speak from personal experience, but my brother Colton swears the only time he got any rest was when his twins were asleep." Cash glanced at the carrier.

Renee blew out a frustrated-sounding breath. "I seriously doubt I'll ever close my eyes again after what happened. I've literally never been so shaken up in my life." She shook her head and pinched the bridge of her nose. "That must make me sound a little crazy."

"Not really. I saw how much having children changed my brother. I'm pretty sure crazy comes with the job." The fact that she laughed at his joke made his chest puff out a little bit more than he should probably allow. It was the first break in tension and she very much needed it. Being on alert that long and overstressed wasn't good for Renee. Cash had seen it countless times with witnesses in his protection.

"I'm beginning to see that now." Her smile didn't exactly reach her eyes, but he'd take it. It was progress. She was quick to add, "I still think it's the best job in the world."

He had no idea. No plans to figure it out, either. Cash had seen his brother go through falling in love, having kids. And then having his heart cut in half when his wife walked because law enforcement was too risky a job. It was true. Only a special kind of person could hang in there not knowing whether or not the love of their life would walk through the door at night. Many men and women couldn't handle their spouses putting their lives on the line on a daily basis.

Cash would argue figuring that out after getting married and birthing babies was ridiculous. Colton's wife had known the risks going in. His brother had been sheriff for the past five years. Vows meant something to an O'Connor. There was no backing out after going to the altar. And Cash was in no rush to jump feet first into that pool.

Renee was different. She beamed at the mention of Abby. "It suits you. Being a mother. Looks good on you."

Her cheeks flushed at the compliment and she was even more beautiful. His heart betrayed him again by clenching and making him wish he had more time to get to know Renee outside of his job.

"Thank you. I have a long way to go before I get a handle on parenting, so I'm surprised it looks good on me." She laughed. It was a small win, but he'd take it. Making Renee relax a little bit after what she'd been through made him feel good.

"You make it work." He smiled back at her. "Do you mind if I ask a personal question?"

"Go ahead. I have a feeling after all this is said and done you will end up knowing a lot more about me than you probably even wanted to." The comment came off flippantly, but he picked up on the serious undercurrent in her tone. He'd seen that dozens of times, too. A regular law-abiding citizen who suddenly finds themselves on the wrong side of crime. It was shocking and could completely throw them off balance. Totally understandable under the circumstances and another reason he liked making her laugh and breaking down some of the shock.

"What made you decide to adopt?" Not that he thought there was anything wrong with it. Taking a baby into her home was admirable. He found that he was curious about *her* decision in particular and wanted to know more about what made Renee tick.

"There were a lot of reasons. I guess in the end I realized I wanted to start my family and that no longer meant being traditional about it. Any time I brought up the subject of putting down roots and starting a family to my ex, he got squirrely about it. The crazy thing is that we'd just lived together so long marriage and family seemed like the next logical step. Being with him became a routine. Then, suddenly, I pulled into the parking lot of the place where we both worked in different departments. My life with him flashed before my eyes and I started crying. Like really crying and I am so not a crier. I didn't want to go inside the building. I didn't want to go home. It was crazy because I felt like we had already made this commitment to each other that we had to honor, and we weren't even married. We'd never even made our relationship official. When his lease was up five years ago after we'd been dating for two years, he asked what I thought about saving on rent and him moving in with me. I remember shrugging my shoulders and telling him that would be fine. There was nothing romantic or special about it. It felt like a business exchange. Isn't that weird?"

"So many people settle for less. It's easier to stay together than to break up after a certain point." He'd been in a similar relationship early on. "I dated someone once who, despite using serious precautions, told me she was pregnant with my child."

"What did you do?" Renee's hand came up to her mouth to cover her shock.

"Stuck around. There was no way I could walk away from my own child. There were rumors circulating that she'd been unfaithful on more than one occasion when I had cases that had me out of town for days on end. The relationship seemed to be winding down when she turned up pregnant, which left a few unanswered questions in my mind. I held off on the marriage until I was certain the child was mine. He wasn't." Those last two words had never made him feel so raw before. Damned if he hadn't stuffed those emotions down deep and tried his level best to forget. Talking about it now with Renee made him able to dredge up the past.

"I'm sorry." Her compassion shed a spark of light in the darkest places in his soul. It wasn't so much that he'd wanted to have a child with Stephanie as it was the loss of the kid he'd believed might be his.

"Thank you. It means more than you know to hear you say that." He meant those words. Cash tried to convince himself that he was sharing personal information with Renee to help her relax. It wasn't true. He liked talking to her and wanted to get to know her better. Part of that process was giving up a little about himself. But it was time to shift the conversation back to her. "What did you do while sitting in the car? Did you decide to go to work? Stay with him longer?"

"I knew in that moment the relationship was over for me. Does it sound crazy?"

"Not in the least. It's easy to stay with someone out of habit. It's easy to get comfortable." Cash could relate. He was pretty damn careful not to send mixed signals to the women he'd dated after Stephanie. He never would've moved in with someone he didn't have the intention to marry. Not because he was taking some moral high road, it just seemed like that meant he would already be committed. He'd seen a couple of his brothers go down that road only to have it bite them afterward. It was an easy mistake to make.

"Considering the fact that I was a leaky faucet, there was no way I could go to work. I texted my boss and said that I needed to take a sick day. Instead of going home, I went to this park near our apartment. I lost track of time sitting there in my car, watching kids play on the playground equipment. I was transfixed." She breathed out a heavy sigh. "I resolved to get my act together right then and there. Having a family was important to me. Having a husband was not. Eventually, I got the nerve to go home. But before I could end the relationship, Jamison got the call about his mother. Her doctor gave her six months to live. She survived for a year. I couldn't walk away under those circumstances with a clean conscience. Color me the fool."

"It's not foolish to be kind. Jamison sounds like a selfish jerk who doesn't deserve someone like you." Cash couldn't help but come to her defense when he saw how much she was beating herself up over her decision to stay long after she stopped caring for her ex. "It shows incredible courage to stick around in a situation like that."

Renee took a minute to respond, like she wanted to really digest the words he'd just spoken. Her gaze lifted to his and there was something unexpected in her eyes, a spark that hadn't been there before. Frustration turned into vulnerability. Vulnerability quickly changed to something else altogether...desire?

In the space of a few seconds, the room heated and that spark in her eyes sent electricity shooting through him, seeking an outlet. A small explosion detonated in the center of his chest and Cash knew in that moment just how much trouble he was in when it came to the single mother.

Chapter Eight

Renee could get lost in Cash's steel eyes. She knew the instant her world had tilted on its axis and she'd stopped fighting the attraction she felt toward Cash—an attraction that had nearly bowled her over from the minute she'd opened the door to find him standing on her porch.

Having strong feelings for someone she barely knew should be odd, not comfortable, not like it was the most natural thing. Reminding herself they'd barely met did nothing to quell the squall gaining steam inside her. And yet, she'd known Jamison for almost a year before they'd started dating and look how that had turned out.

Looking back, it had been Jamison's persistence that had won her over. She'd listened to her head when it had said a man who kept after her for a date for a solid year would be there for her in the long run. It was almost comical when she looked back at their relationship.

A thought struck. Had she traded love for security? If she had, the joke was on her.

The sizzle of attraction and longing that she felt for Cash was foreign. But then, Renee never would've allowed herself to truly fall for anyone no matter how much she tried to convince herself that she liked them.

Or was that just the lie she'd told herself to protect her own heart?

Being with Cash had her questioning all her beliefs about love. Because somewhere along the line, she'd convinced herself that true love was about sacrifice and digging her heels in to stay with someone because he needed her without regard for how little she got in return. Had she settled with Jamison?

The real answer was a slap of reality. In a word…yes. She'd settled for someone who needed her rather than hold out for the person who stirred feelings she wasn't certain how to handle. This out-of-control feeling she had in Cash's presence freaked her out more than she wanted to acknowledge.

Keeping a handle on her emotions was how she'd survived her childhood. As much as she wanted to lean into the feeling of being near Cash, it was too much, too fast.

The buzz of his cell phone broke into the moment happening between them. He checked the screen before glancing up. This time when they made eye contact, she could keep her emotions in check. Barely. Her cheeks flushed at how transparent she was being. The man had just shared something very personal with her and in the process made her feel special. How special was she to him?

Cash O'Connor worked in law enforcement. His job would make him good at getting people to trust him. Clearly, he was good at his job because she'd gone all in for a few minutes with him. She blinked and leaned back in her chair, trying to regain more of her composure—composure that was a slippery slope around this man.

"Colton has a couple of interviews lined up for early tomorrow morning, starting with the crew leader from your moving company." He glanced up at her after double-checking his screen.

Renee's heart jackhammered the inside of her rib cage, slamming out a staccato rhythm. She needed a break from the heat pinging between them and figured it would die down on its own as she spent more time with him. So far, it was a rising tide turning into one helluva wave ready to crash into shore. "We should get a few hours of sleep."

Cash responded to the text before catching her gaze. A warning shot straight to her heart with the look on his face. He put his hands up in the surrender position. "I think I already know the answer to this but I wanted you to think about leaving Abby at the ranch. It might be safer for her here with Stacy."

"She's safest with her mother." Those words rolled off her tongue so easily they gave a boost to her confidence as a new parent.

"I thought you might say that." He quirked a devastating grin and a look that seemed an awful lot like approval. "Let's grab a few hours of sleep and we'll head out at first light."

RENEE WAS SURPRISINGLY able to nod off for a few hours. Abby woke at first light, so Renee retraced her steps to the kitchen to make a bottle. Cash sat at the table, staring at the screen of his laptop.

"Did you sleep?" she asked.

"Enough." He immediately got up and helped make the formula. They worked as a team and when Abby had been tended to, Renee put her daughter on a blanket that was on the floor of the guest room long enough to freshen up.

She gathered baby supplies and then returned to the kitchen where Cash handed her a bagel.

"Shall we?" he asked after she polished it off.

She nodded before following him to his vehicle where he brought a to-go coffee for her. She couldn't think of a safer place than a sheriff's office, so she felt confident in her decision to bring Abby along. Besides, the little girl wasn't leaving Renee's sight. This child would know how much her mother loved her. Once this ordeal was behind the two of them, Renee planned to shower her daughter with what kids needed most—unconditional love and acceptance.

After securing Abby's seat in the back, Renee climbed into the passenger side and buckled in. Maybe it was the moment that had happened between them a few hours ago that seemed to linger, but she wanted to know more about Cash O'Connor. Since she had no idea where to start, she folded her hands in her lap and sat quietly.

Thankfully, he broke the silence. "Is your family originally from Dallas?"

"Yes. I grew up inside the Loop, which means Loop 12 if you're not familiar. My parents owned a resale shop south of the Trinity River. I worked there summers and after school, which taught me a lot about running a small family business. I also decided it wasn't for me so I now work for a global company."

"Really? What didn't you like about the small family business?" He started the engine and navigated onto the long driveway as the sun started to rise.

"I could tell you that a lot of it was because of the

long hours and no health insurance. You probably know best that family businesses basically means working all day and bringing work home. But, honestly, my parents fought all the time. When I think of owning a business, that's what comes to mind. Unhappiness. Arguments. Blaming. Screaming at each other. There was no way I was going to repeat their mistakes." She hadn't really thought about that until now. The realization hit home. It also struck her that she and Jamison rarely ever argued. In part because she had always been easygoing, but also because she let him have his way. What was there to fight about?

"It's important to be able to separate work from home." His comment made her thoughts shift to his situation. Now that his father was gone, would he be expected to step into the family business? It wasn't a question she felt she had the right to ask. But it must be on his mind. Then again, he'd thrown himself into her investigation. She got it. Work was a good distraction from grief and despair. Her work had been a saving grace getting her through that last year with Jamison. Despite Renee's challenging relationship with her parents, she'd loved them. Losing them both so suddenly had been the most difficult thing she'd ever had to deal with until recently.

"Your family seems to have their priorities in the right place. Not only do I admire them for it, I hope to emulate their example with my daughter." Jamison's mother had put her son before everything else. Renee wasn't bothered by the relationship at first. She had confused it with love back then. It wasn't until Jamison's mother had pulled Renee aside to say that her son had complained about Renee's almost constant nagging for him to pick up after himself around their apartment that she realized how unhealthy the relationship was. She'd been mortified. A quick decision was made right there and then. His mother didn't get to tell Renee what to do. And, besides, how awful was it that the person who should be her partner was doing nothing but complaining about her to his mother?

"Believe me when I say we know how fortunate we are. My parents married young and started a family soon after. I think they survived Caroline's kidnapping by making damn sure they always put us first. As strong as my mother is, I doubt she would've survived if she hadn't learned she was pregnant with me a few weeks after my sister was taken."

"I'm so sorry, Cash. I'd like to say that I can't imagine how that would feel and, truly, I count my blessings that Abby is in this back seat instead of..." She couldn't finish the sentence without getting so choked up she could barely breathe. What his mother, his family, went through was inconceivable. "After what we've been through in the past twenty-four hours, I can only imagine it's the tip of the iceberg compared to what your parents have endured. Bad things shouldn't happen to such good people."

"To be honest, I don't think my mother ever stopped looking for Caroline or hoping she'd show up one day out of the blue." The pain in his voice struck a chord. One event could change the course of someone's life so completely. The randomness of life hit home.

"Hope can be a beautiful and yet painful thing," she acknowledged.

"Truer words have never been spoken." He rocked his head and tightened his grip on the steering wheel.

His voice softened when he said, "Thanks for listening to me talk about my family, by the way. You're the first person I've wanted to talk to about them."

"Thank you for trusting me, Cash." Hearing that he'd opened himself up to *her* and shared his pain with *her* sent another dangerous shot of warmth to her heart.

"I just thought you should know that you're special to me."

Renee's heart really beat double time hearing those words. She wanted to tell him that she felt the same more than anything. But the words died on her lips and all her defenses flared. What was wrong with her that she couldn't? How broken was she that she couldn't utter the words trying to form on her lips?

Instead of talking, which she'd never been all that good at anyway, she reached out and touched his arm.

One touch shouldn't bring so many parts of her to life—her body, her mind, her heart.

Saying that she was in trouble when it came to the devastating man sitting beside her would just be stating the obvious. Truly opening herself up would require more than desire, more than heat so intense it pinged between them even now. She *wanted* to be able to let her emotions take over and go with the feelings pulsing inside her. But she couldn't.

The tapes embedded so deep in the back of her mind played a different message. They sent a warning. They told her that every relationship would end up like her parents' toxic one. They said everyone would eventually let her down. They said that she couldn't really trust another soul.

Her situation with Jamison was sad. She felt a fool for staying longer than she should've. But a man like

Cash could devastate her if she got into a relationship with him and it ended. And considering she was no good at relationships, it would end.

Renee withdrew her hand and apologized.

"Why are you sorry?" The hurt in his voice put another chink in her carefully constructed armor.

"I just am."

CASH COULD FEEL the temperature in the cab change the minute Renee pulled her hand back. Had he done something wrong?

The fact that he'd wanted to talk to her about his family and his past still shocked him. He tried to convince himself that he was putting his witness at ease by sharing a common bond. The voice inside his head—the one that didn't put up with any snow job he tried to sell—called him out.

He'd opened up to Renee because he felt a connection to her unlike anything he'd ever experienced with another person. Instead of acknowledging how special she was, he took another route. Cash decided that he was ready to deal with the events from the past. This case was good for him, he reasoned. It caused him to confront his demons so he could move on. Maybe he was ready to unpack the past and move on from it... trust again.

The situation with Pops had Cash twisted up emotionally. There was no way he could deal with losing his father without first reconciling the loss of his sister, Caroline. And he'd searched cold case files for years... still did...with the hope that one day he'd be able to bring closure for his parents. Now that Pops was gone, the opportunity was lost with him.

It was like a bullet slammed into Cash at the thought. The man he'd put on a pedestal and respected his entire life was gone. A heavy blanket dropped on his shoulders.

Dammit. Dammit. Dammit.

Rather than wallow in the feeling, Cash put it into perspective. His mother needed him to be strong. His brothers needed someone to lead them. Well, that thought was almost comical. His brothers were grown men. Still, being the eldest, he sometimes saw his siblings as his responsibility. Either way, Cash's feelings came in a hard third. Stuffing his emotions into the box he was so good at finding, he tucked it away and refocused on the case in front of him.

After a long silence, he pulled into a parking spot at his brother's office. Caroline was on his mind. He didn't regret talking about his sister with Renee even though discussing her at all with someone outside the family wasn't done. "I told you about what happened to my sister because I wanted you to know that you're not alone. Caroline was taken from her crib in my parents' old house—"

"Hold on a second. Didn't you say she was the same age as Abby when it happened?" Renee asked.

"Yes. Before you get too riled up it has been more than three decades since Caroline went missing with no other similar crimes in or near Katy Gulch in between. There have been cases of parent abductions of babies around the same age, but none reported with a child being taken from his or her crib, and no cases of someone trying twice." He'd already thought about the other incidences because he knew this one would dredge up painful old memories for his mother. He'd read the cold case file on his sister. All living relatives had been interviewed, some several times. As an investigator, it made sense to him that the focus would be on next of kin. More than three quarters of abductions involved a parent. Stranger abductions accounted for less than one percent of cases. And those were some of the least recoverable.

"Part of me hoped no one close to me could be this cruel. I guess that might not be the case." Her chin jutted out with what seemed to be determination. "Guess I have to get used to the reality there are bad people in the world."

"The birth mother might have changed her mind. You already heard that the attorney you used to adopt has been linked to a few questionable adoptions. We'll have a better idea of what's going on after hearing from suspects in the interviews."

Renee nodded before climbing out of the passenger seat and opening the back door to take Abby out of her car seat.

"Can I help with anything?" He wanted to lighten her load in any way he could.

"Would you mind taking the diaper bag?" she asked.

"Not a bit." He made a move to pick it up from the floorboard when he thought she was taking a step back. Signals crossed and she ended up leaning into the vehicle at the same time as him. Their shoulders bumped and more of that electricity shot through him. He suppressed a small smile. The electricity pinging between them was inconvenient. Although he told himself it was good on some level. It meant his heart was capable of taking the leap with someone, at least. Getting to know Renee did little to tamp down his attraction. If anything, her intelligence made her that much more physically appealing.

He backed up first. "Go ahead."

She smiled at him as she took a step back. "Sorry. I was trying to help you."

"Since your hands are full, how about I do the honors?"

"Deal." Seeing the way she beamed at the little girl in her arms made the image of a family come to mind. After his experience with Stephanie, he didn't consider himself the settling down type.

One of Cash's uncles had lived perfectly fine without a wedding band. Uncle Brady had made the choice never to wed and had lived his life on the ranch until sickness took him too young. At fifty, he'd dated the same woman for a decade and neither had felt the need to live under the same roof or go before the Justice of the Peace.

Cash could see himself in a similar arrangement. At least, he could until he'd met Renee and Abby. The two of them were carving out a special place in his heart. Again, he told himself being open to the possibility of one day meeting and falling in love with someone who made him want the whole package was a positive. Commitment had just seemed so permanent to him before. There'd never been a person he'd want to wake up to every day—day after day—without getting bored or needing a change. Also, he considered himself married to a job that would always come first. Most of his early relationships proved what his brother had learned the hard way. Law enforcement jobs and long-term personal relationships weren't always a good mix.

He'd dated a few women who'd convinced themselves they could go the distance if things got serious. The attitude lasted, on average, three months. The first time he'd miss an event special to his girlfriend, an attitude shift occurred by the next date. He'd learned the hard way the countdown to the end of the relationship began at that point. His relationships were predictable. He had it down to a science.

Abby cooed, blew spit bubbles and gave Cash the biggest smile he'd ever seen. The kid was all big eyes and cuteness. "You have quite the charmer there."

Renee's cheeks warmed as she looked at Abby. "I'm going to have to keep an eye on this one when she turns fifteen."

"I'll help you find a stick to beat the boys away." His joke was met with a genuine laugh and he realized what it could imply—that he would be there when Abby turned fifteen. Instead of thinking too deeply about that, he put his hand on the small of Renee's back as the two walked into his brother's office building.

Chapter Nine

The minute they stepped inside the lobby, Gert Francis rounded her desk to greet them. His brother's secretary was in her late sixties and could be best described as lively. She had a twinkle to her brown eyes and a grandmotherly smile that was disarming. Folks had nicknamed her Oprah for her ability to get people to open up like the popular TV host, Oprah Winfrey.

Gert threw her arms around Cash first and brought him into a sincere hug. "Stacy called the minute she could. I'm so sorry to hear about your daddy."

"Thank you, Gert." He was still trying to process the fact Pops was gone. "Your sympathy means a lot."

When she looked up at him, tears streaked her cheeks. She pulled back and squeezed his forearm. "I've already said this to Colton, but I want you to hear it, too. You let me know if your family needs anything and I mean *anything*. You hear?"

"Yes, ma'am." Her kindness was greatly appreciated. She'd worked for the last sheriff before he'd retired and Colton had been elected. She'd been a valuable team member, helping Colton get up to speed on his job. They'd known her for years but she'd become like family since he'd taken over as sheriff.

"I already told Stacy that I'm making a casserole to drop off at the ranch after work," Gert said matter-of-factly. She was the roll-up-her-sleeves type. Her husband had passed away five years ago. Since she'd suffered the same loss as his mother, she would be a good person to lean on for advice on how to get through the coming days.

"Mother will appreciate your good cooking and your company." Talking to Gert was making his father's death more real. Cash had been able to put his emotions on hold, allowing himself to get wrapped up in Renee's case. He didn't dare open the floodgates now. "You know how special you are to our family."

Warmth radiated from her when she looked up at him and then to Renee.

"You must be Renee. I'm Gert." She was devoted to Colton and to the county. When she wasn't at work, she watched a constant stream of popular police and detective shows. Her quick wit proved helpful in many cases—cases that she liked to try to solve before Colton. Being sheriff in a ranching community meant crime that mostly involved missing pets, bicycles and rowdy teenagers who were blowing off steam in cow pastures. Hard crime was rare in Katy Gulch and the surrounding community. Although, it did happen. Case in point, his sister's kidnapping. Although, that was more than thirty years ago. Still, he feared this was the tip of the iceberg. His fear came from instinct honed by years of training and experience.

"Very nice to meet you, Gert," Renee said, her fingers tight around the carrier holding Abby.

Cash had never seen Gert pass up an opportunity to

ask to hold a baby. She seemed to realize that Renee wouldn't let go of her child after what had happened.

"I'm real sorry about what you and your sweet angel are going through. We have some of the best lawmen in the state working on your case. Katy Gulch is a better community than this, a safe community." Gert prided herself on living in a place where people helped each other. The sentiment had been built into ranchers and farmers since long before Cash was born and it was part of the reason he would never leave his hometown. Cash O'Connor was right where he belonged.

"Thank you." Renee said the words on a small sigh. She smiled and he could've sworn those words put her more at ease than he'd seen her so far.

"I don't want to keep you. Colton said to bring you straight to the interview room and then let him know when you're there. Follow me," Gert said.

The lobby had Gert's desk on the left and a long counter on the right. There were glass doors that required a special ID badge directly in front of them. Once behind those doors, the building was shaped like a U. Colton's office was to the right and down the hall. The route to the interview room was behind another locked door to their left.

Cash brought up the rear as Gert led Renee through the locked doors and down the hallway to the witness room, which was roughly the size of a walk-in closet.

Abby was busy blowing raspberries on her fist. The minute Renee stepped inside the room, she froze. In barely a whisper, she asked, "Can he hear us?"

"No." Cash kept his voice low.

The lights were dim and there was a small speaker with a box and a button. The button was used to communicate orders to the people inside the interview room, which was on the other side of the two-way mirror.

Gert turned tail. Before she disappeared, she said, "I'll let your brother know that you're in here and you're good to go."

"Thank you," Cash said.

Studying the man sitting down at a metal table, she confirmed the identity of her moving crew's chief. "That's the guy who introduced himself as Paul."

A few minutes later, Colton joined them. "I wanted to stop in here before the interview to see if you recognize this man."

"Yes, that's Paul."

"Paul Miser," Colton confirmed. "According to Gert, he has a clean record with no known priors. He's not a college student." No one seemed surprised about that despite the moving company's name, College Boy Movers. "But he has been working for the company five years. Got moved up to crew chief two years ago. He supports his mother, who is on disability."

Cash wasn't surprised Gert was able to dig all that up in a matter of hours. The woman worked magic.

"His girlfriend is six months pregnant," Colton continued. That pretty much ruled Paul out for personal reasons in Cash's book but he still wanted to hear what the suspect had to say. There was still a possibility that a person with a kid on the way might be desperate for cash. A deep dive into the guy's financials could clear up whether he needed money or not. Of course, Colton couldn't just dig into someone's bank account without a warrant but that didn't mean he couldn't ask permission. Innocent people usually volunteered information to help a case and a guy with a kid on the way might be more cooperative in an attempted kidnapping investigation.

"Your job was the only one he and his crew had. He says he arrived home afterward and took a nap on the couch. His mother woke him in time for dinner and he was home after that. His mother corroborated the story that he was alone in his room. She doesn't work, so he lives there to help her with her bills. His girlfriend's job is too far away so she lives with her family through the week. However, the mother went to bed at eight thirty and didn't see him again until nine o'clock the next morning."

"Not exactly an ironclad alibi," Cash observed.

"No, it isn't."

"Let's see what Mr. Miser has to say." Colton excused himself and closed the door behind him. He strode into the interview room with an entirely different demeanor. Shoulders stiff, he introduced himself to Paul Miser. Paul was solidly built. Most would describe him as stocky. He had on a short-sleeved company T-shirt with dark denim jeans and tennis shoes. His brown hair was almost military short, his eyes were serious and his forehead had deep worry lines for a young man. He carried himself with dignity. Cash's training and experience made him good at reading people. Granted, there were times when he was wrong but those were rare.

The minute Colton had entered the room, Paul stood and readied himself for a handshake. On first appraisal, Paul Miser didn't seem to be the jerk they were looking for.

After introductions were made, Colton got right to the point.

"Where were you this morning, Mr. Miser?" Colton asked, motioning toward the chairs.

"Home." Paul took a seat across the table from Colton, then leaned forward and rested his elbows on the table with his hands clasped. His body language signified that he was nervous and ready to cooperate. "My mother's house, that is."

"Can you confirm her home is located in Big Rock, Texas?" Colton asked.

"Yes, sir." The location in Big Rock would make it impossible for him to be in Katy Gulch during the second kidnapping attempt.

Even though Paul was looking less and less like a suspect, he might be able to provide valuable information about his crew and especially the mystery mover.

"Can anyone verify your whereabouts this morning?" Colton asked the missing piece, which was for someone besides his mother to corroborate his whereabouts.

"My mother was home," Paul stated.

"Is she the only person you saw?" Colton asked.

Paul shook his head. "No, sir. My fiancée stopped by before her shift."

"What time was that?" Colton leaned back in his chair, a sure sign Paul had moved from suspect to witness in his eyes.

"Around seven o'clock." All Colton needed to do to clear Paul was verify the information.

Using two fingers, Colton pushed a pad of paper and a pen over to where Paul could easily use them. "Can you write down her name and contact information for me, sir?"

Paul obliged.

"Thank you." Colton took the offering and motioned for a deputy to come inside. Deputy Sal Frank entered the room as Colton ripped off the top sheet. He held out the piece of paper. "Can you give this to Gert and ask her to call the number and verify that Mr. Miser was home this morning?"

"Yes, sir," Sal said before taking the name and leaving the room. The door closed behind him with a soft clink. He'd been a deputy for ten years when Colton took the job as sheriff. Sal was a respected and trusted colleague.

"It says on your company's website that all employees are bonded and insured." He turned his attention back to Paul.

"We are." His right heel tapped against the concrete flooring.

"Does your company bond and insure its employees?" Colton asked.

"Yes, sir. It does. I sometimes send people in to HR to interview. Some of them get the green light. Others don't make the cut. I don't have anything to do with that part of the process."

Colton nodded. His relaxed body posture seemed to be putting Paul more at ease. "Do you always work with the same crew?"

"Yes, sir. Most of the time. Occasionally we'll get a last-minute sub like on the other morning's job. One of my regulars came down with the flu. So, I got a sub. He's the younger cousin of one of the owners."

"You have a name for this guy?" Colton again moved the pen and paper to Paul.

"All I know is his first name, Jo-Jo."

"Do you know if Jo-Jo is a smoker?"

Paul cocked his head to the side. "No, sir. I didn't see him light anything up and I don't know much about him personally."

"So you didn't see him with a lighter at any point?"

"Not him. But I lost my Zippo. Did someone find it?" He looked Colton in the eyes and then glanced away. Making eye contact with the investigator gave Paul a little more credibility in Cash's book.

"The lighter belongs to you?" Colton maintained his relaxed composure and Cash realized it was taking some effort. He knew his brother well. The connection to the Zippo was important. Or so they'd thought. If Paul's alibi checked out—and he fully believed that it would—that piece of evidence was no good.

"Yes, sir. I quit smoking a long time ago. The Zippo belonged to my father, who passed away ten years ago. He'd had it made special with a dragon on it. He loved dragons and had one just like it on his motorcycle jacket. He wasn't a bad guy. He never got into any gangs. He liked to ride his Harley on Sundays." The Zippo's importance in the investigation just dropped down a few notches. As long as Paul's whereabouts could be confirmed, he was in the clear, anyway. Besides, it had been a little too much to hope that the lighter they'd found on the site would be able to clear up the case. It happened. This just didn't seem to be one of those cases based on Paul's statement.

It was probably safe to cross Paul off the suspect list. The sub on his moving crew, Jo-Jo, might be another story. Considering he was related to the owners of the company, he shouldn't be too difficult to track down.

Renee moved closer to Cash without taking her eyes off Paul. "Do you think he's telling the truth?"

"I do. And his story will be easy enough to verify," Cash supplied. "I had hoped the lighter might lead us to the perp. Doesn't look like that's the case here. It must've slipped out of Paul's pocket during the move, which would explain why we found it near the ladder next to the side of the house."

"Sounds like an important family heirloom. I'm sure he would've backtracked and contacted me sooner or later to see if I'd found it." Her observation skills were dead on.

"What do you think about Jo-Jo?" Her voice was practically a whisper.

"If the story of him being a relative turns out to be true, I have my doubts that he'd be stupid enough to commit a crime on a job he can be linked to. Don't get me wrong, I've seen worse, but it's unlikely. We'll follow the trail anyway and see where it leads." Cash felt like he'd seen or heard it all when it came to crime and criminals, but he'd probably only scratched the surface in his decade-long career in law enforcement.

In the interview room, Colton thanked Paul before instructing Sal to escort the witness out of the building.

When it was clear, Colton opened the door and came into the room with Renee and Cash.

"I'd like to hear your assessment," Colton said to Cash. The two ran scenarios by each other from time to time when a fresh set of eyes was needed on a case. In his view, that might be overkill with this witness, but Colton was obviously dotting every i and crossing every t. Cash relayed the same thing he'd told Renee. Colton rocked his head the entire time, indicating his agreement.

"What's your take on Jo-Jo?" Colton asked when Cash was finished.

"Probably the same as yours," Cash said. "He'd be too stupid to commit the crime on his cousin's dime."

"Agreed." Before Colton could continue, Gert appeared in the doorway.

"Okay if I interrupt, sir?" she asked Colton.

He waved her in.

"Mr. Miser's story checks out with his fiancée. She confirmed that he was home on the morning in question at seven a.m. when she stopped by to see him before her shift. She said his bedroom is in the front of the house and his mother's is in the back, so his mother wouldn't know one way or the other if he had visitors. She offered her employer's name and number to verify that she had to be at work at seven thirty, which I called and verified that she had been."

"Looks like his story checks out. Great work, Gert. Thank you." Colton's compliment elicited a satisfied smile from Gert. She took great pride in her investigative work and it showed. She was thorough, and Cash would have her on his team any day.

"Let me know if you need anything else," she said with a wink. She also had the ability to brighten any room with her spunky personality.

Colton handed her the notepad with Jo-Jo's name along with the name of the moving company on it. "Mind finding out who this guy is? His cousin is one of the owners. We need to track down his whereabouts from this morning."

"On it, sir." Her eyes sparked at the new assignment. "I just got a call from Deputy Mark Ernest and there's something you should know." Her excitement was replaced by concern. "Would you mind stepping into the hallway and closing the door?"

Cash's interest peaked.

"Certainly." Colton glanced at Renee before shooting an apologetic look to his brother. "I'll be back as soon as I know what this is about."

What was so important it needed to be discussed out of earshot and in the middle of an investigation? Cash would dismiss it as having nothing to do with Abby's attempted abduction except the look on Gert's face threw him for a loop.

"Everything okay?" Renee seemed to pick up on the distress in Gert's voice.

"I guess we'll both know in a few minutes."

Chapter Ten

Renee gently bounced Abby. There was no way she was handing her daughter over to anyone else even though the child was as heavy as a bowling ball at this point and she could use a break.

Colton knocked on the door before opening it. His facial muscles were tense and the worry lines on his forehead seemed deeper. He and his brother exchanged a worried look and the knot that had formed in Renee's chest tightened.

Abby started working up to fuss, interrupting the moment. "Maybe she's bored."

In the short time Abby had been her daughter, Renee was starting to get a feel for her daughter's needs. Granted, she had a long way to go before she would feel confident, but this was progress and she'd take any she could get when it came to motherhood.

"Might want to take a walk. We'll be more comfortable in my office where we can close the door and talk." Colton's tone of voice tightened the knot even more.

She followed Colton, who took the lead.

"Do you want to wait in my brother's office while I grab a cup of coffee?" Cash asked in the hallway in front of his brother's office.

Renee didn't want to be rude, but she'd rather stick with Cash. Being near him had a calming effect on her and she could use all the good vibes she could get. "Mind if I come with you?"

"I have a phone call to make anyway." Colton gave her an out and she'd take it.

Cash nodded before continuing down the hall. He stepped into a small break room that had a kitchenette with dual coffeepots like the kind in a restaurant. They reminded her of the years she'd waited tables in college. Other than those, there were two high-top tables with three chairs tucked underneath each.

He went to work grabbing a clean cup and filling it with fresh coffee. She watched as the cotton of his light blue button-down shirt stretched over his muscles with his every move. The guy was muscles and strength, and…sex appeal. Yeah. There it was. He was gorgeous and she knew this was the worst possible time to notice or care. But unfamiliar feelings were building inside her—feelings that should scare the hell out of her.

Except that everything about Cash O'Connor was different. She was curious to see what that meant. With a new baby, new house and new town, she wasn't looking to add any complications to her life. She almost laughed out loud. Life seemed to be doing just fine throwing complications at her without extra help.

And, of course, she'd meet an honest, caring and intelligent man at this point. Because it made no sense in her life.

Renee sighed sharply as Abby made her hunger known, now having worked up to a real cry. The baby tried stuffing her fist in her mouth and missed more than anything. She also started rooting. Her daughter's tears were just about the most heartbreaking things Renee had ever seen.

Cash asked a colleague to grab one of Abby's formula bottles from his vehicle before he moved to the table and offered Renee a fresh cup of coffee.

"Thank you. You've been really great with Abby and me." Renee managed a genuine smile.

"I already told you about Colton's twins. To be honest, it's been a minute since I fed either one of them, though." He wiped a hand over his face and muttered a curse. "I gotta be a better uncle than that."

"They're lucky to have you. It's sad to say that I almost forgot about them considering everything that's been going on." She blew out a breath and figured she looked about as rough as she felt. A renegade strand of hair managed to get caught in her right eyelash. She blew at it to no avail. With both hands on Abby, she couldn't manage to get the hair off her eyelash and it was bugging the heck out of her.

"May I?" Cash locked gazes with her and her heart fluttered in her chest like a teenager on her first crush.

"Please."

He tucked the loose tendril behind her ear. His hand lingered there just long enough for more of that warmth she felt whenever he was near to circulate through her.

"Better?" he asked.

"Much." She heard the huskiness in her own voice. Staring into his steel eyes, she saw something that stirred a place deep inside her, a place that had been long neglected. Forgotten? There was a primal need in his gaze that brought out the same in her. Again, she cursed the timing of meeting him. Life could be so frustrating.

Yeah, her attraction to Cash was inconvenient. It was also a force unto itself that seemed impossible to set aside. There was also something hugely right about being this close to him, so close she could breathe in his masculine and spicy scent.

A noise in the hallway broke into the moment. One corner of his mouth upturned in a small smile before he took a step back and crossed muscled arms over a broad chest. The cotton of his shirt did that stretchy thing again. She forced herself to look away.

Renee expected someone to walk into the room but the person must've changed course or gone into one of the offices or small conference rooms. Renee reluctantly stood up. She wobbled and Cash's strong hand held her steady.

The deputy Cash had sent for the bottle returned. Renee prepared it then fed and changed her daughter, grateful for Cash's spontaneous help. The man could tape a diaper. The three of them returned to Colton's office. He'd been studying his computer screen until Cash interrupted him by knocking on his doorjamb.

Colton glanced over at them before waving them in. The fact that he didn't answer sent her pulse racing.

He stood up and motioned toward the leather couch and chairs on the other side of his expansive and neatly ordered office. She also noticed that he closed the door before joining them.

When he sat down after she and Cash took seats on the sofa and chair respectively, he leaned forward and rested his elbows on his knees. He clasped his hands together, and then he stared at the carpet for a long moment like he was searching for the right words.

Renee's heart was in her throat by the time he looked

up again. Instead of focusing on her, his gaze was fixed on his brother.

"Ruth Hubert was found murdered in her garden." Colton's voice was low as his gaze dipped to Abby and back.

Cash stood up and started pacing. "She moved to the outskirts of town a few months before our sister was kidnapped. Years later, we reviewed the case files and found out that she'd been interviewed multiple times. The sheriff at the time seemed to believe she'd brought bad blood to town. It was also believed for a time that she was using her remote location to traffic people through the area." Cash stopped long enough to rake his fingers through his hair and then rub the day-old stubble on his chin. He shifted his attention to his brother. "What happened?"

"GSW to the back of the head."

Even she realized *GSW* meant *gunshot wound,* although she figured he was using the acronym to soften the news in front of her.

Cash's hands fisted at his sides. "Did I hear that right?"

His brother nodded.

"So, you're telling me that she was killed execution-style in her garden?" Cash held his brother's gaze, waiting for confirmation. She understood the need for repetition. Hearing the news made her sick to her stomach.

"Afraid so." Colton blew out a sharp breath. "Sal is the one who saw her on his nightly rounds. He always checks on the houses of Katy Gulch's most remote residents. Even though Ms. Hubert lives on the outskirts of town, he makes a point to drive by her property at least once a week. She's not the friendly type so he just makes sure different lights are on if he's there in the evenings."

"Any relation to Renee's case?" Those words were daggers to the heart and Renee realized she'd been holding her breath, waiting for the answer.

Colton didn't immediately speak. Then came, "Sal checked her phone, which had been kicked off the porch, to see if there was an ICE." Renee knew that meant an *in case of emergency* contact. Colton delivered a bomb next. "Most of her contacts had no names. They were just phone numbers."

"Did he recognize any?" Cash made another lap around the room.

"Yes, he did." Colton shot an apologetic look toward Renee. "There was one. Kipp McGee."

Renee gasped. Hearing her lawyer's name in the context of this conversation sent a mix of fear and anger swirling through her. Questions assaulted her. What if her lawyer was responsible for murder? What if her lawyer was the one who'd sent someone to snatch Abby back after the adoption? And then the question that nearly gutted her came… What if Abby's adoption was illegal and she was taken away for good?

Renee couldn't possibly lose the little girl who'd been born in her heart so many years ago and was now very much alive in her arms. It didn't matter that Abby had come into Renee's life only recently because the moment she'd held that little girl in her arms, she'd given her heart away forever.

"His name seems to be coming up a lot lately." Cash moved next to Renee as she cradled her little girl. Based on her reaction and the look on her face that dared anyone to try to take her daughter away, he figured she was afraid she could lose Abby. Cash had four words for that scenario: *over his dead body.*

"It sure does," Colton agreed with a weary look.

Cash would do anything and everything in his power to ensure Abby stayed with Renee where she belonged. A few *what ifs* haunted him. What if the baby had been stolen from the birth mother? What if the birth mother gave consent for the adoption and then changed her mind? The other *what ifs* were more cut-and-dried. What if the birth mother wanted nothing to do with her child and handed her over for an illegal adoption? What if a higher bidder came along? What if McGee got Renee involved in a sketchy adoption that could result in her losing Abby? One look at the mother-daughter duo said Renee had gone all in with the child.

He hoped it wouldn't come down to a situation where Abby could legally be removed from Renee's home. He'd heard of a similar scenario happening and it was not only horrific but unfair to the adoptive parents.

The coroner would have to determine Ms. Hubert's time of death and they could start unpacking what the hell had happened. Colton buzzed Gert. "Can you get Kipp McGee here as soon as possible?"

"Yes, sir."

Gert buzzed back a few minutes later. "He's on his way."

"Really?" Colton sounded shocked. "So fast?"

"Let's just say that I convinced him it would be in his best interest to talk to you of his own accord. I sided with him and told him that he just needed to have a quick conversation to help clear up a misunderstanding."

"Remind me how good you are at your job before your next performance appraisal," Colton said. The joke lightened some of the heavy tension.

"Oh, I plan to," she quipped. "We might as well order lunch because it's a couple hours' drive for him."

CASH HAD TAKEN a turn holding Abby so that Renee could get a break. He'd even convinced her to take another nap on the sofa in Colton's office.

Gert knocked on the door, waking her.

"Kipp McGee is waiting to enter the interview room," she said. "There's a shortcut from my office across the courtyard. It'll be faster than circling around and we can get you in place before McGee is walked back." Colton was already at the door by the time Renee pushed up with her free arm.

She reached for her daughter and Cash brought her over immediately. Cash remembered when his nephews were around that age. They didn't seem heavy until he'd been carrying them for an hour. Then they became like lead weights in his arms. He'd offer to continue to carry Abby if it wasn't for the fierce look of determination on Renee's face. He understood her need to keep her daughter close. Hell, he didn't blame her one bit. The thought of having her little girl ripped out of her arms after she'd bonded with her was unimaginable.

Cash was familiar with the shorter path his brother took them on.

"I'll close the door," Colton said after stopping in the hallway to let them pass by to take position.

After thanking his brother, Cash leaned against the

wall. He studied Renee, who looked exhausted. "Can I get you a chair?"

"That would be so nice." Her demeanor had changed and he noticed her shoulders were starting to sag. There were also dark circles under her eyes and she bit back a yawn. They could get through this one interview and then he'd offer to take her back to the ranch to get a break from his brother's office. Cash wanted to chew on the details of what they knew. Taking the rest of the night off would give Colton and his deputies a chance to dig deeper into the case.

Investigations took time. He had no idea if the Hubert case was connected to Renee's. Answers weren't likely tonight and especially now that resources would have to be reallocated to Ms. Hubert's place. And then there was all that was happening at home. Cash wanted to check on his mother and see how she was holding up.

A quick run next door and he netted one of the chairs from a conference room. He placed it directly in front of the two-way mirror a few seconds before he heard noise coming from down the hallway. He made a quick move to close the door, guarding their identities from her lawyer.

It was probably for the best that McGee didn't know his former client would be watching. Although, he might suspect someone was. This wasn't his first time in an interview room from the news Cash had read over the years. He'd heard the man's name mentioned repeatedly, but the two had yet to meet and a charge had yet to stick.

Kipp McGee wasn't the crisp-suit type that Cash had expected to see. The lawyer looked to be in his early forties and would be considered tall by average standards, maybe five feet, eleven inches. He had on a suit, dull gray in color, and his appearance could best be described as sloppy. One side of his white button-down shirt was untucked. He didn't wear a tie and the top couple of buttons were undone. He looked to be average weight except for his gut, which seemed a little overstuffed. His ruddy complexion gave him an aging amateur golfer or tennis player look, and his hair looked like it had been finger combed rather than brushed.

"Do you mind standing right here, Mr. McGee?" Colton pointed to a spot not five feet in across the mirror and directly in front of Renee. She flinched and leaned back in her chair as McGee moved into position.

Cash placed a hand on her shoulder to offer some measure of reassurance as he leaned toward the mirror and studied the lawyer. Much about his demeanor was disarming, except the slight twitch under his left eye.

"Right here?" McGee asked. On the surface, he looked eager to cooperate.

"Yes, sir." Colton always watched his p's and q's with a suspect and that wouldn't stop now. It was also one of the many things that had earned him a reputation as a one of the best in the state while still young in his career. He had a knack for reading people, knowing when to push and when to take a step back. As a fellow law enforcement officer and his brother, Cash couldn't be prouder.

"That's all. Thank you for your cooperation." Colton moved toward the table and chairs in the middle of the room.

McGee stared at the mirror a second longer than seemed appropriate, which was an odd thing for him to do. He had to realize he wouldn't be able to see who was standing on the other side.

Was the move meant to intimidate a victim or witness? Cash made note of the behavior and moved on. Granted, his opinion was tainted by the man's reputation—a reputation that, based on appearances, seemed to have been earned.

"How can I help you today, Sheriff?" McGee took the seat across the table from Colton. He took off his jacket and draped it over the back of his chair. Cash noticed sweat stains. If it hadn't been for the eye twitch and the fact the man had tried to stare into the mirror, Cash might have written the man off as harmless.

Paul Miser had claimed the dragon lighter. That piece of evidence no longer seemed to come into play, which was unfortunate. Forensics might have gotten lucky with prints. It had been less than twenty-four hours and that would increase their chances.

"I appreciate your willingness to cooperate," Colton began.

McGee's arms came up and he waved his hands in the air. His wide smile belied narrowed eyes. "Happy to oblige, sir."

Bet you are. McGee didn't come accompanied by another lawyer, which was strange but also seemed like a ploy to make him appear innocent.

"He seems different to me." Renee finally spoke up, her gaze still locked on to her lawyer. "It's like he's putting on a show to hide the fact that he's nervous."

"I agree."

Renee had keen observation skills.

"And he's working too hard. You know?" Her elbow

accidentally touched his, sending more heat swirling from contact.

"It crossed my mind," Cash said.

She blew out a sharp breath. "Tell it to me straight. You're an officer of the law and I imagine you've seen or heard just about all there is to. What are my chances that I could lose Abby?"

"I'd like more than anything to say none, but I can't tell you that in good conscience."

There was no response, just a palpable sadness. When she turned to face him, her chin jutted out and her expression tensed. There was a whole helluva lot of determination there, too.

"I'll do right by Abby. Even if that means I have to give her up if it's best for her in the long run," she stated.

"We don't know if the adoption was illegal yet." It was important to follow evidence all the way through. Worrying beforehand—although he completely understood—wouldn't do anyone any good.

"True," she said on a sigh. "I'm just preparing myself for the worst. Don't get me wrong, I'll fight tooth and nail for this angel. But a few scenarios come to my mind that mean it wouldn't be right to keep her no matter how much she feels like my daughter already."

"You're an amazing mother—"

"How can you tell?" She blinked clear blue eyes at him.

"You're ready to put her above everything and everyone else, including yourself. She's barely been in your life and yet it's easy to see that you'd walk through fire for her." The fact that she smiled despite going through what must be one of the worst days of her life caused a thunderbolt to strike him in the center of the chest.

With those big beautiful eyes wide open, she thanked him.

Yeah, he was in trouble.

Chapter Eleven

"Can you account for your whereabouts for the past forty-eight hours?" Colton pushed the same notepad she'd recognized from earlier across the table. A pen rested on top.

Renee waited on the edge of her seat for the answer to that question.

Kipp made a show of being caught off guard by the question. His actions up to this point seemed very off to her compared to the confident lawyer she'd dealt with.

"Do I need to?" Kipp's expression morphed into shocked indignation.

"Yes, sir." Colton quickly added, "Purely in the spirit of cooperation."

"Okaaay." Kipp drew out the word. "I'm usually on phone calls throughout the day. I met with a client at lunch yesterday."

"What time exactly was that?" Colton leaned forward like he was hanging on the lawyer's every word.

"It was late. Around two o'clock." Kipp checked his wristwatch.

"Seems like an unusual time to eat lunch," Colton said.

"I go where my clients need me to. There are days

when I work through lunch." Kipp's eyebrow shot up. "I'm sure you understand that."

"Yes, sir. I'm a little too familiar." Colton seemed to be trying to ease the tension. Even Renee could see that a wall had just come up.

Kipp leaned back in his chair and steepled his fingers.

"How did you qualify your lawyer?" Cash asked.

"I didn't. I took him at face value." She should've done more digging around, checked into his background a little more. It had never occurred to her that the adoption wasn't anything but aboveboard or that she could give her heart to a child only to have her ripped out of Renee's arms. It wasn't like she'd acted on impulse, either. She had been carefully considering having a family for years. Of course, she'd believed that she and Jamison would've been married first. A cold chill ran down her back at the thought of being trapped in a marriage with a partner like him.

Looking back, she had no regrets. If she'd walked away from Jamison while his mother was dying, Renee would have felt like an awful person. By the time his mother had passed away, Jamison's affair was out in the open.

There was no denying the fact that Renee had made a snap judgment on hiring her attorney, but she'd carefully thought out becoming a mother. It was something she'd wanted to do for years and maybe for her entire life.

Looking back on what had led up to the adoption wouldn't do any good. Renee refocused on the here and now. If there was an unwitting birth mother out there somewhere who'd had her child taken from her by anything other than her own free will, Renee would do the right thing by Abby and ensure the two were reconnected. After having her child nearly abducted in her own bedroom, Renee could imagine the horror a birth mother would go through to find her child missing.

"I'm sure you'll understand my need to respect the privacy of my clients," Kipp's voice cut through her heavy thoughts. Her mind was starting to spin out. She had always been an overthinker and this was a lot to chew on.

"Does that mean you won't provide the names of anyone who can verify where you've been in the past forty-eight hours, Mr. McGee?" Colton's voice caused the hair on the back of her neck to prick.

"No, sir. I will not." Kipp stood up and wrangled his arms into his suit jacket. His actions so far weren't flattering or instilling any confidence.

"Sir, if you don't mind, I'd like to ask one more question before you walk out of this interview." Colton didn't stand up but he nailed Kipp with his glare. His tone had switched to all business. Kipp straightened his back like he was preparing for a fight.

"Go right ahead. I don't have anything to hide." Renee wished with all her heart that was true. As much as she didn't want someone she knew to be responsible for terrorizing her and Abby, if her lawyer had done something illegal to push the boundaries then her life could drastically change. If Jamison or the creepy guy from the office was responsible, an arrest would solve the problem. The jerk would end up locked behind bars and Renee would be able to resume her new normal life with her daughter. But the lawyer on her adoption case…

She couldn't go there again because disaster was written all over the scenario involving McGee.

"What is your relationship with Ruth Hubert?" Colton asked. Renee picked up on the fact he hadn't used past tense even though the woman had been murdered in her garden.

Kipp glanced from the door to the mirror and then back to Colton. He rubbed a hand over his chin. "I don't have one." Kipp couldn't walk toward the exit any faster. He paused at the door but didn't turn around. "Now, if you'll excuse me. I'm late for a meeting in Houston."

"Do you travel around the state frequently for business?" Colton's eyebrow shot up.

"I go where work requires." McGee focused on the closed door.

"You're free to go. A deputy is waiting in the hallway to see you out." Colton rose to standing. "Mr. McGee."

Kipp stopped just outside the door. "Yes."

"Are you planning to travel outside of the state anytime in the near future?" Colton's question caused Kipp to bristle.

"No, sir." There was more than a hint of worry in his voice now.

"Good. Please let my office know if that changes." Colton's tone didn't waver.

"Yes, sir." Kipp couldn't get out of there fast enough.

"That's so not good," Renee said quietly.

Cash was by her side in the next beat, his reassuring hand on the small of her back.

"No, it wasn't." His steel voice was low. "You want to get out of here and head back to the ranch?"

"Yes, I do," Renee answered quickly. In fact, there

was little else she wanted at the moment besides a safe place to unwind. She needed to get a permanent fix for Abby's window and hadn't done that yet. Lack of solid sleep was catching up to her and she was getting so tired her bones ached.

The door opened and Colton filled the frame. "The lawyer is gone. It's safe to come out now."

"It's been a long day. Renee agreed to take off with me so she can settle her daughter in and get some rest." The fact Cash so easily spoke of Abby as Renee's daughter brought more warmth to her heart. In a world that could be twisted and crazy and unexpected, that those words felt so right confirmed everything Renee had fought for in order to become a mother.

"I was just about to suggest the same. We're still trying to track down Mr. King and Ms. Tran." Colton rubbed the back of his hand over red-rimmed eyes. With one-year-old twins at home and a more-than-full-time job as sheriff, Renee could hardly imagine.

Cash embraced his brother in a hug and more of Renee's heart melted. She could learn a lot from these brothers about family, and part of her wished she would have the opportunity once this case was behind them. "Will you call if there's any change or news?"

"You know I will." Colton turned to Renee. "We'll do everything in our power to find the person responsible for both attempts." He didn't say kidnapping and she was grateful. Hearing the word spoken out loud brought back all those helpless feelings when she was caught off guard at home. The second time had been scary but she'd been more prepared. And determined.

Plus, there was something different about the second attempt. Granted, there were more people and the location was public. Was that why, looking back, she felt safer now? She had people around? People who cared about her and had her back?

"Thank you for everything you're doing," she said to Colton before kissing the top of Abby's head. "Becoming a mother is the greatest thing that's ever happened to me. I have every intention of doing whatever's necessary to keep her safe."

Colton nodded. "We promise to do the same. My office will be in touch."

"I'm taking them to the main house at the ranch," Cash informed his brother. Colton's eyebrow shot up but he didn't speak. "I'd like her to be around people and the ranch is the safest place I can think of until she gets her bedroom window fixed and a security system installed. I'm getting Russell on the job. He's the best, but he's also booked solid. He said he'd fit her in soon, but he might be calling last minute."

"Sounds like a good plan," Colton agreed.

Cash held his hand out toward the door and locked eyes with Renee. "Shall we?"

She retraced their earlier steps to his brother's office with Cash right behind her. Colton's secretary was on a call. She put her hand over the phone. "Nice meeting you."

She smiled and waved as they moved through the lobby. After securing Abby's car seat, Renee shook her arms to get some feeling back in them. Both had gone numb more than an hour ago. She climbed into the passenger seat and buckled in.

"Are you okay with going back to my family's ranch?" he asked. "I'd offer to stay at your place but with everything going on with my family I'd like to check in at home. We can stay at the main house again in a guest suite and—"

"Yes, I'll go. I don't want to go back to my house right now with everything that happened, and your family needs you. It's the safest compromise until I can get an alarm installed. Speaking of which, thank you for setting up a contractor." She'd cut him off because he didn't have to oversell the idea. Being with someone who had her back while she attended to her daughter's needs was exactly what she needed right now. If Cash was willing to be that person...even better.

A small part of her enjoyed being with a capable adult male for a change. The O'Connors seemed to have quite a few of them. By the end of her relationship with Jamison, she'd felt more like his caregiver than his life partner, and he'd become incredibly needy. It had come at a price of neglecting herself and her needs. She would never do that again in any relationship.

"The main house it is." Cash smiled, turned the key in the ignition and started his vehicle. Renee tried to ignore the part of her heart that wanted to convince her she could really like this man. Any relationship besides the new one she had with Abby was more than enough to handle even though her heart wanted to argue there was room for more.

A COUPLE OF steps inside the massive entryway to the main house, a noise sounded from down the hallway. Cash turned to Renee who was standing close behind him. Her arms literally felt like they might fall off at this point, but she couldn't put Abby down, either.

"That sound came from my mother's library. I want her to hear the news about Ruth Hubert from me. Are you okay with meeting my mother now? Because I can take you to the guest room first if you're not ready." Cash was sweet to consider her feelings.

"I'm fine, actually. I'd like to meet your mother very much. In fact, once this is all over, I'd like to get some parenting advice from her considering what an amazing job she's done with the sons I've met so far."

His genuine smile spread warmth through her chest and a desire to stand close enough to be in his sun.

She followed him to the opened double doors, where he knocked. "I'm sorry to interrupt you—"

"Don't be silly. Come on in. I could use the company." Margaret O'Connor had the kind of gentle but firm voice that took Renee back to third grade in Mrs. Malone's class. Renee smiled at the memory of her favorite teacher.

"I have a friend with me." The casual reference shouldn't cause disappointment. She mentally shook it off, figuring she was lucky to call an O'Connor a friend.

"The more, the merrier." Even though Renee didn't know Cash's mother, the words sounded like they were spoken with a forced cheeriness and she completely understood why.

One step inside the library halted Renee in her tracks. First of all, the floor-to-ceiling bookshelves were delicate and impressive. The room had endless layers of patterns and brass accents. Even the ceiling had a bronzed hue and a pattern that mirrored the rug. A granite frame and mantel flanked the fireplace on the opposite wall from the French doors. A deep orange sofa with leather club chairs made up the seating area. A pale blue ottoman anchored the room with a rug covering the floor beneath it. There were so many books it would be impossible to count them all. She took note of stacks of mysteries and true-crime novels.

The impressionist painting over the fireplace looked familiar and Renee was struck by just how wealthy a family the O'Connors were. Neither Cash nor Colton came off like they'd been born with silver spoons in their mouths. In fact, they were two of the most down-to-earth people she'd ever met.

"This is Renee Smith and her daughter, Abby," Cash said to his mother, who sat straighter as Renee walked toward her.

"Pleased to meet you," Mrs. O'Connor said in that genuine tone that brought Renee back to one of the few bright spots of her childhood. "Do you have time to sit for a minute?"

"Yes, ma'am—"

"Please, call me Margaret," she said with gray eyes that twinkled.

"It's a pleasure to meet you, Margaret." Renee took a seat as offered, grateful to get off her feet.

Margaret's smile widened when she looked at Abby, another thing that made Renee's heart swell.

"Your daughter sure is beautiful," Margaret said.

"Thank you." Renee couldn't help but beam at the compliment as she looked at her sleeping angel. "I'm so sorry about your husband."

Margaret looked up with the saddest eyes and nodded.

"May I hold her?" If it had been anyone else asking, the answer would have been a hard no. Margaret had the kind of gentle and elegant demeanor that put people at ease around her. Renee leaned toward her newfound friend and handed her daughter toward open arms.

Margaret's entire face lit up as she cradled Abby against her chest. Renee was beginning to see the magic of babies. She herself was pretty spellbound by the little angel and figured she could sit and hold that little girl for hours and completely lose track of time. Renee had never been much of a couch potato. She always liked to be up doing something, whether it was organizing a pantry or closet or trying—and mostly failing—to figure out how to craft.

Cash took a seat across the ottoman from Renee. She glanced at him and her heart took another shot seeing the look on his face while he watched his mother hold a little girl. It occurred to Renee that he was about to deliver news about the attempted abduction. Abby was around the same age as his sister, Caroline, when she'd been taken from the family.

He didn't seem in a hurry to open that old wound. His cell buzzed in his pocket as Renee leaned back in the chair, grateful her arms were getting a break. She'd never met a person she trusted so immediately or so completely. Instead of being strange, it felt like the most natural thing.

"Excuse me," Cash said to the two of them. His gaze lingered when it met Renee's. She caught a worried look as it passed over his features. Margaret was too wrapped up to notice much else besides the miracle in her arms.

He walked into the hallway and his voice lowered to a hum. Renee couldn't make out what he was saying.

"I'm new to motherhood," Renee said to Margaret as she bit back a yawn. "I've met two of your sons so far and am so impressed with the amazing men they are. Any and all parenting advice is appreciated."

"The only thing a child really needs is love," Margaret said without hesitation. Those words shouldn't make tears threaten and yet they did. Unconditional love wasn't something Renee had a whole lot of experience with and her relationship with Jamison had caused her to doubt her ability to love or be loved by anyone. Abby was an exception as Renee knew a child would be. Rather than become angry at her parents for their self-involvement above all else, she felt sorry for them. Because they'd missed out on the greatest joy in Renee's life to date. Becoming a parent filled a longing from a place deep inside her. A place her parents had never reached with her. Or at least that's how it had felt.

Even when she'd been sick as a young child, they'd told her to stay inside her room. They would turn off her light and she was lucky if they remembered to check on her before they went to bed. Renee had come to accept her parents' lack of interest in her as normal behavior since it was all she'd ever known. She couldn't imagine doing the same now that she'd become a mother.

The family business had kept her parents up late hours arguing about money and dealing with all the paperwork that came with owning a small business. It was one of many reasons she'd considered early on that had led to her decision to work for someone else.

At five thirty every day, she was done with her job. Any web updates that needed to be made after that had to wait until morning. Once she left the building, she was off. She rarely had to work overtime or on a weekend. Although, she'd thrown herself into work and school to get where she was. When she worked overtime, it was her call.

The O'Connors seemed to be the exception to pretty much every rule. They obviously prioritized family over business and yet they ran one of the most successful cattle ranches. They had more money than they could spend, but it didn't seem to rule their lives.

Renee bit back another yawn as Cash stepped inside the room. With deep grooves in his forehead and a gaze that searched first for his mother and then for Renee, his expression was that of someone who was about to deliver more bad news.

Chapter Twelve

On instinct, Renee sat straighter as though a rigid spine would prepare her for any blow that came next.

Margaret was so busy being enthralled with Abby that she barely glanced up at her son. But when she did, she locked on to his gaze. "What's wrong?"

Cash reclaimed his seat. "Ruth Hubert was found murdered in her garden a few hours ago." That much, Renee already knew.

"Oh." With several sons who worked in law enforcement, Renee figured there wasn't much that shocked Margaret. "That's terrible news."

"Did you know her very well?" Cash asked his mother.

"Not really. I knew of her, but she mostly kept to herself. Our neighborhood committee has reached out to her several times over the years to see if she'd like to get involved in civic activities but she was never interested. She kept to herself mostly." A delicate eyebrow arched. "Why?"

"Deputies are going through her computer and phone records. They found links to a person who is widely suspected to be an officer in a trafficking ring that has been running for years."

"How far back does it go?" Margaret's interest seemed very peaked now.

"Decades." That one word seemed to let the air out of Margaret's lungs. She seemed to catch herself, as if her mood might impact Abby, and she straightened her chin and took in a breath after a quick glance at the baby in her arms.

"Does this link her to Caroline?" There was so much bravery in the steadiness of her voice in that question.

Cash heaved a sigh. "It might."

"Oh."

Renee's mind immediately snapped to Abby. Before she could open her mouth to speak, he nodded.

"There was an attempt to kidnap Abby," he said to his mother. "And Colton is investigating any possible links between the two cases."

"Kipp McGee." Renee said her lawyer's name practically under her breath.

Margaret looked confused. "Who?"

"He was the adoption lawyer for Renee," Cash supplied, his voice a study in calm. He had to have a million emotions drilling through him right now, too. There might be a break in his sister's case, on top of the fact he'd lost his father who was clearly a man Cash loved and respected.

Margaret's gaze flew to Renee. "I'm so sorry this happened to you and Abby." The sincerity in her words brought on more of those inconvenient emotions. *Acceptance* was another foreign word to Renee and yet it practically vibrated from Margaret.

"Thank you. It's been a difficult few days in a new city," Renee said. Even the quick burst of adrenaline that came with hearing the news couldn't stop her exhaustion from wearing thin.

"I can imagine," Margaret said with a look of solidarity. An invisible tether linked them and for the second time, Renee didn't feel alone. "You haven't slept much, have you?"

"To be honest, I'm afraid to do more than close my eyes for a few minutes. I'm scared that I'll wake and she'll be gone." A rogue tear escaped and slid down Renee's cheek.

Margaret's gray eyes widened before she nodded understanding. "Would you like to take her back?"

"Part of me wants to. But the other part knows that I can trust you and my arms need a break," she admitted. "Unless you're tired."

"I could hold this angel all day." Margaret's words were soothing and there was so much sincerity in her eyes Renee didn't doubt the woman for a second.

"I brought them here to stay in the main house in the guest suite if that's all right with you," Cash said to his mother.

"What a great idea. Stay as long as you like." Margaret smiled through what must be difficult news to hear about her own case. This might be the first real break law enforcement had had. "Would you like to be shown to your room? We can set up a bassinet in the guest suite and Abby can sleep right next to your bed."

"If it's all right with you, I'd like to stay right here." The oversized club chair was the perfect size to curl up in and there was something so very comforting about being near Margaret. It was like Renee could finally let out the breath that she felt as though she'd been holding her entire life. The first time she'd experienced it had been with Cash.

"Make yourself at home. I'm more than happy to sit here awhile with your angel." Margaret's tone combined with the smile on her face said she meant every word. She started a low hum to one of Renee's favorite lullabies. Abby seemed perfectly content to stay put, so Renee slipped her shoes off and curled up in the chair.

Cash walked over, bringing a light blanket with him. He placed it over Renee with so much care tears pricked the backs of her eyes. She told herself that she was just running on empty and that was the reason for the emotion, but it was so much more than that. He was exactly the type of guy she could really fall for if she could take that step. She couldn't. Her past would always creep in, telling her she couldn't really trust anyone. She hugged the throw pillow and rested her head on the arm of the chair.

The next thing she knew, she was out.

CASH DIMMED THE lights in the library, trying to ignore how full his heart was at the scene of his mother holding Abby while Renee slept.

"Can I get anything for you?" he asked his mother quietly.

"Tea would be nice." The news about the investigation must have hit her hard but in true Margaret O'Connor form, she kept a handle on her emotions. Seeing her sitting there holding a six-month-old girl like she was the biggest prize hit him in a place very deep.

"I'm on it." He needed to step out of the room anyway before he lost all objectivity when it came to Renee's case. Or, if he was being honest, Renee.

Walking down the hallway toward the kitchen, he thought about all the times he'd heard about love at first sight but didn't believe it. Sexual chemistry? There was no doubt about that. Sexual chemistry was instant and there was plenty of that between him and Renee. He'd convinced himself that love at first sight was equivalent to a Bigfoot sighting. Lots of interesting characters claimed to have seen one over the years but always fell short when it came to producing evidence.

Whatever was going on between the two of them, he felt that lightning bolt hit square in his chest the minute he laid eyes on Renee. The feeling was different than anything he'd experienced before. He'd leave it at that.

The tea was in the exact same spot in the pantry as he remembered. He and his brothers had made it for their mother during holidays and special occasions. Her favorite black tea was there alongside a few he didn't recognize.

Heating water on the stove was old-fashioned and took more time, but he was feeling nostalgic today and, besides, he wanted a little extra time before going back to the library. The possibility that the person responsible for his sister's kidnapping could have been right underneath their noses his entire life sat like a hot poker in his stomach.

He leaned over the granite island and gripped his mother's favorite teacup. Realizing how delicate it was, he loosened his hold.

Ms. Hubert moved to the area roughly six months before Caroline's kidnapping. The MO was identical and yet no similar kidnappings had taken place in Katy Gulch in between. It felt possible the two kidnapping cases were linked. Improbable, but possible.

What would the connection be? Two kidnapping cases decades apart?

Caroline and Abby were the same age at the time of the incidents. The heat brought on by Caroline's kidnapping back in the day might've caused the operation to shut down here in Katy Gulch. Maybe Ms. Hubert felt it was safe again to shop in her own backyard. Or, it was possible Abby fit the needs of someone willing to pay dearly for a child who looked like her. The elderly woman might not be the one calling the shots.

A burst of hope that his sister could somehow still be alive after all these years struck. Going down that road again—the one that made him believe he could find her for his parents—reopened a deep well of pain. Going there again was like walking into a fire without any gear.

Cash decided he needed to know everything there was to know about Ruth Hubert. He'd start there and see where the trail led him. His thoughts shifted to his brother Colton, who would be on the exact same track. Then there was Garrett. There was so much Garrett didn't know about here at home that he needed to be brought up to speed on.

Firing off a group text to his brothers, sans Garrett, Cash let them know the MIA status of their rogue sibling.

A few texts came back almost immediately. Figures, one of his brothers said. Sounds about right, came back from another. What did you expect, still another said. Colton was the only one who didn't respond, and he'd already been updated.

Any ideas on how we can find him? Cash asked.

The responses came quickly. They were all some version of *we'll see what we can do.* The teapot on the stove shrieked. Cash poured hot water over the tea bag and turned off the stove. Pocketing his phone, he brought the tea to his mother.

He set it down on the tray in front of her. Renee was asleep in the chair and his mother spoke quietly to a sleeping Abby. There was something a little too right about this whole scenario.

But he was also reminded of the circumstances that brought Renee to his family home. Then there was the loss of his father and a deep well of grief that had yet to fully surface.

"I never thought much about Ms. Hubert." His mother looked up at him. "She was so quiet. Folks whispered about her living all alone on the outskirts of town on enough land to grow pretty much anything she wanted, legal or not. She had visitors, folks said, so she'd be all right. People worried about her living out there all alone. And so did I. All this time she might've been the one…" His mother stopped herself before adding, "She might have been in plain sight all this time."

"I'd hate for you to be disappointed again," he said after carefully choosing his words. The last thing he wanted was to give his mother false hope. It had already stirred in his chest and was written all over her face.

"Your sister was a beautiful baby." She beamed down at Abby. "All of you were."

"She would be thirty-six now." His comment was met with a wistful smile.

"That's right." Her expression took a turn. "Do all your brothers know about your father yet?"

"Everyone but Garrett. We're trying to track him down." He held back his opinion about his irresponsible and hotheaded younger brother. Cash had always been the eldest sibling despite his sister's age. With her gone, he'd stepped into the role.

"Oh. Any idea where he might be?" His mother's eyebrow shot up but she didn't look surprised. She seemed to accept that Garrett would drift in and out as he pleased.

"We checked his last job. He didn't exactly leave on good terms."

"He should never have worked for that family anyway. They've been branding our cattle and poaching from us for longer than I care to remember." His mother didn't normally talk badly about others. She'd always been the quiet type, preferring her library and her books to parties and gossip. The events she hosted usually benefited a charity and she played hostess in order to raise money, not out of a need to be the center of attention. She'd done a lot of good in the world. She deserved answers to her greatest personal misfortune—answers that investigators weren't able to give her and answers that neither Colton nor Cash had been able to provide.

She wouldn't see it this way, but it was impossible not to feel like he was letting her down in some way by not finding out what had happened to Caroline. Now that Pops was gone, she would need her family around even more.

Cash needed to think through his role on the ranch, which would be more than helping out in a pinch and with the busy season.

"Your father always wanted his sons to take over the ranch when they were ready." Her words hit him to the core.

"I have a career." Not only did he have a career, but

he had one that he loved. Texas, this land, would always be part of his soul but his heart was in law enforcement. With the renewed possibility that they might have stumbled onto a lead in his sister's case, his blood was pumping again.

"Yes, you do. I didn't mean to make you feel guilty." She didn't give him a lecture and it occurred to him that she was planting a seed more than anything else. With their father gone, the family would need to have a meeting about how best to handle family business moving forward. Hard discussions needed to be had. There was no way Colton would desert his job as sheriff. Cash was certain about it. Other than Riggs, Garrett had the most experience working a cattle ranch, but could he be trusted to stick around? And, honestly, could he be trusted at all? Dawson was also a US marshal and he helped on the ranch as much as he could, much like the others, same as Blake who worked as a cop in Houston.

"Am I wrong to admit that I haven't given much thought to my role here on the ranch should anything ever happen to Pops?"

"No, you're not. No one saw this coming. Not me. Not your father. His doctor certainly thought he had more time." As far as young marriages went, she and Pops had beaten the odds. They'd met in high school and been sweethearts ever since. He'd opted to go straight to work for his family's ranch while she'd gone to University of Texas at Austin. Her parents hadn't thought Pops would be a suitable candidate for marrying their daughter since he hadn't gone to college. They'd told her that he might come from money, but she'd get bored of him because all he'd ever be able to talk about was cattle. Her father had refused to give his blessing for a marriage.

When Mother had told Pops, he'd cautioned her to think long and hard about her choices. Being cut off from family wasn't something he could have ever considered. Family had meant everything to Pops and it had to Mother, too. Pops had known deep down that she would have never been happy without her parents. He'd told her to take all the time she needed to think about it. That when a man met the woman who he was supposed to spend the rest of his life with, he could wait a few weeks or months for her to be certain of her choice to be with him.

He hadn't made it to his pickup truck before she'd asked, arms folded across her chest, if he was done with his speech. He'd said that he was. She'd told him to wait out front because she was going inside to get her bag.

Pops had always said waiting for her was the longest ten minutes of his life. When she'd returned, she'd told him that her parents might not approve but her heart did. She'd figured they'd come around once they saw how happy she was. The only regret she'd had was that she wouldn't finish college.

There was no desire that Pops didn't want his bride-to-be to fulfill. He'd refused to let her sacrifice her education for marriage. He'd said that he might not be able to bring her parents around, but he could ensure she got her degree.

So, she'd lived in a dorm Sunday night through Friday afternoon. Pops had driven to Austin every weekend to pick her up and bring her home to the ranch. Then he'd turned around and driven her back to campus. He'd made that trek for two and a half years without complaint.

As for the wedding? The preacher had been set to perform the ceremony at the ranch. Mother had invited her parents, but their seats had been empty with ten minutes to the wedding. Pops had overheard Gayle, Mother's best friend then and now, telling a friend that Margaret's mother had been heartbroken not to be able to witness her only daughter's wedding. It was the father who'd been holding out.

Pops had had everyone pile into the back of a couple of pickup trucks and had moved the entire ceremony to her parents' porch where his future mother-in-law could watch from the front window. Eventually, her father had come around and Pops had forgiven him. Because of Pops's big heart, Cash knew both sets of grandparents.

Cash would never consider himself a hopeless romantic by any means, but he loved hearing his parents' story. He looked at his mother when he said, "It's like a piece of us is gone without him and we will never be able to fill the hole."

"I know," she said with her characteristic warmth.

"The whole medical news came out of the blue," he admitted. She'd been right before. They would have to consider what to do next and especially if no one wanted to step up and help run the ranch. "I need a minute to think about my next steps."

"This place has been in your father's family four generations. There's so much history in these walls. I always felt privileged to be part of the O'Connor legacy." She looked him straight in the eyes. "Your father wanted to be here. It was his choice. He wanted the same for all of his children and that's the reason he never pressured any of you to work for him. He wouldn't want you to be miserable."

That was the thing, Cash didn't hate the idea of working more at KBR. He hadn't considered a life outside of law enforcement mostly because he figured Pops would live forever. There'd been no other possibility in his mind and especially since the man seemed in his prime physically. Cash had locked on to his career early and never looked back. "Maybe it's time to consider what's best for the family."

"What's best for each of you *is* best for the family."

While he understood what she was saying and appreciated her for it, he also realized that he didn't want the O'Connor family legacy to die with Pops. Cash and his brothers needed to talk about what their roles would be, if any of the others wanted one. Riggs was already on board. Yet, it wasn't fair to let all the responsibility fall on his shoulders. "I'll do my part to keep this place running."

There was also the question of what would happen to their mother if no one stepped up. KBR ran like a well-oiled machine, it could go on autopilot for the time being. Pops had hired an incredible team to take care of the cattle. He was one of the most respected men and employers in the state. Slim Jenkins was top when it came to his job as foreman. The man was like family. But Finn O'Connor was the captain who held the ship together. How long could it keep running smoothly without him?

Cash rubbed his forehead in an attempt to stem the headache trying to take seed. "First things first, I have to keep that kiddo and her mother safe. We need to lock away the bastard who tried to take this angel from her bed and then rip her from her mother's arms in a parking lot."

"The person came back a second time?" Mother sounded startled by the news.

"Yes."

She clucked her tongue and then looked down at Abby. "Sounds like someone wants this little girl very much."

"That's the way I'm looking at the situation. She has an ex I don't like. There was a creep from her office who can't be ignored. I'm following the evidence but this feels personal." And that most likely meant it was totally unrelated to Caroline's case because there was no connection between the families that he knew of.

"Why risk coming back?" Margaret O'Connor had observation skills that would rival any good detective.

"The second attempt was made in the grocery store parking lot."

"In such a public place?" She balked.

"Exactly. It's been bothering me, too."

"Do we know who the birth parents are?" his mother asked.

"Not a clue. Colton interviewed her adoption lawyer a little while ago. We were at his office watching before we came here."

"And? How do you think it went?" She made a tsk-tsk noise. His mother could always be counted on to let people know how she really felt. She'd never been one to disguise her emotions, even when she put on a brave face.

"Poorly. He basically stopped the interview when Colton asked him to prove his whereabouts for the past forty-eight hours." Cash had taken note of McGee's body language and it didn't inspire confidence the man was innocent. Of course, the lawyer was already known to be shady, so that could very well be the reason. His nervousness might not have anything to do with Renee and Abby. He could, however, be connected to the Hubert murder. The lawyer might have believed the Hubert case was the reason he was being questioned. "He came across as squirrely to me."

"The guy sounds like a shady character." His mother had developed keen investigative skills over the past three and a half decades. He remembered the stacks of books in her library that she'd read and reread. Eventually, those gave way to mystery books.

"He's definitely someone to keep watch of, but that doesn't necessarily mean he was involved in the kidnapping attempts. He doesn't fit the description and trying to climb a ladder with his physical fitness level would be a challenge. The person who climbed in and out of Abby's window made the round trip quickly."

"Wouldn't Renee recognize her lawyer or anyone else she knew?" his mother asked.

"She couldn't see very well without her glasses on, so all she had was a general shape to go on. She didn't think it was him personally, which doesn't mean he's not involved and especially now that we found a link between him and Ms. Hubert."

"A man who hides behind his office wouldn't commit the crime himself." Her gaze narrowed. "No, he'd have henchmen do his bidding."

Cash sat for a long moment, contemplating his next question because it wasn't directly related to the case.

"Does it ever go away?" he finally summoned the courage to ask. No one ever spoke about Caroline directly unless it was her birthday and then his mother would recount the precious few memories she had.

"Missing Caroline?" she asked.

"Yes. That ache. Does it ever get easier?" Even saying those words caused painful stabs in his chest.

"I'm afraid not, son."

"I'm sorry that happened to you and Pops," he said, wishing there was some way he could go back and fix the past to make it less painful for his parents.

"It happened to all of us."

Chapter Thirteen

"Abby." Renee sat bolt upright and searched the dark room for her daughter.

"She's right here." Margaret's soothing voice calmed Renee's nerves.

"Sorry." She blinked through blurry eyes, still half-asleep. It felt like the whole world was moving in slow motion, but that was probably just her. As her eyes adjusted to the light, she moved to the sofa next to Margaret.

Renee shook her head, trying to clear the fog.

"You tell me when you're ready for her." Margaret's kindness was water in a drought when it came to mothers.

"Is she okay?" Renee asked.

"She's an angel. We've been bonding."

"Does she need anything?" Renee could use a bathroom and a splash of cold water on her face to wake her up.

"She ate an hour ago and I changed her diaper after. I stayed right here in the library in case you woke. Cash did everything else and held her when my arms needed a break." Margaret smiled down at Abby. "She's a sweet baby."

"Thank you." Renee glanced around the dimly lit room. "Where is Cash?"

"In the office making a few calls. He didn't want to disturb you by making them in here. Should I call for him?"

"Maybe in a minute." There was something oddly comforting about being in this room with Cash's mother and Abby. It was obvious this woman would lay down her life before she'd allow anything bad to happen to either one of them, which struck Renee as remarkable considering they'd just met only a few hours ago. "How long was I asleep?"

"Probably not nearly long enough." Margaret chuckled. "About three hours."

"Your arms must be ready to fall off. I can—"

Margaret clucked her tongue. "I've had plenty of breaks with Cash around. Don't take her back until you're ready. Besides, it's been a really long time since I've held a little girl as lovely as Abby."

"She is a good baby, isn't she?"

"She really is." Considering Margaret's vast experience with little ones, Renee would take the compliment.

"Is there any chance I could trouble you for a cup of something warm?" Renee asked.

"Kitchen is down the hall. Help yourself to anything you want." Margaret nodded. "Or I could call Cash."

"No. That's okay. I don't want to be any trouble. I'll do my best not to get lost." She smiled but she also meant that very much. The main house was massive and beautiful from what she'd seen of it so far.

"I've lived here so long the place doesn't seem as big to me now as when I first moved in. This was my in-laws' place. I renovated once they handed over the reins in order to make it my own but I'd forgotten how over-whelming the place can be at first blush." She beamed back at Renee. "I hope you and Abby will make your-selves at home here. Cash is my oldest and he's not one to open up to people right away. That's always been my biggest worry with him. That he holds everything in." She sighed. "I'd like to tell you there's a point when you stop worrying about your children, but there isn't. Not until you see them happy." She paused a beat. "He's different when he's around you two. He could use a… friend." The way she said the last word made Renee think it was a substitute for the real one she wanted to say. There was so much warmth and love when Mar-garet spoke about her son. It was the same sunshine-on-a-warm-spring-day feeling she'd had when she first walked into their home. And, if she was being honest, when she'd first met Cash.

"I'm not sure what Abby and I would've done without your son." She felt her cheeks warm when she talked about him and was grateful for the dim lighting. Hope-fully, his mother wouldn't see her physical reaction to talking about Cash.

"I couldn't be prouder of the man he's become." Mar-garet beamed. "Kitchen is down the hallway and to the left. I think you'll find everything you need there."

Renee thanked Margaret and headed out of the li-brary. She pit-stopped at the bathroom and did a double take when she got a good look at herself in the mirror. Margaret had said to make herself at home, so Renee opened the medicine cabinet and located a few sup-plies for freshening up. It was the closest she could get to taking an actual shower. The toothbrush and tooth-paste were like manna from heaven.

After washing her face and wrangling her curly waves into a ponytail, she headed toward the kitchen. The sound of fingers on a keyboard hit before she turned left. Someone was in the kitchen working. Cash had five brothers and there was plenty of hired help at the main house. This late, though, she figured she would most likely run into someone else in his family.

She didn't want to surprise whoever was in the room and especially one of these men who were used to carrying weapons, so she cleared her throat as loudly as she could as she rounded the corner.

The minute she entered the room, Cash turned to face her and he stood up. Man, did her stomach perform a gymnastics routine the second their eyes met. Her body seemed to have a mind of its own when it came to the handsome lawman. Her brain was definitely out of its league when it came to controlling her physical response to him. The heart could want what it wanted all day long as far as she was concerned. Renee knew better than to let go of control like that despite how strong the urge was to do just that.

"Hey there," Cash said as his masculine voice conspired with her heart. "Did you get a good rest?"

"Surprisingly, yes." She tucked her hands inside her pockets for lack of something better to do with them. Knowing where to put her hands had never been a problem before now. She took in a deep breath and tried to remember why she came into the kitchen in the first place. "Tea." She didn't realize she'd said the word out loud until Cash nodded toward the counter.

"I'd be happy to get you a cup while I refill mine with something stronger."

"Oh, no. Don't go to any trouble—"

"I mean, it's no trouble. I was just about to get up." There was so much chemistry pinging between them that she thought she picked up on it in his voice, too. It was reassuring the attraction didn't seem to be one-sided.

"Okay. Well, if you're already getting yours." Her hands came out of her pockets and she shrugged in the most awkward of body movements. She knew exactly what she wanted—Cash. Her mind argued against the timing of an attraction as strong as this one. Logic tried to say that she felt this way only because he'd saved her and her baby…he was their rescuer or something like that.

Cash moved toward the counter and she was relieved when his back was turned to her so she could let out the breath she'd been holding. It was so much easier to think when those steel-gray eyes weren't locked on to hers.

Refocusing her attention on where he'd been sitting, she noticed he had a laptop and notepad on the massive oak table. "Find anything interesting?"

"Not really." As Cash brought over a steaming cup of tea that smelled like absolute heaven, his cell buzzed on the table next to the laptop.

Colton's name lit up the screen. Renee and Cash locked eyes for one second before he made a move to pick it up. The exchange between them, as electric as a hot-wired fence, sent more of that warmth sizzling through her. He set her cup down and answered.

"I'm putting you on speaker. Renee is here with me." The fact Cash seemed to need to immediately let his brother know who was in on the conversation with them made her wonder how much confidential information the brothers usually shared. Between the two of them, they had to be responsible for keeping many of the community's secrets, and she wondered how much of a burden that might be.

"Good." That one word from Colton sent a chill racing down her back because it meant he had news about her case.

She palmed her mug and rolled it around in her hands before taking a sip. The tea would provide much-needed calm.

Colton cleared his throat. "One of my deputies got an anonymous tip to pick up a young guy who works for the Pierson ranch. He was acting suspicious, so my deputy started digging around, asking questions. He told the guy our office would figure out if he'd done something wrong, lock him up and throw away the key. The kid got real nervous because he needs his job and room and board in the bunkhouse."

"Did this guy fit the general height and build of our window creeper?" Cash asked.

"He's a little smaller than the description she gave…"

Renee didn't want to point out that she didn't have her glasses on and so the guy's frame was more a blur. She'd been dead asleep and startled awake. She could've gotten this description wrong. It all happened so fast.

"But he confessed to being in the parking lot with two of his buddies. He said a man paid the trio a thousand dollars in cash to scare the mother."

Cash blew out a breath. "And you believed this kid?"

"By the time my deputy brought him in here the kid was almost inconsolable, especially when he found out what had happened a few hours before. He swears that he had no idea. He and his buddies thought the whole thing was some kind of twisted prank," Colton continued.

"So, these guys agreed to harass me and my daughter for a thousand dollars?" It was good to know what her life being turned upside down was worth to virtual strangers.

"The kid gave up his buddies' names and a deputy is on his way to pick them up to get their statements," Colton said.

"Do you believe him?" Cash's question was direct.

"Yes, I do. Obviously, I plan to follow wherever the evidence leads me but I think this kid is telling the truth." Colton didn't say how much this changed the course of the investigation. Cash had mentioned the crime seemed personal. It didn't get more personal than paying someone to…what?…scare her?

Renee took a sip of tea before taking a lap around the island. This place was the whole deal: farm sink, white granite countertops, double ovens. It looked like something out of a design magazine. And, yes, it did strike Renee as odd that she was noticing the decor when she'd just been thrown a curveball. Actually, she took that back. This was a fastball aimed right between her eyes.

"Why would someone do that?" She heard the words coming out of her mouth and revised. "Why would anyone pay another person to scare me."

Jamison came to mind. So did another name. The contractor from work. "Darion Figg."

"I had a chance to follow up with your boss earlier." Cash tapped his fingers on his mug.

Oh, darn. With everything going on the past few

days she'd forgotten to give Rikki a heads-up about the call coming. "What did she say?"

"Mr. Figg seemed to develop a fixation on you and a couple of other female co-workers. Your IT department found incriminating pictures on his computer and he was fired not long after you complained about him. Once he lost his job, his girlfriend found out about what happened at work and left him."

"Seems like a pretty good reason to try to get back at me," she said. The creep deserved more than to be fired if he was snapping pictures of her and co-workers without their permission. She, for one, knew she'd never been asked. Another cold chill gripped her spine thinking about Darion. How many times had she turned around to suddenly find him standing behind her in the parking lot? In the beginning, she'd tried to be polite. She'd say, "Excuse me." Then, she'd walk away. He must've mistaken her politeness for interest because he'd pushed his body up against hers in the elevator, pinning her for a split second before she was able to shake off the shock of what had just happened and bring a knee up to his groin.

"The problem is that he's in county lockup on a drunk and disorderly charge. He got into a fight with a neighbor over where he parked his pickup," Colton said.

Cash shot a disappointed look her way. "That would make it impossible for him to be here."

Renee took another lap around the kitchen.

"Who did the kid say paid him? He must've met up with the guy if money changed hands." Cash was right on track with what her next question was going to be.

"The kid said the whole transaction was handled in the men's room at the gas station. The money was slipped underneath a stall in a paper bag. Half up front. Half when the job was finished." Colton paused. "The kid flipped out when he realized how much trouble he was in. He's willing to cooperate but he doesn't know much about the guy who paid him. He was insistent that he was paid to scare her not to steal a child."

His statement explained why the suspects took off, and Renee found it reassuring they hadn't been out to steal Abby.

Who would hire someone to scare her? Who would pull a jerk move like that?

HEARING THIS, WATCHING Renee wear a path in his family's kitchen, Cash could see her tension building. She already had a white-knuckle grip on her mug of tea when the conversation started. Her stress levels seemed to be skyrocketing. Not an unusual reaction for someone who'd recently experienced one of the worst days of her life. But he wanted to do something to ease her stress. Since nothing came to mind, he asked Colton if there was anything else.

"That's what I have for now. I'll keep you posted if anything changes," Colton said before saying goodbye and ending the call.

"Darion could've been behind what happened in the parking lot," she said as she approached the table with a whole heap of apprehension on her face.

"That's true. What would his motive be? Revenge?" Cash was just thinking out loud.

"It's weird to think someone could hate me that much. I did knock the wind out of him when he came on to me."

"Good for you. I hope the bastard thinks twice before he tries to force himself on another person. And I sure hope you nailed him where it counts." Cash would like five minutes alone with any person who tried to prey on someone they assumed was weaker than them.

"I doubt he'll look at women quite the same after the incident. He looked pretty shocked that I fought back, actually. He wasn't expecting a knee to the groin."

"Well, he deserved one." Cash picked up the pen on the pad of paper and twirled it around his fingers.

"My mind is flooded with possibilities. Darion could've hired someone from jail," she offered.

"A drunk like that isn't usually capable of arranging a money exchange. He wouldn't have been in contact with anyone on the outside if he was sleeping off a binge, so it would've been impossible for him to communicate." Cash was already running through possibilities in his mind.

With Renee standing so close to him, he could smell her floral scent. She smelled like spring flowers after a good rain. He was also aware when she shifted from frustration to need. It wasn't uncommon for someone who'd been through trauma to want proof of life.

When she locked gazes with him, her glittery blue eyes sent a shot straight to his heart. He was taking on fire being so close to her. He should remain partial and step away, despite the signals she was sending.

"Cash." Her warm honey tone wrapped around him.

"Yeah." He could hear the huskiness in his own voice when he spoke.

"Can you do me a favor?" Her body language wasn't difficult to read and yet he still wasn't prepared for the next couple of words that came out of those soft pink lips.

"Depends on what it is." There was a lot of ground her question could cover. Cash didn't make promises he couldn't keep. His word was his honor.

"Kiss me."

Chapter Fourteen

Cash took in a sharp breath, closed the distance between him and Renee in a couple of steps and leaned in.

She closed her eyes and leaned toward him. He knew exactly what he wanted…her. Was it smart? Was he crossing a line that couldn't be uncrossed if he finished what he'd started?

Granted, she'd never felt like a victim to him, no matter how much his protective instincts flared when she was around. The pull toward her was stronger than anything else he'd ever experienced. But cross that line and there was no going back. His professionalism was at stake in a career he'd worked his tail off to build.

"Cash." His name came out as barely a whisper.

He flexed and released his fingers because they itched to get lost in her hair. His mouth was so close to hers. Damn. He rested his forehead against her.

"Believe me when I say that I couldn't want to kiss you more than I do right now."

"But…"

"It would be a game changer for me." He meant that on so many levels even though he couldn't articulate the reasons if he tried. On instinct, on a primal level, he realized Renee was different. She was intelligent and determined and beautiful on more levels than he could count.

"I can't afford game changers in my life right now. Not after my breakup with Jamison. I'm sorry," she said.

"My job is to protect you, not confuse you." Everything in Cash wanted to take that final step, consequences be damned. He didn't get to where he was today by giving in to impulses. He'd been calculating about his life choices and would be the same way if the right circumstances happened for him and Renee to move forward with what they both so obviously wanted in the moment.

Cash didn't do or give regrets.

"I'm pretty damn clear about what's good for me. Kissing you falls into that category. Doing anything else, anything more…not so much."

"Take a step down that slippery slope and we can't come back." One kiss wouldn't be enough with Renee. Where would that leave them? One great kiss followed by a helluva lot of nothing. Because it couldn't go anywhere in the middle of an investigation. Granted, it was his brother's investigation, but Cash was acting as consultant on this one and since he'd stepped in on the initial call, he was committed to seeing this through. The annoying voice in the back of his mind called him out as a liar. He'd never once brought a victim to the main house for protection no matter how personally responsible he felt for their safety. Cash knew himself. He had a tendency to go all in whether it meant family or work.

Was that part of the reason he'd shied away from relationships? He didn't have it in him to go all in with a woman?

Why the hell did his mind pick this moment to reveal that his heart had already fallen down that slippery slope he'd been talking about a few seconds ago.

"No." She paused for a thoughtful moment. "But we could hang on to each other while we brace for the fall."

Cash needed to refocus. He needed to force his thoughts away from those full pink lips of hers. He needed to think about something besides how silky her skin would feel if he reached his hand up. And he sure as hell needed to stop imagining what she might taste like because this close he figured it would be a mix of tea and peppermint, basically Christmas.

He brought his hands up to cup her face. Temptation was two inches away from his mouth and stood at five feet, seven inches tall. He could feel her pulse racing, the tempo matching his.

Cash's cell buzzed again, indicating a text had come in. Since it could be news about the case, he dropped his hands on a hard sigh. "Think we can talk about this...*us*...later?"

"Yeah." She was breathless when she spoke and a little satisfied smile quirked the corners of his mouth up. Renee Smith had one hell of an effect on him. It made him feel better than it should that she seemed to have the same reaction to him. Under any other circumstance, she was exactly the kind of person he'd want to get to know better. He envisioned them dating and...

Holy hell. His thoughts had a mind of their own when it came to Renee. They needed to stay in check. He reminded himself of the facts. She'd been through a lot. She was most likely just reaching out for comfort. It wouldn't have mattered who'd been standing there...

He couldn't sell himself on the last line because her reactions to him had been too real. No matter how much he tried to convince himself otherwise, whatever was going on between them was special. He'd be smart to keep a firm handle on his emotions.

It had been a really long time since he'd cared about someone *this* much, and he barely knew Renee Smith.

"Why are you smiling when I'm this...*frustrated?*"

"This is how I handle frustration." It was true.

She laughed and it broke the tension between them. Granted, it was sexual tension but that was the most intense he'd ever felt. Laughter was a good thing about now.

"What does your phone say?" She picked up her tea and took a sip. Immediately, she scrunched up her face. "Well, that went cold on me fast."

That comment really made him laugh. She locked gazes with him and broke into a wide smile when she picked up on the undercurrent.

"I'm just going to leave that comment alone and heat my tea." She made a show of looking for the microwave.

"That way." He pointed to the opposite end of the kitchen.

"This place is so big. I don't think I've ever been in a kitchen this large before and I was a waitress once."

Cash studied the screen and didn't respond. He heard the microwave beeping and figured she'd found her way. A half-dozen bombs were exploding inside his head as he reread the message.

"Cash?" Renee studied him as she made a beeline toward him. "What is it? What's wrong?"

"It's the Hubert case. We found email ties to the Ludlow kidnapping ring. The feds have been gathering information about them and their involvement with bigger crime organizations. Basically, they are considered one of the biggest illegal adoption operations in the Southwest."

"She can't be connected to my case, can she?"

"It's possible. She might've paid the kids to scare you to throw us off the track," Cash stated.

"Or the person she reported to might have done it after the kidnapping attempt was messed up."

"True. Your crime has felt personal but that could just be what they want us to think. Like you said, throw us off the trail after botching the job." Cash had seen pretty much everything in his life as a marshal.

Renee gasped. "She might have been murdered to prove a point."

"Or to keep her quiet. Maybe whoever is really in charge thought she brought too much heat to the organization. Believe me when I say these operations run better than most Fortune 500 companies. They have to. There's so much more at stake than disappointing shareholders with earnings. These are live by the sword, die by the sword people. Literally."

"I know she's safe but hearing this makes me want to go check on Abby." Worry lines creased Renee's forehead.

"I'll go with you. My mother needs to hear the news." He bit back a curse.

"Your sister?"

"I don't want to get my mother's hopes up because there's no concrete evidence to link Ms. Hubert to Caroline despite the timing of her moving to town," he hedged. "My mother should hear this news from one of her sons and not through the grapevine or a news outlet."

"Small towns do breed a tight-knit community. It's

one of the many reasons that I wanted to leave Dallas. I love my city, but it's grown so much that it can feel impersonal at times. Neighbors don't really know each other anymore and especially not in the suburbs where I lived."

"I can't imagine not knowing the people I lived around. Stacy has become like family as much as everyone who's worked here a long time. But then, my job reminds me we only know the face people show us. Doesn't mean it's who someone truly is." Cash picked up his cup of coffee. "Better head to the library now. Are you coming?"

"Yes, but I'll only stay if you want me to."

There was a lot he wanted from her. He'd settle for this. "My mother has been through a lot. And now with Pops—"

"Yes, of course. You probably want to be alone. This is family time." She sure knew how to backpedal. If she had on running shoes she'd probably be hitting the door about now.

"I was actually about to say that having you and Abby here is a bright spot in what has otherwise been an awful couple of days. I've never seen her hold a six-month-old girl before. My brother has sons and she loves them with all her heart. There's always been a special spark in her eyes when she looks at a little girl."

"DON'T TELL ME stuff like that. Okay?" It was pure protective instinct causing her to speak up. The fact that Abby was welcomed by Margaret sent more of that warmth spiraling through her. She couldn't afford to let anyone else in right now.

Cash studied her before he responded. She'd expected him to get angry or demand a reason like Jamison would've. Instead, he crossed his arms over his chest and seemed to look right through her. "Mind if I ask why not?"

"Because right now getting my bearings on being a mother is my absolute first priority. It's all I have time for." Letting anyone else in her heart when it had just been so broken seemed like a suicide mission. She'd taken her time getting to know Jamison, at least she'd convinced herself that she knew him, and look how that had turned out. Her heart had been stomped on. And it should feel…it should feel a lot worse than it did. She'd convinced herself that she was having some kind of delayed reaction.

She'd been mad as hell at him when she'd found out about the affair. It had never gutted her in the way losing a man like Cash would.

Damn. Was that her real concern? Not that Cash couldn't care about her but that her feelings for him might run too deep? So deep that if he walked out one day her heart might not survive?

Cash's eyebrows drew together. He studied her for a long moment and he looked at her like he could see right through her. It should startle her. Instead, there was a comfort like she'd never known. Acceptance that she'd wished for her entire life.

Now, she realized, it was good that he didn't act on their mutual attraction no matter how much she'd wanted him to. Kissing him *would* be a game changer. She would leave it at that and back away from the thoughts in her mind telling her it was about time the game was changed.

"You're welcome to come back here and use the laptop. I'll be back in a few—"

She waved her hands in the air to stop him from finishing his sentence. Margaret O'Connor had been nothing but kind to Renee since she'd walked in the door. She trusted the woman enough with her daughter to fall asleep as well as leave the room once she woke. If Renee's presence could provide some small measure of comfort to the person who'd been so kind, so be it. "Never mind, Cash. I'd like to stay with you."

He probably had whiplash from her change in plans.

"She'd like that, Renee."

Instead of overthinking the offer, she turned and walked toward the library.

The sight of Margaret O'Connor holding Abby stirred more emotions. Renee had never felt so vulnerable to something so little or so emotional.

"She really is a good girl," Margaret cooed.

"Is she awake?" Renee performed a double take. Abby's eyes were wide open. Instead of being afraid of the stranger, she smiled and cooed right back. The grandmotherly image brought out a longing for something that Renee hadn't even realized had been missing. Abby had no grandparents. And with Renee's parents long gone and no other side of the family to count on, it was just going to be the two of them. The statement had never felt lonely until now, until the O'Connors, until Cash.

"She's been awake since you left. I think she sensed you were gone. She's comforted by you being here." Margaret's words made more of those hot tears prick the backs of Renee's eyes. She wanted more than anything for them to be true. "We've been keeping each other company, though. I figured you needed a minute. How's the tea?"

"Good," Renee answered quickly. Probably a little too quickly.

The astute woman's eyebrow lifted ever so slightly. Her gaze went to Cash and held. "You have something on your mind."

"Yes, ma'am."

"You are both welcome to sit down. And, as much as I've loved holding this little angel, she's ready for her mother." Margaret must've felt Renee's apprehension as she handed over a happy Abby.

Renee took a seat on the couch next to Margaret. It was easy to feel at home with the O'Connors and especially with her daughter in her arms.

Cash reclaimed his seat from earlier. "I got a text from Colton a few minutes ago. The investigation into Ms. Hubert's death is turning over a few stones and I don't want you to be caught off guard."

"The media will be back full force, asking questions. They'll figure out a way to get my cell number and hound me again." She looked at Renee with the most determination she'd seen. "They used to pay folks to give my number to them after Caroline was taken. That was back in the day when we had house phones and land-lines. Finn and I couldn't leave the property for fear of being followed. I had my bumper tapped on the way to town once by a reporter. We figured it wasn't safe to go on the roads until everything died down. Of course, back then we thought they'd find her and bring her home. We endured the publicity because we thought it might help bring her back to us."

"I can't begin to understand what you went through.

I'm so sorry." Renee patted Margaret's hand. Much to her surprise, the older woman gave a reassuring squeeze.

Margaret turned to her son. "What do they know so far?"

He leaned forward and filled his mother in. He spoke with so much compassion. The love and respect between him and his mother was big enough to fill the room.

"And now you fellas are thinking Caroline's case might be connected?" She seemed to already know the answer to her question but asked anyway.

"I just wanted to warn you of the possibility. You know how many twists and turns there can be in an investigation. Ms. Hubert's case spans a lot of years. No doubt, the media will make the connection and folks will be talking about Caroline again." Before he finished his sentence, his mother was nodding.

"Any kidnapping news that involved a child under the age of one caused her name to be brought up. You'd think it would bother me. I never minded, though. I figured it couldn't hurt to talk about her again. The nagging feeling that someone must've seen something that night never left me. The person might not have even realized they'd seen anything important. You hear about these stories of crimes being solved ten or twenty years after the fact because a witness pops up out of the blue not realizing the red sedan they'd witnessed driving away from some crime scene would lead investigators to the offender. That's always been the problem. Whoever took Caroline was able to blend right in."

Renee took note of the stack of true crime books on the table next to her. There were stacks of mystery novels, too.

Margaret motioned toward a particularly large pile. "I can't even count the number of hours I've spent in here trying to train my brain first to think like a criminal and then a detective."

Cash's hands were folded together and there was so much reverence in his eyes. It clicked with Renee that he and several of his brothers went into law enforcement for their careers. She wondered how much of it had to do with the very real pain still present in Margaret's eyes.

It struck her just how much one event could alter the course of someone's life forever. If Abby's kidnapper had succeeded...

Renee couldn't continue with that train of thought.

Caroline's kidnapping had shaped this family. For Renee, her parents' car crash had altered her life in so many countless ways. While she'd closed herself off from the world, the O'Connors seemed to have used their tragedy to pull together and form even tighter bonds. Maybe that was the difference between growing up alone versus being in a large, loving close-knit family.

"I failed her—"

Margaret's voice broke. She shushed Cash when he tried to offer words of comfort. Those three words amounted to Renee's biggest fear. She'd felt that same helplessness when she woke the other night. The man in Abby's room couldn't possibly have been there only to scare Renee. She'd caught him red-handed picking up her daughter from the crib.

The cover-up might have been intended to throw them offtrack. The idea that Caroline's case could be related to Abby's all these years later was a terrible possibility.

"News will get out about Abby soon. I guess the

comparisons are coming no matter how long it's been. I'm more worried about that to be honest." Margaret clucked her tongue in disapproval. "I want to find out what happened to my daughter, but I don't want to over-shadow your investigation. It's no good if people get distracted."

"No, it isn't," Cash agreed. Those words scared Renee. She wouldn't be able to leave her daughter's side or sleep alone in a house again until the perp was caught.

Freaking out every time the doorbell rang or being too scared to go to the store sounded like living in a prison.

Margaret fell quiet for a long time. She looked tired, weary. The glow from holding Abby had faded.

The older woman pushed up to standing. "We won't solve anything tonight. I'd probably better try to get some sleep." She turned to Renee. "Thank you for let-ting me hold your angel. She's a lucky little girl to have you as a mother. I hope you'll come to me with any questions you have. I'm not sure that I know much, but I'm happy to share what I've learned over the years."

"I will take you up on that. I'm grateful for any ad-vice." Renee meant every word. She was rewarded with a warm smile.

"Cash, will you show her to her quarters?"

"Yes, ma'am." He stood and wrapped his mother in a hug. Another one of those rogue tears leaked from Renee's eyes. She ducked to cover it while she wiped it away. His mother had to know Renee already knew where her room was, so she took the suggestion as a sign Margaret wanted to be alone.

"Do you want me to take her?" he asked, nodding toward Abby.

"No, thanks." She needed her daughter to keep her arms busy. Especially because what they wanted was to reach out and touch Cash.

Chapter Fifteen

Renee reviewed the facts once she was settled in the comfortable guest room.

The mystery mover's identity had been revealed. He had a solid alibi as did his crew chief, Paul. They'd learned earlier that the lighter, a piece of evidence she'd hoped might lead to the perp, belonged to Paul.

Darion Figg was in jail, which didn't necessarily rule him out but made pulling off the crime more difficult. He had the perfect motive along with an equally perfect alibi. He had harassed other women at the office. The reason he'd been fired had to do with the pictures found on his work computer and wasn't necessarily the direct result of her complaint about him. Some of her other office mates had come forward, too. So, the trail of revenge should be longer than just Renee.

Kipp McGee was tied to a murdered woman who was linked to a kidnapping ring. Why give Abby to Renee in the first place if he was only going to turn right around and take her back? She needed to think through why someone would do that. What would his reasoning be? Didn't he have to have a motive?

She looked up at Cash. "Something has been bothering me about Kipp McGee. Why give Abby to me only to take her back a month later? Why not cut out the middleman altogether if he had the baby in his care in the first place? He was the one who brought her to me."

Cash leaned back in the chair beside the bed. "For one, to throw people off the trail of who the baby was really going to. You hired him to do a job. He delivered. He collects his fee and makes you think he moved on."

"He's never been inside my new house. Didn't you say early on the perp seemed to know the layout?"

"Being from the area and having been in countless homes, it wouldn't be difficult for McGee to guess the layout." He made a good point.

"I know it wasn't him that first night, though. It sounds like you're saying he would've hired someone to…*do it* for him." She couldn't bear to say the words *take her.*

"Right," Cash agreed.

"So, someone botches the first attempt and then tries to cover with the guys from the grocery store parking lot. And then an anonymous tip leads the investigation to him, but he can't give any details about the person who hired him. It doesn't make sense to me," she said. "Why would someone go to all that trouble?"

"To change the motive. To distract investigators and lead them down a different path," he stated.

"Jamison is missing and so is Yolanda," she reminded him.

"The investigation is all over the place right now, which could indicate the perp is an amateur. He might've started to take your child and then panicked when you caught him. It was maybe supposed to be a quick in-and-out job. But you ruined that so he had to hire someone to throw us off." Cash rubbed the scruff on his chin, a habit she'd noticed him doing when he was stressed.

"And then there's Darion." She crossed her arms over her chest and hugged them. It was strange thinking about who might have a grudge against her.

"Getting drunk and being locked up gives him an airtight alibi," Cash said.

"For both attempts."

"He couldn't have known the first attempt would fail and I seriously doubt he could pull off the second one from jail," Cash reasoned.

"It sounds safe to erase him from the suspect list then." At least they were able to cross a couple of names off the list so far.

Cash nodded. "Unless new information comes up to change our minds, we can go ahead and rule him out for now."

"You said something early on that has stuck in my mind ever since. You stated that the crime seemed personal because of the second attempt happening so soon. Have you changed your opinion?"

"My personal opinion? No." Cash's cell buzzed. He checked the screen and then gave her a look that sent her stress levels soaring before picking it up. The look was becoming familiar and meant Colton had another message.

Cash studied the screen. "There were no prints on the ladder."

"Wouldn't there be *someone's* prints on there?" Someone had to have touched it at some point. Right?

"It was wiped clean. Considering the perp took off after being interrupted, he had to have wiped the ladder beforehand. And it also means he wore gloves so we're not likely to get any viable prints at your house, either." He issued a sharp sigh. "There's something else. Yolanda Tran answered Colton's call. She said that she and Jamison are on a babymoon and that he's been with her since the doctor's appointment."

"Does that mean he's ruled out?" A part of her wished it was true. She didn't want someone she'd once cared about and trusted to be responsible for one of the most horrendous acts against her.

Cash looked up from his phone. "I'm never thrilled when a person's alibi hinges on someone else who has a lot to lose. Plus, their story seems to be changing from a doctor's appointment to a babymoon."

"Paul's mother might have a lot to lose, right?" It clicked why. It was probably common for a person to lie, cheat or steal to protect someone they loved. The reasoning made perfect sense and yet it all still had a huge ick factor. Renee had always been one to follow the rules. Then again, she'd never been in a situation where she'd had to protect someone she loved. She glanced over at Abby's crib. Her protective instincts were already so strong. But what example would she set for her daughter if Renee was willing to do anything at all costs to cover for her. Protecting and covering were two different things in Renee's book. Clearly, not everyone shared her morals.

"Right. Besides, he could've tricked her into thinking he was home when he wasn't." What he was saying made perfect sense.

"Yolanda has a lot to lose if Jamison goes to jail right before she gives birth to their child."

"What else can you tell me about your ex, though?" he asked.

"Like?" Renee would like to forget as much about him as she could, but this might be important to the investigation. Again, it should seem strange sharing so many personal details with him. Instead, it was like talking to someone she'd known her whole life.

"What were his habits? How did he deal with stress?"

"He changed a lot over the years. I mean, when we first got together, he could be a little possessive. I tried to break up with him over it but he convinced me to stick around. He was great in the early days. He once drove two hours round trip to put a single flower on my car with a note telling me to have a great day. But it grew from there and started to worry me that he was getting too attached, too soon. When I put my foot down about him showing up unannounced at the restaurant where I worked, he stopped." Or so she'd thought, until now. It was highly possible that he'd been keeping track of her over the years without telling her.

"From the sounds of it, he pursued you pretty hard."

"Looking back, I guess that's true. He definitely had to convince me to go out with him in the first place," she said.

"You weren't interested in him?" An eyebrow arched.

"Not him. Not anyone. I'd lost my parents the year before we started dating and their relationship had left a sour taste in my mouth. I was working at a restaurant to pay for classes at my community college. The business my parents owned was in bad financial shape. It's part of the reason they fought all the time. I'd been living at home, working my way through school when the accident happened."

"I'm sorry for your loss." Those words soothed her

soul. Despite not having a great relationship with her parents, she was still sad they were gone.

"Thank you. While they were alive, there was still a chance to make things right. You know?"

He nodded his understanding and she appreciated his compassion, but how could he know what it was like to come from a broken family?

"Our home was foreclosed on and I had to find a place to live. I rented this tiny apartment over an older couple's garage. I had no way to bring furniture. I couldn't afford to buy anything, so I slept on a pile of blankets on the floor. I kept working despite everything I was going through. I managed to stay in class, barely able to afford to keep going. But I did and I got an associate degree and tech certification, so now I can support myself and my daughter."

"Wow." He sat back and blinked at her like she'd just dropped a bomb in his lap. "I knew you were strong and capable when I first interviewed you but this... most people would buckle under those circumstances, not fight."

It was strange to hear from an outsider's perspective considering she'd never talked about her past with anyone. Even Jamison seemed content to take her at face value when she said that she and her parents weren't close, but that she'd loved them. He'd never once seemed amazed by what she was able to accomplish, but then she'd never really gone into much detail, either. Looking into Cash's eyes now, his admiration was almost overwhelming. "I did what I had to in order to survive. Anyone in my position would do the same."

She tried to shrug off his compliment.

"I'd say you're doing a helluva lot better than surviving. Not many people could pick up the pieces of their life and thrive, considering the obstacles life threw at you early on."

She was surprised she wanted to tell Cash about her past. She was used to downplaying or hiding it.

"I never talk about the past. Part of me thinks I've bottled all my emotions up for so long that it's just become the elephant in the room of every friendship, every relationship." Renee was surprised at how much she wanted to open up to a stranger. Except that Cash O'Connor didn't exactly fit into that category. There was a spark with him that she'd never felt before with another man. The connection between them couldn't be faked. And she should be embarrassed that he'd rejected her advance before but she wasn't. The fact he'd wanted her as much as she wanted him—well, almost— comforted her. She was on the right track. He felt the chemistry between them as much as she did. And he made it seem like it was taking all of his self-control to keep their relationship platonic.

"It's easy to do. Tuck an emotion into a box and stuff it down deep." He stared at the wall when he spoke. As wonderful of a mother as Margaret had to have been, losing her firstborn in the way she had would've altered the rest of her life.

"The work you do is dangerous. Does that ever bother you?" She wanted to know more about his decision to go into law enforcement versus the family business.

"There's not much more danger than ranching."

"How?" She was genuinely curious. She'd talked enough about herself and wanted to know more about Cash.

"Poachers, for one. Cattle rustlers are another serious threat. Wild animals have taken down a few men over the years. Wild hogs are nasty and dangerous. Human error while running equipment can be deadly, and is one of the biggest killers. And then there's Mother Nature herself."

"Wow. I had no idea. The biggest threat in the suburb where I used to live was traffic." Dallas traffic was a force to be reckoned with for sure.

"I still have a whole helluva lot of respect for what you've been able to accomplish despite tough beginnings." He managed to cycle the conversation back around to her.

"You managed to make something of yourself despite growing up in a place like this." She was still in awe of the O'Connor family home. It was something to behold.

"Are you saying that I could've ended up a trust fund baby? Because I doubt that would float on a hard-working cattle ranch like KBR." He laughed and it broke some of the intensity of the conversation. She figured it was part defense mechanism to laugh when the conversation turned serious. She'd been guilty of that herself, which made it easier to recognize in someone else.

The break in tension was a welcome reprieve. It also made her think of normal things, like taking a shower.

"Any chance I can grab a shower while she's sleeping?"

His smile was devastating. He shook his head. "Probably not a good idea to put the image of you naked in my...never mind." He nodded toward the en suite bathroom. "I already had your clothes brought to the main house and the others have been washed. You should find them in there."

Being with Cash, with someone who thought about her needs, stirred more of those falling-into-the-deep-end feelings in her chest. She took in a breath, smiled to herself and walked into the bathroom.

"YOU'LL BE OKAY with her if she wakes?" Renee stopped at the door. He didn't want to notice the soft curve of her hip, so he adjusted his focus.

"Did okay with twin nephews at this age. I think I can handle one." Technically, he'd been alone with them only once. This wasn't the time to discuss his qualifications, or lack thereof. As close as he was to Colton and all of his brothers save for Garrett, Cash had always been married to his work. If Abby stirred, he could figure out a way to handle the situation while Renee showered. She seemed to trust him and quietly closed the bathroom door behind her.

Cash opened the laptop he'd brought with him from the kitchen, which pulled up one of his favorite family pictures. It was the summer before senior year. Cash and his brothers had been working the ranch and, for reasons he couldn't pinpoint now, he and Garrett had gotten into an argument. The day had been a scorcher. The temps had topped off at one hundred and seven for the third day in a row. All six boys had been working the ranch since four o'clock, his father's usual wake-up time. It was the time of year in Texas when the weather never cooled off.

So, it was probably teenage hormones baking in a hot sun all day that had him and Garrett on edge with each other. Garrett had popped his mouth off about something or other and Cash had stomped over and gotten in his brother's face. Wrong move. As an adult, he'd learned to reason his way out of most situations. Foolish pride had him challenging Garrett, poking the angry bear.

Garrett had always been a hothead, so it hadn't been difficult to get him riled up. Cash had probably just needed to blow off some steam. Garrett had thrown the first punch. The two of them had ended up on the ground in a wrestling match. Until their mother had caught wind of what was happening.

She hadn't raise her voice. They'd had no idea she was even there until the bucket of ice-cold water doused them.

Two people had never jumped up so fast in their lives. Both ready to fight because they'd had no idea they'd be staring Margaret O'Connor in the face. Even then, she'd been a tiny storm best left untouched. The rest of his brothers had stood in a semicircle, snickering, which had gotten Cash and Garrett in even more trouble because they'd both started cracking up. Their mother hadn't seen the humor in her sons getting into a fistfight.

Pops had heard the commotion from the barn. Next thing Cash knew he'd been staring down both of his parents. Pops had asked what had happened.

Garrett had started by saying, "Well, sir. My brother here is a donkey's backside."

At those words, Cash had lost it. Just when he'd expected to be reamed out, Pops had laughed, too. That'd made their mother crack up. She'd walked to him and Garrett and pulled them both into a hug. Her dress had been soaked. Pops had picked her up and pretended he was about to toss her into the pond. She'd been as calm as she could be when she'd dared him to do it.

Even Pops had known not to cross his wife. She was five feet, five inches of pure dynamite. Slim Jenkins had watched the scene unfold. He'd told everyone to squeeze in for a picture. All of the boys had groaned. But they'd done it. The picture was of Pops carrying his wife and their boys flanking them, two of whom were soaked to the bone in pond water.

Everyone had a silly smile plastered on their face. All of which were the real deal unlike those Christmas card pictures their mother had liked to force on them. At least she hadn't insisted they all wear the same sweater. It could've been a lot worse.

But this was Cash's all-time favorite family pic. It was messy. The boys were precocious. Their parents loved the family no matter what, dirty pond water and all.

This was the real O'Connor family. Despite Garrett's current shortcomings, he needed to know what was going on. Pops had never wanted a real funeral. He'd be angry that everyone was so sad when there was work to get done.

No doubt, Margaret O'Connor would respect her husband's wishes. There would be a small ceremony, a remembrance, a celebration of his life. A few tears slipped out at the thought of Pops never walking through the back door again, sweaty from a hard day's work and still dressed in a long-sleeve button-down shirt. Although most cattle ranchers used pickup trucks to herd cattle nowadays, Pops considered himself a renaissance man. He rode his horse every day to check fences to see if any part needed repair. Most people would be surprised at just how much of a cattleman's life was spent doing paperwork and checking fences to ensure the safety of their livestock.

Wiping blurry eyes, Cash zeroed in on his email. With his cell phone almost constantly being available, he hadn't thought about sending his brother an email. Since no one else had come up with any better ideas, Cash pulled up their last exchange. He checked the date. It had been three years ago. His brother wasn't the type to have a social media account, so this was his best bet for the time being.

But what should he say over email? He didn't want to puke the news out without preparing Garrett for what was coming. He also needed the note to sound urgent enough to get his brother's attention.

Garrett,
I realize we've been out of touch. You're needed at home. There's serious news. Call or come home.
Your brother,
Cash

It wasn't Shakespeare, but it got the point across. He added his cell number under his name in case Garrett wanted to reach out.

Cash took a deep breath and hit Send. There was no good time to deliver bad news, and he hated that Garrett didn't already know.

Rubbing his temples, he tried to stave off one helluva headache. The shower water was on full force in the adjacent bathroom. He could hear it even through the door. And, yes, his thoughts immediately went to Renee standing naked in the shower. But he managed to refocus.

Staring at a computer screen wasn't helping the throb above his eyes, and besides, his mother had always repeated the phrase about a watched pot never boiling. As he lowered the screen, a message popped up.

It was from Garrett.

Lost my cell. On my way home.

Chapter Sixteen

Cash couldn't sleep if he tried. He'd gone days without shut-eye before while working a case and this one was shaping up to be no exception. Rather than fight it or dread it, he settled in as he heard the water turn off in the adjacent room.

He texted his brothers to let them know Garrett was on his way home. Then he messaged their mother. She needed to know her son was coming.

Unless they were missing something, there were three suspects left in Renee's case: McGee, Jamison and Yolanda.

The lawyer reopened old wounds with his connection to another town resident. A feeling of dread that Ms. Hubert could be linked to his sister's case was growing, niggling away at the back of his mind. The reality of losing his father was also starting to sink in. It had been one helluva couple of days since meeting Renee.

Much of Cash's life was being turned upside down and there was still a sense of rightness in the world with Renee and Abby in the picture.

Just as he thought about Renee, she came walking out of the bathroom. His heart took another dive. Renee was beautiful, inside and out. Watching her love for

Abby was nothing short of inspirational and mesmerizing. Learning about her past and how far she'd come rocketed her into a whole new stratosphere of respect.

"What is it?" Grooves deepened on her forehead as those sky blue eyes penetrated his armor.

He started to speak but no words came. She seemed to understand as she walked straight to him and sat down on his lap. Her leggings and T-shirt hugged her curves. Beads of water rolled down her neck.

He looped his arms around her waist as she turned to straddle him. No words seemed necessary as she brought her hands up to his face.

"I know you can't kiss me because of the investigation." She leaned forward. "But that doesn't mean I can't kiss you."

Cash started to protest but it would be half-hearted. He brought his mouth to hers and pressed his lips to hers with the feeling of being home.

With a groan, he deepened the kiss. Her soft pink lips tasted like heaven. Peppermint toothpaste filled his senses. Peppermint was his new favorite flavor.

Her tongue delved into his mouth as she scooted her sweet, round bottom closer to his length. The effect she had on him was instantaneous, and a force of its own. He pressed his palms to the soft curve of her lower back and she rocked back and forth as she moaned her pleasure.

Her fingers dug into his shoulders, her nails against his hot skin as she dropped them to his arms was pure sin on Sunday. A need so intense Cash could scarcely fathom it welled up. He dropped his hands to each side of her hips as she rocked a little more.

His pulse raced, matching the tempo of hers. Reason escaped him as blood flew south. He tried to convince himself that lack of oxygen to the brain wasn't enabling him to break the rules. The annoying voice in the back of his mind returned, though. Repeating the two words that had the power to stop him in his tracks. *Game changer.*

With enormous effort, he pulled back.

"Believe me when I say that I want this to happen more than you could possibly imagine." His words came out through labored breaths.

"Why stop then?" She managed to say through her own heaves.

He didn't immediately respond. He needed a minute to slow his heart rate, and another to convince himself he was doing the right thing. "My job, for one."

Her shoulders deflated with his cop-out. "You're not exactly forcing me to do anything. In case you haven't noticed, I've been the forward one."

"That's not an issue for me. I like it a little too much when you take the lead." This time, he looked her straight in the eye because she needed to know where he stood. "Here's the other thing and it's the most important one. I've come to realize that you wouldn't be a casual fling for me, Renee. And your life is complicated right now. I'd be in the way. Plus, you've already said you're not ready for anything more than friends. What would we be doing here?"

"Not sleeping." She stared at him for a long moment. "I'm sorry I basically attacked you but—"

"Come on. We both know I was a willing participant."

"Plus, I doubt anything between us could be less than mind blowing," she said in a tone of voice that implied he'd offended her. Damn. He hadn't meant to do that. But she was temptation on a stick and he needed to keep a handle on his attraction.

"You're not making this any easier on me." He wanted nothing more than to block out the rest of the world and get lost with Renee even if it was for only a few hours. Once would never be enough with her. He'd want more and wouldn't be able to give it.

"You are right about one thing. My life is complicated." She climbed off his lap and sat on the bed. Her cheeks turned beet red and she toyed with the edge of the blanket. "I apologize for—"

"Don't. Believe me, you didn't hurt my feelings. You couldn't hurt my feelings if you tried. It's just not the play right now. You know?" He was doing a bad job explaining himself. "I know what I said before about not being ready to commit to anyone right now. But you're changing that for me. Being with you is a game changer. I don't know exactly what that means but I've never felt this way about anyone before you. If you decide you're ready for the possibility of something more…"

"You were right to stop things before they got out of control." The blush to her cheeks made him feel guilty.

"Being out of control with you would probably be one of my best days." His attempt at humor fell flat. If he'd met her a couple of years ago and she wasn't someone linked to his case, this would be a different situation. Kissing a beautiful woman was high on his list of things he enjoyed. But his heart wouldn't appreciate being stomped on as she walked out the door.

Damn. Was that the real reason he'd stopped her?

Cash forced the question aside and glanced at the clock. "All kidding aside, the little one won't be asleep much longer. I'm here. I'll probably just sleep on the chair. You can go to bed."

Now she really did laugh. "I'm betting that I'll be safe on the bed *with* you on it. You haven't slept in longer than me. You might as well claim the spot right here." She patted the pillow. "I promise to keep my hands to myself."

What she said was meant to be a joke, but Cash couldn't bring himself to laugh. In fact, there was nothing about her promise to leave him alone he thought was funny. How was that for proof that his priorities were upside-down?

"I probably won't be able to sleep, but I'm going to give it a shot anyway." She curled on her side on top of the covers, so he cut off the light.

Getting in bed with her was a bad idea. Instead, he waited until he heard her soft, steady breathing before easing his weight off the chair and heading toward the bathroom. A quick, cold shower woke him up. Damn good thing because he needed to be able to think clearly.

Cash walked over to the bassinet to check on the sleeping baby. Once he knew Abby was good, he returned to the chair and sat down. His head wasn't throbbing anymore, but it wouldn't hurt to close his eyes for a second or two.

The next thing he knew, the room was filled with light. He snapped his head up and glanced around. He rubbed his blurry eyes, looked down and saw that Renee had covered him with a blanket.

"Good morning." Her honey voice washed over him. She was sitting on the floor with a blanket spread out, playing with Abby.

"Morning," he grumbled. "I need coffee. Can I bring you a cup?"

"Already got one." She nodded toward the mug on the dresser.

A smile formed on his lips. He liked the fact she'd made herself comfortable at the ranch. "Baby's fed?"

"Fed, bathed and changed."

"How long was I out?" He checked the clock.

"Not too long. The minute she moved, I picked her up because I didn't want her to disturb you."

"I'm usually a light sleeper." He raked his hand through his hair.

"You needed the rest." There'd be no argument there.

"How about breakfast? Did you eat?" He needed to grab coffee for himself and, at the very least, a piece of toast.

She shot him a look. "Now that you mention it, I didn't eat. Any chance you have something light in the kitchen? Yogurt? A banana?"

"Do you like eggs and bacon?"

"Oh, bacon. Who doesn't love bacon?"

"How about a refresh on the coffee?" He walked over to the dresser to pick up her mug after she smiled and nodded.

"You should also know that once your mother found out about my tech skills, she offered me a job here."

Cash liked the sound of that a little too much.

"Did you take it?" He tried to sound casual.

"It's tempting. I told her that I'd think about it."

RENEE WAS IN serious trouble when it came to Cash. He had that whole ruggedly handsome bit down pat. He was also thoughtful and kind, and strong. She'd blinked her eyes open to see him checking on Abby last night and then pretended to be asleep. Her heart was pure liquid butter in her chest at the sight of him looking after her daughter.

To say she liked talking to him was a lot like saying beef came from cows. Looking back, it was strange to think how bad things got between her and Jamison before she'd decided to call it quits. The decision had been so hard at the time and now she only wished she'd done it years ago.

How many times had she read a book or disappeared into the bedroom to avoid having a conversation with Jamison in recent years, and especially the last three or four? More than she could count.

In fact, it had become her habit. She'd listen to him talk about his day, smiling and nodding as he went into great detail about his general frustrations or his problems with a client. And when he was done, he would grab a beer and head off to watch football in the other room or spend time in front of the TV or on his laptop.

Early on, he'd been more attentive. There'd been a lot more shine on their relationship. The fact that he'd been the main topic of conversation hadn't bothered her in the beginning. She'd chalked it up to the fact that he was more of a talker than her instead of what became obvious to her later. He was self-absorbed. Jamison could be a charmer when he wanted to be, and especially when the relationship was new.

But that part of her life was moving into the past now. Renee took in a deep breath as she looked down at her daughter, the future. The little girl was happily cooing and talking the language Renee was certain only other babies understood.

Being here at the ranch with Cash and her daughter, her crazy, mixed-up world had righted itself. Even if it was for only a short time, she'd take it and then figure out how to make more of it. This was the feeling she wanted her daughter to grow up surrounded by. This felt a lot like unconditional acceptance...love?

Renee wasn't kidding about Margaret offering the job. The crazy part was that Renee was actually considering taking her up on it. Her boss had been understanding when Renee had spoken to her after the police. She'd asked for a few days and Rikki had agreed to them. But she wasn't known for being flexible with time off and having a baby was shifting Renee's priorities. She needed a steady job but she also wanted the flexibility to be with her daughter when she needed.

For now, her thoughts couldn't go in the direction of having anything more with Cash. Logic said they'd known each other only a short time. Her heart tried to argue differently because she'd taken it slow with Jamison and look where that had ended up. They'd been together for years and still hadn't made the marriage leap, a thought she was thankful for now.

Renee's cell dinged. She moved to her purse and checked the screen. Her battery was getting low. She needed to charge it.

The text caused her pulse to skyrocket.

Hey. Are you okay?

It was from Jamison. Why would he reach out to her while on his babymoon? Not that she believed any of it.

Should she respond? Technically, he was a suspect. Cash had said that Jamison's alibi was weak. Nothing in her wanted to have been in a relationship with someone who could want to hurt her, but she couldn't ignore the fact that he might want to take her daughter away. Kidnapping her newly adopted child ranked right up there with one of the worst offenses she could think of.

A thought struck her as odd. He asked about her and didn't mention Abby.

Cash walked into the room. She blinked up at him. His expression morphed to concern the second he looked at her. "What's wrong?"

She held her phone up, palm out. "Jamison just reached out to me."

Cash brought her plate of food and handed over her coffee mug that he'd been balancing. "What did he say?"

"He asked if I'm okay."

Cash grunted. "He's letting you know that he's aware of your situation and trying to come off like he cares."

"The only person Jamison King cares about is himself." Shouldn't he be worried about his pregnant girlfriend? The fact that he'd landed squarely in the middle of a kidnapping investigation was most likely stressful for Yolanda. The fact the woman had had an affair with Jamison while he was still living with Renee didn't exactly rank high in her book, but he should still be focusing on her and not on Renee. "I'm not answering it."

"Maybe you should." He put his hand up to stop her from arguing. "Hear me out before you decide."

She nodded but he was walking into scary territory.

"I'd like to set up a meeting. Colton would be involved and you'd be nowhere near the scene. He's set up a sting before. That way, we could draw him out so he can be picked up for questioning." The way he put it made it sound like the risks would be nonexistent and she had no doubt Cash wouldn't put her in an unsafe environment.

"If he's behind the attempt, I'm still trying to figure out how he knew where I was moving and the fact that I'd adopted Abby. I kept that information close to my chest."

"Did he ever know your password to your laptop or your phone?" He quirked a brow.

"No." Well. Hold on a minute. She thought about the time he'd said he needed to check her inbox for a message from his mother's doctor. "Now that you mention it, I'm realizing that he did ask for my password a while back. But that was a long time ago. He said he needed to check my inbox because he'd given my email by mistake to the doctor's office where his mother was a patient. He asked them to send a referral. I can't remember how long ago it was. That whole time period toward the end is fuzzy. It was a year ago, maybe?" She shook her head to jog her memory. "I guess I forgot about him asking because I immediately changed my password that night."

Cash's eyebrow formed a perfect arch. "You didn't trust him?"

"Not after I found him checking my calendar early in our relationship and then questioning me about where I'd been and who I'd gone somewhere with." More red flags that Jamison was a jerk.

"Controlling men often install spy apps. All he would've needed was a window of opportunity to infect your system." Cash's lips formed a thin line.

She should have suspected him more. She'd been too trusting and he'd become way too possessive. His mother's illness had changed him, amplified his bad qualities. Made him more self-absorbed. And angry. If he caught anyone talking to her at the office longer than he thought was appropriate, he'd fly off the handle with her later.

"Installing spyware would've been easy enough to do." She bit back a curse as she thought back to the few times that he seemed to slip. Looking back, there'd been the time when she'd told him that she was meeting one of the consultants for lunch and he'd dismissively told her that he knew that already. He'd saved his slipup by convincing her that she'd told him that morning, which was odd. She'd specifically remembered telling him that she'd been planning to meet with Rikki.

He'd made a joke about her being so busy that she was forgetting what she told him and what she didn't. Considering all the stress she'd been under trying to organize the move to Katy Gulch, she'd believed him.

How long had he known about her plans to adopt Abby? How long had he realized she was leaving him before she'd mentioned it? A hollow feeling expanded in her chest.

"I need to get Colton on the line." Cash's cell was already in hand but he seemed to be waiting for her to give a nod of approval. His thoughtfulness was foreign territory and she wanted to tread lightly. Her heart seemed to have other ideas when it fluttered wildly against her ribs. Cash was strong and considerate. He never seemed to feel the need to throw his weight around or force someone to do or say something they didn't want to.

"The guy from the lot was paid to bring his friends and scare me." She bit down on her bottom lip. "Why?"

"It could've been to throw the investigation off track." He'd said that before.

"The second attempt was very public," she said.

"Which could send a message that he can reach you anytime and in any place." He made good points—points that she hadn't thought about.

Cash's cell buzzed while still in his hand. He checked the screen and looked up. "It's Colton. He wants us to come to his office. Yolanda is in a fight with Jamison and just recanted her babymoon statement."

Chapter Seventeen

There was no way that Cash was going to ask Renee to leave Abby at the ranch, even though he thought it was the safest idea. She was determined to protect her daughter at all costs and would never leave her that long. He couldn't blame her.

"How long will it take to get her ready?" he asked.

"I just need a minute to put on real clothes." With that, Renee was up and rummaging through her weekend bag. She glanced at Abby and then him. His damn heart skipped a few beats, and he knew he was in deep water. He'd been in trouble from the minute he set eyes on her and figured he was just beginning to see the depths of where that was taking him.

Renee stepped out of the bathroom in a summer dress that bared the skin of her shoulders. Cash hadn't realized just how sexy shoulders could be until he'd seen her exposed. He tamped down his attraction and helped pack up a few supplies for Abby.

Within five minutes, the three of them were inside his vehicle and on their way down the country road leading to town.

"The car seems to put Abby at ease," he noticed.

The ride to Colton's office had put the babbling baby to sleep. It had been the same with the twins.

"I love learning these little things about her." Renee smiled and more of that annoying warmth settled over him. There was a wistfulness to her tone and Cash realized that it most likely had to do with the possibility of losing the little girl who had already won Renee's heart. If the abduction attempt had been orchestrated by Kipp McGee or was somehow tied to Ms. Hubert, the possibility couldn't be ignored. But this case was looking more personal.

Cash realized he'd white-knuckled the steering wheel as he pulled into a parking spot at his brother's office. Renee was out of the passenger door before he could get around to her side, so he held open the back door as she unlocked the carrier from its base.

Cash leaned in and took the bag from the floorboard. He shouldered the strap and closed the door behind them.

Walking into the building, he caught their reflection in the glass door. Renee with Abby and him looking about as domestic as they come, a diaper bag over his right shoulder. It was like a lightning strike that packed a punch straight to the chest when he realized they made a damn fine-looking family.

She'd been clear on where she stood and he respected her position. Since those thoughts were about as productive as trying to get milk from a turnip, he shoved them aside.

Was he attracted to Renee? The answer to that question was a hard yes. To say the possibility of a relationship was complicated was an understatement.

His momentary shock at the realization they looked

like a family was mirrored in his brother's expression the second the three of them walked into Colton's office.

"Good morning." Colton did a great job of hiding his thoughts but Cash knew his brother too well to let anything slide.

"Morning," Cash grumbled before pulling his brother into a hug. After Renee greeted Colton, he got right down to business.

"Ms. Tran is in the interview room, waiting. She got here ten minutes ago and has done nothing but pace the floor ever since." Colton shot a sympathetic look toward Renee. "Have you seen her in her present condition?"

Renee blinked. "Do you mean pregnant?"

Colton nodded.

"No."

"Is that something you're ready to—"

"The way my relationship with Jamison ended wasn't good, but I'm not in love with him." And then she added quietly, "I'm not certain that I ever was and any feelings I might have had died a long time ago."

Cash set his personal feelings aside and tried not to be too transparent about how happy those words made him. They made no difference to the case and that was all he needed to focus on. But Colton needed to know about the text she'd received earlier and he hadn't had a chance to bring his brother up-to-date yet. He glanced at Renee and their gazes locked for a second longer than they should've.

Colton caught the look between them.

"Jamison reached out to me this morning on my phone, asking if I was okay," she said.

"Text or phone call?" Colton asked.

"Text." Her gaze darted to her purse. "My phone is in here if you can grab it." She looked to Cash.

Without hesitating, he reached into her handbag and produced the cell, handing it over to his brother.

"I can unlock it with my thumbprint." Her eyes widened. "My thumbprint." She repeated the words again. "He could've used my thumbprint when I was asleep, couldn't he? Before Abby, I slept like a rock. Now, I doubt I'll sleep until she's eighteen. Point being, he could've pressed my phone to my thumb at any time during the night to gain access to my emails."

Cash rocked his head. He didn't want to think about Renee being with the kind of jerk who would do something like that. In his line of work, he heard about scenarios like this more than he cared to. A jealous boyfriend or spouse could go to some pretty damn drastic lengths to keep tabs on a person. How they felt justified in doing so, Cash would never know or understand.

"A lot more about his behavior makes sense now from the past year." Renee's cheeks flamed when she got angry. She glanced at her daughter. She seemed to decide not to spit out the few choice words that were on the tip of her tongue.

A person like Renee came around once in a lifetime. Only an idiot would blow his chance with her if he was lucky enough to get one. And only a complete asshat would take advantage of her loyalty and devotion. Jamison King must not realize the value of those traits in a person.

"She was planning to give you a heads-up when we got the text to come here. Figured it was easy enough to tell you in person," Cash said to his brother.

"Mr. King reaching out to you is interesting considering the timing of his very pregnant girlfriend showing up in my office." Colton cocked his head to one side.

"I thought so, too." Cash couldn't agree more.

"I'm even more interested to hear what Ms. Tran has to say now." Colton's gaze bounced from Renee to Cash. "Shall we?"

With her lips forming a thin line, Renee nodded. If steam could come out of her ears, it probably would.

The betrayal was bad enough. Having to stand across the mirror from the evidence of it would devastate most people. Renee was strong, which didn't mean she wasn't suffering. Cash could see it in the tiny stress cracks around those clear blue eyes of hers.

Instinctively, he put his hand on the small of her back as they walked toward a person who she wouldn't be able to easily shut out of her mind when she closed her eyes that night.

Being done with her ex was a good thing. The bastard deserved to be strung up by his heels and left in the hot sun a day or two. Betrayal hurt. It stuck around. It festered if left to languish. He should know.

Betrayal, Cash understood.

Colton stopped in front of the viewing room. "Will you be okay in here?"

WHETHER OR NOT Renee was okay seemed to be the question of the day. For the record, she was not okay. She might never be okay again. But it had little to do with a very pregnant Yolanda Tran and Renee's ex.

The sad fact was she now hoped Jamison was responsible because that would mean her adoption couldn't be revoked.

Renee settled Abby's carrier on the seat of a chair,

wedging the plastic in between the arm rests to keep her daughter's carrier secure.

The feeling of betrayal should have overwhelmed her when she walked into the small, dimly lit room adjacent to the interview room. Yolanda was beautiful. She had long, straight silky-black hair that fell to her waist. She had a round face with dark brown eyes. She was a tiny thing except for the big belly announcing to the world that she was carrying a child.

Instead of betrayal, Renee felt closure.

The woman, who was pacing around the room, worked her hands together. Her fingers laced and then she balled a hand. It seemed like she couldn't be still in any part of her body. The stress of being with a man like Jamison, who could be so charming until he wasn't, was written all over her actions and especially all over her face.

The all-too-familiar stress that Renee had felt at being with a man who ignored everyone else's feelings and thought only about himself. Yeah, Renee recognized that look in Yolanda because she'd stared at it in the mirror once. It was the reason she'd decided to leave and start over.

Watching Yolanda was just the reminder Renee needed. Jamison was a coward and a jerk.

Although Yolanda's morals were seriously off to have an affair with a man she knew was in a relationship, Renee felt nothing but pity for the woman who would have Jamison's child in a matter of weeks.

"I should probably hate her," she whispered to Cash, who stood right beside her. "I can't."

He studied Yolanda for a long moment. "She looks

like she's carrying the weight of the world on her shoulders."

"It was the same for me at the end and the reason I finally walked away. Makes me kind of stupid, doesn't it?" She barely finished her sentence and he was already shaking his head.

"Caring about someone else doesn't make you stupid. It makes you human. Making a mistake does the same thing. Besides, you would've left the jerk a long time ago if his mother hadn't been sick, and he sounds like a master manipulator." Every word of what he'd just said was true.

"It's hard not to feel like a sucker." Admitting it, saying the words out loud made them lose some of their power. She'd been so embarrassed that she'd let the relationship go for so long without breaking up that she'd been quiet. Then again, the only person she ever really talked to was her boss, who'd always encouraged Renee to stick it out with Jamison. Renee didn't have the first idea why she'd listened to Rikki.

"Being loyal to someone doesn't make you bad." Cash turned toward her, his strong body standing within inches of her. He brought his hands up to her face and cupped her cheeks. "Your ex was the idiot. He doesn't deserve you." And then under his breath, he said, "If you were with me, I'd know how to treat you."

Renee's pulse skyrocketed and her stomach freefell. She pushed up to her tiptoes and pressed her lips to his. Bringing her hands up, she dug her fingers into his shoulders.

Voices coming through the speaker shocked them back a step.

"Ms. Tran, my name is Sheriff Colton O'Connor. We

spoke on the phone." Colton walked over to her and extended his right hand. She accepted the offering. Her face was sheet white.

"I'm not sure if I should even be here." Her hand dropped down to cradle her stomach as she surveyed the room.

Anger toward Jamison was a flame inching toward a dry field in the middle of a draught. The thought a child would be caught in the middle made Renee burn.

Colton gave Yolanda a look that Renee figured was meant to reassure Yolanda. Being so stressed while pregnant couldn't be good for her or the baby. A couple of times in the last few minutes, the woman's face tensed and she seemed like she was blowing air slowly out of her mouth like she had a cramp.

"Would you like to sit down?" Colton motioned toward the chairs. He seemed to catch on, too. The chairs had been moved from across the table to one side. The arrangement seemed more intimate and less confronting.

Interesting.

"No, thank you." Yolanda wasn't done pacing. She brought her hands to her hips. Anyone could see that she was debating walking out the door and taking her information with her.

"How about you talk to me a little bit about why you're here." Colton's voice was steady. Renee assumed it was meant to keep Yolanda calm and it seemed to be working when she blew out a slow breath.

She chewed on her lip, seemed to be reconsidering stopping in.

"I don't have to remind you that lying to an officer

of the law counts as impeding an investigation. You could be held in contempt. Jailed."

She gasped.

"It's not too late for you to make it right. Tell me what brought you here and what part of your earlier statement you're recanting." Colton crossed his arms over his chest.

A few seconds that felt like minutes passed by without her opening her mouth.

"A baby was almost kidnapped." Colton's gaze dropped to her belly where she was cradling her bump.

"I'm sorry about that. I can't help you after all." She took a step toward the exit.

"Walk out that door and I find out that you lied there'll be trouble at your door in a heartbeat."

"I didn't do anything wrong." She froze.

"If you're covering for someone who did, you could go to jail as an accomplice." Those words got the tears rolling. She was teetering on a ledge. Renee hoped the woman would tip over. As awful as it was, Jamison trying to kidnap Abby was so much better than a botched adoption. It could've been one of his friends that first night. With Jamison, it was personal.

Yolanda's expression dropped and more tears came flooding. "He told me to say he was with me, but he wasn't. I don't know where he was, who he was with or where he's been but he told me his ex was trying to frame him for something he didn't do. I had no idea there was a child involved. He… He…"

She broke down crying and it was difficult for Renee not to force her way into the adjacent room and try to offer some comfort to the woman. At the very least for the child's sake. Colton picked up the box of tissues from the table and offered them to Yolanda.

"Do you know where Jamison King is right now?" Colton asked when the tears stemmed.

"No, I don't. We've been in a hotel room off the highway. We had a huge fight because I wanted to go home and he told me that he didn't want to have this baby with me. He said that I wasn't anything like his ex and that he still loved her. He was always comparing me to her during our relationship. Renee this and Renee that. He talked about how perfect she was. At first, I accepted it because…" She hesitated long enough to wipe a few more tears. "I knew he was still with her when we started dating. He convinced me that it had been over between the two of them for a long time but that he didn't want to leave her with everything happening with his mother. Renee loved his mother."

"That's news to me." Renee nearly choked hearing those words. Renee had never really gotten along with the woman.

"I thought maybe he'd gone back to her when I found out she was near. My boss left a few messages saying he'd talked to a sheriff." Was Yolanda trying to get back at him for leaving? Despite feeling sorry for her, Renee wouldn't trust that woman as far as she could throw her. And, yes, the tears got to Renee. It was difficult seeing a pregnant woman so upset.

"We'd like to talk to Mr. King if you see him or if he contacts you." Colton was a study in calm.

"I can't believe he'd do anything to break the law. I thought I knew him better than that," Yolanda said.

Renee coughed. Seriously?

Yolanda cradled her bump and Renee wasn't sure how much of that was now being played for sympathy.

"She sure likes to remind my brother that she's pregnant," Cash said low and under his breath.

"You noticed that, too?" Of course he would in his line of work. Renee wasn't used to being around someone so observant.

"That's probably the fifth time she's made a show of touching her bump," he noted.

"At least." The air seemed to thin and breathing was difficult. "I need to take a walk. Get some air. If I look at this show anymore, I might lose my temper." Renee glanced at her angel who was still sleeping in the carrier. "Will you keep an eye on her for a minute?"

Cash looked like he was trying to make a decision. Then came, "Yeah, sure. Do me a favor, though?"

"Name it."

"Stay at the front door where Gert can see you at all times." A chill raced down her spine at the reminder of the danger she was in.

"Deal."

This time, it was Cash who hauled her against his chest. He pressed his lips to hers. "Good. I can't have anything happening to you."

Didn't those words melt what was left of Renee's resolve. Logistics be damned, she was starting to believe she could open her heart a little more to Cash. She *wanted* to.

"I'm safe as long as I'm with you."

He pressed a slow, sweet kiss to her lips before stepping back and refocusing on the witness.

Renee walked out of the room, down the hall and past Gert's desk. She was on the phone but she glanced up and waved. Renee pointed to the front door and Gert nodded.

There was no amount of time that could erase the damage that Jamison had done to their relationship. Seeing his new girlfriend pregnant with his child was a slap of reality—one she needed. Caring for Jamison wasn't the problem. Those feelings were long gone. Seeing him ruin another person's life and bring a child into the world when he'd been clear that he never wanted children set the blaze. The child deserved better. Every child deserved better.

As Renee walked the sidewalk in front of the building, the devil himself walked up from behind her.

"I thought I'd never get you alone again." Those were the last words she heard before a blow to the head caused her world to go black.

Chapter Eighteen

Renee blinked her eyes open. Jamison was shoving her into the back of his car. He was trying to force something over her mouth. A cloth? There was a smell she didn't recognize but it was strong. She tried to scream. He grabbed her by the throat cutting off her voice.

When did he become this strong? He squeezed so hard she thought her eyeballs might pop out. Drawing up her knees, she pulled on all the strength she could muster and kicked with everything she had inside her.

There was enough force to knock him back a step and loosen the grip.

"No." He bit the word out with so much anger. "You don't get to leave me again, Renee. Ever. I was just trying to scare you into coming home but you won't scare. You don't need a child, Renee. She's in the way. You need me."

"I don't love you, Jamison," was all she managed to say before his hand was back on her throat.

Kicking and screaming—her cries were muffled—she unleashed hell on him.

"You forgot how much you love me. It'll come back or you'll love no one. I sure as hell won't let you stay with that cowboy." He tightened his grip as she dug her fingernails into his hand.

During the struggle, she'd lost her glasses and all she could see was a blurry mess in front of her, on top of her. Despite her efforts, she couldn't make him budge.

She scratched his face, digging her nails into his cheeks deep enough to break the skin.

"You shouldn't do that, Renee." He tightened his grip until she thought she might black out again.

With all her energy, she twisted and rolled onto her side. She landed hard on the floorboard but at least managed to break his choke hold. He came down on top of her and she felt his hands struggling for purchase. Despite the fact her windpipe hurt and she gasped for air, she managed to buck him off.

"Cash." She screamed the word, praying someone would hear her. It was broad daylight. The statistic that most women were abducted under these conditions came to mind. It was high.

Not her, not if she had anything to say about it.

Suddenly, Jamison's weight was ripped off her. She heard a voice—Cash's voice—giving her the first sign of hope.

Scrambling to her feet, she managed to get out of the car on her own. Her throat hurt and she couldn't count the number of bruises forming on her skin but she could feel every one.

"Cash." He was a blur but she would recognize him anywhere. She fumbled around for her glasses and found them. When she put them on, she looked in time to see Cash's fist rear back before landing a punch that caused Jamison's head to snap back.

Blood shot from his nose as Cash made quick work of tackling Jamison to the cement, face first.

"You're going to spend the rest of your life in jail if I have anything to say about it." Cash rammed his knee into Jamison's back, holding him in place while Colton pulled zip cuffs from his belt and then cuffed him.

The second Jamison was secure, Cash closed the distance between him and Renee in a few strides. She saw the worry lines scoring his forehead.

"I thought I lost you." He cupped her face in his hands and searched her eyes.

"I'm okay, Cash. I'm here. Safe. Where's Abby?" She glanced around, frantic.

"Gert's bringing her out. She didn't want the little girl anywhere near Jamison."

Renee pushed up to her tiptoes and kissed him.

"What about Kipp McGee and the adoption?" she asked when she pulled back.

"He might be tied to the Hubert case, but he's not involved here, which means this adoption is real," Cash said.

"I'VE NEVER BELIEVED in love at first sight," Renee said to Cash after everything settled down and they were alone in Colton's office. "I wouldn't know how to trust it."

"Really?" He looked at Abby. "Because I don't believe you. How long did it take for you to realize you would make any sacrifice for Abby? Did you know her?"

"In my heart, I knew her all along. Meeting her was the next logical step," she said without hesitation.

"When it came to Abby, you let your feelings take the lead. You didn't question them or put up a wall." He wasn't sure if he was getting through to Renee, but he had to try. "I'm not saying what we have is the same as a love for a child, don't get me wrong. The two are very different animals. Since I met you, I became a believer in love at first sight. I knew you were going to be important to me from the minute you opened the door and I stood on your porch. I just didn't know how. It would be a shame not to see where that takes us because I've never experienced a lightning bolt like that with anyone else. If you don't feel the same way, I'll walk out the door and leave you alone. Say the word and I'm gone."

She was making quick work of the baby cloth in her hand. Her head was tilted to one side and he could see how much she was chewing on his words. He meant every one of them. All she had to do was tell him to walk. He'd hate it. But he'd respect her wishes.

"What if I said that I do want to spend more time together, but life is in the way right now. I have Abby to think about. I can't exactly see myself leaving her with a babysitter. Relationships take time. Getting to know each other takes time."

"If someone had said the same thing to me last week, I would've agreed."

Renee took in a deep breath. She usually did that when she was fortifying herself to say something that was difficult or face a new challenge. He had no idea which way she would go on this one. All he knew for certain was that her words would either open a door or close one. With Renee, she would go all in or walk away.

"I knew you were special the minute I saw you. I had no idea what that meant until you stepped up time and time again for me and my daughter. I should probably be afraid of my feelings for you. You have the power to shatter me, Cash." There was so much vulnerability in her words and he could see that it was taking great effort for her to admit her feelings. "So, don't."

"Does this mean what I think it does? You'll give us a chance?" Hope ballooned in his chest.

"No."

That one word had the power to devastate him.

She continued before he could respond. "A chance implies there's an option to fail. I love you. I've known it since the second we met. I want to run toward it instead of reason my way out. Because it's clear to me that I'll never find someone who fits me in the way you do. I'll never find someone who makes my heart flutter and yet still makes me feel safe even though I'm risking all I have, all that I am. I choose you."

"In that case." Cash took her hand in his and dropped down on one knee. "Let's make it permanent. Let's start our family today and not look back. I love you, Renee. I'm never going to find someone who challenges me to be the best person I can be like you do. I've never been so in love before I met you. You're it for me and I want the world to know. I want to adopt Abby and make our family official in the eyes of the law. I want our little girl to have every right afforded an O'Connor. We can proceed any way you like. But, if you'll have me, I'd be honored if you'll agree to marry me."

"Yes, Cash. I'll marry you. With all my heart, I'll marry you."

With those words, he stood and brought her into his arms.

She blinked at him and said, "I can't wait to make our family official but I don't need a piece of paper to know what's in my heart. You're my family and I can't imagine a better father for Abby."

"The kid struck gold when she landed you as a mother," he countered. "Both of you won my heart. And, now, I'm ready to build a life together."

"I can't think of a better way to spend the next fifty or sixty years than with you and our daughter." When she looked at him, her eyes sparked. "And maybe a couple of siblings for Abby."

"My job in law enforcement is important to me for now. I'm not ready to give it up. Are you okay with that?" he asked.

"Don't ever change for me. I love you for who you are. When and if you're ever ready to take more responsibility at the ranch, I'll support that decision."

He looked at her and his chest nearly burst with love and pride. He kissed her, slow and sweet.

"My mother has offered you a job at the ranch. Any chance you'd consider taking her up on it? You'd be an asset on the ranch, especially with your technical abilities. What do you think about helping her run the place? KBR is as much yours as it is my brothers', mine and Abby's."

Renee beamed. "I'd like to use my skills to continue the legacy we'll hand down to our children. So, that's a yes from me."

"I love you, Renee." With those words, Cash found home.

Epilogue

The open door to Mother's library stopped Cash in the hallway. It was early, even for her.

A light was on, telling him she was inside. She always made a point to walk through the house before bed and turn off lights. She called it putting the house to bed and told him even the house needed to rest.

Taking in a deep breath, he took the couple of steps until he stood in front of the door.

"Morning." Her voice cracked enough to let him know she'd been crying. Crying wasn't something he'd seen his mother do very often.

"Hello, beautiful. What are you doing up at this hour?" He wished he could reel the question back in the minute he'd asked it. She was grieving and, based on the fact she had her favorite book in her hand, searching for comfort.

She held up the worn paperback.

"Mind if I join you?" There was something about her expression that made him want to stick around a few minutes. See if he could provide some comfort to the woman who'd spent most of her life taking care of him and his brothers. How did he even begin to repay the kind of loyalty and dedication she'd shown to him and his brothers?

"Please do." The warmth in his mother's eyes returned. Thinking about taking care of Abby and the weight of the responsibility ahead of him—responsibility he gladly took on even though he was way out of his league—made him appreciate everything his parents had done for him and his brothers. It also made him resolve to clear the air with Garrett. Losing their father made Cash realize how important family was and how much he'd taken for granted that they'd all be there. Wounds could be healed *someday*. Time would wait for them to catch up.

Flawed thinking. A little voice in the back of his mind said the best way to honor his father's memory was to pass on his unconditional love, his easygoing nature and his unwavering belief in his children. That same voice reminded Cash that his investigative work wasn't done. Not until Caroline's story was told, not until he gave his mother closure, whatever that meant—and that might mean delivering news no son wanted to give his mother in a case like this.

"I don't have many regrets with your father," his mother started after he claimed a seat. "We had a beautiful marriage. Not perfect, mind you. But it was better than I ever dreamed possible considering I never saw my parents show affection one time. I think they came from a generation of 'united front' mindset."

He chuckled. His grandparents had been stiff people. He couldn't remember a time when his grandmother wasn't dressed to the nines, wearing her pearls, sipping tea from a delicate cup. "Remember when I poured Nana's tea into a coffee mug once?"

Margaret laughed. "I thought she would have a heart attack."

"But she was too proper to scold me."

"Her back went straighter than a board." Margaret slapped her hands together. It felt good to make her laugh. Damned if she didn't deserve to smile again. Grief would be a cloud over her, the ranch, for a while. There was a time for grief and a time to laugh. He'd grab every happy moment he could. "But her face was priceless."

"Her lip was stiffer than the queen's."

Now, his mother really laughed and it was a musical sound.

"What about Ruth Hubert?" Margaret leaned forward and her serious expression returned.

"Remains to be seen." He needed to set realistic expectations. "It'll most likely take time to unravel that tangled mess."

"Her files?"

"They'll take a while to unpack." Cash knew exactly what his mother was asking. Could Ms. Hubert possibly be connected to Caroline's disappearance?

Time would tell.

"Abby's adoption?" she asked.

"Is legitimate. Colton will be working with the feds on the Hubert adoption ring. We won't give up until we find out if she had anything to do with Caroline's case." He looked at his mother, who was surrounded by her books in the library. He wished he could give her the answers she needed.

"You got hold of Garrett." She smiled.

"He's coming." Cash nodded.

"Your father wouldn't want me to be sad." She had that part right.

"No. He wouldn't."

"He wouldn't want you to be, either."

"It's hard not to miss him." Another point there was no argument for. "He left big shoes to fill."

Margaret clucked her tongue. "You've always been your own person, Cash. Your father wouldn't want it any other way. He would never expect you to become him in any way and that means working here at the ranch. You can do anything you want, be anything you want."

"My place is here. I *want* to be here and take my place on the ranch. What you guys built here should be carried forward for—"

She held up her hand to stop him. "You love your job. It's important to do work that you feel passionate about."

"I love this, too." He nodded in the direction of the backyard. There was one case that he hadn't solved and it was his reason to go to work every day. "I'm not ready to give up my job just yet. Make no mistake about it, this is my home. This ranch, this land is exactly where I belong. This is ultimately where my heart says I should be. I've never been more certain of anything in my life."

Cash looked for a sign of disapproval or acceptance in his mother's face. She gave no hint of her feelings. When he really thought about it, she'd always been there for him. Never judging him. Always making him feel like he couldn't go wrong. He thought about Abby and how ready he was to become her father. The fact that he even wanted kids at all was news to him. The little girl held special magic in her smile if it made him want to sign on to parenthood.

But then, she was special. She deserved parents who

gave her the same kind of unconditional love Cash had grown up with.

"Take your time. A place will always be here waiting for you," his mother said and he realized she'd been studying him.

"The only thing I know for certain right now is that I want to make Renee my wife and adopt Abby."

His mother beamed. "I like her a lot." She paused. "She accepted my job offer to work on the ranch."

"Seems like a good way to get to know the family business." In losing his father, Cash realized how very short time actually was in this life. Instead of it making him depressed, he saw it as a call to action.

"I want to be part of the business again and I don't want to wait. If we could take it slow for now and work up to me being here full-time one day, that would be ideal." He would come to his own in the family ranch. He wanted to be part of it. But not yet. He hadn't solved his biggest case yet.

But for now, he was focused on Renee and Abby. And that was enough.

* * * * *

WHAT SHE KNEW

Chapter One

Amber Kent didn't normally pick up calls from numbers she didn't recognize on her personal cell. She tapped her toe on the floorboard while waiting for Harvey Baily to finish loading hay bales onto her truck. He'd insisted she stay in the cab in order to keep warm.

The temperature hovered just above forty degrees. The sun was covered by thick gray clouds. She stared at her buzzing phone. The call could be coming from a distant relative. She'd had a few of those since losing her parents a few years ago. It was past the holidays.

Glancing in the rearview mirror, she noticed that Harvey wasn't even close to being done loading. She had a couple of minutes to spare.

"Hello," she said. The silence on the other end had her thinking answering was a bad idea.

"Amber, this is Rylan Anderson..." The familiar voice came through the line clearly. He didn't need to say his name for her to know that voice. It was deeper now, but that unmistakable timbre goose bumped her arms. Talk about a blast from the past. How long had it been? Eight years? Nine?

"I heard you moved back to town, but I thought people were pulling my leg." After nearly a decade of being gone, she was surprised he'd come back to Jacobstown, Texas.

"Yeah, sorry I didn't get in touch." That was an odd thing to say. Had he planned on seeing her at some point?

"It's fine," she said quickly. Too quickly?

"I know it's been a long time but I need a favor." At least he didn't pretend this was a social call. So why did disappointment wrap around her? A little piece of her wished he was calling to see how she was, or if she wanted to meet up for coffee. Hearing from him after all these years was a shock to the system.

"What can I do for you?" she asked, suppressing a small sigh.

She heard something *or someone* in the background. Then again, it could be a TV. She couldn't make out the noise clearly.

"I didn't have anyone else to call who could handle..." His voice trailed off, and that really got her curiosity going. He didn't sound like himself. Although, what did she expect? He'd gone dim on social media after leaving Jacobstown to join the military. Platforms had changed, phone numbers had changed and she didn't keep up with him.

"What is it?" she asked. Curiosity was getting the best of her. What on earth could make him call after all this time?

"It's hard to explain. Can you stop by my house?"

"Um, sure." She didn't have a clue about why. "Are you in some kind of trouble?"

"Yeah. Kind of," he hedged. "I don't know—"

"The bank's closed if you need mon—"

"It's not like that." There was a hint of defensiveness

in his voice that she hadn't meant to put there. "You know what? Never mind. This is a mistake."

"Hold on, Rylan—"

It was too late. He'd ended the call.

Amber wasn't letting him get away with that. She called him back.

He picked up on the first ring. The noise in the background confused her. "Where are you? What's going on?"

He issued a sharp sigh.

"Rylan, I can drop by. Don't be a mule," she said.

There was a long pause. "I'd really appreciate it."

He sounded like someone with a migraine coming on, and for a split second she wondered if he needed medical attention.

"You're okay, right? I mean, you're not injured," she said, and she didn't bother hiding the worry in her tone.

"It's not like that." At least she'd ruled out a trip to the ER.

"Text your address and I'll stop by on my way home." She should probably turn and drive in the opposite direction from her brother's former best friend. The trouble was that she'd counted Rylan as a friend once, too. Plus, it was just beyond the holiday season. Rumors that he'd moved back to town were true. And he shouldn't be on his own. How could she refuse his plea for help? The text came through immediately after the call ended. She knew exactly where that was. Mrs. Parker used to live there, and Amber had stopped by many times to drop off a meal before the widow moved away.

Harvey tapped on Amber's truck bed as he closed the tailgate. He waved. His job was done. She rolled down the driver's side window and shouted a thank-you through the howling wind. A chill settled over her, and she realized the temperature had dropped another ten degrees. It was going to be a cold night if the rest of that front moved through town.

Jacobstown was an hour's drive south of Fort Worth. It was considered a bedroom community that had been a safe haven until recent weeks when some twisted individual started mutilating the left hooves of animals. The perp had started with small animals and then worked his way up to heifers. Several had been found on the Kent Ranch, a place she owned with five brothers.

Amber navigated onto Main Street and across town to Mrs. Parker's old house. It was Saturday, and there weren't many vehicles on the roads. She imagined grocery stores were probably busy with everyone anticipating the weather. She tapped her right thumb against the steering wheel. There was something about the tone of Rylan's voice that wasn't sitting right. Her first thought was that she should've asked him to come to the ranch. But she was close enough to stop by his house on her way home from the feed store, and she figured part of the reason he hadn't contacted her yet was because of the blowout he'd had with her brother Will. Eight years was a long time to hold on to a grudge. It wasn't like Will to do that, either.

Whatever had transpired between the two of them was kept quiet, no small feat for a town that seemed to know everyone's business in real time. People weren't nosy. They cared. Ranch families had a long history of looking out for one another.

Fifteen minutes later Amber pulled up in front of Rylan's bungalow-style house and parked. At least the place wasn't on fire. She'd worried his emergency was something like that based on the urgency in his voice, but she also realized he'd be calling the fire department and not her.

Her curiosity had her mind running through half a dozen wild scenarios before she'd arrived. Last she'd heard, Rylan was a Navy SEAL. There probably wasn't much that he couldn't handle on his own. Needing her made even less sense as she rolled over possible problems in her head.

By most accounts Rylan had been in Jacobstown for two weeks already, and she had yet to see him. He'd basically pushed her out of his life before he'd signed up with the military eight years ago. He'd walked away without looking back not long after the one kiss they'd shared, but this wasn't the time to rehash that memory. Besides, he probably didn't even remember it.

Amber hopped out of the truck, took a deep breath and moved to the front door. There were ten-gallon buckets of paint littering the covered porch. Paint chipped off the outside of the building. She stepped over a ladder in order to get to the front door.

Rylan didn't seem to expect any visitors. She knocked, and it felt like it took forever for him to answer. It didn't. She had a case of nerves. She'd tried to shake them off before seeing him again and clearly hadn't.

"Thanks for coming, Amber." Rylan opened the door for a peek, blocking her view into his home. He looked a little too good in what she could see of his jeans and long-sleeve T-shirt. Her heart performed an inappropriate little flip-flop routine at seeing him again. She didn't want to have those feelings for him, like the childhood crush she'd had. She was an adult now, and there was no room in her life for childish pursuits.

Rylan's dark curls had been clipped off, but that did nothing to take away from his good looks. The military had filled him out even more, and she had to force her eyes away from his chest, which had always been at eye level.

"You're welcome." She tried to look past him and see what he was blocking. "What's going on, Rylan? I don't hear from you in eight or nine—"

"Eight," he interjected.

"Fine, eight years it's been, and now I get an emergency call from you out of the blue? I don't see your house burning down, and you're not letting me inside. I'm a little confused as to why I'm here."

"Damn." He muttered something else under his breath that she couldn't make out. "This is harder than I thought."

"What is it, Rylan? Why did you call me?" Impatience had her tapping the toe of her boot on his concrete porch.

"Did you buy this place?" She hoped Mrs. Parker was okay. She'd moved six months ago to be closer to her daughter in San Antonio.

"I'm in the process," he said, and an emotion she couldn't quite pinpoint darkened his eyes.

"It's good to see you, Amber." He closed the door a little tighter against his side. He was massive at six foot three inches. He'd always been tall, but now he was filled out, too. It made a huge difference in his size and aided his ability to completely block her view.

Amber planted a balled fist on her hip, ignoring

the reaction her body was having at seeing him again. "What's so important that my hay had to wait?"

A baby let out a wail.

"Come on in and see for yourself." He looked at her with the most helpless expression.

"What have you done, Rylan Anderson?" Amber stomped through the doorway and froze. Her jaw must've dropped. Rylan stared at her, but all she could focus on was the baby on the floor, lying on a blanket with couch pillows tucked all around her. "Is this yours?"

"I don't know," he admitted.

"What do you mean by that?" Okay, she understood what he was saying, but it was more like a *seriously? How could this happen? And how could you not know if this is your child?*

"A random person showed up at my door with her." Rylan looked helplessly at the little girl who'd settled back down already. He really did sound lost and confused. His dark eyes had that lost quality, too.

"Where's her mother?" Amber scanned the place. Her blood boiled that a person could drop a baby off and run like that.

"That's a great question." His voice held a mixture of frustration and desperation.

Thankfully, the baby had gone back to sleep.

"How did this happen?" She walked over and stood near the little pink bundle. She was young, a few months old if Amber had to guess. She'd been around her brothers' children enough to know a little bit about babies.

Looking down at that sleeping angel caused Amber's heart to squeeze. The air thinned, and it became difficult to breathe. She would never be able to look at such a young baby without remembering her loss. She reminded herself that it was a long time ago. And she still couldn't go there, couldn't allow her thoughts to run rogue without the world trying to crash down around her. She refocused on her former friend.

Rylan stood there, looking at a loss for words and staring at her like she had three foreheads.

"Okay, fine. I'm not that naive. I know *how* this happened. I'm just wondering…never mind…you got coffee?" She figured she was going to need some serious caffeine if she was going to think straight. She shook off the cold and shrugged out of her coat, which he immediately took from her and tossed onto the chair near the door.

"I put on a pot." He turned toward the kitchen. "Here, let me—"

"No, thanks. You stay in here in case she wakes up again." Amber didn't want to explain the sudden burst of emotion that made tears well in her eyes. She knew better than to let Rylan see them, or he'd have too many questions. She stalked past him and into the adjacent kitchen.

She opened a couple of cabinets before she found the right cupboard. The coffeemaker was near the sink and easy to spot. There were unpacked boxes stacked against the wall in one corner. "You want a cup?"

"Yes. Please."

Amber wiped her eyes and straightened her back before filling the mugs she'd taken from the cupboard and returning to the living room with two steaming coffees.

"Here you go." She handed one to him and then took a sip of hers, enjoying the burn. She needed to clear a few cobwebs in order to think clearly. She plopped down on the floor, near the baby.

"Come join me, Rylan," she said.

He did.

"You've been in some messes before, Rylan Anderson, but I can't even begin with this one." She took another sip and lowered her voice. "You don't know if you're the father?"

"This is the first time I've set eyes on her," he admitted. "I had no clue that she existed until someone knocked on my door looking panicked, asked me to hold her and then ran. She was crying, and I had no idea what to do. The person said her mother asked him to drop the child off. He also said I'm her father, apologized and was gone before I could stop him."

Amber looked down at the sleeping baby. She had Rylan's dark curls, which didn't exactly mean she belonged to him. She just looked like she *could* be his daughter. The thought of Rylan being a daddy hit her hard in the chest.

"Okay. Here's what we'll do. You can get a DNA test down at the store. I think they're pretty easy to take. If she's yours, we'll take the next legal steps for you to claim her." Her statement didn't get the reaction she was hoping for.

"How accurate can a drugstore test be?" Rylan looked even more lost. "I need to track down her mother, and I can't do that if I don't know who she is."

"How many women have you been with?" Before he could answer, she held up a hand. "Don't answer that. It's not my business."

"This situation is complicated, Amber. But I'm not some jerk who runs around getting women pregnant and then ditching them. I just got out of the military and, yes, there've been a few women, but none who were important, and I'm *always* careful." The indignation in his voice shouldn't make her want to smile. Rylan would be considered hot by pretty much any woman with eyes. He was also smart and funny.

"I'm not trying to judge you unfairly, Rylan. I'm really not." It was a mistake to look into his dark brown eyes while sitting this close.

He looked away and took a sip of coffee. "It doesn't matter. She's here and I have no idea who she is, where she came from, or if she's mine. But I can't help wondering who would track me down and play a twisted prank like this, either."

"Did you say the stranger dropped off a diaper bag?" She was already looking around for one.

The living room had a sofa, chair and boxes. On the opposite wall was a perfectly set up and organized flat screen. There were two-by-two-inch swatches of paint colors taped to the wall that got the most natural light.

"It's over there." He pointed next to the sofa.

"Did you check it for a name?" she asked.

He shook his head.

Amber retrieved it and opened the zipper compartments one by one. She blew out a breath. "I don't see anything."

She held up the bag. A name was embroidered on the front pocket in small letters. *Brooklyn.* She showed it to Rylan. "The bag might've been borrowed, but we can call her Brooklyn for now."

"It's a start," he agreed.

"What about social media? Surely, if you spent time with someone intimately you'd be following them or the other way around." Discussing Rylan's sex life wasn't high on her list of post-holiday musts. Jealousy took another jab at her, so she straightened her shoulders. A man as hot and charming as Rylan had sex with women, probably any women he wanted. It wasn't her place to judge. She'd had sex, too. She figured the only difference was that they were presently talking about *his* sex life.

"I'm not much on that computer stuff," he said, that lost look in his eyes returning. "But, Amber, wouldn't I know if I had a child?"

Chapter Two

Rylan didn't expect seeing Amber again to hit him like a physical blow. It did. All he'd known when he'd made the SOS call was that he was in way over his head and he needed a female perspective. His mind had immediately snapped to Amber. He'd tried to tell himself the reason was that he'd dated most of the women in Jacobstown, which wasn't much once high school was over, and that he figured Amber was safe. He nearly laughed out loud. Amber Kent safe.

The knockout youngest member of the Kent family could not be more fireworks and temptation. She was beautiful as ever. No, check that, she was even more beautiful than before. And that wasn't exactly good for Rylan's heart.

Her nutmeg-colored hair was in one of those thick French braids. A few strands broke free and fell beside her heart-shaped face, framing eyes that could best be described as a warm, light brown. She was the total package, full pink lips and creamy skin. She stood at roughly five foot seven and had legs that went on for days. Her hips were curvier than he remembered, which only made her sexier. He knew better than to let those unproductive thoughts occupy his mind.

As much as he liked looking at a pretty face and a hot body, Amber was so much more. Her intelligence and sense of humor had been the first things he'd noticed about her. Well, after they'd both gotten over those awkward teen years. She'd come through it all so easily. Not him. He'd become angry and headed down a bad path with the wrong people, which had led to him shutting out his best friend. This wasn't the time to dive down that slippery slope of shame and regret.

"I'm drawing a blank on who the mother could be." Embarrassing as it was to admit, he had no clue. He had no excuses, either.

"This baby looks to be few months old. My best guess is around three," she stated.

"How do you know?" He had no clue.

"We've had a baby boom at the ranch." She shot him a look like she just realized he wasn't caught up on her family's life. "Don't ask."

He glanced at her ring finger. Relief he had no right to own washed over him when he saw no gold band. "Didn't plan to."

"Good. The mother would've been pregnant for nine months. So where were you…" She paused looking like she was making a mental calculation and counted on her fingers. "Twelve months ago, give or take?"

Rylan rubbed the scruff on his chin. He looked away from those distracting eyes. "There was a weekend that I don't remember much about. I must've had too much to drink."

"No one drinks so much that they can't remember where they were or who they were with, Rylan," she argued.

He thought back to where he might've been a year

ago and drew a blank. "The thing is… I used to drink and that got me into a lot of trouble. I quit. Even when I drank, I never partied so much that I was careless enough to…" He motioned toward the baby.

"Well, that's good to know." She blew out a breath. "She's probably not even yours. This is most likely a mix-up."

Amber pulled out a piece of paper from the diaper bag. "I didn't see this before."

"What is it?"

"A note from someone. The mother?"

Guilt stabbed at Rylan. There was that one time he'd gone to a party and woke up the next day in a motel room, alone. A hazy memory said there was a woman with him that night. Everything was foggy, and it felt more like a dream than reality. He'd felt off for a few days afterward, most likely the effects of alcohol after not drinking anything stronger than a cup of coffee for years.

She skimmed the note. "It's not signed. But it's addressed to you, and the baby's name *is* Brooklyn."

Rylan thought back to that weekend. Was that twelve months ago? It seemed longer than that, which meant he couldn't be the father of the child. What would the odds be of those dates matching up? They had to be slim. "What else?"

Amber held up the piece of paper and shrugged. "That's it. At least we know her name for certain now."

Rylan studied Amber. She had that same lost look from when she first saw the baby.

"I need to call Zach." Rylan referred to the sheriff, who also happened to be Amber's cousin.

"What can he do?" she asked.

"I don't know. Call in Child Protective Services?" There was no conviction in his words. "Find this kid's mother?"

"And what if she is yours? Do you plan to ignore that fact, Rylan, because if you do I won't recognize you anymore." She was all anger and ire. Damn that she was even more beautiful when she was scolding him. He shouldn't find it amusing or cute as hell.

"I would never deny my own child." It was true. Rylan knew firsthand what it was like to have a father who couldn't be bothered with his child. When Rylan was young, his mother had told him that his father had gone camping. He later realized that she was covering for the fact that Rylan's father had walked out on them both. The man didn't look back. He just disappeared one day, leaving Rylan's mother to care for him long before Rylan had any memories of his father.

His mother had worked two, sometimes three jobs to pay the bills. He'd loved her and respected her, but he never knew her. Loralee Anderson was always gone, working, trying to make a living. When she became sick and passed away when Rylan was in high school, he had rebelled. He'd gotten out of control. And then the night he'll never forget happened. Even now, he couldn't go there mentally.

The US Navy had become his family once he decided to get his act together and join. Then, his brothers on his SEAL team were his only family. And yet he'd never quite been able to erase Jacobstown from his mind.

Now that his time was up in the military, and he'd had no designs on a forever career, Rylan came back to the only place he'd ever known as home. Except nothing was the same anymore. Strange how moving away from the place he grew up made him think it would somehow be frozen in time when he returned. It didn't work that way. Life moved on. People grew up and grew older.

"Are you listening?" Amber interrupted his heavy thoughts. She blinked at him.

"Yes. Sorry. What were you saying again?" He took another sip of coffee to wake up his mind. He'd stayed up too late last night unpacking the kitchen, but at least the place was close to livable now. He planned to move a wall in order to open up the living area to the kitchen. There were other renovations on deck. Once the place was updated, Rylan had planned to decide if it was worth sticking around Jacobstown.

"Where's your laptop?" Amber set her coffee on the table next to the couch.

"Ah, over here." He retrieved it and sat next to her.

She opened it and asked him to log into his social media page. She looked at his story and skimmed all the people—mostly women—who followed him.

He could've sworn she'd blown out a frustrated breath.

"There are a lot of names here, Rylan." She studied the screen.

"Yeah, I know a lot of people thanks to traveling all over the world," he said.

"Thank you for your service," she said, and there was a hint of admiration in her voice. It made him proud to hear it.

"You're welcome," he said reflexively. He'd heard it dozens of times over the years, but it sounded somehow sweeter coming from Amber. He told himself that he couldn't afford to care about what she really thought of him, even though a little voice in the back of his head called him out on the lie.

"Okay." She refocused on the screen. "Let's get to work on these names."

She pulled up picture after picture, but he didn't remember being with any of the faces. Especially not in the time frame that would be necessary for one of them to be the mother of the child.

"It's no good." He was getting frustrated.

"We'll figure it out," Amber reassured him.

It was easy for her to say. Everything in life came easy to Amber Kent. Beauty? Check. Brains? Check. Great family who loved her? Check. Money? Check.

"Everything can't be fixed by the Kent charm." He nudged her shoulder with his. A surprising amount of electricity pulsed from where they made contact. Well, that was a bad idea. One Rylan had no intention of repeating.

His attraction to Amber came roaring back, but he remembered the promise he'd made to his best friend. Will Kent knew Rylan better than anyone else, and if Will thought Rylan dating Amber was a bad idea, then it was. Period.

Besides, Rylan would never break a promise to his former best friend.

"Ha-ha. Very funny. You know, luck visits those wearing overalls more often than someone who can't be bothered to get his hands in the dirt," she shot back.

"True." He picked up her hand and showed off her manicured nails.

"Just because I know how to clean up doesn't mean I don't put in the work, Rylan Anderson." Hearing his name roll off her tongue shouldn't sound so good. He should also ignore the electricity bouncing between them. Those were things that had gotten him into trouble before, and he'd touched the hot stove once.

Rylan liked to think that he learned from his mistakes.

The baby stirred. Rylan had never been around kids and he hoped, no prayed, the little thing wouldn't wake before someone from CPS could get here. He had no idea what to do with a baby, and was grateful that Amber had shown up before the little girl woke and started crying again. Her wails had damn near broken his heart before she tuckered herself out and fell asleep.

Rylan had never felt so useless or helpless in his life. He'd practically worn a path in the carpet making circles in the living room as he held her against his chest. It was the only position she seemed remotely soothed in.

"I know you work hard," he conceded. "I also know that you're smarter than me. So, what do I do with this?" He motioned toward the black-haired angel. "Because I'm out of my league here. I surrender."

"Like you said, we can start by calling Zach. You know my cousin will come right over. News will get out, too. News that you're possibly a daddy. News that I was here." She flashed eyes at him, and he realized she was asking if he was prepared for her brother to know she was at his place. "Are you prepared for her to be tied up in the system until the courts figure out paternity?"

He hadn't thought of it that way. He'd been too focused on trying to ensure he wasn't left alone with her for long. He didn't have the first clue how to care for a baby. But Amber made a good point, and it was something he needed to seriously consider.

"No. If she's mine, then I want her with me. I'd also

like to figure out who her mother is either way. I mean, having this dropped on my doorstep has rocked my world, and I want to know if this is a babysitting detail or if some person is going to show up in six months with a court order demanding her baby back."

He didn't do the unknown real well, especially with stakes this high.

Chapter Three

Amber's cousin, Zach McWilliams, happened to be nearby when she called to explain Rylan's situation. The sheriff was on his way over. Questions were mounting, and Rylan needed answers. He could hardly imagine that a person could abandon such a sweet child. Even when Brooklyn had cried in his arms earlier she'd done it softly.

There was something delicate and tiny about the little girl that brought out Rylan's protective instincts. She had the roundest cheeks, the thickest head of curly hair and the most angelic features he'd ever seen.

Granted, Rylan hadn't been much on babies before, and had no intention of having one of his own until he had something to offer. That was one of many reasons he hoped this one had a different father. But as far as babies went, he'd be lucky to have one like her.

A soft knock sounded at the door, and Rylan immediately walked over and let Zach in.

"Thanks for coming on such short notice," Rylan said.

"Good to see you again." Zach's wary expression made sense given the circumstances. All Amber had told her cousin was that she needed to speak to him at

Rylan's house, and that she'd explain everything when Zach arrived.

His gaze bounced from Amber to the sleeping baby to Rylan. Amber gave her cousin a hug. He eyed the stacks of unpacked boxes.

"I'm still getting settled," Rylan said by way of explanation.

"I heard you were back," Zach said. "Welcome home."

Rylan thanked him. He hadn't been sure of the reception he'd get from anyone connected to the Kent family. But then it wasn't like Will Kent to go spreading rumors.

Amber motioned toward the couch. "Sit down."

"I'm good." Zach stood in an athletic stance like he was preparing himself for just about anything. He looked to Rylan. "What's going on?"

"A guy shows up at my door. He's holding a baby in a carrier and has a diaper bag on his shoulder. I just moved in so I figure he has the wrong address or is looking to visit Mrs. Parker, who used to own this place."

"She moved to San Antonio to be close to her daughter," Zach confirmed. He'd pulled out a notebook and pencil. He looked up from the notes he was scribbling.

"Yeah. The place had been empty and she needed the money. I figured we'd both win if I bought it," Rylan said.

"So, you're planning on sticking around?" Zach asked.

Rylan glanced at Amber before returning his gaze to Zach. "That's the idea for now. I figure I can always rent the place out if I decide to move to the city."

"People need affordable housing." Zach was nodding.

"The guy who showed up. Had you ever seen him before that you can recall?"

"First time," Rylan said. "He shows up and asks if I'm Rylan Anderson. I tell him yes and then his cell goes off. It wakes the baby and she starts crying. He looks flustered, asks me if I can hold the baby carrier while he answers his phone. The minute I take the carrier he drops the diaper bag at my feet, tells me the kid is mine and then bolts."

"Did you chase him?" Zach asked.

"By the time I set the baby down and kicked the bag out of the way, he had too much of a head start. She was crying, sounding pitiful, so I didn't have it in my heart to leave her. I looked up, but by then the guy disappeared in between the neighbors' houses." Rylan was still annoyed that he'd been outplayed.

"What did he look like?" Zach jotted down notes.

"He was around five feet nine inches. He had blond hair and blue eyes. He was young. I'd say in his early twenties. He was slim, looked like a runner. He had thin features," Rylan stated.

"Think you could work with a sketch artist?" Zach asked.

Rylan nodded as the little girl stirred. She immediately started winding up to cry. Again, Rylan felt useless. He looked toward Amber.

"She's probably hungry," Amber said, picking the baby up like it was as natural as a Sunday walk. Bouncing the little girl kept her from wailing. "You two keep talking. I'll figure out how to make her a bottle. Do you have a microwave?"

"Yes," Rylan said. He turned his attention back to Zach as Amber disappeared.

The baby cried louder once in the kitchen, and he figured Amber had her hands full. She probably needed help.

Rylan followed the sound. "What do you want me to do?" He had to do something. He couldn't stand helplessly by and watch Amber do all the work. He wasn't a jerk.

Zach waited with the patience of a Sunday-school teacher in church.

Amber mixed a packet of formula with bottled water that she'd heated. She filled the bottle and secured the lid. The little girl latched on and then settled in Amber's arms. Rylan didn't want to notice how natural Amber looked holding a baby. *His baby?*

"I have no idea if the child is mine. There was one time I was with someone, but I'm not even sure the dates match up," Rylan admitted.

Zach asked a few routine-sounding questions that Rylan didn't know the answers to.

"What happens now, Zach?" Rylan needed to know what was going to happen to the little girl.

"This is where we call in Child Protect—"

"Let's say that wasn't an option," Rylan interrupted. "What then?"

Amber's gaze darted from the little girl in her arms to Rylan and back.

"A case could be made for her to stay with a parent," Zach informed him.

"We haven't established paternity." Rylan had no idea if he was the little girl's father, but no kid deserved to be dropped off and left behind. Being rejected by the two people who were supposed to love a kid the most made for a bad upbringing. Although Rylan was never a bad kid, per se, he'd managed his fair share of trouble over the years, especially in high school. Thinking about restitution for the trouble he'd caused the Willow family was a large part of the reason he'd moved back to town. He owed them and had every intention of making good.

"I'll make that call and see who's available at CPS," Zach said. "Before you tell me you don't have to meet the CPS worker and that you have a comfort level with the child, I'll make that call to see who's available. The other option is to let her stay here."

Rylan looked at the little girl, who seemed content to curl up in Amber's arms. "I'll meet the person you send."

Brooklyn Anderson? He did like how that sounded.

Zach excused himself to make a call. He returned a minute later. "Elise Shelton is on her way."

"What will happen to her?" Rylan motioned toward Brooklyn.

"She'll be placed in a temporary home until her identity can be established via a DNA test and her parents are located," Zach informed him.

Rylan appreciated Zach for not automatically assuming she belonged to him. If she turned out to be his daughter, he would figure out a way to make her feel at home in his house, in *their* home.

"Any chance I can keep her here until this mess is sorted out?" Rylan didn't have a legal leg to stand on. Maybe there was a loophole? If not, he'd have to rely on Zach's good nature.

The sheriff's eyebrows shot up in surprise. "You would want to do that? Don't get me wrong, it's a noble gesture but babies need a lot of care. Do you know how to make a bottle or change a diaper?"

Rylan shrugged. "I wouldn't sign up for it voluntarily but here she is. Being dropped off here must've been traumatic for her, and the thought of sending her off to someone and changing her environment again doesn't sit right. And here's the thing, what if she *is* my child? Then what? She gets bounced back here right where we started?"

"I see your point." Zach's expression was calm, serious. "What if she's not your child? What if a mother is running away from someone? What if she picked your name off a mailbox and found a random person to tell you this story?"

"That's all the more reason for me to keep her. I can protect her." Rylan was dead serious about that. His military training made him the best qualified to handle a threat, foreign or domestic.

"Do you know how to care for a baby?" Zach asked again. "Don't take this the wrong way, but they're a handful."

Rylan needed to think long and hard about his next move.

"I'LL STICK AROUND and help with the baby until her paternity gets sorted out," Amber volunteered.

Zach's gaze flew to her. She shrugged, trying to dismiss the innuendo that she was offering for another reason, like she was attracted to Rylan.

"You sure that's such a good idea?" Zach asked.

"I'm not going to turn my back on a friend, Zach. Besides, he's never taken care of a baby before as far as I know, and you just pointed out what a handful one could be." Throwing his own words back at him usually worked in disagreements with her cousin. She knew he had her best interests at heart, but she also knew her own mind. "Do you really want this sweet little girl bounced around? And, as Rylan said, there's a chance you'll be bringing her right back here at the end of a couple of days anyway."

Zach stood there, staring at the carpet. She knew she was getting through to him.

"I doubt this will take long to decipher, and then I'll be back at the ranch doing my own thing again," she added for good measure.

"What if the DNA test reveals that Rylan is the father?" Zach was tapping his toe. "What then?"

"He'll have to figure out his next moves when that time comes," Amber admitted. "Until then, I plan to give him a hand."

Rylan would have to hire help. There were a few grandmothers in Jacobstown who had free time on their hands and who wouldn't mind a babysitting job. Amber could think of three off the top of her head, and she'd be happy to supply names. Heck, at least one of them would babysit for free just to have something to do. Granted, individually they couldn't handle Brooklyn all day by themselves, but something could be worked out.

"Your heart's in the right place, Amber. It is," Zach started. "But you have a full plate at the ranch right now."

"I can do some of the work from here. Calves aren't due for another couple of weeks, so that gives me some time," she said. Zach could only give her advice. Amber was old enough to make her own decisions, and she would. He knew it, too, based on the look in his eyes.

"If that's the decision, I'd better track down this little one's parents," he finally said.

"What about a home paternity test? Don't they sell those at the drugstore?" Amber already had her cell phone out, checking out names of tests on the internet. "Do you think those are accurate?"

"Sometimes they are. Sometimes they aren't. This is too important to leave to chance," Zach stated.

"You're right about that." Rylan folded his arms.

"The courts will want me involved to prove paternity," Zach said. "They'll want me to control the chain of evidence. We'll get Dr. Logan out here to take the sample. Let me text Elise and tell her not to come. She probably won't want to get out in this weather anyway."

The fact that Rylan could be a father slammed into Amber. She couldn't see him waking up at three thirty in the morning for feedings or diaper changes until this moment. There was something about the look in his eye that said he would do whatever he needed to in order to care for his child.

Amber's chest squeezed at thinking about the baby's mother showing up and wanting to be a family. It was silly, really. Amber and Rylan had never dated. A relationship with her older brother's friend was completely out of the question, especially considering no one would clue her in as to why they'd stopped talking. And yet an inappropriate stab of jealousy struck anyway.

Did she want another baby? Was that the reason for the strange emotions coursing through her? The one she'd lost with her ex had nearly done her in emotionally. She couldn't even talk about the baby that had been stillborn, the divorce that had followed.

When she really thought about it…no. Amber had too many responsibilities at the ranch and in town.

Thinking about babies struck her as odd. She'd never been the type to sit around and daydream about weddings and kids. She'd never really been certain that having a family of her own was the right decision for her, especially after losing her parents, her baby, and then getting divorced before she turned twenty. She'd seen a few of her brothers find happiness and settle down. Marriage had been good for them.

Amber couldn't fathom trying again. Besides, she had too much to accomplish. And she may never decide to have a family of her own. It would take a special guy in her life to make her want those things again. He would have to be someone incredibly special to make her able to face another pregnancy.

And the funny thing was that she wasn't even ready to begin looking for him.

But, sitting in Rylan's kitchen, holding what could be *his* baby, she couldn't deny a certain pull toward the child.

Then again, those big brown eyes and round cheeks had a way of casting a spell on a person. *Quit being so cute, kiddo.*

Amber refocused on the conversation going on between Zach and Rylan. It involved a doctor and the court and words she never expected to hear in a conversation about Rylan. Fatherhood. Wow. It looked like he was about to grow up if this was real. Looking at his body—a body he'd filled out during his time in the military—it looked like Rylan had already accomplished that on his own.

Her heart stuttered when he caught her gaze. He also

busted her staring at his chest. Her cheeks flamed. This was turning out to be a red-letter day.

He walked close to her as Zach made a phone call, presumably to Dr. Logan.

"Thank you for offering to stay, Amber." He started to say more, but she put her hand up to stop him.

"It's nothing." Her heart argued against her offer amounting to nothing. "Don't worry about it."

How long could it take to get answers?

Chapter Four

"I'm sure I would've heard gossip if Amber Kent had had a baby. So, who does this little bean belong to?" Dr. Logan smiled at Brooklyn. She cooed. Wow, Amber thought. Five kids definitely gave him the experience edge. Thankfully, he'd been on his way home from the hospital and didn't mind diverting for a few minutes to lend a hand.

Amber and her family had known Dr. Logan since forever. His green eyes were as warm as ever even though the rest of him was aging. He was graying everywhere else. He was a gentle man, fairly tall at five feet eleven inches but much shorter than Rylan. Dr. Logan kept himself in shape by running.

The times Amber headed into town in the morning she'd see him on a run. He was an honest man who'd been married to the same woman since graduating high school. They'd had five children, and the joke had always been that they needed one more to keep up with the Kents. Mrs. Logan and Amber's mother had been close friends. Amber's heart squeezed. Even though it had been years and she should be used to it by now, she still missed her mother. She missed her father, too, of course. But after losing her child, Amber could have used her mother to help get her through. The recent holidays left her feeling blue without her parents.

"She's not mine. We're trying to figure out if she belongs to Rylan Anderson," Amber said to the doctor with a wink. She'd asked to be the one to answer the door when he knocked.

"I'd heard he was back in town. Didn't realize he brought back a family." Dr. Logan wasn't being judgmental when he said it. He glanced past Amber.

Seeing him made her miss her folks that much more, and between Brooklyn and her brothers' babies maternal feelings stirred inside Amber after shutting them off after losing her baby.

"Zach and Rylan are in the kitchen." She motioned toward the back of the house. She stopped short of walking in the next room. "Rylan had his world shaken up, Dr. Logan. He just learned about this little angel and has no idea if she's his."

"Oh. I see. Zach mentioned there was a question about the little girl. I didn't connect the dots. Forgive an old man." His smile lit up his eyes and made her think about her own pop. He would be close to the same age as Dr. Logan now. Her father's eyes had been hazel, like looking across the sea.

"Thanks for understanding." Amber's eyes started welling up. That was embarrassing. She shoved her feelings aside, wiped a rogue tear and focused on the baby in her arms.

Amber followed Dr. Logan into the kitchen. She'd believed that she'd dealt with her sense of loss with her parents a couple of years ago, but emotion brimmed just under the surface. "Thank you for coming, Dr. Logan," Zach said with an outstretched hand.

He took Zach's offering first and then Rylan's.

"How about you sit right here," Dr. Logan said to Amber, motioning toward the chair next to the kitchen table. "This won't take but a second."

He made goofy faces at Brooklyn. The baby laughed. He played peekaboo, and the little angel's laugh caused an ache in Amber's chest. Doc opened his medical bag and pulled out a swab. He used it to collect a sample from the inside of the little girl's cheek.

Rylan paced circles on the tile floor behind Amber.

She avoided eye contact with her cousin because she could already read the disapproval on his features. He wouldn't want her around Rylan any more than her brother Will would.

Rylan had made a few mistakes, she'd give Will that much. And she knew deep down her brother still cared about his former best friend even though he'd refused to talk about him the first year Rylan was gone. Anyone who mentioned Rylan's name got a dirty stare before Will excused himself and left the room. Something had happened between them, and she couldn't for the life of her figure out what it had been. And she'd tried. She'd quietly asked around, but either no one knew or no one was talking. Knowing her brother, no one knew but Will and Rylan. Will had gone quiet and Rylan signed up for the military.

Will was stubborn. Especially when he thought he was right.

The problem was that she had no idea how her brother felt about Rylan anymore. Her relationships with her siblings had changed after losing their parents. In some ways the loss had brought them all closer. In others it had taken a toll. Everyone had been busy in the last few years changing their lives in order to take over their rightful places at the ranch.

Nothing felt settled. Of course, that could just be Amber. She was the broken one.

Brooklyn cooed once more at Dr. Logan, who could win Dad of the Year based on his exchange with the baby. In fact, Amber figured she could learn a few things from the man.

Again, the thought of Rylan being a dad struck a strange chord. She needed to get a grip. They were old friends and nothing more. He needed help and had been back in town only a week or two. He'd reached out to her as a friend, and she was helping because of their past and because the recent holiday season had her feeling melancholy. That was all. Her body might have an inappropriate reaction to seeing Rylan again, but logically she knew better than to put too much stock into it.

So the military had filled him out and he looked even more gorgeous than before, if that was even possible. That wasn't all. Something was different. They were both eight years older; both had changed.

"One more sample and I'll be on my way," Dr. Logan said, looking toward Rylan.

Amber figured that Rylan would want to know immediately about the results and part of her wanted to know, too. Again, the thought of Rylan being a dad blew her away. He hardly seemed old enough, but he very much was. Several of her brothers were married and had children.

Reality was a hard smack. When had everyone gotten this old?

Okay, granted, being in their twenties and early thirties wasn't exactly *old*. She meant when had everyone matured enough to have families of their own? It felt like only a minute had passed since she'd been running in the fields with one or more of her brothers and some of their neighbors playing Keep Away or Freeze Tag.

And now?

She'd blinked and everything was different.

"Any chance you can share the results with Rylan the minute they come in?" she asked the doctor.

"I think that would be okay as long as the sheriff doesn't have a problem with it," Dr. Logan answered.

All eyes flew to Zach.

"I'm fine with it." The sheriff raked his fingers through his hair. "I'd want to know as soon as possible if this was me. Official word is for the courts."

"Thank you," Amber said, and she could see some measure of relief on Rylan's face. Otherwise, he looked pretty out of his element.

The doctor finished his tests in a matter of minutes. He handed one to Zach and placed one in his carrying case. "I won't have the results until Monday. The lab's closed for the day."

Amber figured it was going to be an uncomfortable night, but they could power through.

"Thank you." Rylan walked Dr. Logan to the front door.

Amber turned to Zach. "There's a diaper bag with a handwritten note in it."

"I'll take it into evidence." Zach excused himself and then returned a minute later with a paper bag.

"It's in there," she said.

Zach was careful to remove the note. "Maybe we'll get lucky with a fingerprint match."

"Mine will be on there. Sorry." Amber wasn't sure

she wanted Brooklyn's mother to be in the criminal database. That would mean her mother had committed other crimes, which was not exactly ideal.

Amber's stomach performed that annoying flip-flop routine when Rylan came back into the kitchen.

"I better run. Let me know if Dr. Logan sends word to you, okay?" Zach held tight to the evidence bag that now had a companion.

"We will," Amber answered before Zach let himself out.

Rylan motioned toward the coffee machine on the counter. "You want another cup?"

"Yes, please." Amber didn't want to think about how right it felt to be in this man's kitchen. There was a lot she didn't know about Rylan, like what he'd been doing for the past eight years. "What did you do in the military?"

He rolled massive shoulders. "Not much. I was a diver."

She'd known a Navy SEAL once who used that line. It also meant that he wouldn't tell her much more. She glanced around the room. "You're still getting settled in?"

"Yep." He turned the tables on her when he asked, "What have you been up to for the past eight years?"

"I'm the one asking questions," she shot back.

"Why is that?" He picked up her coffee mug and walked toward the machine.

"You're the one who asked for my help, remember?" She wasn't ready to talk about her past with anyone.

"Is that how this works?"

"It is if you want me to stick around," she said playfully.

"I do. So, I guess you're in charge." He poured a cup and started the second.

"Be honest. How come you and my brother stopped talking?"

Rylan froze for a split second but then recovered quickly and went back to work. "People change."

"What's that supposed to mean?" Amber didn't see how two best friends could become so distanced in two seconds flat. She understood people growing apart or moving in different directions in life, but this had been like stepping in front of a bus.

"It's not important," he said, dismissing the conversation. He turned around with two mugs in his hands. "But she is, and that's my first priority right now." He motioned toward the baby.

He set the mugs down.

Amber bounced the little girl, who cooed. It was satisfying to be able to help with Brooklyn. Maybe Amber wasn't all thumbs at taking care of little ones after all. She was getting enough experience with her brothers recently, that was for sure.

"There's a cold front coming tonight," Rylan said.

"That does tend to happen this time of year." Christmas was a few weeks ago. It had always been Amber's favorite holiday. Except for the past few years. Since losing her parents, she hadn't found her footing. Being with her brothers and their families had been the best part about it. Amber couldn't help but notice the absence of her parents even more this time of year.

"All I have is what's in that diaper bag." He took a sip of coffee. "She'll freeze in what she's wearing."

"Don't be dramatic, Rylan. She'll be fine. You'll wrap her in extra blankets," she said.

"And what if she kicks them off? I'm a whirlwind sleeper. What if she's the same?" His look of concern was endearing. Her stomach performed another somersault routine. "Let's worry about getting some lunch first. Then we can think about sleeping arrangements later."

Rylan didn't speak for a few minutes. He looked tired and concerned.

"However this turns out will be okay, Rylan. You know that, right?" she asked.

"No, it won't."

RYLAN DIDN'T HAVE the first idea how to be a dad. He was probably going to damage the child beyond repair *if* she turned out to be his. Part of him was still holding out hope that there'd been some mistake. It wasn't Brooklyn's fault. The kid was adorable. He was the problem.

Besides, a mother would have to be desperate to leave her child with someone she hadn't seen in a year who'd never met the child. To make matters worse, he didn't even remember the child's mother. What kind of jerk did that make him?

"Tell me what you're thinking, Rylan." Amber's voice—a voice he'd thought about more than he should admit while he was overseas—cut through his heavy thoughts. Telling his best friend that he'd kissed his little sister before shipping off had been a disaster, especially after the mistakes Rylan had made. He didn't blame Will for not trusting him. Rylan hadn't deserved his friend's confidence.

Even so, Will's reaction had set Rylan off. Will had blown up. Rylan had gotten offended. He'd been so hotheaded back then. Ready to fight the world and, stupidly, his best friend when his reaction wasn't what Rylan was hoping for.

There was more to it than that. Rylan had been pushing boundaries and heading toward dangerous territory. Will had tried to intervene and talk him down from doing stupid things. What had Rylan's response been to his friend's concern? He'd told him to get a life and had gone off and messed up royally.

"I'm thinking that I'm in a whole mess of trouble." The baby was one thing. Rylan had come back to make amends for his mistakes. Now, his life had just gotten a whole lot more complicated.

"Well, it's no use feeling sorry for yourself," Amber said a bit more emphatically than he liked.

He couldn't help but smile. "That's not what I was doing."

"What do you call it then?" There was a hint of mischief in her eyes, and he didn't want to think it was sexy even though he did.

He missed talking to Amber. With her, conversation wasn't work like with most people. She had a quick wit and sharp sense of humor, but it was her intelligence that drew him in. Seeing her again was supposed to stop him from thinking about her. That, like many of his plans of late, had gone to hell in a handbasket the second he put eyes on the woman.

She was still beautiful. More so now that she had a few curves. She had big eyes, not saucers because that description would be way too plain. And they were the most beautiful shade of brown. Her nutmeg-colored hair fell past her shoulders in that braid. She'd grown it out a little more, and it looked good on her.

"Where do you think her mother could be?" Amber

asked. She must've noticed that he'd been staring at her with the way her cheeks flushed.

"That's a great question," he said.

"A woman would have to be awfully desperate to convince a person to drop off an angel like this at a man's house sight unseen." Amber's brow shot up. "Why'd you really come back to Jacobstown?"

Rylan shrugged. He wasn't ready to talk about the real reasons, and there were many. He settled on, "It's where I'm from."

"I figured you'd end up in the city," she admitted.

"Fort Worth? Nah."

"No, I was thinking someplace farther than Fort Worth. Austin, maybe. San Antonio. I didn't think you'd come back here," she said.

"Austin's nice. I have work here, though," he said. What he meant to say was that he had work to do. He had retribution to pay, and would never be able to get on with life as a man if he didn't right a wrong. He didn't want to go into the details until he figured out how to go about it.

There was another reason why he'd come back to Jacobstown. He had nowhere else to go.

"You came back for a job?" she asked.

"Something like that," he said. "Why all the questions? Don't you think I should be here?"

"I never said that," she said quickly. "I'm just surprised. I figured you put this town behind you and didn't want to look back."

"I served in the military. I didn't sign up to live on Mars." A big part of him didn't want to look back at Jacobstown; facing this town again was harder than he expected. But he could never move forward until he made amends for the past. The Willow family deserved that and more.

"Why not?" she asked with a smirk.

"Mars doesn't have a Jacobstown," he quipped.

"You always said you couldn't wait to leave this town, to get out and make your mark on the world." She took a sip of coffee, which wasn't an easy feat with a baby in her lap. She managed to balance both without letting Brooklyn grab the cup.

"I was fifteen years old the last time I said that. What did I know?" He stood and walked over to the window. The wind had picked up, and he could see the oak tree in his backyard sway.

"Your head was filled with ideas about what you were going to do when you turned eighteen," she continued. She fell quiet for a few minutes, bouncing and playing with the baby on her lap. "Did you find what you were looking for out there?"

Rylan didn't answer.

Instead, he took another sip of coffee and contemplated the storm.

"It's going to get a lot worse out there. You okay with being here if it really comes down?"

Amber looked up at him and locked on to his gaze.

"A storm never stopped me, Rylan."

Chapter Five

"It's important to get the exact brand of formula or she can get an upset stomach. Think you can find everything on the list all right by yourself?" Amber asked Rylan after giving him a few items to purchase from the store for an overnight with the baby.

"Yes." The one word answer gave more of a hint that he was so far out of his element he didn't know where to begin.

Amber couldn't help but smile. Her heart pounded her ribs as she thought about spending the night alone with the former SEAL. She could admit to having had a childhood crush on her older brother's former best friend. Speaking of which, she still had a lot of questions about what had happened between the two of them. Based on the earlier conversation with Rylan, she wasn't going to get easy answers.

"What's so funny?" He stood at the front door, searching his pockets for his keys.

"Not a thing." Amber shouldn't break what little confidence he seemed to have when it came to the baby. "But when was the last time you went shopping?"

"Yesterday," he shot back.

"Your keys are on the kitchen table, by the way." She couldn't help herself from smiling again.

Frustration came off Rylan in waves. He made eye contact, which did a whole bunch of things to Amber's stomach. Unwelcome things at that.

"Thanks." He stalked into the next room, and she heard his keys jingle a moment later. "You sure you'll be okay alone with her?"

"Yes." The fact that he was worried about the little bean caused Amber's heart to squeeze. There was something incredibly sexy about a strong and outwardly tough man's vulnerability when it came to protecting a baby.

Amber reminded herself that Brooklyn had a mother out there who could walk through that door any second. The woman had obviously tracked Rylan down. She held the cards until the paternity test came back. Again, the thought of Rylan being a dad hit hard.

"Where's the list I gave you?" she asked an uncharacteristically frazzled-looking Rylan.

He glanced around and checked his pockets again. This time, he came up with a crumpled piece of paper.

"I should come with you," she said.

"No child seat in my Jeep. Remember?" For a split second she saw the relief in his eyes. It shouldn't amuse her.

"Fine. I'll take her for a walk instead. She could use some fresh air." Amber stood.

"You sure it's not too cold outside?" His concern was evident in his wrinkled brow.

"Get out of here, Rylan. We'll be fine. I'll wrap her in a blanket if I have to." She shooed him out the door and followed him onto the porch. "Call if you get stuck on something, you hear? I'll have my phone with me at all times."

He nodded and then hopped off the porch.

Amber glanced around at the land, land that was as much part of her soul as the ranch her family owned. Texas was everything to her.

Rylan stopped before climbing inside his Jeep. He looked like he wanted to say something. It took a few seconds as he seemed to be searching for the words. "I owe you one for this big time, Amber."

"Go on, Rylan," she urged. Figuring out a way to keep an emotional distance was difficult when he stood there staring at her. Her stomach decided to flip like a gymnast again, and she took a deep breath in order to calm it down. She needed to collect her thoughts and keep control of her mental game.

He smiled one of those devastating Rylan smiles before backing out of the drive.

There was a serious chill in the air. Amber decided on that blanket. She walked inside and moved into the master bedroom, ignoring the sensual shivers racing across her skin at being in Rylan's personal space.

"Where's a blanket that won't swallow you whole?" she said to the baby.

Brooklyn smiled up at Amber.

"You sure are a cutie," Amber soothed, pleased that the little girl seemed to be happy. Amber was good with her nieces and nephews, but she'd had practice with them. This baby was little, and she couldn't hold this bean without thinking of her nieces and nephews as well as the one she'd lost.

More of those adorable dimples showed. Amber wiped a rogue tear and refocused. She couldn't go there mentally with the one she'd lost. It still hurt too damn much even though it had happened years ago.

The only blanket Amber could find was on the bed. She didn't want to wrap Brooklyn in the one he used for sleep. She moved to the bathroom and opened the cupboard, looking for a good-size, thick towel. She noted the size of the bathroom was perfect for one person.

In fact, the two-bedroom house was made for a single person. The space was in disarray, which was not Rylan's fault, but it was no place for an infant. There were unpacked boxes in the bedroom, too. It looked like one of the walls had been marked for demolition. Old wallpaper hung from walls in the bathroom and bedroom. This place was a construction nightmare. Also, the carpet seemed as old as the house. It had probably been a nice color of beige at one point. Now it was stained and had ripples so big from wear a person could trip over them. There was no way a baby could safely crawl around on this germy floor.

"How long did he say he'd lived here?" Amber said to Brooklyn because the little one seemed to like the sound of Amber's voice.

She located a towel in the hall cupboard, held it to her nose and sniffed it.

"Clean," she announced to the baby. "Are you ready to go outside for a walk?"

Brooklyn stuffed her fist in her mouth. Drool dripped from her chin.

"Are you an early teether?" Amber hadn't seen any teeth so far, but that didn't mean one wasn't trying to peek out of her gums. Three months old was early to be getting her first tooth, but it wasn't unheard of. Six months was the general rule of thumb, but with her nieces and nephews Amber had learned that while there were general guidelines, when it came down to it every child was unique.

Without her nieces and nephews, Amber would be lost right now. She'd never been the babysitting type until her oldest brother Mitch and his wife, Andrea, had had twins. Rea and Aaron were the first Kent babies and kicked off a baby boom at the ranch that Amber wanted no part of personally. She loved every bit of being an aunt. But babies of her own after what had happened? Amber didn't see herself going down that path again.

Besides, she'd always been the outdoorsy type and loved working long hours on the ranch. A fact she blamed on having five brothers. She was also the youngest, which probably should've made her spoiled rotten, but she had too much of her father's hard-working attitude for that nonsense. She'd never been one for inside chores. The only kind of cooking she was good at was for holidays or daily survival. The only remotely motherly thing she ever did was cook at Christmas, and that was because her mother had insisted. Lydia Kent had been revolutionary for her generation. She hadn't seen cooking as women's work, and Amber couldn't agree more. Mother had made a point of having all of her children pitch in for holiday meals. Everyone had grumbled about it growing up. And now, Amber couldn't be more grateful.

Because of her mother's ideals and stubbornness in the face of opposition, Amber and her brothers had been continuing the tradition of Crown Pork Roast with Cranberry Pecan Stuffing as a main course along with Make-Ahead Yeast Rolls and desserts like Apple-Bourbon Pie and Orange Bundt Cake. They baked molasses crunch cookies, staying up too late in the week leading up to Christmas after daily chores were done.

The smiles on everyone's faces once they quit grumbling about helping and started rolling up their sleeves and working easily made up for the lost sleep. Their mother would turn up the radio that was locked on to the station that played nonstop Christmas carols. She practically danced around the kitchen. She used to joke that Dad got the children most of the year after the age of five but Christmas belonged to her.

She'd blocked out holiday memories in the years after losing her mother. Her father, a devoted husband, had joined his wife a few short years after her death.

Amber's mother was the bright light, the warmth, that everyone had migrated toward.

Brooklyn stirred in Amber's arms, and she ignored the pang in her chest as she stared at the little girl happily sucking on her fist. Amber put on her coat and then wrapped the baby in the towel like a burrito. She gathered Brooklyn in her arms and headed outside for some fresh air, reminding herself that she always got a little melancholy after the holidays.

Rylan lived in town in a neighborhood with quarter- to half-acre lots. It was nice to walk around the area. Make no mistake, she loved living on the ranch but this was pleasant, too. It seemed like a change of pace, and she could see how a kid might enjoy having neighbors close by. Amber had grown up with brothers and around ranch hands. Her only respite was her cousin Amy, who was also Amber's best friend.

Speaking of which, she owed Amy a phone call. She had been the one to warn Amber that Rylan had come back to Jacobstown. Amber had been caught off guard that her cousin had felt the need to approach the subject with caution. When Amber had cornered Amy about it, she'd acted like it was no big deal. But her cousin always had a reason for her actions. She was probably warning of the fireworks to come between Rylan and Will.

She'd traveled two blocks from Rylan's house before she snapped out of her mental walk down memory lane. There was a school playground at the end of the street, so she picked up the pace.

"You'll probably like going to the playground, right?" Amber was keenly aware that she was enjoying a conversation with a little one who had no ability to talk back. She was trying to distract herself from thinking about Rylan too much. He was never far from her thoughts.

The playground could use some updating, Amber thought as she climbed the four metal stairs to the smallest slide. She held on to a rail as she positioned herself at the top and then slid down. Brooklyn laughed. The park consisted of a slide, three swings and a seesaw. The wood chips needed replacing, she thought as she made her way to the swings. She made a mental note to tour other parks and see if she could form a neighborhood beautification committee. Everyone in the community would benefit from updated playground equipment, and there'd been great strides making the features safer in the last five years. A committee could evaluate parks across Jacobstown, identify the ones in the most need of new equipment and start from there.

Amber also needed to call home and let everyone know she wouldn't be back tonight. She had a load of hay in the bed of her truck that needed to be taken home at some point. Their bulk order was delayed and this would be enough to get them by until it's delivered.

"You like the swing, don't you?" Amber asked, pleased with herself for being able to make the little girl happy. Besides, she needed to keep her mind busy because her thoughts kept wandering to Rylan, and that was as productive as milking a boar. Get close enough to one of those and she'd end up hurt, too.

She half expected to hear from Rylan at some point. That he hadn't called so far was probably good news, but also worried her. Was he *that* lost? Or *that* embarrassed to ask for help? Her brothers wouldn't stop for help unless the car was on fire.

"You ready to go again?" she asked Brooklyn, and Amber's heart melted a little more when the little girl with the big eyes smiled up at her.

If the slide was popular, the swing was like Christmas morning to Brooklyn. Amber held on to the little angel while swinging so long her arms felt like they might fall off.

"Okay, little miss. We better head home." She figured the baby would be hungry soon.

It was chilly outside so they'd had the entire park to themselves, which was good given the size. There were enough houses nearby to warrant further digging into an expansion.

Amber held Brooklyn to her chest and marveled at the warmth from the little bundle. As she turned the corner toward Rylan's house, the hairs on the back of her neck pricked. She had a strange feeling that someone was watching her, but it was probably just her imagination. Her nerves were on edge.

Amber glanced behind her and quickened her pace.

She heard a car in the distance. It was otherwise a quiet Saturday afternoon. She surveyed the sidewalk across the street, looking for movement. There were tall pines and mesquite trees lining the street. It was windy, and the temperature felt like it was dropping with every forward step she took.

Something or someone moved down the street. The person was too far away to get a good look. Amber quickened her stride, needing to get to Rylan's house as soon as possible. It felt like fire ants crept across her skin. She'd feel more comfortable behind a locked door at this point. Unfortunately, that meant moving toward the person—and she was certain the object was a him now—who'd ducked behind a tree.

Amber hugged Brooklyn tighter to her chest. The baby didn't seem to mind. She happily cooed and blew raspberries on her fist, unaware of the possible danger.

Another twenty feet and Amber would have the baby inside.

This probably wasn't the time to think about the fact that she'd left Rylan's door unlocked. Of course, she didn't have a key.

The figure moved. It was tall and broad, so her initial guess was right. He had to be male.

Brooklyn stirred and let out a sad little cry. Amber's heart battered her ribs as she soothed the baby. She hoped that Zach could get a hit from the description Rylan gave of the man who'd dropped Brooklyn off and ran.

Who did that? Granted, people could be desperate for money. She'd been blessed to grow up in a house where she never wanted for anything. But this was a life, a child. Who could be so cold as to drop a baby and run?

Amber couldn't get inside the house fast enough. She'd lost visual contact with the male, and her nerves were pulled taut. Rylan's house was close. So, Amber broke into a run. Brooklyn fussed louder as she was bounced up and down so Amber slowed her pace to a fast walk.

"It's okay," Amber soothed.

She cut across the front lawn, praying the man was gone. She wasn't exactly fast with a baby in her arms, and Brooklyn was most likely picking up on Amber's stress. She'd read somewhere that babies could do that. They could absorb emotions and react. She willed herself to be calm and soothing.

It was too early to be relieved, but making it onto the porch felt like a win. Noise from behind startled her. She spun around to investigate.

Her back thudded against the door when she saw him. He was too close. There was no way she could get inside before he got to her.

The tall male wore a hoodie, scarf and jeans. Sunglasses shielded his eyes. Amber couldn't make out the details of his face.

"Fire," she screamed at the top of her lungs. She'd been taught by her law enforcement cousin never to yell for help in a situation such as this. He'd taught her that people reacted to hearing the news of a fire. It might be self-preservation instinct and them wanting to make sure their property wasn't about to burn, but she didn't care.

Brooklyn went into full-on crying mode, and Amber could only pray someone heard her own screams over the sound of the baby.

The male sneered at her as he closed the gap between

them, his mouth and nose were the only things visible. As he neared, she smelled tobacco and figured the scent would be burned into her nostrils for the rest of her life.

"Fire," she shouted again, but feared the neighbors were too far away to hear. It was cold enough for windows and doors to be closed, and the wind howled. She had to think of something. She had to assume the man was there to take Brooklyn, and no way was she letting him walk away with the innocent child without a fight.

Running would do no good. Amber wouldn't get far while holding a baby. Besides, this guy had to have run behind the houses in order to sneak up on her like that, and he didn't seem winded. He was tall, maybe six feet, with a runner's build.

When the male was close enough to reach for the baby, Amber started memorizing details of what little she could see of his face. His skin was light, pale. His eyebrows red. He had a small mole on the left side of his nose.

"I don't have anything for you," she shouted with more authority than she owned. "Step away."

His gloved hands were reaching for the baby. No doubt he'd be stronger than her. Amber had seconds to make her move.

She let him get close, so close she could smell his awful breath. In one quick motion, she stepped into him and brought her right knee up hard into his groin. She ducked out of his grasp as he winced and coughed.

She'd barely bought a few seconds. Making a run for her truck was her best option. She'd left the keys under the mat on the driver's side and maybe could make it inside without him catching up by some miracle. Driving with a baby in her arms was not ideal.

Brooklyn was screaming at the top of her lungs as Amber hopped off the porch. She made it all of two steps when his hands gripped her arms. She struggled against his grasp, but it was like being locked in a vise-like grip.

All she could think to do was to drop down, but he stopped her. He was strong. Too strong. Brooklyn was fussing and fidgeting. It was all Amber could do to hang on to the little girl.

In the next second, Amber was being spun around and the baby pulled from her arms. She couldn't let this happen. She couldn't let this man get away with Brooklyn. And she couldn't stop him, either.

He ripped the crying baby from her arms.

It dawned on Amber that he would have the same problem she did. Trying to run with a baby was next to impossible. So, Amber grabbed onto his neck. She didn't want to risk hurting the baby, but if she let this criminal take off with Brooklyn, the child's life could be over before it got started. What kind of a person tried to steal a baby?

Amber fisted his metal frame sunglasses as she was dragged forward a few steps. She crushed them against his face.

He ground out a few curses before giving a shake that was so hard she lost her grip. She kept repeating the word *fire* at the top of her lungs, praying someone would hear her.

Amber clawed at his right arm until she was able to get in front of him. She grabbed Brooklyn and before he could rip the baby out of her arms again, she heard the sounds of an approaching vehicle coming. She risked a glance and saw a Jeep.

The assailant must've seen it, too, because he sprinted in the opposite direction.

Amber held Brooklyn to her chest as she checked the little girl for any signs of being hurt. Tears streamed down Amber's face at the thought of what had just happened, what *could've* happened.

The Jeep came roaring up and came to an abrupt stop. In the next second, Rylan was out the driver's door and giving chase to the attacker, who'd disappeared behind the neighbor's house.

Amber wasted no time locating the keys. She wouldn't give that jerk an escape route if he doubled back.

Heart pounding, she darted toward the house and locked them both inside.

Hands shaking, she managed to calm the baby by rocking her.

Stomach lurching, she conceded to being rattled as she sat down and balanced the baby in her lap so she could call Zach.

Chapter Six

Rylan lost track of the hooded male two blocks east of the park down the street from his house. The guy was a good sprinter, and Rylan figured that he had a vehicle tucked away over there on the ready. He must've planned for the run scenario, which meant there was premeditation on his part. Any thought this could have been a spur of the moment decision, however minuscule, died.

Frustration was a gut punch. The only reason the jerk got away in the first place was because Rylan had hesitated at the get-go, wondering if he should stick with Amber and the baby in order to protect them.

The decision to run was predicated on two things. Trying to find out who that little girl was and who she belonged to. Both of those might still be a mystery, but someone seemed determined to take her from Amber.

Blood ran hot in Rylan's veins. The kid didn't need to belong to Rylan for him to want to make sure she wasn't put in harm's way.

Was this the reason the girl's mother had found him? More questions surfaced as he broke into a run back to his place. Was he even the father? Or had a desperate woman sought him out for his ability to keep her baby safe? Had this been the move of a woman who had no choices left?

Rylan of all people couldn't judge another person for those actions. He'd been in his fair share of circumstances that had caused him to act out of character. Hell, he'd taken and run with a lie and tangled his best friend in it, too. That had cost him—he'd lost someone who he'd considered to be the brother he'd never had. Will Kent wasn't a liar, but he'd lied to keep Rylan out of jail. Rylan had been young and stupid. He'd made too many mistakes thinking he wasn't worth anything. Not even his best friend could convince him otherwise.

Rylan had a stubborn streak a mile long. And just to prove his friend wrong, Rylan started drinking and hanging around with the wrong crowd in nearby Collinsville. He'd done things to be ashamed of. Yeah, he could play the abandoned kid card all day long. Down deep, he'd known better. The military had helped him get his anger out. He'd gone in looking for a fight and found one. He'd hoped that he'd come out a better man for it.

If that baby turned out to be his child, he wouldn't shy away from the responsibility. He did need to find the kid's mother and learn what the drop-and-run routine had been all about.

"Rylan, what happened? I was scared half to death. Get in here." Amber's eyes were wide as she stood in the open doorway, the baby fussing in her arms.

"I lost him." He stepped inside, chest heaving, allowing her to usher him in.

"At least he didn't get her." Amber closed and locked the door behind him. "Zach's on his way. I called him immediately. He should be here any minute."

For the moment Rylan needed to catch his breath.

"He was wearing sunglasses, and I couldn't get a good look at his eyes. He wore a hoodie and scarf, too. His skin was pale, and his eyebrows were red. And he had a small mole on the left side of his nose." Stress lines creased her forehead. "I smashed his sunglasses into his face to stop him from running away. Maybe there's a piece out there. It might give Zach some DNA to work with. I'm pretty sure I scratched his face up, so he'd be easily identifiable if he showed up in public. Plus, there should be some of his DNA under my fingernails."

"That was smart thinking, Amber." He should have known she'd be savvy enough to leave a trail for Zach. Facial marks would be difficult to hide in a public place. If this person was part of the Jacobstown community, he wouldn't be able to walk around freely until his face healed. All law enforcement would be on the lookout.

"What about prints? It looked like you two were struggling for the baby," he said.

"Zach won't have any luck there. The guy wore gloves." She shook her head for emphasis.

"You know what?" Rylan paced. Nothing inside him wanted to say these next words. "After you give Zach your statement, I want you to go home. Brooklyn and I will make it through the night okay. We'll figure it out."

The thought of being alone with a baby for an entire night sent an icy chill up his back. He had no knowledge of babies and no particular skills with them, either. Hell, he hadn't been around any until this little one.

"Absolutely not, Rylan."

"Look. I have more supplies in the Jeep. I'll get those and take over with her." He could be stubborn when he needed to be, and this situation called for it. Putting Amber in danger was never meant to be part of this deal. Now that he realized his mistake he needed to fix it ASAP.

"Don't go out there yet," she warned. "And I'm not leaving you alone with her. Do you even know how to change her diaper?"

"How hard can it be?" he asked.

She harrumphed and her jaw set, like when she was determined about something.

"Don't go digging your heels in the sand, Amber," he warned. "When I called for help earlier, I had no idea what I was committing you to. If anything happened to you it would be my…"

The look of understanding that overtook her features stopped him dead in his tracks.

"You called me because you knew I could help. How could you have known there'd be an attempted kidnapping?" She stared at him. "I'm not leaving you stranded when you need a friend, Rylan. I'm not built that way, so it won't do any good to argue. Besides, she's taken to me and I won't abandon her until we know who this angel's mother is and why she saw fit to drop her on your doorstep. Now that that's settled—"

A knock at the door interrupted her speech.

"That's probably Zach. I got this." Rylan knew Amber well enough to know when he'd lost an argument. It might've been years, but that same stubborn streak he'd noticed when they were teens seemed to have grown.

Zach stood on the porch. Rylan opened the door and invited him inside.

"Is the baby okay?" Zach asked before crossing the threshold.

"Yes."

"And how about Amber?" Zach didn't miss a beat.

"She is."

"Make sure she stays that way." Zach's tone issued a warning.

"Hold on there, Zach." Rylan put his hand on the sheriff's shoulder. "I just spent the past five minutes trying to convince her to leave. If you think I brought her into this knowing it could turn into a cluster—"

"Don't put words in my mouth, Rylan." The welcome home tone was gone from Zach's voice now. The man's words had hit hard.

"I didn't." Rylan heard the defensiveness in his own tone—defensiveness because the conversation he needed to have with her brother Will was on Rylan's mind.

AMBER DESCRIBED THE ATTACKER the best she could as she recounted her story to Zach. Her cousin nodded and scribbled down a few notes while she spoke. She could almost see his wheels turning, and he did a heck of a job not freaking out that she'd been part of the attack.

Rylan had already warned her about sticking around. After spending a little time with Brooklyn, Amber was hooked. She couldn't step aside while that little girl's future was so uncertain. Besides, Kents weren't made to walk away from danger. Kents stuck together and Kents stuck around. Her brothers and cousin hated to admit it during times like these, but she was no different from them. Not one would turn a blind eye to someone in need or in danger. Granted, she was the baby of the family and that fact had her siblings trying to play protector from time to time. Lucky for her, she'd grown up with five brothers to ensure she could handle herself in almost any situation.

Case in point, the attempted abduction had been stressful and her nerves were still shaky, but she'd managed to ward off the attack. Brooklyn was safe because Amber had been there.

"I broke his sunglasses, and I'm hoping something is left of them in the front yard." Before she could finish, Zach was on his way to the door. His back was turned so she couldn't see the look of panic she knew would be there at the admission.

The baby had had a bottle, which seemed to be enough to keep her satisfied. She was back to sucking on her fist. So, Amber hopped up, settled Brooklyn in her arms and followed.

The sun was starting its descent. This time of year, that meant it was a little after five o'clock. The yard was visible as they searched.

"This is where it happened." She pointed to the spot, and thinking about what had happened gave her a chill. So much could've gone wrong. Brooklyn could be in the hands of that man, who couldn't want her for good reasons. An honest man with good intentions would've knocked on the door and explained the situation calmly. Only someone with something to hide would try to rip a child out of a stranger's arms.

She knew to stay back and let Zach do his job. Trampling all over his crime scene wouldn't help. Rylan seemed to realize it, too. He stayed with her, and she could see the anger on his face. She figured the anger was for what had almost happened to Brooklyn even though a little piece of her wanted the anger to be for her, too.

It was a silly notion and one best left alone.

Amber tucked that idea away with all the other up-to-no-good thoughts racing in her head whenever he was near. He'd always had that effect on her. Well, not always. She'd thought him to be pretty darn annoying in middle school. High school had turned around her feelings toward him. But then his mother had died and he'd gone inside himself. He shut out all his old friends, and rumor had it that he'd gotten involved with a bad crowd in Collinsville.

She'd kept busy with the ranch and with school over the years. And then her mother had gotten sick. She and her brothers became orphans when her dad died a few years later. Granted, they'd been adults when that had happened. But none of them had truly ever gotten over losing their parents. Did anyone ever?

Coming from a tight-knit family had made them feel the losses that much more. And then everyone had scattered like buckshot in order to handle family business. She'd always known their family had each other's backs; that was a given. But no one ever talked about losing their parents or how that had changed everything. How that had changed the family's dynamic.

"Got something." Zach put on a pair of rubber gloves and retrieved a paper bag from his SUV. He returned to the spot he'd zeroed in on, careful as he stepped so as not to trample on evidence, and then squatted. Metal glinted in the sunlight as he picked up what looked like a piece of sunglass frame. He held it up toward the sun like he was examining a prize. "Between this and the

DNA under your fingernails, we might have the break we need."

Amber had been around law enforcement long enough to realize this was too early to expect good news and that the evidence would have to be sent to a crime lab. Getting results could take weeks if not months depending on how busy the lab was.

After examining the area, Zach motioned for them to go inside. He was a few steps behind them because he put the evidence bag into his locked SUV for safekeeping.

Zach spun around on her the minute the door was closed. His gaze flew to Rylan. "Do you mind giving us a minute to talk?"

Rylan locked gazes with Amber like he was checking to make sure that's what she wanted before he complied.

She nodded.

"I'll be in the kitchen if anyone needs me." Rylan winked and she smiled as he left the room.

"I don't like you being anywhere near this case." Zach cornered Amber. She sidestepped him and moved to the couch.

The minute she turned on him, ready to put up an argument, he brought his hand up to stop her.

"I do realize that I have no authority in which to make that request, and I also know that you aren't the type to be told what to do under any circumstances. But hear me out because I'm only saying this because I care about you."

"Fine. What do you want to say to me, Zach?"

His gaze moved from her to the baby and back. "She hasn't left your side since the last time I was here, has she?"

"Nope." Amber had no plans to abandon this little angel, either. She also had no plans to defend herself or try to convince him this was different.

Before she could respond, Zach blew out a sharp breath.

"I figured that would be the case." He sounded resigned to that end.

"So, what's next?" There was no use going down the road of him trying to talk her out of staying.

"I'm not finished," he said.

"Really? Because you know as well as I do that I'm not leaving this house until this girl is in safe hands. She's been through a lot already, and I don't want to traumatize her further by abandoning her." Those last words nearly caught in her throat. She coughed to clear them. "I know this situation stinks and none of us realized how dangerous it was going to be, but none of this is her fault. She's taken to me, and I have no plans to leave Rylan alone overnight with a child when he has no experience caring for one."

Brooklyn had leaned into Amber, and she was rubbing the little girl's back.

"What if that guy comes back? What if he brings others with him? We have no idea what we're dealing with here."

"All good points. I was thinking that maybe I could ask Rylan to stay over at the ranch tonight—"

"I'm not going where I'm not wanted." Rylan appeared in the doorway to the kitchen, and she'd known he was listening.

"I just invited you," she countered.

"You're not the problem." Rylan positioned his feet

in an athletic stance and folded muscled arms over his broad chest.

"Then who is?" she asked.

"That's between me and your brother. Trust me when I say that door is closed." Rylan's voice was steady, even. She wondered if it took much effort to come off that way. He and her brother had been close. It made no sense that they were still at odds.

"I can speak to my brother—"

"Like I already said, not an option. Can we just leave it at that?" Rylan's granite features gave away nothing, and he was a bull when he wanted to be. "You didn't leave when I told you to. I respect that. Now, you need to return the favor."

He made a good point. One she knew better than to argue.

"It might not be safe to stay here, Rylan. Have you considered that?" Those words seemed to sink in as he nodded.

"What are we dealing with here?" he asked Zach.

"The worst-case scenario is an illegal baby adoption ring. These groups are high stakes, and there's a lot on the line since they work outside the law. People who don't want their name in the press or who can't adopt a baby by legal means turn to folks like these." Zach wasn't trying to scare them. Amber knew that. He was putting his cards on the table. "There's generally a lot of money at stake, and that tends to draw very good criminals to the business."

"One of which I was able to stop because of the training you and my brothers gave me growing up," Amber pointed out.

"Once they know who and what they're dealing with,

they'll come back more prepared next time." Zach's jaw set.

"They aren't the only ones," she started to say, but her cousin interrupted with a hand in the surrender position.

"Granted, what you did a little while ago might've saved the baby's life. Hell, I'm proud of you. The problem is that we don't know who she belongs to. We haven't established paternity, and technically have no rights to keep her." Zach's words hit harder than Amber had thought possible.

Being with Brooklyn was always going to be a temporary situation. So, why was Amber letting herself get so attached to the little bean?

She decided it was nothing more than protective instincts kicking in. Who wouldn't want to ensure this kid was okay? And maybe there was something motherly inside Amber after all. She'd doubted it after losing her own child within hours of his birth. Prior to getting pregnant, she'd never considered herself the marriage and kids type. But, hey, there was nothing wrong with being a fabulous aunt. Those were in short supply from what she'd heard.

And she loved the land, working on the ranch, being part of something bigger than just herself. She was helping build her family's legacy. How would she leave all that behind? She'd become a mom and then what? Scale back her work? Feel exhausted all the time? Not this pony.

"Something's off here. Doesn't this sort of thing usually happen with newborns?" Amber asked.

"I agree with the first part of what you said. But, no, this is a problem for the first year, to year and a half.

Generally, kids older than that are safe from these kinds of people because couples want babies." Zach tucked his notebook inside his front shirt pocket and his eyes zeroed in on Amber. "If you insist on being here, I'll put extra security on the block just in case."

"Thank you, Zach." That should deter the jerk from making a return trip.

"Trust me when I say you don't want your brother finding out about this from someone other than the two of you," Zach said.

"Honestly, this situation might right itself by morning. We'll get Rylan's test results back and go from there." What were the chances he was the father anyway? They had to be slim, right? He couldn't remember being with anyone during the time in question.

And, besides, she'd make the call to Will.

Enough time had passed. Whatever had happened between her brother and Rylan would surely have blown over by now. How bad could it have been?

Chapter Seven

Zach was gone. The baby was fed, washed and asleep. Amber had washed her own face and borrowed a toothbrush in order to brush her teeth. Thankfully, Rylan had an unopened spare. They'd dined on leftover pizza earlier, and the day's events had left her beyond tired, considering days on the ranch started at four o'clock in the morning.

"Got any clothes I can change into?" she asked Rylan, who stood at the bathroom door holding Brooklyn.

It was probably just the day Brooklyn had had, but trying to put her down to sleep on a makeshift bed on the floor was totally out of the question. That little girl's eyes had shot open the second there was no more human contact. At least she hadn't been so disturbed that she couldn't go back to sleep right away the minute she'd been picked up and cuddled.

Rylan had Brooklyn, and Amber was almost amused at how uncomfortable he looked. This was the first break from holding Brooklyn that Amber had had since meeting the little bean. Her arms burned and literally felt like they might fall off. Amber also tried to ignore how right it felt to spend the day with Brooklyn.

She was a good baby. That was the extent to which

Amber would allow herself to examine her feelings. And it was most likely the marriage and family boom at the ranch that had her comfortable with a child in the first place. If this had been a few years ago... Amber stopped right there. *This* never would've been a thing.

The family cattle business had never been so successful, and her innovation with organics had heralded the ranch into the future and was a large part of the reason for the success.

Of course, she could admit to feeling like she was missing out on something lately. But that *something* couldn't possibly be a baby. Amber had spent a long time convincing herself of that. Even so, being with Brooklyn fulfilled a need Amber didn't realize she had. It was probably just the growing Kent brood that had her questioning her stance on no longer wanting children of her own. Besides, she'd never survive that heartache again if something went wrong.

"I can take her back once I'm settled," she said as he stood there looking at the two of them.

An emotion passed behind Rylan's dark eyes that under different circumstances she'd recognize as desire. But that was probably just her mind playing tricks on her, seeing what it wanted to see. Rylan had never seen her as more than a little pain in the rear who'd followed him and Will around like a lost puppy. Okay, the lost puppy bit was probably being dramatic.

"Follow me," he finally said. She did and tried not to notice how cute his backside was. It was, no doubt about it, but that wasn't what she liked about Rylan.

Her high school crush had that mysterious troubled quality. He was a bad boy who was good deep down. Seriously hot. Wasn't that what every girl wanted? Finding a good bad boy was like owning a sweet horse that ran fast. Or meeting a unicorn.

Amber pushed those unproductive thoughts aside when she nearly bumped into said cute backside when Rylan abruptly stopped in front of her. It was probably her overwrought emotions that had her thinking about such silly things, like high school crushes.

First and foremost, she and Rylan had been friends. He'd been two years ahead of her in school.

And as long as she was admitting things to herself, she'd go ahead and say that he was a good guy. Sure, he'd started down a bad path but going into the military seemed to straighten him out.

A lesser man would've pushed this baby on the first person he could. He would've insisted Zach take her or allowed Child Protective Services to whisk the little girl away with a random family. No matter what Rylan said or thought of himself, he was a decent person.

"There are boxers in that drawer and T-shirts in the one below it." He motioned toward the dresser. She had to remind herself to breathe for seeing that baby sleeping so comfortably on his shoulder. A lightning bolt struck, like she needed to be more attracted to the man. What was it about a tough guy who could be so tender when handling something so vulnerable? A man like that was far more tempting than ice cream. And Amber liked ice cream.

Rylan walked to the door. He stopped at the threshold and hesitated for just a few seconds. Heat flushed through Amber, warming her in places she didn't want to think about with the baby in the room. With a sharp breath he left the room and closed the door behind him.

By the time Amber changed and walked into the living room, Rylan was studying his phone. He didn't look up, but he nodded toward the couch.

"You sure you don't want to sleep in the other room?" he asked.

"Definitely." She didn't want to sleep in sheets that had his masculine outdoorsy and campfire scent. She was no idiot. She wasn't doing that to herself on purpose. It was silly that she felt this strong of an attraction to Rylan after all these years. And embarrassing. Especially since he clearly still saw her as a friend. Even if he didn't, what would that mean? The two of them would never make it in the long run. They were about as opposite as two people could be. She loved the stability of the ranch and having family around, while staying in one place seemed to suffocate Rylan once he'd turned eighteen. As soon as he fixed up the Parker place, he'd get the itch to move on. Amber had no plans to get remarried. She'd shut that possibility off years ago when she'd married at eighteen, gotten pregnant almost immediately and lost both husband and child in less than six months. She'd begun her adult life as a divorcée, and that wasn't exactly a title she'd wanted to keep on her résumé.

She'd been young and infatuated. Amber had never been the type to sit around and dream about her wedding day. If she did get married again and, honestly, she couldn't see that as a possibility, then she'd go down to the courthouse and not make a big to-do over it.

Thinking back, her marriage had been the unhappiest time in her life. Before that, she'd felt free and full of possibilities. When she was little, her brothers used to tease her that she and Amy were like wild horses. Amber especially because she used to sneak into the barn and open the pens to let out the stock. Pop used to round them up and put them back in the stable. Amber would get in a whole mess of trouble, but she'd argue right back. When she was right, she was determined. When she thought she was right, she was unstoppable. She could hear her argument, her words to her father now. Wild horses had to be broken in order to be tamed. Not loved, broken. She couldn't think of a worse fate.

Being married had felt a lot like being shoved into a pen. Amber had accepted the proposal on impulse. The pregnancy came six weeks later, and she'd already realized being married wasn't for her. She'd kept quiet for the pregnancy's sake, figuring it was meant to be. That was the last time she second-guessed her instincts. They rarely failed her.

Amy and Isaac, from ranch security, had been on and off for the past couple of years. They were doing a terrible job of keeping their relationship a secret. Apparently, they were *on* again. What did it say about Amber that she was the Lone Ranger now?

There was a makeshift bed on the sofa. Rylan had pulled the back cushions off the couch and placed a rolled up blanket to soften the edge.

"You'll wear a hole in that carpet if you don't stop." Amber watched Rylan take another lap around the room.

"I was afraid if I stopped she'd wake up and cry again. I didn't want you up all night because of my rookie mistake," Rylan said.

"You want me to take her now?" Amber held out her arms because one look in his desperate eyes gave her the answer. "Looks like you've finally met your match, Rylan Anderson."

He gave her a resigned look.

"What do you need?" Relief brightened his stressed-out features when he handed over the baby successfully.

"Nothing I can think of. We'll be good." She lowered her voice to church-quiet as she balanced the baby and positioned herself in a somewhat comfortable position on the sofa. "Other than maybe the lights."

Rylan shut off all lights but one, a side table lamp with a soft glow.

"You going to sleep?" Amber bit back a yawn.

"Doubt if I can." He settled into a side chair.

"Deputy Perry is parked out front. Zach will most likely patrol the area all night. It's probably never been safer to grab some sleep. But if it would make you feel better, we could go in shifts." Her cousin wouldn't risk anything happening to her. He'd always been protective just like her brothers. Things had gotten even more tense with the crimes that had seemed to follow the Jacobstown Hacker and that first heifer discovery weeks ago.

"I'll wake you if I get tired, but I'm used to going days at a stretch." Of course, he would be. He'd only just gotten out of the military. She was pretty sure a mission wouldn't have him sleeping every night at the Ritz.

Silence stretched between them. The only sound Amber could hear was the baby's breathing. So many thoughts raced in Amber's mind. Technically, she didn't know Rylan any longer. He had no idea about her life, what she'd been through since the last time she'd seen him. And she had no idea who he really was anymore.

"Why'd you call me?" she asked out of the blue.

"You want the honest answer?"

"If it's a good one," she teased.

"I have no idea. You were the last friend I had in Jacobstown and the first one who came to mind," he said. "You've changed—"

"Well, so have you," she quickly countered, hearing the defensiveness in her own voice.

"Hold on. I meant that in a good way. You're older—"

She issued a grunt, stopping him cold.

"You're not a little kid anymore. You're a grown woman. Beautiful."

"Well, now you're doing a little better." She figured he'd added that last part to keep her from giving him a hard time. She'd accept the compliment anyway. "You ever think about becoming a daddy, Rylan?"

"No. I'm not anywhere near where I want to be in life, and I don't want to do that to a kid. But if the test proves she's mine, it doesn't matter what I think, does it?" The question was rhetorical. His tone left no room for doubt that he'd do the right thing by Brooklyn.

There was another long pause where neither spoke. After all these years, it should be awkward to be in a dark room alone with someone she knew from her childhood. But this was Rylan. She couldn't feel anything but at home with him. An annoying little voice warned her that she was alone with a stranger, but it wasn't difficult to quash.

"What are we going to do if he comes back?" she asked.

"This time, we'll be ready." That statement had so much finality to it Amber had no doubt that Rylan meant every word. He had the skills to back it up, too.

Amber shut the thought down. Because Rylan's protectiveness over the baby lying across her chest stirred Amber's heart in ways she couldn't allow or afford.

Conversation trailed off when Amber could no longer hold her eyes open. When she opened them again, she heard Rylan's steady breathing. His shirt was off, and in the dim light she could see his muscled chest.

An ache welled up from deep within.

RYLAN BLINKED HIS EYES open the second Amber shifted her weight.

"You're awake," she said, sounding caught off guard.

"I was never asleep. My eyes were resting." He rubbed the scruff on his chin and then raked a hand through his dark, thick hair.

"Said every man I've ever met who was actually sleeping." She laughed. Her laugh, hell, her voice, had a musical quality to it. This wasn't the time to get inside his head about why it was her laugh he'd heard when an enemy gunman stood over him with an AR-15 pointed at the center of his forehead. He'd told himself it was natural for childhood memories to come back when a man faced death. And she did have a great laugh.

"I've been thinking about where I might've been about twelve months ago. I was stationed in San Antonio last year and had a few weekends off. Several of us guys used to drive over to Austin. They did some partying." The disappointment on her face struck like a physical blow. "I haven't had a drink in six years, three hundred and twenty-four days. Except possibly that weekend."

"Oh." The one word and the way it was spoken conveyed pity. He didn't want that from Amber. "I'm sorry. I didn't realize that about your drinking. I knew it had gotten a little out of control before you left but—"

"My low point was good for me because it made me

realize that I had a problem. I saw the man in the mirror one sober morning and knew that wasn't who I wanted to be. Not on weekends, not on leave, not anymore," he said. "Before that I did a few stupid and reckless things. None of which involved not using protection no matter who I was with or how much I'd had to drink."

The women he'd spent time with knew the deal. He was upfront about his mind-set. He'd always shied away from any woman who was interested in anything more than one night of mutually consensual and amazing sex.

"I'm sorry you went through all that," she said, and the sincerity in her voice made him realize just how alone he'd been all these years.

It was fine. His choice. But this was the first time his life seemed lonely when he thought about it. The possibility of fatherhood was probably what had him going inside himself, searching for redeeming qualities that might make him worthy of bringing up that little girl on his own. He had no plans to let her down.

Amber tried to sit up and the baby stirred.

"I need to use the restroom. Think you can handle her for a few minutes?" she asked.

He nodded, deciding not to point out the fact that he might be doing that for a heck of a lot longer than a few minutes. The idea should stress him out, and it did, but not as much as he expected. He'd had a few hours to let the possibility sink in.

There was no going back now. If the call that came in said he was Brooklyn's father, so be it. He'd make sure that girl had a real childhood with dolls and dance classes even if he had to work two jobs to do it. Reality was a gut punch. Wasn't that what his mother had done? His father hadn't bothered to stick around long enough to get to know Rylan. That wasn't the life he wanted for Brooklyn. Staying in Jacobstown might not be an option. Work was sparse here. He'd have better luck and get more pay if he moved to Fort Worth or Dallas.

The thought of leaving Jacobstown hit harder than expected, but he could finish updating this house and then rent it out for income. He stopped himself right there. One step at a time. He didn't need to know how to finish the journey. He only needed to take the first steps. And that meant being okay with whatever news Dr. Logan delivered.

But first he needed to track down the baby's mother and find out what trouble she'd gotten herself into. Only a desperate mother would abandon her child.

Brooklyn squeezed her eyes shut before letting out a little cry. Panic set in. Was she hungry? Did she need a diaper change? Of course, she would need that. Didn't babies go to the bathroom almost constantly?

Thankfully, Amber returned before the baby could wind up a good cry. She brought a bottle back with her, and Brooklyn settled down almost immediately. She'd shown him how to feed the baby earlier, so he took her, figuring he needed the practice.

"You want me to burp her?" she asked him almost the second Brooklyn finished her bottle.

He nodded. There was an emotion behind Amber's eyes when she looked at the little girl that Rylan couldn't exactly pinpoint. Whatever it was ran deep.

"Will you teach me how to change her?" he asked as Amber passed the baby back to him. He did his level best not to sound as helpless as he felt when it came to taking care of the baby.

"It's easier than you think. Come on." The spark in

Amber's eyes shouldn't stir his heart like it did. She could always make the most mundane thing seem like an adventure.

She dropped to the floor next to the diaper bag in the middle of the living room and waved him over. "Put her down on her back."

He was probably as awkward-looking as all hell, but he managed to set Brooklyn down gently without causing her to cry. The minute he withdrew his hands she kicked up a storm, and her sad face nearly broke him. "What did I do wrong?"

"Hold on there, little bean." Amber patted the little girl's tummy. Brooklyn wound up to cry, but Amber tickled her belly and Brooklyn laughed instead. The sound of her voice had a calming effect on the child, and he couldn't imagine doing any of this without Amber. He wasn't sure what he owed for the favor this had become. "Take a diaper from the bag next to me."

He did, ignoring the sizzle of attraction he felt when his arm brushed against her shoulder.

Amber unzipped the pink onesie pajamas and pulled each tiny foot out. Her motions were fluid, and she made it look so easy. She opened and closed the tabs on the diaper the baby already had on a couple of times as a demonstration.

"Open yours up. Figure it out. Pretend it's something mechanical and take it apart. There's not much to one of these." She leaned over and bumped his shoulder. The electricity pulsing between them from contact sent a jolt of heat rocketing through him. "My brothers' kids each seemed to have a different kind of diaper when they were this age. One needed a certain no-leak protection and another needed a specific night guard fabric."

"You mean there's more than one kind of these?" He couldn't imagine why.

"Afraid so," she said.

Rylan played around with the diaper, pretending he didn't just have the over-the-top chemistry reaction to Amber Kent. "This is pretty basic."

"Until you try to put it on a wiggly baby." Amber was making cooing sounds, and Brooklyn seemed enraptured.

He figured he could use the distraction to change a diaper.

Removing the other diaper was easy. The rest was a bit more complicated, but with Amber's help he managed his first successful diaper change.

"Does she have any other clothes in the bag?" Amber picked up Brooklyn while he checked.

"Nope. She has what she had on yesterday." There was nothing other than formula, diapers and wipes. But that was a lot, considering the way he'd received Brooklyn. "Someone cared about her, didn't they?"

"I hope so." Amber was busy putting the pj's back on her.

"Who takes the time to write a note, pack diapers and wipes but not extra clothing?" His mind churned. "For the most part it seems that someone wanted her taken care of. I mean, there are diapers at nearly every convenience store, but her mother wanted to make sure she had the ones Brooklyn uses."

"That's a good point. It makes me think she'd been considering her options for a few days at least," Amber said.

"Brooklyn might not be my daughter. Her mother could be someone I know. I still have no idea who she could be." Whoever the woman was must know that he wouldn't take a random person's word for it that he'd fathered a child.

"Maybe she figured it would take a couple of days for the paternity test to come back and by then she'd be out of trouble and able to take her daughter back," Amber agreed. "She could've picked you because you're loyal and might be the only one she knew who could handle himself in a dangerous situation."

Which made the odds Brooklyn wasn't his child drop pretty damn drastically if he was right. But then, he'd most likely spent one or two nights with the woman in question. Wasn't exactly a recipe for knowing him, and the idea that she'd been desperate didn't sit well.

A knock sounded at the front door.

Amber gasped.

Chapter Eight

Amber didn't mean to startle the baby. She reminded herself just how much little ones picked up on the emotions and energy of everyone around them.

"It's okay, sweet princess," she soothed.

"I'll take care of whoever it is." Rylan pulled a weapon from underneath the cushion of the chair he'd been resting in earlier. The sun was up but it was still early.

Several thoughts raced through Amber's mind. Was the baby's mother back? Amber should want that, but her heart squeezed thinking about Brooklyn leaving so soon. Had the guy from yesterday returned? That was all kinds of awful, too. It could mean that Deputy Perry had been jumped or worse. She didn't want to consider the possibility that he was outside somewhere hurt because of her.

It could be good news, like Zach had found the perp who'd tried to snatch Brooklyn from Amber's arms.

Rylan checked the peephole. "I'll be right there, Zach."

He returned his weapon to its hiding place before opening the door and ushering her cousin inside.

One look at the tension lines on Zach's face and she knew something was wrong.

"You need to come back to the ranch." His lips formed a grim line. "A body was found near Rushing Creek. Female. Early to midthirties. You can ride with me if you like."

"Oh, Zach. That's terrible." Every possible worst-case scenario fought for attention in Amber's mind. "Is everyone accounted for at home?"

"Yes. Your sisters-in-law and Amy have all checked in." Zach's brows furrowed. "You gave us a scare, though. I must've called your cell ten times trying to reach you."

"My battery must've died." She regretted her word choice under the circumstances and wished she could take that last one back. She couldn't, and it wouldn't change what had happened on the ranch. It was heartbreaking.

"Everyone would rest easier if they could put eyes on you. Plus, the family wants to meet and talk about what's happening," Zach said.

Amber picked up Brooklyn and held her to her chest to keep the little girl from crying, and to give herself something to do besides give into the mounting panic attack. A woman was dead. A family was about to receive the worst possible news and suffer an unimaginable loss. Her heart ached for the victim and her family.

"Everyone on staff has been accounted for," he added. She couldn't feel much relief considering some poor soul had been killed.

"He used the same MO as the Jacobstown Hacker," Zach continued.

Her gaze bounced from Zach to Rylan. His confusion was knitted across his forehead, and she realized he must not have kept up-to-date on Jacobstown. Of course, he hadn't. He'd cut himself off from the family and, as far as she knew, hadn't been in contact with anyone recently. "Over the past few weeks, someone has been killing animals. He's specific in the way he kills them by hacking off their left paw or hoof. Up to now, the jerk had focused on animals. Now everyone's fears that he would move onto people are being realized."

"I didn't know." There was so much compassion and reverence in his voice.

"Come with me, Rylan. *Please*." She added that last part as a plea because she didn't want to leave him or the baby. Whatever had happened between him and her brother needed to be set aside, and she'd remind him of that if push came to shove. She hoped it wouldn't come to that.

"I'll get your coat," he said. She expected an argument from Rylan and was pleased when she didn't get one. There was no time. Her heart hurt for the woman at the creek. Anger burst through her that someone could get away with that on her family's property.

Rylan located her coat, which he'd hung in the closet and helped her into it. Zach stood by the door, waiting for them to get themselves and the baby ready. Amber caught him watching her as she interacted with Brooklyn, and she knew exactly what was on his mind.

Amber stopped short of the door. "We don't have a car seat for her."

"I borrowed one from Deputy Perry. He's buckling it in my SUV now." Zach opened the door and the trio followed him, with Rylan closing in from behind. His home was a half hour from the main house at the ranch.

This early in the morning Zach made good time cutting across town.

Isaac was working security at the front gate. He waved them by. Amber wasted no time exiting the SUV. She tried to help unbuckle Brooklyn, but her hands shook too hard. Rylan took them in his—a move that shouldn't calm her but felt like a lifeline to sanity—and caught her gaze. He didn't say anything and yet his presence comforted her.

Amber took in a calming breath and managed to usher in Rylan's masculine scent, all pine and outdoors.

"Go on in. I'll be right there," he said.

"Okay." She couldn't imagine that it was easy for Rylan to face her family home again, and it meant the world to her that he'd come along. Strange as it might seem to an outsider since she'd only been around him and the baby a short time, they felt like part of her family, too. She told herself it was because Rylan and Will had been attached at the hip for so many years up until the summer before senior year when Rylan's mother had passed away. Then, he'd stopped coming around and Will seemed a little lost without his best friend. Amber had confronted her brother about abandoning his friend when Rylan needed him most. That had gone over about as well as sriracha on a ghost pepper.

Mitch, the eldest brother, greeted Amber in the entrance to the main living room. She could hear low chatter coming from the kitchen area. The low hum buzzed toward her, and the tone made the air heavy, like dull gray rain clouds hovering in the sky before it opened up into a show of thunder and lightning.

"The kids are at my place with Joyce. Everyone else is here, including Will," Mitch said after a hug. Joyce had been their loyal caregiver since the day the twins were born. His twins had been the first babies in the Kent family. Being the eldest brother, he probably felt more responsibility for taking care of everyone in the family. Which was most likely the reason he'd taken Amber outside to tell her when his wife had become pregnant a couple of years ago. He'd chosen his words carefully. He'd been keenly aware of what she'd been through and even time didn't seem to heal the wound of losing her child. Amber appreciated Mitch for caring. But she really didn't expect the rest of the family to stop living their lives because of her loss. It was hers.

"Does he know where I've been and who I've been helping?" She wouldn't change a thing about the past twenty-four hours; she just needed to know what she was up against.

"Yes," Mitch admitted.

Amber took in a deep breath. "Let's go."

Four brothers and three sisters-in-law sat around the large hand-carved wooden table in the massive kitchen. Seven sets of eyes landed on Amber when she walked into the room. She picked Will first. Better stare him down straightaway so he knew better than to call her out. His wife, Kelly, sat to his right. The pair had been through hell and back when Kelly was almost forced to marry a Fort Worth millionaire who was out for revenge. Amber's brother Deacon and his wife, Leah, sat across the table from the others. Leah used to work for the city of Fort Worth as a detective. She'd been targeted by a murderer posing as a copycat. In the process of investigating her case, she'd met and fallen in love with Deacon. The other couple at the table was Nate and Chelsea. She'd moved to town after an inheritance from an aunt she never knew gave her a new lease on life. But trouble soon followed, and Nate stepped up to protect Chelsea and her daughter. In the process, she and Nate had fallen in love, married and the three, plus Linda, her mother, had settled into his house on the ranch. Which left Jordan and Amber, the single siblings in an increasingly small club.

Mitch and his wife, Andrea, sat side by side. He held on to her hands, and witnessing the comfort the pair—and all the couples—seemed to provide each other struck Amber. She'd never felt hollow inside. So, where was it coming from now?

Amber expected to find disapproval in Will's eyes, but he mostly seemed concerned. He acknowledged her with a grim smile. It was most likely the weight of the situation at Rushing Creek that had him casting his gaze down and not his disappointment in her.

Zach entered the room last, and all attention went to him as Amber took a seat at the granite island toward the back of the kitchen. She couldn't be in this room anytime around the holidays without thinking just how alive it had been in past years. Maybe it was time to change that, to bring some of that love and vibrancy back to the main house. It was a point worth considering because it was so easy in life to focus on what she didn't have instead of seeing and appreciating all that she did.

"Here's what we know so far." He looked up from his notes. "This information stays inside this room, by the way."

"Goes without saying," Mitch added.

"There hasn't been confirmation of the victim's identity." Zach paused. He took caring for the people of Jacobstown seriously, and a murder in his backyard was a big hit. Especially considering the murder had happened at the family ranch.

"She was found by Lone Star Lonnie on his morning rounds. He went farther north along the creek bed chasing wild boar." Lone Star Lonnie was the foreman of KR aka Kent Ranch. "Coroner says she'd been dead for less than twelve hours. I have deputies on the scene, and Lonnie refuses to leave."

Last night was Saturday. Amber's hands fisted in her lap. This shouldn't have happened. "I realize there hasn't been confirmation, but do we have any idea who the victim might've been?"

"Lonnie did the right thing by not contaminating the crime scene. He kept his distance. Mike will text me the minute he knows something." Zach referred to Mike Travis, the county coroner.

A thought struck that Amber couldn't ignore. Could the victim be Brooklyn's mother? The baby was outside with Rylan. Was that part of the reason he'd refused to come inside? Was he thinking the same thing? It was unbearable to know any life could be cut short. Amber's heart clenched thinking that Brooklyn's mother might be the one…

"Town will want answers today about the victim, her killer and how this happened," Mitch said. He was always thinking two steps ahead, and Amber appreciated that about her brother.

"Every woman will be looking over her shoulder from now until we catch the perp," Deacon chimed in.

"I'll help in any way I can," Leah offered.

Zach thanked her.

"My office won't release information until we have

all the facts," he said. "But it never hurts to issue a statement about making sure folks lock doors and keep vehicle keys with them, like we've requested in the past."

Rylan walked into the adjacent room with Brooklyn in his arms. One look at his face, and Amber could tell she'd guessed right a few minutes ago. He wore a heavy expression like he carried the weight of the world.

"If y'all will excuse me." Will stood and then walked out the back door.

"Will," Amber started, but stopped when she saw the momentary hurt darken Rylan's features. For a split second, Amber considered going after her brother. Will needed air, and he needed to accept the fact that she and Rylan were friends. Granted, what was happening felt like more than friendship to her, and she thought Rylan experienced that same heat when the two of them were in the room together. But those were facts she didn't want to examine at the moment.

Amber refocused on Will. She knew her brother well enough to realize he needed space. Rushing out there now would only hurt her cause, and both of them could end up saying words they'd regret.

"Welcome back to town, Rylan." Mitch extended the first olive branch. "I'd offer a handshake, but I can see yours are full at the moment."

"Thank you," Rylan said, and she'd never heard two more sincere words from a single soul.

"Who is that sweet little girl in your arms?" Kelly, Will's wife, asked after introducing herself.

"That's a great question." Rylan gave a quick rundown of what happened yesterday. "All we know for certain is that her name is Brooklyn."

Leah seemed to catch onto the implication that

Brooklyn's mother could possibly be the victim. She introduced herself to Rylan before saying, "If you need someone to go with you to the morgue, I was a detective in a past life."

"I appreciate the offer. I'm hoping it doesn't come to that," Rylan admitted after thanking her, as well. Seeing the family, save for Will, welcome Rylan so openly caused Amber's heart to squeeze.

Andrea introduced herself, followed by Chelsea.

While introductions were being made, Amber thought back to what Rylan had told her about his sobriety. The simple truth was that he may not be able to positively ID the victim if she was Brooklyn's mother. His mind was still fuzzy about what happened that weekend, and she took to heart the seriousness in his voice when he spoke about being sober. There was so much regret and self-reproach at the possibility he'd slipped up and had a weekend binge. The fact that he hadn't had a similar one since the very early days of his sobriety struck a chord.

Zach, who had been studying his phone, walked over to Rylan. "I put the description of the man who dropped Brooklyn off at your place in the database. I flagged the file as urgent. I also just heard back from the sketch artist. She can meet this afternoon if you're still game."

Rylan was already nodding. "Of course. I want to do whatever I can to help."

"I'm probably just being Pollyanna here, but maybe we'll get lucky and the baby's mother will show up to reclaim her," Chelsea offered.

"That would be a best-case scenario for the little girl. Of course, there are legal ramifications for dropping off a baby and disappearing," Zach pointed out.

"There are no easy answers on this one." Rylan held on to the little girl, who was starting to fuss. Her gaze was locked on to Amber. From the looks of it, she found a new friend.

Mitch issued a warning look. There would be concerns from her family. They loved her and were keenly aware of her loss. Deacon was discreet, but she caught him watching her a little too intently. For now, she wanted to keep the focus on the victim and not bring up what she was doing with Rylan—other than helping an old friend after the holidays who'd been put in an impossible situation.

"It's not safe back at my house." Rylan was finally alone with Amber in the kitchen after a round of everyone wanting to meet Brooklyn. He couldn't deny the kid was cuteness times ten. She'd reeled him in almost immediately. He appreciated the kindness the Kent family showed to the little girl.

Will walking out after Rylan had come inside was a blow. He couldn't say he didn't deserve it or have it coming. It just hurt.

"After what happened last night on the ranch, I don't think it's safe anywhere." Amber blew out a defeated breath. Then she looked up at him. "I'm going with you."

"I'd argue with you but I've seen that face before," Rylan said. His cell buzzed in his pocket. He fished it out and checked the screen. "It's the doctor."

He and Amber exchanged glances. This phone call had the ability to alter that little girl's future in a big way.

"I'll hold her." Amber took the little girl, who seemed more than happy to make the switch.

Rylan answered the call and walked over to the sink. He could see the sun bathing the yard in light. "Thanks for getting back to me so soon, Dr. Logan."

"I drew two samples, one for Zach to be locked up as evidence and the other to be sent to a lab for analysis. I had a friend open the lab and speed up the process as a favor. You deserve to know what you're dealing with, although this is unofficial word when it comes to the courts." Doc paused. "She's your daughter."

Those three words should be a gut punch. They weren't. He'd allowed that little bean to worm her way into his heart. Rylan had expected the news to hit hard. A piece of him was relieved. He tried to convince himself it was for Brooklyn's sake, that he would do a better job of protecting her than anyone else. That part was most likely true.

"Thank you, Doc," he said into the phone.

"I hope you got the news you were hoping for," Dr. Logan said.

"I appreciate the sentiment, Doc." Rylan stared out the window for a long moment, absorbing the fact that he was someone's father. And then he turned to face Amber, who'd already moved beside him, and nodded. "She's mine."

"Are you okay with the news?" she asked.

"She's a great kid. She deserves to have someone looking out for her who cares. I'm ready to be that person." Rylan meant every word. "This might not be the way I'd envisioned becoming a father. Hell, I've never held the wife and kids fantasy. But here she is. I have every intention of doing right by her."

"Excuse me." Zach's voice came from behind them, interrupting their conversation. Based on his tone, he wasn't there for casual chatter.

Rylan turned around.

"My deputy just called. We got him. The man you described who dropped off the baby and ran yesterday morning is in custody." Zach put a hand up. "Now, I know what you're going to say and I'd probably want to do the same thing if I was in your shoes—"

"I doubt you do." Hearing the words inside his head that he was a father was about as foreign as it got. "I'm going down to your office with you."

"I wasn't about to say that you shouldn't come. I need you to identify him. All I wanted to be clear about is that you can't speak to him. You have to give me your word you'll stay on the other side of the mirror and not try to catch him in the hallway when he's being moved back and forth." Zach must've seen the tension building in Rylan's features because he kept talking. "Think of it this way. We make the right moves with this guy, and we find this girl's parents."

"Let me stop you right there, Zach. I just got a call from Dr. Logan. You'll get the official results soon enough, and they'll reveal that I'm Brooklyn's father."

Chapter Nine

After delivering the news that Rylan was Brooklyn's father, there wasn't much else that needed to be said. He had the rapt attention of everyone in the room. He turned to Amber. He'd tell her not to come with him, but he wasn't one for wasting time. She'd insist. "Are you ready?"

"Yes." The word was spoken in a firm and confident voice. No one could argue she knew what she wanted. "Can we borrow a few baby clothes before we head out?"

"We keep a few things here at the main house. I'll go grab some," Mitch said.

"While you guys wait for those, I'll get on the road. I need a five-minute head start." Zach left first.

Amber picked up the diaper bag and slid the strap over her shoulder. She looked at her family like she was daring one of them to speak. Will, the one person Rylan wanted to speak to the most, was outside somewhere, most likely in the barn. Work did a lot of good to clear the mind. It was also a great outlet for anger, an emotion Rylan understood all too well.

"Thank you for your hospitality." Rylan meant those words.

Mitch returned with a few items that he handed to Amber. He walked over and put his hand on Rylan's shoulder. "It took a lot to show up here, Rylan. You always were like family. If you need anything come back any—"

"Thank you, but I doubt everyone shares that sentiment." He motioned toward the barn.

"You know Will. He needs a minute. But he'll come around." Mitch set his jaw, looking confident in those words.

"Some people don't deserve forgiveness," Rylan said to Mitch.

"That's where you're wrong. Everyone does." Mitch squeezed Rylan's shoulder before leaning in close to his ear. "She'd kill me if she knew I said anything. But take it easy with her."

Rylan issued a grunt. "Amber can—"

"Hear me out," Mitch interrupted. "She probably didn't tell you but she was married before."

"Amber?" She never said anything about a husband. Why did it hit him so hard that she'd kept something so big a secret?

"It didn't go well for her. There was a child involved and—"

Those words hit like another rogue wave. It was starting to make sense why the family seemed so concerned when she'd taken Brooklyn in her arms. Anyone could see those two were natural together. Had she been married to a man who'd had a child in a previous relationship? It made sense as to why she'd been so cautious with him.

"Based on your expression I'm guessing you had no clue about either one of those things," Mitch said.

"Not a one." Rylan was still trying to absorb the first of the two revelations.

"I shouldn't have said anything. Those are not my secrets to share. I just don't want to see her heart ripped out—"

"You're trying to protect her."

Amber walked into the kitchen. She froze when she saw the two of them in intimate conversation. She balled a fist and planted it on her hip. "What's going on in here?"

"We were just talking," Rylan started, but she grunted.

"I figured that much out. You plan on telling me what you were talking about?" she asked.

"We can talk on the way over to Zach's office. Did you pick up your phone charger?" Rylan hoped the distraction would work.

It seemed to when she spun around and walked out of the room. She returned a few minutes later looking more than ready to go.

"Zach was our ride," Rylan pointed out. And he'd left minutes ago.

"I have more than one vehicle, Rylan. And I keep a car seat in the back of my small sport utility." Amber's gaze moved from Mitch to Rylan. "What were the two of you talking about?"

"I was just giving Rylan some kid advice," Mitch said, sidestepping the question.

"You sure that's all?" Amber asked her brother.

"I told him to be cautious with you and that if he hurt you I'd be on his doorstep." He walked over and put his hands on her shoulders.

"You know I'm a big girl, Mitch. I appreciate you

having my back, but I'm capable of fighting my own battles," she said.

"Maybe I think you shouldn't have to fight anyone anymore." Mitch pulled her into a bear hug. "Love you, sis."

"I know you do." Amber returned the hug cautiously. "But we've gotta go."

Rylan took the lead, walking toward the door. Part of him needed to know what had happened to her. He wanted, no needed to know if what Mitch said had anything to do with the seriousness in her eyes. Years ago, she'd been all spunk and spark and fire. Her heart was bigger and more open than the Texas sky. And he could still see those qualities in her, but some of that spark had dimmed and he wondered how much it had to do with her ex, with having a child taken away from her.

Thinking about anyone hurting Amber caused a fire bolt to swirl through Rylan.

Leah stopped them at the front door. "Have you guys considered leaving the baby here until you figure out what's going on at Zach's office? We have plenty of qualified family members here to take care of her, and there are lots of kiddos on the ranch. I doubt anyone would notice one more."

Before Rylan could form an argument, Amber answered for him.

"She'll be safer with us, and Rylan wouldn't be able to concentrate if she's away from him," she said. She was right, and he was surprised that she could read him so well. "But we're grateful for the offer."

"Let us know if that changes. Any one of us could come pick her up at Zach's office if the situation drags on or gets too tense." Deacon moved beside his wife, nodding his agreement with what she said. He put his arm around her, and Rylan was struck at how happy they seemed.

"Thank you," Rylan said, and he meant it for both of them.

Amber added an extra blanket over the baby. Rylan opened the door for Amber, who walked outside and into the brisk afternoon air. She shivered. "It's gotten even colder."

A blanket of gray clouds covered the sky, making it feel later in the day than it was.

Amber handed him the keys to her small sport utility after helping to buckle Brooklyn into her car seat. She stopped long enough to ask, "What did Mitch really say to you in the house?"

"Enough to make me curious about your past," he admitted before taking the proffered keys and moving to the driver's seat.

Amber put some muscle into closing her door after getting inside. "Did he tell you that I was married?"

"Yes. But that's all. He said it was a long time ago." Rylan turned the key in the ignition, and the engine hummed to life. He put the gearshift in Reverse.

"What else did he say?" she demanded, and her voice was a study in calm. He couldn't decide if that was good or bad.

There was no point beating around the bush, and he didn't like the idea of hiding information from her, so he came out with it. "Did your husband have a kid?"

"*I* had a child, Rylan. He was stillborn—"

"I'm so sorry, Amber. It's none of my business. You

don't have to talk about it if you don't want to." His heart fisted in his chest thinking about the pain she must've endured as he pulled off the drive and put the transmission in Park.

He turned to her as she stared out the front windshield. "I was out of line bringing it up, Amber. And so was Mitch. He never should've stirred that pot."

"That's the thing, Rylan. I never talk about him. My family always tiptoes around the subject and I get it. They're afraid of dredging up the past, and I love the fact that they want to protect me. From what I can see that can be rare in families, and I wish more people had loved ones who would do just about anything for them." She paused and he let her catch her breath as a few tears rolled down her cheeks. "But I'm done talking about this for now. We have a little girl in the back seat who needs all of our attention."

"When you're ready to keep going, I'm here." A dozen questions fired off in his mind. This wasn't the time for any of them. He couldn't help but wonder if losing a baby was what caused the sadness in her eyes. It was a flash, and he'd almost missed it a few times already. There was another emotion present when she held Brooklyn that made sense to him now.

"That means a lot to me, Rylan."

She turned to face him, and he leaned over the armrest to brush his fingertips across her cheek. "I wish there was something I could say or do that could take that pain away from your eyes, Amber."

"No one can take that away, Rylan. But you can do something," she said.

"Name it. I'll do anything." He meant it, too.

"Kiss me."

"THAT'S NOT A GOOD IDEA," Rylan said, but there was no conviction in his tone.

She leaned toward him, and they were so close she could breathe the same air. His masculine scent filled her senses, destroying her ability to think clearly. "No. It's not. But it's too late for me."

With that, he dipped his head and claimed her mouth. She parted her lips for him and teased his tongue inside. For something that should be avoided at all cost, kissing Rylan sure felt right in the moment.

But then she'd thought about the one kiss they'd shared in high school more times than she cared to admit. She could be real about it. He'd most likely been drinking. In fact, back then she thought she tasted alcohol on his breath. When she'd accused him of kissing her because he was drunk, he'd laughed and told her he kissed her because he realized how beautiful she was. That night at the bunkhouse, where she'd often gone to clear her thoughts, he'd looked at her like it was the first time he'd really seen her. She'd changed over the summer and had grown two inches, to her current height.

And ever since he opened the door yesterday, she'd been wanting him to kiss her again to see if it would be as magical as it felt that night.

Rylan's hands came up to cup her face, and she brought hers up to get lost in his thick dark hair.

She'd never experienced so much passion in a kiss with any other man, not even the one she'd been married to.

The skill with which Rylan kissed Amber caused her mind to snap to other pleasures she figured he'd mastered, as well. She could only imagine the sparks that would fly in the bedroom based on the heat she was experiencing right then.

The baby cooed in the back seat, breaking into the moment.

Amber pulled back first, and he stopped her with his hands. He looked into her eyes, and it felt like he was looking right through her.

"Damn," he said under his breath. That one word was about the sexiest thing Amber had heard.

She laughed at herself and he cocked an eyebrow.

"That's not a response I'm used to in situations like this," he said, but then he smiled, too.

"I don't doubt you have a lot of experience in situations like this, Rylan Anderson," she quipped.

"That might be true. But none have ever felt like this."

Now it was her turn to say the word *damn*.

With that, he turned his attention back to the road ahead. He navigated back onto the driveway and onto the farm road.

Amber didn't ask how long Rylan planned to stick around. Staying in one place seemed to suffocate Rylan once he turned eighteen. He'd never been good at holding on to a possession for more than a few months. The pattern was always the same. He'd get a new motorcycle, and it would be all the rage for a few weeks. He'd tire of it and sell it only to buy a four-wheeler a few days later. The only certainty was that he'd get bored with his latest toy and move onto something *or someone* else. She figured some people didn't stick. They moved in and out of cities, jobs, lives. She would do well to remember that, because he'd moved out of hers once already. An annoying little voice reminded her that he'd come back to Jacobstown and that technically he didn't *leave* her.

Having a daughter would change him but nothing would tame him. He'd always walked the edge. He didn't grow up with money. He'd worked for every penny. But that didn't mean he spent it wisely. At least back then. She remembered the time he bought an old Jeep and then got bored with it before he was finished paying for it and lost money on the deal. It wasn't the money she worried about. Young people didn't have the same understanding of finances that someone with real responsibilities did. It was his attention span that bothered her.

Thick gray clouds rolled across the sky. Amber had a bad feeling in the pit of her stomach.

Luckily, Brooklyn had a full stomach. She was cooing happily by herself in the back seat. The two-lane farm road leading away from the ranch was empty at this hour on a Sunday. The temperature was dropping. The cold front was blowing through, and the temperature had dropped into the thirties. At least the temperature was above freezing and it was dry outside.

The conditions threatened to worsen, but the best thing about Texas weather was that it changed on a dime. People always said if someone didn't like the weather, all they had to do was stick around for five minutes and it would change. And if not five minutes, then a couple of days before the sun would shine and the days would warm up again.

Rylan cursed as he checked the rearview mirror.

An all-black sporty sedan roared up behind them. There were no markings on the vehicle. Amber took note of the plate. "I think we should keep an eye on this guy."

"Maybe we should turn around and head back to the ranch where we have backup," Rylan said. They'd driven halfway to Zach's office.

Amber briefly thought about making a call for help. She'd charged her cell enough at the house to be able to make a call. This far away who would be able to get to them? Amber's heart galloped. Trees lined both sides of the road. Turning around was their safest, and only bet. She studied the car behind them. "It almost looks like an unmarked vehicle."

"Why would law enforcement be out here on this farm road?" Rylan made a good point.

"Wish I knew." She glanced back at the sedan. "This doesn't feel right to me, Rylan. We rarely ever have another agency here in town that Zach doesn't know about. Maybe we should give him a call just to check in with him."

"That's probably smart," Rylan said.

Amber called her cousin, who picked up on the first ring. "We have a suspicious vehicle on our tail and Brooklyn is with us. Do you know anything about outside law enforcement being in the area?"

"I haven't heard a word. That doesn't mean another agency couldn't be involved, especially if Brooklyn was taken across state lines. We have no idea what we're truly dealing with, and I can't speak for another office," Zach stated. "What does the vehicle look like?"

She described it.

"What about the license plate? Maybe I can run it through the database and get a hit," he offered before seeming to think better of it and adding, "Although, any undercover operation would be blocked."

"It's worth a try." Amber chanced a glance behind.

Everything was quiet for a few seconds save for the sound of tires on the road and the unaware baby in the back.

"While I'm waiting to see if we get a hit, which vehicle is Rylan driving?"

"We're in my small SUV."

"Is that the one you take on cattle runs sometimes?" Most cattle ranchers used ATVs or pickup trucks and not horses like her family usually did. It was a tradition her father had started when they were young, and everyone kept it up most of the time.

"Yes."

"Have your weapon at the ready just in case there's trouble." She located her SIG Sauer in the glove compartment. Granted, it was normally her brothers going up against dangerous poachers, but she knew how to protect herself and she, like everyone else, carried anytime she went out on the property. A coyote could be lurking behind any tree or bush. Wild hogs were mean creatures, not to mention dangerous. And then there were poachers. She'd encountered the first two more times than she cared to count. She'd been spared the latter so far.

"I have DPS on the line. I need to put you on hold." Zach waited for acknowledgment, which she gave.

A grin lifted one side of Rylan's mouth. "I'd ask if you know what to do with that SIG, but I know better. Remember the time you shot a hole in my favorite ballcap?"

She couldn't help but laugh at the memory.

"You were just lucky it wasn't on your head at the time," she quipped, grateful for the momentary break in tension.

But then the sports sedan sped up toward the bumper.

"What do we do here, Rylan? What's our move?"

Chapter Ten

Lights swirled from the black sedan behind them. Amber wished Zach would come back on the line so he could tell them what to do.

"Anyone comes at us with a weapon we protect ourselves." Rylan pulled onto the shoulder of the two-lane road as he surveyed the landscape.

"This is bad," she said.

"If that little bean wasn't in the back seat and you weren't here, this would be right up my alley," he stated with one of those devastating smiles that was all Rylan. She tried to convince herself that it was the heat in the moment that sent a rocket of electricity shooting through her, and not the fact that she had a very real *and growing* attraction to the man in the driver's seat. "As it is, I have to consider both of you."

"Thanks for the confidence in my shot." Amber snorted.

"I just mean that if either of you got hurt because of me I'd never forgive myself. So, I can't be my usual self on a mission." His voice dipped when he spoke those words aloud. It always had a deep, musical quality that she could listen to all day. His voice poured over her like Amaretto over ice cream, melting her insides as it washed through her.

He covered her hand with his, and electricity pulsed through her. It was his masculine and all-male presence that did that to her, made her want things she knew better than to think about.

"I can take Brooklyn and run into the woods. No one would know this area better than me, and that would give you time to handle these guys on your own," she said.

The lights continued to swirl, but the driver didn't exit his vehicle. A pickup truck did come speeding up on the road in front of them, barreling toward them.

"Whatever happens next, I'm glad you came back, Rylan," she admitted. She wanted, no *needed* him to know that.

"Don't count me out yet, Kent," he countered with the sexy little smirk that dented the corner of his cheek. He was in his element.

A man in what looked like a state trooper uniform exited the vehicle. His tan uniform and hat seemed authentic.

"Something feels off, but I can't quite put my finger on it," Amber said.

The truck was getting closer as the officer walked toward them.

"Wouldn't he wait? I mean why get out of his vehicle on a two-lane road while a truck is steaming toward us?" Rylan had good questions.

"I'm concerned about this, Rylan." She scanned the officer and it struck her. "Zach never makes a traffic stop without his hand on the butt of his gun, in case of trouble. I've never seen any officer just walk up like this. Also, notice how much is missing from his belt?"

Rylan muttered the same curse she was thinking. Turning the steering wheel a hard left, he mashed the gas pedal. "Take the safety off and get ready to shoot if he so much as looks like he's about to pull his weapon and fire."

The tires peeled out as Rylan banked a U-turn and then navigated the small sport utility on the shoulder and past the black sedan.

"I sure hope you have a plan that doesn't involve getting rammed in the bumper by a pickup truck that weighs far more than my car." She braced for impact, and her thoughts immediately snapped to the little girl in the back seat. Even in a car seat she could be hurt by an impact.

The black sedan's engine revved, and then the vehicle spun around to follow them.

Rylan's reflexes were spot-on as he shifted to the right and swerved so that the pickup missed the bumper.

Zach returned to the line, and Amber gave her cousin the quick rundown and told him they were headed back toward the ranch with two vehicles on their tail. She ended the call. "He promised to send the closest deputy. He's also calling my brothers, so help should be here in a few minutes."

Rylan pushed the SUV as fast as it could go, outmaneuvering the other pursuing vehicles, and she could see why he was the best at what he did. His confidence was earned. She and the baby were handicaps that he wasn't used to accounting for.

Amber was ready with her SIG, but she really didn't want to get a shooting match started. There was no telling where a stray bullet might end up, and she wouldn't risk Brooklyn's safety.

The road zigzagged ahead, and Rylan drove like an Indy driver on a hot track. He checked the rearview mirror a couple of times before she could visibly see tension leaving his shoulders as the other vehicles moved out of sight.

"They're gone. But I have bad news. You're stuck with me until this whole situation is settled."

"I get that we'll have to hide, but where can we go with an infant?" Traveling with a child wouldn't be easy. If Brooklyn cried at the wrong time, it could be game over. Even Amber realized that.

"Call Mitch. Let him know what just happened. Security needs to be made aware of another threat to the ranch. We can't take anyone's safety for granted." He was right.

The phone call home was short. She relayed the details. Everyone was already on high alert due to the murder that had happened last night. All Amber could think about was getting to her cousin's office and hearing what the mystery man who'd dropped off Brooklyn had to say. Certainly, he'd be able to describe the woman who handed over the baby, and that might jar Rylan's memory. Would she match the victim?

Right now, they had little to go on, and Rylan didn't seem able to remember being with Brooklyn's mother, or any other woman, during that time frame. He'd insisted that alcohol likely played a role in his memory loss, but after being around him she highly doubted that had happened. They would find another explanation if they looked hard enough. She believed that with her whole heart. "Do you think the guys who were following us will expect us to show up at the ranch? They could be circling back."

"I know a back way to Zach's office from here." Rylan made a couple of turns that would have them doubling back. His gaze was intense on the stretch of road in front of them. "I'm sorry I got you involved in this, Amber. I truly am."

"You didn't do anything on purpose." How could he have known how this would all shake out?

"I have no idea what Brooklyn's mother got herself into, but this isn't good and I'd bet anything now she got involved in something illegal." He gripped the steering wheel. That steel resolve was in his voice, but she didn't like the undercurrent of resignation that she picked up on, too.

"We'll find out soon enough. This guy at Zach's office will lead us to Brooklyn's mother—"

"Who might not still be alive," he stated.

"We can't think like that until we know for certain. I'm sure once you hear a description of her it'll all come back. We'll find her and figure out what made her leave this beautiful little girl and take off. I mean, she must've cared about her daughter because she did find a way to leave her with her father," Amber stated.

"What if—" He stopped himself. "No. Never mind."

"Go ahead. Say what you're thinking," she urged.

"I wasn't in a good place that weekend if I had a drink, Amber. There's a chance her description won't ring any bells. And then what? I've put you in danger for nothing." It wasn't exactly defeat in his voice that she heard, but she didn't like where this was going.

"If this guy gives us good information and if it clicks who he's talking about right away, then great. We still have to locate her, and from what I can gather so far, she seems to be in pretty big trouble. Look at that angel in the back seat. She's been well taken care of for three months. Her mother wouldn't do that if she didn't love her. And anyone who takes that good care of her baby can't be all bad. Maybe she got herself in a tough spot and went to the wrong people for help." Amber could only hope her words were sinking in. "It'll be okay. You'll see. This'll all be over soon, and you can start figuring out your next move. You can look forward to getting to know your daughter, Rylan. What could be better than that?"

Amber wiped away an unexpected tear as Rylan navigated into the parking lot of Zach's office, and then parked in a spot close to the front door.

THE SEDAN AND the pickup truck were gone for now. That most likely meant the drivers were on a scouting mission. Experience had taught Rylan that the men would return, ready to strike next time. They'd be better prepared. That was the only explanation for why they didn't shoot. Which led him to the conclusion that someone wanted Brooklyn.

They'd have to kill him to get to her. And based on the protective look on Amber's face as he walked beside her into her cousin's office, the same went for her.

Rylan had had bad days in his life. Hell, most of them could be considered bad once his mother passed away. There was something about that little girl in Amber's arms that gave him a sense of hope. He chalked it up to the innocence children brought, the new perspective on life. Brooklyn was a good baby, which most likely meant she'd been well cared for up to this point. Her whole life was ahead of her.

A thought struck Rylan as he held the door open for Amber. What if her mother never turned up? Or, worse, what if she turned out to be the victim? What if the thing she'd gotten herself into caused her to lose her life? Other thoughts joined. What if she was sick? What if giving Brooklyn to him was a last-ditch effort to give the baby a chance at life?

All those thoughts amounted to a hill of beans when it came to thinking about anything happening to that little girl. Was there a court in the world that would take her away from him? He hoped the hell not. Because he was all-in when it came to Brooklyn from now on. It was a foreign feeling to him. He hadn't felt like he belonged to something bigger than himself in too long.

Shoving those thoughts aside, he entered Zach's office.

"We're going down the hall." Zach pushed off his desk, stood and focused on Amber. "There were no hits on the vehicles you described."

"They'll be back," Rylan stated.

"We'll be ready." Zach's resolve almost had Rylan believing the man could handle whatever entered his county. But Rylan didn't have time for false hope. This was bigger than Zach and his deputies. Besides, they had a murder to investigate. "But first, follow me."

Rylan put his hand on the small of Amber's back and ignored the heat pulsing through his fingertips from the contact. This wasn't the time to notice the attraction sizzling between them or think about the kiss they'd shared. Or the fact that he'd never experienced a pull this strong to any other woman.

He forced the thoughts to the back of his mind and refocused on the man who started all this. The blond.

The small room down the hallway from Zach's office had low lighting, no doubt because of the one-way mirror. The room itself wasn't much bigger than a walk-in closet. The space on the other side of the mirror doubled in size. There was a table and two chairs placed opposite each other. The white tile seemed sterile and like what Rylan would find in a hospital hallway. The walls were barren and gray. The only wall decoration visible to Rylan was an analog wall clock. It was circular, about a foot in diameter with large black numbers. The timepiece hung above the only door in and out of the space.

Everything about the room was meant to make someone uncomfortable. It was damn smart because Rylan was uncomfortable looking inside.

The door opened and a deputy walked in with a man in cuffs shuffling behind him. Rylan recognized the man immediately as the one from yesterday, and he felt the tension stiffen his shoulders. He rolled them back to loosen the knots, but it didn't do any good.

"Is it him?" Amber was studying Rylan, and he figured she already knew the answer to that question.

"He's the one." Those three words confirmed what she clearly had already guessed.

The man wore a camouflage hunting jacket, blue jeans and boots. He was much shorter than Rylan, not six feet tall if he had to venture a guess.

Deputy Perry instructed the suspect to sit. From opposite the table his shoulders were square with Rylan, which was good. The man was close enough for Rylan to see clearly. The interview room was small, and he figured it was designed that way on purpose.

He felt Amber move beside him with the baby in her arms.

The deputy's back was to them. "State your name."

"Chester Hunter III, but my friends call me Chess." Chess sat on the edge of the seat as he wiped his palms on his thighs. Rylan could only guess the man had sweaty palms. Chess displayed other signs of nervousness. Sweat beaded on his forehead, and he blinked at a rapid pace. He spoke a little too fast, and his voice was a higher pitch than Rylan remembered.

Zach opened the door and popped his head in the viewing room. He looked at Rylan. "Can I get a positive ID?"

"I'm certain it was him," Rylan responded.

"He's not denying his involvement. The deputy asked him to wait to give a statement until I could make it in." Zach put a hand on Rylan's shoulder. "Let's hope we get the answers we're looking for."

"Do you live in Jacobstown?" Deputy Perry continued.

"No, sir. I'm from Bremmer City." Bremmer City was to the south of Jacobstown. Rylan had done some partying there in his youth before signing up for the military and righting his life.

"Did you bring a child to a residence in Jacobstown yesterday?" Deputy Perry jotted down a couple of notes. His posture was the opposite of Chess's. The deputy sat comfortably in the metal and plastic chair. His feet were apart, and he leaned forward on the table in between him and Chess.

"Yes, sir." Chess's right leg started shaking. The man looked to be in his late twenties.

"What's your occupation?" Perry asked.

"Mill worker," Chess replied. "I work for my father's construction company. He builds custom homes."

Perry asked a few follow-up questions.

"Can you describe the child in question?" Fact-checking was a routine part of any investigation.

"She was a little girl. Small enough to fit into one of those carriers you see people with all the time. Her hair was black, curly." He'd gone from a shaking leg to tapping the toe of his boot against the tile floor. "She was a cute kid."

"How old was she?" The deputy's voice was a study in calm. He was almost conspiratorial.

"I don't have enough experience with kids to tell. All I know is she was young enough and small enough to fit into the carrier." The words came out rushed.

"Did she have anything else with her?" Again, the deputy was confirming facts.

"Yeah. She had a diaper bag."

"Can you tell me how you came to be in possession of the child?" Rylan's ears perked up.

"Of course. I was pumping gas at the 401, the one by the Pig's Ear down on farm road 26. That's the one I always go to because gas is always cheaper than by the interstate." He blinked up at the deputy like competing gas prices were common knowledge.

The deputy nodded.

"So, I'm pumping gas when a woman holding a baby in a carrier comes up to me. She looked scared and her eyes were saucers, like a cornered animal's. She comes up to me and starts begging me to help her out. I'm looking all around expecting someone to charge up to us, or something—"

"Can you describe her?" Deputy Perry asked.

Rylan leaned toward the glass and listened.

"She was pretty. Her hair and eyes were brown, like coffee beans. She stood about yay high." He held his right hand up to his chin, which would make her about five feet five inches.

Rylan drew a blank.

The deputy scribbled more notes. "Can you describe what she was wearing?"

"Yeah. She had on some kind of shirt with jeans. The shirt was short-sleeved. Oh, and flip-flops. I noticed because I thought it was weird she wasn't wearing a coat or real shoes since it was so cold out." His gaze was fixed but there was nothing on the walls to stare at, and it was one of those blank stares like when someone recalled facts.

To Rylan's thinking, the guy seemed legitimate. He was definitely the man from the other day. There was no question. Rylan had wondered if Chess was involved. Based on his reactions and what he said so far, there was nothing to make Rylan believe that was true.

Deputy Perry glanced up. "Did you say flip-flops?"

"I thought that was weird, too," Chess stated. "The kid was bundled up, though. She had a warm blanket over her and a hat on."

Flip-flops on a frigid day. No coat. The mystery woman was in a hurry, which supported the idea that she'd been in grave danger. Could she be from the area?

Chess's statement made Rylan think the mystery woman had found out at the last minute that someone was coming for her or the baby. The last thought struck a chord. Was the mystery woman in trouble herself and trying to off-load the baby, or was someone after Brooklyn instead?

The fact that someone was *still* after the little girl—his daughter—gave him the strong impression she was the target. Had they gotten to Brooklyn's mother? Had she disappeared in time, afraid to show up while the men chasing her were in town?

There were more questions than answers in this case.

Amber looked to Rylan expectantly.

He shook his head. "I don't know who she is."

"Did she have any distinguishing marks? Scars? Birthmarks? Tattoos?" Deputy Perry returned his focus to the notepad as he scribbled.

"Not that I can think of." Chess returned his focus to the spot it had been before. And then his face twisted. "You know, now that you mention it she did have a birthmark on her neck. It was low, close to her collarbone. On her left side because facing me it was on the right."

That struck a chord. A vague memory tried to take shape in Rylan's mind, but it was still a blur. He'd been running on no sleep for weeks during a mission in Kandahar. And then he'd gone to San Antonio for the last three months where he'd remained until getting his papers and moving to Jacobstown.

There was a time in his life when finding out he'd had a child after a weekend of partying wouldn't have surprised him. Granted, he wouldn't be proud of himself. But he wouldn't be shocked, either.

Looking back, shame for the way he'd handled his stress, his life, engulfed him like an out-of-control forest fire. Now that his head was clear, he could acknowledge that he'd used alcohol to deal with the stress of losing his mother before he was out of high school. He'd worked hard and partied even harder until that last time when he was so out of it he caught the Willows' crops on fire. He'd been so out of it that he'd almost died. It was a wake-up call. After that, he realized he needed to deal with his pent-up emotions in a healthier manner. Truth of the matter was that he'd wanted to be a better man. The desire had spread like a wildfire after Will had lied in order to protect Rylan.

Becoming sober hadn't been easy. He'd attacked it like everything in his life. He'd gone all-in. He'd realized that he needed to open up and talk, let people in rather than hold everything inside. He'd started talking after that instead of ignoring his pain and little by little was able to let the past go.

Admitting he'd needed help went against everything inside him as a soldier who'd been trained to rely on himself and take care of everyone else around him. Until he realized it made him far more of a man to own up to his mistakes, to his weaknesses. The hardest damn thing had been taking an honest look in the mirror.

Rylan would never be free of the shame, the guilt until he made things right in Jacobstown. He had two apologies left to make. One to the Willow family and the other to Will Kent. He owed the Willows retribution. But how did he repay Will? How did he square with the man who'd stepped up and blamed his own negligence for the fire that devoured the Willows' crops and almost their livelihood?

Mr. and Mrs. Kent had stepped in to get the Willows

back on their feet. He couldn't apologize to them or thank them for what they'd done. But he owed the Kent family. He sure as hell wasn't repaying them by getting Amber mixed up in his life. That made two Kents who should know better than to put their trust in Rylan.

Chapter Eleven

Amber stared at the one-way mirror. Hearing details about a woman Rylan had had a fling with shouldn't have this effect on her. So, why did it?

One kiss, no matter how electric it had been, did not a relationship make. Besides, getting involved with Rylan beyond friendship would be a mistake. He seemed to realize it as much as she did.

She bounced Brooklyn on her hip, reminding herself that she had no claim on Rylan. The two were friends and he'd come to her for help, not for a relationship. Was there chemistry between them? She'd be a fool to deny it. They'd always been able to laugh and joke around when they were younger. She'd always felt a little spark whenever Rylan was over. That spark had ignited into a full-blown attraction.

And how smart was that on her part?

Pretty damn stupid.

Rylan might have a child—and she had no doubt this little girl would be the one thing that Rylan would stick to—but that didn't change who he was. He would always move on. Those words, that honesty shouldn't feel like a knife wound to her chest.

Amber needed to create a little emotional distance.

She took a step away from him as she examined the face of the man being questioned. Strange that he lived one town over but she had no idea who he was. It seemed like everyone knew each other in Jacobstown, but that wasn't exactly true. People moved in and out without being known.

Zach entered the viewing room. "How's it going in here?"

She knew what he was really asking. *Was any of this ringing a bell?*

"Not as well as I would like," Rylan responded.

"The coroner is sending over pictures of the victim in the hopes of a positive ID." Zach's voice held the respect of a deacon during Sunday morning church service.

Amber's heart went out to the little girl in her arms. It made sense that her mother would've given her to someone else if she suspected something was about to happen. Had her mother seen death coming? Was that why she'd made a bold move in making sure the child got to Rylan?

It was strange that Brooklyn's mother could be somehow tied to the Jacobstown Hacker. Or maybe she wasn't. Amber leaned toward Rylan and asked, "What do you think the odds of her mother being connected to the Jacobstown Hacker are?"

"I thought about that, too. Maybe she was an innocent victim of his, the perfect opportunity for him to finally strike." Rylan folded his arms across his broad chest.

Amber hugged Brooklyn a little closer to her. She couldn't imagine growing up without a mother. It was difficult enough to lose a mother as an adult. But as a child? Amber was even more grateful for the time she had with hers.

An argument could be made that Brooklyn's mother wasn't at the top of her game. She'd obviously gotten herself into some kind of trouble. She knew to stash her child away safely. Now that the paternity test had come back, it was certain that Rylan was the child's father.

What could Brooklyn's mother have possibly gotten herself into that could force her to hide her daughter? Coming to Jacobstown must've been a last-ditch effort. But showing up in flip-flops in late January, not wearing a coat?

Granted, it appeared as though she wasn't here on her own accord. She'd wrapped up the child in blankets and a hat before handing her off to a stranger and, what? Hoped for the best? That screamed of desperation. The woman didn't take time to put her own coat on.

The interview in the next room continued, and Amber realized she'd spaced out for a second.

"Did you ask the woman with the baby her name?" Deputy Perry continued.

"No. I didn't really think to at the time—"

"A woman thrusts her child at you and you weren't the least bit curious about her background?" Perry lifted a brow.

"It wasn't like that. She came up to me and begged me to take her baby. She said she needed help, but I told her to go inside the convenience store and tell the clerk. I told her to call the sheriff but—" His words came out faster this time. He'd already been rushing his speech, but he shifted in his seat and put his hands up to his face. "She said she couldn't involve the sheriff. Or something along those lines. I'd finished pumping my gas and was putting the nozzle back in the receptor by then. My first thought was that she was on something, but as she talked I realized she was scared."

"And what was your response?" There was no sound of judgment in the deputy's voice. Amber was too emotional to work in law enforcement. The thought of a man refusing to help someone in need riled her up too much. She'd never be so diplomatic. But then, that's probably one of many reasons she was a cattle rancher and didn't wear a badge.

"My mind immediately snapped to someone abusing her. That's when I looked for signs," he stated.

"And did you find any?" Deputy Perry spun the pen between his fingers as he waited for a response.

"That's when I saw the birthmark. No bruising, though. But that doesn't mean it wasn't somewhere on her body. She rattled off an address and said she needed to get the baby there ASAP." He paused for a beat. "She also said to make sure I wasn't followed."

"How did you respond to her?"

"I told her that I couldn't help her. She needed to go to the law." He flashed his eyes at the deputy. "I had a cousin who got shot for trying to help a friend of his who was in an argument with her boyfriend. I don't stick my nose where it doesn't belong."

Domestic violence was a serious issue. Amber had heard from Zach countless times those calls were the most dangerous. Domestic violence calls and traffic stops ranked up there as the most threatening to officers.

Still. Every one of Amber's brothers would stop to help any person in need. There'd be no question. She could tell by the way Rylan tensed that he would've done the same. That was his personality. He might be the type to move around and never settle in one place for long but he wouldn't turn down anyone who asked him for a hand.

"What happened next?" Deputy Perry kept the interview on target.

"She got a panicked look. Started looking from side to side like someone might jump out from behind the gas pump. I'd finished my business so I told her that I had to go inside and pay. I told her to come with me and call someone. That's when she took off running." He paused another beat. "I figured that was the last I'd see of her or her baby. But when my back was turned she sneaked the baby in the driver's seat and took off."

"How'd you remember the address?" Perry made a good point.

"Easy. My mom moved out that way when she and my pops divorced. I'd been over there more than a few times to visit. Mom used to live next door to Mrs. Parker." Chess seemed satisfied with himself for the answer.

Amber turned to face Zach. "Any chance he could be *him*?"

"He would've been the last one to see her alive if the victim turns out to be Brooklyn's mother, which makes him our top suspect," Zach stated. "And he just admitted to being familiar with the area."

"I picked up on that, too." A shiver raced down Amber's back. She turned and studied the man sitting at the table. Would she even know if she was staring at a killer?

"Does your mother still live at the same address?"

There was a slight difference to Perry's voice. She doubted Chess picked up on it.

"No, sir. She moved two years ago." If Chess was the Jacobstown Hacker, would he admit to knowing the area so freely? "My stepdad got work in Houston so they headed south."

"Do you come back to Jacobstown to visit friends?"

"Didn't have any. I'd stop by my mother's for lunch on Sunday a couple times a month. We didn't go out. I'd watch the game with Paul, her husband, and then head home," he admitted.

Zach's phone pinged. He checked the screen. "Coroner is sending over pictures of the victim."

Amber searched Rylan's face. He may not have had a relationship with the woman who could very well be the victim, but that didn't mean this would be easy. He'd spent time with her. They'd had a child. Granted, he didn't know about Brooklyn until two days ago, but a child connected people whether they wanted to be or not. She thought about the child she'd lost. About her ex, Red Coker. Losing their child had broken their relationship. Every time she thought about what happened to her baby, she ached. The pain hit her full force, like it had happened yesterday.

She shoved the thoughts down deep and refocused on Zach, who was pulling up an image on his phone.

He must've texted the deputy in the next room because he told Chess to sit tight and then left the room.

Chess fidgeted with his hands before leaning forward and resting his elbows on his knees. His right leg was going a mile a minute.

Zach stared at the image on his phone as he shared it with Rylan.

"There's no birthmark on her neck," Rylan pointed out. "It can't be her."

"Can I see? I might be able to help." She handed the baby to Rylan before walking over and standing next to her cousin. She wanted to protect the innocence of the child even though Brooklyn would have no idea what she was looking at. It didn't take but a second to recognize the victim. "I know who she is. That's Breanna Griswold."

Zach muttered a curse under his breath. "I remember that family."

"They moved away a few years ago saying they wanted a fresh start after Breanna got into trouble here. We were in the same grade in school, but we didn't hang out. She used to skip a lot. I think she got held back for nonattendance after freshman year of high school. I always felt so bad for her. She seemed sad all the time." Amber had invited her to sit together at lunch, but Breanna flat-out refused. "She kept to herself and never socialized. I saw her a few times hanging out with the McFarland boys, and we all know they turned out to be bad news."

Rylan suddenly got very still. She remembered overhearing a fight between him and Will about those brothers years ago. She figured this wasn't the time to reopen those old wounds. It was obvious by Will's actions earlier that he hadn't forgiven Rylan for whatever happened between them in the past.

She turned to Rylan. "Did you know her?"

He shook his head. "I have no idea why she would've been on the ranch."

Brooklyn tried to jam her entire fist inside her mouth. She started fidgeting in Rylan's arms.

"She's probably getting hungry," Amber stated, ignoring the look Zach issued. He could look all he wanted. It wouldn't stop her from getting to know Rylan's daughter. Besides, that man needed a hand if anyone did. He admittedly had no idea how to take care of a child. He didn't exactly have time to learn, either. She'd literally been thrust in his arms two days ago. "Can I help you get a bottle ready in the break room?"

Rylan glanced at Zach. "I don't want to get in the way of a family discussion."

He must've picked up on the feeling of being the monkey in the middle. She wasn't trying to put him in that position.

"Zach, you have anything else you want to say to me?" Amber's balled fist was on her hip now.

Her cousin shot a defeated look toward her. "I'm good."

"Then it's settled. I can take you to the break room. There's a microwave in there where we can heat up her bottle." Amber motioned for Rylan to follow. She thought about the offer to keep Brooklyn at the ranch and figured the idea deserved more consideration.

With a glance in Zach's direction, Rylan joined her in the hallway. He turned back to the sheriff. "Let me know if Chess says anything worth hearing."

"You bet."

"I can take her or the diaper bag. Which is a better help?" Rylan asked.

"You want to hold this muffin so I can figure out how to heat her bottle in that microwave? I never come here anymore," she admitted.

Brooklyn fussed the minute her daddy took her in his arms. "I don't think she likes me very much."

"You'll get the hang of it, Rylan. Give yourself a chance. The two of you just met." Amber looked at the baby, who was working up to belt out another cry. Her heart fisted while everything inside Amber rushed to comfort the baby. Yeah, she was in deep trouble. "I'll take her back and you can make the bottle."

"She met you *after* me." Rylan admitted defeat as he handed over the little girl. He followed Amber down the hallway and into the break room.

Amber rattled off instructions for heating the bottle as she rocked Brooklyn, offering what little comfort she could when all the baby really wanted to do was fill her belly.

Fifteen minutes and one crazy messed-up bib later, Brooklyn was sucking on a bottle of formula. It was dangerous to get too attached, Amber thought. And then she looked into those beautiful brown eyes that looked so much like the baby's daddy.

Thoughts of Breanna struck, of her family and how they would have to hear the worst news ever. Now Breanna's parents would suffer the heartbreak no parent should ever have to endure. Granted, Amber didn't wish that particular brand of pain on anyone. Having heard rumors about the family, she knew they wouldn't be described as close-knit. Did that really matter?

To her thinking, pain was pain. Loss was loss. And she wished she'd made even more of an effort to reach out to Breanna back in school. Would it have made a difference? Amber would like to think that everyone's actions could. Was she living in a fantasy world?

Maybe she didn't want to live in a world where they didn't.

Looking at Brooklyn, at her innocence, Amber had

to believe that everyone could make a difference in someone else's life. She would already do anything for the little girl in her arms. The thought was dangerous. Could she open up her heart again?

Chapter Twelve

Rylan studied Amber as Brooklyn slept against her chest. Ellen Haiden, Zach's secretary, had dimmed the lights in the break room, and Amber had moved to a leather club couch that was backed up against the east facing wall.

"I'm sorry about your friend," Rylan said.

"That's the thing—she wasn't."

He cocked an eyebrow.

"She had trouble at home. I heard rumors that she had it pretty rough. I invited her to sit at my lunch table, but she refused. I gave up even though I knew I shouldn't have." Her voice was laced with regret.

"How old were you?"

"I was in ninth grade. Old enough to know better," she said.

"Most kids that age can't be bothered to think about anyone but themselves. The fact that you noticed says how special you are." He took a seat on the arm of the couch and touched her cheek. Outside of the break room, activity was a blur. Here, with Amber, time seemed to slow and the setting felt intimate. It was just her. Being with her stirred places inside him. He still wasn't ready to figure out what that meant, but he was intrigued. No one had ever held his attention like she did. He'd never felt a draw this strong or wanted to reach out and touch a woman this badly.

And that's where he put on the brakes.

Amber was a friend, probably his only friend. He didn't need to go messing around with that. As long as he was in Jacobstown, and for the first time in his life he was thinking about sticking around somewhere more than a minute, he needed that friend.

Part of him wanted to say that he needed her, but he shut it down before it could gain any traction. Rylan didn't *need* anyone. He did, however, appreciate her help. So he wouldn't repay her kindness by taking her to bed, even though she gave him signs and his body tried to convince him it wouldn't end in disaster.

Besides, Will hated Rylan enough already. He didn't want to hurt his former best friend any further.

When Rylan had called Amber, he thought he was asking for a favor that might last a couple of hours. He never would've signed her up for what was going on. "You sure you want to keep doing this?"

"Doing what?" She bit back a yawn.

"Stick with me. I realize you're in danger, Amber. And you have a heart bigger than Texas, which is saying a lot. But there are places you could go to be safe," he said.

"Where? Like the ranch?" She twisted her mouth. "Look how well that worked out for Breanna."

She made a point. And he was still trying to figure out why she would've been on the family's ranch in the first place.

"Besides, Rylan, how do you know you didn't save my life?"

Now she was going overboard. "What does that mean exactly?"

"If I'd been on the ranch, that could've been me. This jerk was ready to strike. He's been ready. He's been biding his time, waiting for the right opportunity. What if that had been me out there instead of Breanna?" He couldn't argue the logic. And he appreciated her trying to take the burden off him.

"I hear what you're saying. We go back a long time," he started, "so don't take what I'm saying the wrong way. But I'd never forgive myself if anything happened to you because you were helping me."

She stared at him for a long moment. He expected her to put up a fight, but she seemed to be contemplating his words instead. She pursed full pink lips, and then she spoke. "I understand."

Silence sat between them, and he gave her a minute to rethink her position.

"I hear you, Rylan. I do. You've said it more than once. No matter how much this investigation heats up, I'm committed to helping you and this baby. You have a family, Rylan. How wonderful is that?" She put her hand up before he could comment. "Granted, I know the circumstances are not ideal. We'll find this baby's mother and figure out who she's running from. But at the end of the day you have a healthy and beautiful baby girl. That's a blessing some people never get."

Her words, her loss, was a gut punch. He must seem pretty damn selfish to her, considering she'd lost a child. He couldn't argue the point that Brooklyn was a beautiful kid. He had bigger fears about what the child's mother had gotten all of them into. From the sound of Chess's statement, Brooklyn's mother was scared half out of her mind. "We don't have any idea what's really going on. If I have a chance to protect you from it, I will."

"I know that, Rylan. I appreciate the fact that you care. Right now, you need me. You don't have the first idea how to take care of this little angel." Amber held that child tight against her chest. It was easy to see that someone would need pliers to pry Brooklyn from Amber's hands.

Rylan knew when he'd lost a battle. He wanted Amber's help, just not at the risk of losing her.

So, he conceded the argument for now and paced while he waited for word from Zach.

A half hour ticked by while they waited for Chess to work with a sketch artist.

The man was scared and, better yet, willing to cooperate. He was also the last known person to see Brooklyn's mother alive. Rylan could only hope she wasn't physically harmed. After hearing the story from Chess, it was clear that Brooklyn's mother was in serious danger.

About a year ago, Rylan remembered spending a lot of his leave time with a buddy. This was as good a time as any to make the phone call he'd been needing to make. Fishing out his cell, he told Amber about making the call and excused himself. It seemed wrong to talk about his time spent with another woman in front of her, like a betrayal.

Roger Hendricks answered on the first ring. "Rylan, man, are you in town?"

"Hey, Roger. Nah. I'm back in Jacobstown."

"Yeah? I heard you got out. Thought you might be up for a party," Roger said.

"Another time." Rylan had no plans to follow up on that. "I was hoping you could help me out, bro."

"Anything. You know I'd do anything for you, man," came Roger's response. The two had gone through basic training together before different deployments sent them to opposite ends of the world. They'd stayed in touch. Rylan had set his sight on elite forces, where Roger had served and then gotten the heck out, as he'd put it. His friend had said the only sand he wanted to see for the rest of his life was on a beach in the US. Rylan couldn't blame the man. Places like Kandahar weren't for everyone. "What's up?"

"I'm trying to locate a woman—"

"Who am I? Tinder?" Roger joked.

"Funny, bro. It's someone from last year. A friend of Sandy's." Sandy was Roger's girlfriend.

"Ah, yeah, Sandy. We had a good time together. But, man, we broke up months ago," he informed him.

"No worries, bro. What's Sandy's last name? Maybe I can find the person I'm looking for on her social media," Rylan explained. "It's important that I find her. I think she might be in some kind of trouble. I'd like to help her out."

"Good thinking. Bonds is her last name," Roger replied.

"Cool. Thanks, bro. I owe you one." Rylan didn't want to get into the whole baby business with his buddy. Not yet anyway. He was still coming to terms with the fact that he was that little girl's father.

He ended the call and located Zach in his office. The sheriff had a serious expression as he studied his computer screen.

Rylan knocked on the doorjamb.

"Sorry, I didn't see you standing there." Zach seemed caught off guard. "I have the sketch."

He motioned toward his desk and studied Rylan as he walked over and picked it up.

"I don't know." Rylan racked his brain. She seemed kind of familiar but he wasn't certain. "It's not ringing any bells."

"Sorry," Zach said. His tone said he meant it.

"I have the name of my buddy's ex-girlfriend. I just got off the phone with him a few minutes ago. I might be able to use her social media page to locate our mystery woman. Do you have a tablet I can borrow? Amber and I can search social media sites and see what we can come up with," Rylan said.

"Great idea." Zach searched around on his desk, and had to move a couple of files before he uncovered a tablet. He held it up. "Here you go."

Rylan thanked him and returned to the break room with the tablet in hand. He sat next to Amber. "Let's see what we can find on this."

"Who are we looking for?" Amber's shoulder touched his, and he ignored the impact the contact had on him. When the time was right, he planned to address it. He also planned to see how far another kiss would take them even though he knew better than to go there in his mind.

"I have the name of one of Brooklyn's mother's friends. Sandy Bonds. I thought we could check social media now that we have a face to go on."

He set the sketch of the mystery woman on his leg while he pulled up a popular social media site on the tablet and performed a search for Sandy Bonds. Several faces popped up. He searched each one until he recognized her.

"There she is. There's Sandy Bonds." Amber studied the page.

"Who has seven hundred–plus friends?" Rylan asked under his breath. Close friends he could count on one hand. Okay, maybe his best friend was sitting next to him. And that was another reason why he shouldn't be thinking about the kiss they'd shared or wanting more than that from her.

"I never did get into social media other than for the ranch. I started our page and post every once in a while on it," Amber said. "It helped get word out when we were changing our practices in order to provide organic meats to our customers."

Rylan remembered that he'd read something about her being a pioneer in the beef industry. He admired her business savvy, but he also knew she respected her animals.

He scrolled through the faces, searching for a resemblance to the sketch. Zach strolled in and joined them, sitting on the opposite side of Amber.

And then it happened. The face he was searching for filled the screen.

"Alicia Ward." Zach said the name out loud most likely hoping to trigger a memory.

"We have a name." Rylan shrugged. "It doesn't ring any bells for me, but at least we have a face and a name to go with it. Let's figure out who she is. Click on her page."

"Mind if I?" Zach clicked on the tile with her face and a profile filled the screen. Rylan would call this progress, except there wasn't much on her page save for a few stock pictures of animals with cutesy quotes underneath.

"How much do people have to fill out in order to show up on one of these sites?" Rylan asked.

"Not much and any information can be faked," Amber said. "There aren't as many controls as you'd think there should be. Pretty much anyone can make a page as long as they don't put up strange or offensive material to get their page reported."

Zach scrolled through the animal pictures, no doubt looking for some kind of clue about the woman they searched for. "There's no information about who she is or where she's from. Do you know if she's even from Texas?"

"We met in Austin while I was stationed in San Antonio for a training exercise. I was in and out in a few weeks. Went to my friend's house a couple of times in Austin. Hit Sixth Street to listen to live music. I'd been through a stressful time overseas, and Roger thought I needed to get out more." Rylan tried to force the memory. He had a beautiful baby girl whose DNA matched his own. He ought to be able to remember the child's mother.

"Sandy should be easy enough to find. Her information is accessible." Some of Zach's confidence had returned. "You said Alicia is Sandy's friend."

"That's right." All Rylan could remember from those few times in Austin was hanging around with Roger. Most of the weekends were clear as a bell. There was one he couldn't make heads or tails out of, and that bugged him to no end. Guilt and a strong sense of shame slammed into him. Rylan had never considered himself weak, so a binge weekend seemed impossible. And yet the evidence sat in Amber's arms.

He fished out his cell and called Roger back. "Hey, sorry to bother you again. Do you mind if I ask a strange question?"

"Not at all, man. Go for it," Roger said.

"Was I sober when we hung out?" The question probably seemed out of the blue.

"You don't remember?" Based on the surprise in Roger's voice, Rylan had caught his friend off guard.

"I know I didn't choose to drink. But that's not the same thing as being sober—"

"Well, I didn't force anything down your throat," Roger joked.

Rylan let the conversation stay lighthearted. It was embarrassing to have to ask. He didn't remember falling off the wagon so why was that one weekend so fuzzy? Why didn't he remember the mother of his child or the making of his child? Hell, he should remember that, at least.

"Let me think back. Damn, it's been a while since we hung out, and you were definitely a saint. No drinking. But, yeah, there was that one time I wondered about you." His friend got quiet.

"What did I do?"

"Slurred your speech. You sounded... I don't know...*off*. Not like yourself. I even asked what you were drinking, but you denied having a beer." Roger paused. "Which was strange because I'm not the saint you think I am. I remember thinking there was no reason to lie to me."

"Was I with a woman that night? Do you remember me being with someone?" Rylan moved his lips away from the mouthpiece and focused on Zach. "Can you send that picture over to him?"

Zach nodded. He got Roger's number from Rylan and texted Alicia's photo.

A minute passed before Roger responded. "Wow, yeah, I remember this woman. What did you say her name was again?"

"Alicia Ward," Rylan said.

Roger drew in a breath. "Of course I remember her. A person remembers someone as good-looking as her. Especially when she comes on to his buddy. I was with Sandy then so it didn't bother me. But she was smokin' hot and seemed pretty locked on to you. You didn't stay in touch?"

"No. I don't remember much about her, and that's throwing me off because I quit drinking and got my act together when I signed up for the military." Rylan wasn't frustrated with his friend. He was frustrated with himself. "I don't remember drinking that night because I don't drink anymore."

"If a woman who looked like that came on to me, I'd remember." Roger's comment issued a strong response from Amber.

She grunted and Zach turned his head to face her. He seemed to know better than to say anything once he got a good look at her expression.

Hell, Rylan knew better than to poke the bear. Part of him—a part he shouldn't give much credence to— liked the fact that Amber seemed jealous. He knew better than to let the thought take seed. "I don't remember much about that weekend, to be honest. Do you remember if I did anything to embarrass myself in public?"

"I had my own thing going, and it's been a long time. Nothing that stands out," Roger said.

It was too soon to be relieved and Rylan wasn't any closer to answers, but if he'd slipped he was fairly certain Roger would've known it. Which didn't explain why he didn't remember Alicia. All he remembered drinking that night was soda.

"Thanks, bro. If you remember anything, will you give me a shout?" It was worth asking even though Rylan doubted anything would spark. A year was a long time to recall something that happened over a weekend. And to a buddy.

"Will do, man."

Rylan ended the call after saying goodbye.

"I'll be able to dig around now that we have a name. I'll get my secretary on a hunt for Brooklyn's birth certificate. That woman works miracles when it comes to research. Now that we know you're the father and we have a mother's name, there are two possibilities for last names, which will narrow the field." Zach's mind was clicking through his next steps. Those seemed like good places to start.

"I keep wondering why the unmarked car from earlier sat behind us for so long without making a move. When we bolted, he didn't try to shoot, either." That was just two of the puzzle pieces not clicking in Rylan's mind. "I keep coming back to the fact they were casing us." He turned to Zach. "There another reason you can think of?"

"I agree with you. They most likely wanted to see who is involved and monitor the threat level for when they come back," Zach stated.

"Why keep coming back at all?" Amber had been

quiet for the past few minutes, and Rylan didn't necessarily see that as a positive sign.

"It's obvious that someone wants Brooklyn." Zach rubbed the scruff on his chin. "You want my honest opinion?"

Amber shot a look that dared him to go ahead.

"The mother got herself in some kind of trouble or decided to sell her baby to a ruthless baby ring. There's big money in black-market adoptions. A couple might have been promised this child and then the mother reneged. Maybe she didn't want to go along with this in the first place but felt she had no choice. So, she figures out another way, panics at the last minute and then backs out of the agreement. These guys aren't having any of that, so they come after the girl. Only these guys don't ask permission. They're used to taking what they want. They get things done. I'll send a deputy out to speak to Sandy Bonds and see if we can get any information about her friend. This could take a few days, so I want both of you to be prepared for that. I need a little time to investigate, and I need to know all three of you will be safe in the meantime. You're welcome to stay at my house."

Brooklyn woke up and started fussing, interrupting Zach. From what Rylan gathered so far about babies, she would need a bottle and a diaper change. "We appreciate the offer, Zach, but we'll figure out a good spot."

"How could anyone abandon a sweet little baby like this?" Amber's eyes sparked as she repositioned Brooklyn onto the couch beside her in order to change the little one's diaper. "Trouble or not, what kind of person could just drop her off with a stranger and run? She had no idea this man would come find you. He could've done anything he wanted to this little girl."

What did that say? Rylan let the thought sit for a few minutes. He liked to think of himself as a good judge of character. Going on a bender and having a baby with a near-stranger weren't shining examples of good behavior. Those weren't making the highlight reel of his life.

Again, he thought about the drinking and chided himself. How could he have allowed this to happen? He'd been to parties with beautiful women before and had never gotten out of control. The urge to drink never went away, but as the years went by sobriety got easier to maintain. He couldn't remember the last time he'd been tempted.

"If you two will excuse me, I have some work I need to get back to. I'll return as soon as I have something more to talk about." He extended his hand and Rylan shook it. "I said it before but welcome back to town."

Chapter Thirteen

"A sheriff's office is no place for a baby." Amber hugged the little girl tighter to her chest. She'd changed and helped feed Brooklyn, but the baby had a hard time settling back down. "She's probably just picking up on all this energy. We're too stressed, and she's reading us and there's too much activity for her to go to sleep."

"Can babies do that?" Rylan paced circles around the break room while gently bouncing Brooklyn. Seeing such a strong man being so gentle with a little one cracked a little more of the casing around Amber's meticulously guarded heart.

"Pick up on energy?" She looked at him. "I believe so. I've seen it with my nieces and nephews. If not that, she could have a fever."

Rylan stopped long enough for her to touch the baby's forehead.

"Is she hot?"

"No. Not that I want her to be sick, but that would explain why she's so fussy." Amber followed as Rylan made another lap.

"Everything she's known for the past three months has changed. She might just be reacting to wanting her mother." He made a good point.

"I can't imagine what would have to happen for me to be willing to be away from my child." Amber's cheeks almost caught fire for how much she burned on the inside thinking about Brooklyn's circumstances.

"I don't remember her." Rylan stopped. "How much of a jerk does that make me?"

"It's weird. Don't you think? You don't remember drinking and, Rylan, I believe you. You vaguely remember spending time with someone, but it's all hazy. Have you thought about the fact that this woman might've slipped something in your—" she paused for a second "—Coke or tea or whatever you were drinking?"

"Coffee."

"At a party?" Amber wasn't a drinker but even she didn't drink coffee at night. And she loved her some coffee.

"It was winter. Cold outside and I'm not much on soda." His honesty shouldn't make her want to laugh. There was something pure in those words and she was more convinced than ever that he didn't drink, even though she couldn't prove it and all evidence pointed to him doing just that. "I'd just gotten back from a deployment and was undergoing some training in San Antonio. I had leave so I called Roger. I wanted to get the hell off base and away from anyone wearing combat boots."

Was he talking about something real with her? Not just cracking a joke when a subject got too intense like when they were kids? She liked the fact that he'd opened up to her. She could see the pain in his features when he talked about the possibility of him drinking.

"Did something happen overseas?" She wondered if that was part of the reason he'd doubted himself.

"A lot happened over there, most of which I can't talk

about. But the worst of it, the worst of human kind came when a grandmother strapped an IUD to her grandson and sent him toward a bunch of us." He stopped like he needed a minute. Brooklyn fussed a little more, and he picked up where he left off pacing.

"That must've been horrific to watch." Again, she couldn't fathom a parent or grandparent who could do something so awful.

"The kid didn't make it near any of us. His life was sacrificed for nothing. Don't get me wrong, I didn't want any of my fellow SEALs to die—"

"I get it. You wanted his life to mean something. He was young, innocent. If he had to die, it should be for something," she said.

He stopped and locked eyes with her for a long moment. It was like time froze and the earth shifted. Sure, he was handsome and she'd been attracted to him from the time they were in high school. This grown-up crush just got real. And she couldn't allow the seed that had been planted to grow because her heart ached for Rylan.

So she cleared her throat and refocused on Brooklyn.

"She probably just needs to get out of here. Your arms must be breaking by now. Do you want me to take a turn with her?" She diverted her gaze because she didn't want to look him in the eyes when she felt so vulnerable.

"I got this. Looks like I'll have to get used to it just being me and her at some point. I appreciate all your help, but I have to learn how to care for my daughter."

"Rylan, do you want to hear a shock?"

He nodded.

"You're going to be an amazing dad."

"I doubt that. But I plan to give it my all. My fail-

ures won't be from lack of trying, that's for damn sure."
He patted Brooklyn's back, but she only fussed more.

"Maybe try sitting down with her." She glanced at
the wall clock. "It's time for another bottle."

It was getting late. They'd been at the sheriff's office
for at least twelve hours. They both knew they needed to
leave at some point. They couldn't stay there all night,
not with a baby who needed some comforts.

Amber made a bottle. She needed something to do
with her hands anyway.

Rylan settled onto the sofa with the little girl in his
arms. He carefully positioned her so he could free his
right hand in order to feed her the bottle. She settled
down almost immediately as she latched on to the plastic nipple. He had that satisfied smile that dented his
cheek. Her heart stirred even though she ordered it to
behave.

That was the thing about being with Rylan. Her emotions were as out of control as he was. Amber wouldn't
change a thing about him, either.

"It might be easier to transport her once she's sleeping. We'll have a few hours to make our move before
she'll need tending to again," Rylan said, his voice a
low rumble.

"Where should we go and how should we get there?"
Amber asked as Zach walked into the room.

"I got a hit on the birth certificate. The baby's name
is Brooklyn Ward, and she was born in a hospital in
San Marcos," Zach informed them. "Her mother listed
her occupation as a homemaker. She didn't list a father's name."

"That's not surprising given the circumstances,"
Rylan said.

"The hospital where she gave birth has a reputation for covering up illegal adoptions," Zach warned. "It seems we were on track with the adoption ring."

"Can a baby be adopted without the father's consent?" Rylan made a good point. Amber didn't have a lot of knowledge of the adoption process, but the question was reasonable.

"In the state of Texas, when there's no father on record or at the birth, judges usually side with the mother," Zach informed him.

"How can we find out if paperwork was filed? Or if an adoption has been started?" Rylan started firing questions.

"She can't be taken away from you legally now that paternity is being established. Technically it already has been, but I'm talking about in the eyes of the law. My favorite lab should be able to confirm what we already know. Brooklyn is your daughter." Zach glanced from Rylan to Amber. "Why do I get the feeling the two of you were about to leave?"

"This place isn't good for a baby. She needs a bath and clean clothes," Amber stated.

"Were you thinking of taking her back to the ranch?" Zach asked.

"That's probably not a good idea. There will be a lot of attention as soon as news of Breanna's murder gets out," Amber replied. "This office will also be inundated. How will we be able to keep this little girl protected with people coming in and out? You know as well as I do the town has been uneasy. Everyone's been fearing what just happened on the ranch, and we have no idea how much pandemonium the news will stir up."

"You're right. We're already starting to get calls.

Word will spread like wildfire from here," Zach admitted.

"Where is it safe for us to go?" Amber was thinking out loud.

"Maybe it's best if we don't say. I know a place we should be safe." Rylan sounded confident, and Amber wished she shared the feeling.

As it was, she felt like she was damned if she did and damned if she didn't. Tell Zach where they were planning to hide out and their location could end up compromised. Don't tell him and there'd be no extra patrol to count on.

Deputy Perry peeked his head into the break room. "Sir, there's a couple here that has requested to speak with you."

"Can it wait? I'm in the middle of something here," Zach said.

"This couple says they're Brooklyn Ward's parents."

"That's impossible," Amber said under her breath. She was on her feet in two seconds flat. "Zach—"

"I know," he reassured her. "Give me a minute to get them inside the interview room, and then I'll send for you. Wait here."

Willpower was in short supply when it came to waiting to see who claimed to be Brooklyn's parents. The expression on Rylan's face, the steel resolve in the face of the unknown made her wish for half his strength. This couldn't be easy on him.

Zach left the room, and she wheeled around to Rylan.

"Let's just hear them out. They can't be talking about her." She offered reassurance from a shaky voice.

"She's my daughter. They'll take her away over my

dead body," was all he said, but those words were loaded with the kind of truth that took on a physical manifestation. There was no room for doubt.

Deputy Perry appeared in the doorway, signaling Amber and Rylan to follow him down the familiar hallway and into the room they'd been in not that long ago. The baby had fussed herself to sleep and was cuddled against her father's shoulder.

After depositing them inside the viewing room, Deputy Perry leaned into the interview room and gave a thumbs-up.

"Please state your name for the record." Zach's posture was relaxed as he leaned over a pad of paper that was sitting atop the table and looked at the male sitting across from him.

There were three people present. A couple who looked to be in their late forties or early fifties and a man wearing one of those crisp expensive buttoned-up collars tucked inside an even more expensive navy blue business suit. The man in the navy suit sat ramrod straight and had an intensity about him, like if he ordered a hamburger at a fast-food restaurant people would immediately get nervous about making it perfect.

The couple also wore suits, cut from material that would classify them as power suits. From what Amber could tell, there was a lot of money sitting across that table. She figured it was old money because everything the couple wore was understated, expensive and classic. There was nothing showy like people with new money gravitated toward.

Wealthy ranchers were a different breed. She noticed the differences all too well growing up. Her father would welcome anyone to the dinner table who was honest and worked hard. Ranch hands often got invited to her mother's legendary Sunday suppers, with food that Amber still could almost taste when she thought hard enough, and missed to this day.

Amber gravitated toward salt-of-the-earth types. If she and Rylan didn't have such a long history, he'd be the kind of man she'd want to date. But then, men she actually wanted to go out with had been in short supply in the past couple of years. Add to the fact that Amber worked fourteen-hour days and she had no time for socializing. It was fine with her except that she could admit to feeling like her life was missing something lately.

She chalked up her change of heart to all the happiness around her. Amy had found happiness with Isaac. Zach recently reconnected with the love of his life.

"My clients' names are Veronica and Cornell Robinson. They received information that their adopted daughter is here in your office." The Suit bent to his right and pulled a manila file folder out of his black briefcase. He set the file on the table between him and used two fingers from each hand to push the file toward Zach.

"What's the basis for Mr. and Mrs. Robinson's claim?" Zach ignored the manila file, and that seemed to irk the Suit.

Amber had seen her cousin at work and in action many times before, and all she could say was the man had found his calling. He had a way of cutting through the layers and getting down to what was really important. He had a way with people and could get them to talk. Being sheriff suited him to perfection.

"Open the folder and you'll see for yourself." The

Suit leaned back in his chair, folded his arms and crossed his legs.

"Whatever's in there won't hold up in court," Zach informed him, and Mrs. Robinson issued an over-the-top grunt. It was her turn to act indignant.

"We can do this the hard way, but I can see that you're a busy man and there's no reason to waste anyone's time." The Suit didn't realize he was already outplayed. At this point, this matchup was like watching a Little League team versus the Texas Rangers.

Amber could only see the back of Zach's head, and she wished for a better view of his face. It was his turn to lean back in his chair like he was in a hammock in the Caribbean. She could almost see his expression, having witnessed it so many times when he was on the verge of winning an argument. And growing up with five brothers and a male cousin who'd spent half his childhood at the ranch, she knew a thing or two about when someone was defeated.

"Do they look familiar to you?" Amber asked Rylan.

"I've never seen these people in my life." He seemed to be going to great lengths to keep a cool head, and she appreciated the fact that he'd taken her seriously about the baby picking up on emotions.

"Strange," she whispered. "The guys in the sedan and pickup from earlier might've been able to take her if they'd really wanted to, but they didn't. They let us go. Granted, you drove the heck out of my SUV in order to get around that sedan, but they let us go."

"I figured they were casing it and planning to come back in with muscle. I never saw this coming," Rylan admitted. "They didn't want to risk her being hurt because these guys want her in one piece is my best guess."

"My clients demand to take their daughter home, and if you would open that file, you'd see they're within their rights to do so and this mix-up can be resolved."

Mrs. Robinson wore her suit and pearls to perfection. Her hair was cut in a bob that flattered her oval-shaped face. She wore enough makeup to cover any blemishes on her face. It was almost too perfect. When Amber really looked at the woman, she noticed that she had on a considerable amount of foundation. What was she covering? Was she sick? Was Mr. Robinson physically abusive?

This couple looked like they could legitimately adopt a child. Based on appearances, money didn't seem to be a problem. So, if they'd used a sketchy adoption agency, there had to be something lurking in their background. Amber agreed with Rylan. Brooklyn would leave this office with them over her dead body, as well.

Zach extended his hand to the lawyer. "Forgive my manners. My name is Zach McWilliams."

The Suit obliged.

"What makes you so sure I have a baby here in my office?" Zach asked.

The attorney leveled his gaze. "Are you denying it?"

Amber rolled her eyes. It was just like a fancy over-dressed lawyer to dodge the question. "Zach has a good point. How do they know the baby they claim belongs to them is here?"

"Brooklyn Ward's birth mother, Alicia Ward, signed over parental rights to my clients," the Suit said.

"Sorry, I didn't catch your name." Zach picked up

the pen in front of him and leaned forward again, ready to write.

"Teague Thompson." The man was playing it too cool. He was either as big of a deal as he would have Zach believe, or he was big-time bluffing.

Zach made a show of looking at his cell phone. Then came, "Will you folks excuse me?"

Teague Thompson pursed his lips and studied Zach before finally nodding.

Mrs. Robinson made a dramatic show of throwing her arms in the air.

"Do you see any real tears?" Rylan asked as he studied the woman's face through the mirror.

"Nope. Not one. I doubt she'd smudge her makeup with any," Amber said in a low voice.

Zach stopped in the hallway outside the opened door. The lights were dimmed inside the room, and it gave an almost intimate feeling.

Amber knew how this worked. As long as it was dark in the room, she was in the clear. The occupants of the adjacent room were none the wiser about who watched. By contrast, the interview room's lights were bright fluorescents.

Zach waved them into the hallway. Deputy Perry stood watch over the interview room door, arms folded against his chest and with his back to the door. He looked like a bull waiting to be baited, and it was obvious that wouldn't go well for the challenger. Amber knew from experience not to mess with a determined deputy. Her cousin hired only the best of the best, and the most loyal. He'd said that he could train someone how to do the job, but he couldn't train personality, work ethic or loyalty.

"This is an unexpected development." Zach raked his fingers through his hair.

"What's your take on the husband and wife?" Amber wondered if he picked up on the signs she saw.

"She's either sick or being abused." He didn't hesitate with his opinion, and it confirmed what she'd already been thinking.

"My thoughts exactly." Amber trusted her instincts but confirmation from Zach left no room for doubt. If Mr. Robinson had a history of abuse, no legitimate adoption agency in Texas would give the couple a baby.

"I can run a background check on him because they have a connection to Brooklyn's mother, who has gone missing. I can threaten to hold them both and interview them all I want. They've already lawyered up, and my experience tells me that they've been coached on how to answer any question I might bring up." Zach made good points. Even though she and Rylan were on the right side of the law, a good attorney knew how to manipulate the truth and find loopholes.

"Think we should stick around?" Rylan asked her.

Of course, in her mind the law always won out, but that was probably fairy-tale thinking mixed with good intentions.

"If you're not here, they can't accidentally see her. I can't lie to them, but I'm not obligated to volunteer information, either." Zach's face was a study in determination.

"I'd like to hear what they have to say. Why they think they have a claim to her," Amber interjected.

"Then stick around. Just know that they most likely will recognize the baby, and it could get messy," he informed her.

Brooklyn stirred and Amber's heart went into free fall. The last thing the little girl needed was to hear shouting or conflict. Zach was right. Even though she'd settled down for the moment, it was only a matter of time before she'd wake again and start fussing.

"What are the chances their claim is legitimate?" Rylan's jaw clenched, and she could see the question wasn't easy for him to ask.

Chapter Fourteen

"If all the players are on the court, I'd say we have the upper hand right now. I've learned not to take anything for granted when it comes to the law. I don't know who these folks might be connected to because I get the impression they're important. If they support someone in a higher office, I could get a phone call. My hands could be tied and that's not a feeling I like. A skilled lawyer could tie up the case for months, possibly years. And even if we get justice at some point, these two could relocate to Europe or Mexico and take Brooklyn with them." Zach spoke the truth and even though it wasn't what Rylan necessarily wanted to hear, he needed to consider every word carefully.

No one was prying Brooklyn out of his hands now that he knew she was his daughter.

"I wanted to give you a heads-up. I'm going back in that room, and at some point during the interview I'll be forced to open the file and see what evidence they think they've presented. If they know she's here, it'll make it more difficult for me to deny that I know her whereabouts. But something's brewing for them to come down here like this and demand custody. I took an oath to uphold the law. My instincts have to take second place."

Rylan figured as much. "What are you planning to tell them?"

"That this is my jurisdiction and every citizen, including the ones not old enough to defend themselves, deserve my protection. Here's the thing. I don't technically have proof that you're Brooklyn's father, and I might get caught in a legal loophole." He scratched his chin. "They might be bluffing, but I don't know what cards they have up their sleeves. Showing up here and boldly demanding custody of Brooklyn leads me to believe they haven't shown all of their hand yet."

Rylan nodded his understanding.

"I better get back inside. Think about what I said," Zach said.

Rylan thanked him and fisted his hands. The sedan and pickup could be outside waiting for them in case they made a run for it. He thought about their dwindling options. He and Amber couldn't take the baby back to his place. They couldn't take her to the ranch, either. There were too many witnesses, and Rylan would never ask another Kent to cover for him.

Amber urged him back into the small viewing room and closed the door.

"We have the right to demand to see our daughter." Mr. Robinson had the authoritative voice of someone used to being in charge at home and at the office. If Rylan had to guess, he'd figure the man for someone who ran his own business and not an abuse victim.

"How old is your daughter?" Zach asked.

"Three months and two days," Mrs. Robinson piped up. Amber was right; there was something off about the woman that didn't sit right with him. The thought that the man seemed to be abusive with his wife sat like a nail in Rylan's stomach. Mrs. Robinson could best be described as…broken. She forced her shoulders straight, but Rylan could see that she wasn't used to being assertive. To make matters worse, Mr. Robinson's posture was tense, aggressive.

"When was the last time you saw the baby's mother?" Zach looked up from his notepad.

"No one said my clients have met the mother," the lawyer interjected.

Mrs. Robinson shot a nervous glance toward her husband, who held a solid glare aimed at Zach.

Mr. Thompson took Mrs. Robinson's hands in his. She bowed her head in dramatic fashion, and her shoulders rocked as though she was sobbing. She put on a good show.

"My clients were supposed to be given access to their daughter three days ago. The birth mother failed to show." It was the lawyer's turn to glare at Zach. "If you'd open the file, you could read all this in the report. As you can see, my client is distraught. We'd like to wrap this up and go home."

Wrap it up?

Rylan's daughter wasn't a present. He didn't like much about the adoptive parents and wondered if Alicia had gotten cold feet once she met them. It wouldn't do a lot of good to speculate, considering they were light on details. But his gut burned with fury.

"What kind of vehicle do you drive?" Zach asked.

"Excuse me?" The question seemed to catch Teague off guard. "What myself or my clients drive is not relevant to this discussion."

"It is to me." Zach paused while Mrs. Robinson pulled out a packet of tissues from a designer-looking handbag. "What's the harm in telling me?"

"My clients don't have to explain what kind of car they drive or what they're doing in town. Their daughter is here—"

"How exactly do you know that?" Zach opened the file and looked at the first piece of paper. "It says here that you're from Fort Worth. Arlington Heights. How do you know what's going on here in my town if you live an hour and forty-five minutes away?"

Rylan knew enough about the city to realize that was an expensive neighborhood. That part didn't surprise him. He, like Zach, was curious how they'd tracked Brooklyn to Jacobstown if they weren't working with the drivers of the black sedan and pickup truck from earlier.

"Fine. We'd hoped that it wouldn't come to this, but we'd like to report a kidnapping." The lawyer had that card ready to play quickly. He'd anticipated some of Zach's moves. With an expensive suit like the one he was wearing, he looked prepared to earn his keep.

"I'm not admitting that the child is even in my county. However, if this alleged child is here in Jacobstown, you need to be very clear on one thing. She won't be leaving without a court order and/or DNA test—"

"My clients have rights, Sheriff. If you look at the second piece of paper in that folder, you'll see that a judge agrees." Teague looked a little too smug.

"And I have a right to investigate a missing person—"

"This is a kidnapping case—"

"I'm talking about Alicia Ward, the birth mother.

My guess is that you already know she's disappeared. What I'm unclear on is why you believe her child is in my county." Zach slapped the folder closed and shoved it toward Teague.

Rylan turned to Amber. "Let's get her out of here."

"Okay. But where will we go?" she asked.

"Maybe it's best if we don't say. I know a place we should be safe." Rylan sounded confident and Amber wished she shared the feeling.

"THOSE PEOPLE COULD'VE ended up raising your daughter and you never would've known any different." Amber had been holding her thoughts in too long. She had no idea what kind of person Alicia Ward was, but the woman must've had some heart to back out of the deal at the last minute. "I have so many questions, Rylan."

"Like?" He got behind the wheel after she'd secured Brooklyn, and he'd made sure no one seemed too interested in what they were doing. It was past nine in the evening and they'd been at her cousin's office for thirteen hours. Her back was stiff and she was tired of sitting.

"If Alicia had known she was going to adopt out her baby, why wait three months? Why take care of her that long and then dump her on a family? Of course, the other question is why change her mind and have her brought to you? Was her pregnancy a scam? She gets herself pregnant and sells the baby but has been on the run for three months because she changes her mind and decides to keep the baby? And then she realizes that someone is after her or someone was getting close and so she tries to get the baby to you, who, by the way, has no idea she's coming or that he's even a father."

"All good points." He paused for a minute as he navigated out of the parking lot and onto the narrow street. "I still don't remember her or much about that weekend."

"And don't you think that's odd?"

"Look, I made a mistake. I must've fallen off the wagon—"

"What if you didn't, Rylan?"

"I'm not ready to let myself off the hook. It's happened before," he admitted.

"Years ago you slipped. But you said yourself that this time was different." Amber wasn't letting him hang guilt around his shoulders like that. Not if he was innocent.

"That doesn't mean anything—"

"You've been beating yourself up over this, Rylan. And if you did it, then that's fine. But—"

"No 'but.' I can't make excuses for myself, Amber. Don't you see that? It's too easy for a person like me to slip and fall down that slope again. I'd been under a lot of stress. I might've picked up a beer."

"You just don't remember it," she countered.

"That doesn't mean I didn't do it, dammit." Frustration poured off him in waves. Guilt and shame seemed to clock him.

"I believe in you," she said calmly.

"Well, don't."

She let that sit between them for a few minutes.

"Can you answer a question?" she asked.

"I can try."

"Those couple of other times that you said you fell off the wagon early on. Do you remember the first drink?" Amber gripped her cell.

"Yeah. I do. Clearly."

"But not *this* time," she continued.

"What, are you a prosecutor now? I already said that I don't remember any of it." His grip on the steering wheel tightened until his knuckles were white. "Are you satisfied?"

"Yes. I am." Amber gave it a moment to sink in.

"I hear what you're saying. It was different that time and that could've been because I didn't willingly take that first drink. It's a nice assumption, and one I want to be true with everything inside me. But I had a drinking problem at one time, and that means I can't make excuses. I have to take responsibility for my actions. Period. Until I know for certain that I didn't willingly take that first drink, I have no intention of cutting myself any slack."

The casual tone she was so used to in conversation with Rylan was gone. He usually covered what was going on inside with a wink and a smile. His charm was so good at seducing women, at making her fall a little bit harder for him. But this genuine side to him was an express train to hurt. Because she was falling for him hard. "I believe in you, Rylan. I believe that you've changed. And I believe that you're sober. I understand what you're saying, and I appreciate your perspective. I can only imagine how difficult it must be for you to think you might've jeopardized your sobriety. All I want you to do is open up to the possibility that it wasn't your fault. We have no idea what Alicia's intentions were. She might've signed up to get pregnant—"

"Why would anyone do that?" Rylan cut her off.

"We don't know her circumstances. Let Zach investigate. You know he's good at his job. He'll uncover the truth," she said, trying to soothe him. His commitment to his daughter only served to draw Amber toward him even more. When she'd given Red the unexpected pregnancy news, he'd come off as supportive in the early days. It didn't take long for his true feelings to surface. Red didn't want a child. Of course, she'd learned that after the wedding. At eighteen, she'd been young and naive. Had she been in love with Red? No. She cared about him, though. And she'd believed a relationship could grow from there. That they could grow to love each other after becoming a family. And then their child had been stillborn. Red had packed his bags and moved out before she made it home from the hospital. Looking back, he'd done them both a favor because being a Kent would've caused her to stick out their relationship. Kents didn't quit.

The divorce papers showed up a month later. Red had moved to California and moved on with his life. It should've hurt, but instead she felt relieved that he was gone. Ever since, she could admit that she never allowed herself to get close to anyone.

Speaking of family, there was something she needed to know before she made the argument that they might be safer at the ranch, just not at the main house. "Rylan, what happened between you and my brother?"

"It's between me and your brother." Rylan's tone had a definiteness to it that she ignored.

"I need to know."

"Why? What purpose could it possibly serve?" He white-knuckled the steering wheel.

"I changed my mind. I think we should go to the ranch for a few—"

"Forget it." Those two words had the sharpness of a blade and the finality of death.

"There's security at the main house. I know what happened to Breanna, and I reacted to that earlier but that was on the property, which we both know is vast," she argued.

"I still don't like the idea," he admitted.

"We can't just drive around all night. Being on the road isn't safe if those henchmen decide to come back and forcibly remove Brooklyn from our arms." Amber had no intentions of giving up easily.

"You said yourself there are flaws in ranch security." He could be a mule when he wanted to be.

Amber bit back a yawn. "There are baby supplies there. How are we supposed to take care of a three-month-old while being chased by these idiots?"

"We'll figure it out." Rylan checked the rearview mirror again, reminding her of just how much danger they were in.

"How?"

"You underestimate my abilities," he scoffed, and seemed genuinely put off by her lack of confidence in his skills as a soldier.

"I've seen how you handle yourself. Believe me when I say that if this was a one-on-one situation I'd have no doubts. But you have two handicaps, me and a baby who needs to eat every few hours and has to be handled with care. She could cry at the wrong moment, and you might not be able to cover in time. I'm not much use while I'm trying to hold her. You know that normally I know my way around a shotgun and I'm not afraid to use one. This is different, Rylan. Even a tough guy like you can see that we'll hold you back and quite possibly cost us everything. I know you're strong physically and mentally."

He grunted at that last word.

"You are, Rylan."

"We need to find Alicia Ward, and we can't do that from the ranch," he argued.

"That's a good point. We can't find her and offer the best protection for Brooklyn. If the Robinsons or their henchmen catch up to us, we might be forced to hand over your daughter and let the courts decide. You heard Zach. That could take months or years. Our family attorney would tell you the same thing if we called him." She gave him a few minutes to let those words sink in.

He concentrated harder on the stretch of road in front of them. She was getting through, making progress.

"The ranch is the safest option for Brooklyn," she added.

"That's playing dirty," he finally said.

"Maybe, but I'll do anything to keep that little angel safe and so will you. The Robinsons are going to leave Zach's office without their baby. They believe, right or wrong, that they have rights to her. Until your official DNA test comes back and proves to the courts that you're the father, we don't have any aces in our hands. Can you live with yourself if someone takes her? We only assume the vehicles were linked to the Robinsons. What if they weren't? Brooklyn could be sold off into some baby ring and literally disappear from our lives forever before we have a chance to find her." Amber risked a glance at Rylan, and she could see that her filibuster was working.

So, she stopped in order to let her argument sink in.

After circling a block three times, Rylan turned east, the direction of the ranch.

"I don't like the idea of putting your family in harm's way," he said.

"Breanna Griswold might argue that you can't protect everyone." Amber's heart fisted thinking about Breanna, about her family, about her lost life even before her death. "We need to get some rest and give Brooklyn a break. I can get enough supplies from the main house to get us through the night without alerting anyone to our presence."

"Where do you expect us to sleep without someone realizing we're there?" he asked.

"The bunkhouse." She could've sworn she saw him tense at the idea of going to the last place they'd been alone together before he left eight years ago.

Chapter Fifteen

The rest of the ride to the ranch was silent. All the noise was going off inside Rylan's head. Thoughts battled for attention. Frustration nailed his gut. And he'd be damned if he wasn't thinking about the kiss he'd shared with Amber that had been so much better than the one in the bunkhouse. There'd been so much promise and intensity and chemistry in that kiss. Rylan could honestly say there'd never been a kiss like it. He wondered if that was what it was like to have something more than a physical attraction to someone. Although he had that, too. In spades.

He had to remind himself that he was falling down another slippery slope and as silly as it sounded, even to him considering he was a grown man, the promise he'd made to Will at eighteen still mattered. The fight the two had had and the position Rylan had put Will in still mattered. Even more so now that Rylan was a man.

But this wasn't the time to dwell on an inappropriate attraction to his former best friend's baby sister. He almost laughed out loud at the *baby* part. Amber Kent was all woman. She helped expand the successful family cattle ranch into the powerhouse it was today and had yet to hit thirty years old. She was a force to be reckoned with. She had a sharp wit, an easy laugh and a heart that knew no bounds. And even though she'd closed off parts of herself, which he assumed had to do with the baby she'd lost, she was still the most open woman he'd ever met. One look into those eyes and he could see right through her.

Rylan refocused his attention. Dwelling on Amber's good points wasn't doing anything to quell his attraction to her—an attraction he needed to keep in check.

His thoughts were weighted with other issues. He wondered if there was a court in Texas that would take his daughter away from him. He didn't remember the girl's mother. How would that make him sound? His playboy ways might catch up to him, and Brooklyn could pay the price.

But then, if the adoption wasn't on the up-and-up, would the Robinsons want to bring this to court? Was that why they'd brought the big guns now? They'd walked into that interview room like they owned the place. When he really thought about it, Teague Thompson had played the confidence card. Mr. Robinson had seemed angry and put out. Those were understandable emotions given the fact that they'd been promised a baby who'd then disappeared. Mrs. Robinson seemed troubled. Rylan got a bad feeling every time he thought about her. And Zach had made a good point about the family's possible political connections.

"I know a private investigator who might be able to help us dig into the Robinsons' background," Amber said as they approached the gate to the ranch. "That way we won't feel like we're wasting time resting."

"That's a good idea." Rylan stopped at the guard shack.

Isaac Vanguard stood six feet one inch. He worked security at the ranch. With short, light brown hair and powder blue eyes, he would likely be considered attractive by most women.

Isaac stepped out of the building. He bent down as Rylan opened the window.

"Amy's worried about you," he said to Amber. "Said you two were supposed to be planning a lunch to benefit a women's shelter, but she hasn't been able to reach you."

Amber leaned toward the driver's side and filled Rylan's senses with her flowery and clean scent. Had she always smelled this good? "I'm sorry. I totally forgot. My cell battery died, and I keep forgetting to charge it. If you see her before I get a good charge, would you mind telling her I'll be in touch as soon as I can?"

Isaac glanced in the back seat. "Will do, ma'am."

He moved back inside the shack and pressed the button to open the gate. There was another security guard in the background, a man Rylan recognized from the other day. It seemed the Kent family was serious about adding extra security, and he saw that as a good sign they could handle almost anything that came their way. "Who was the other guy?"

"That's Blaise Dillinger." Amber rubbed her temples.

"You okay?" Rylan picked up on the tension. Granted, what they'd been through would have anyone stressed. Adrenaline had long faded from their encounter with the pickup truck and sedan, and the surprise of the Robinsons showing up at Zach's office.

"I was just turning over ideas in my head, spinning out. What if my cousin has to follow through with an investigation? The Robinsons could get a search warrant and surprise us. My family would never give us up, but they'd also be put in a bad position if they knew we were here. They'll protect us no matter the cost. They won't hesitate to stand up for us, and that could cost them if they're found in contempt of court."

"We're here. What now?" Rylan figured they were already well in over their heads.

"Would you mind doubling back to Isaac for a second?"

Rylan put the gearshift in reverse and navigated backward toward the iron gate.

Isaac must've realized something was up because he hopped out of the guard shack and jogged toward them.

"Need something?" he asked.

"If anyone asks who's at the ranch, you don't have to answer—"

"Yes, ma'am. I know." He nodded.

"I would never put you in a position to lie, Isaac—"

"I took an oath to protect this family. I've been advised of my legal rights and am aware my actions could be contested in court." Isaac's dedication was noble. "I don't have to answer any questions I don't want to. Ever. Unless I'm in a court of law being asked by a judge. It's my decision whether or not I want to put myself in jeopardy with the system. And in case you're wondering what that means, my loyalty lies with this family."

"I'm not asking whether or not you're loyal, Isaac. I already know the answer to that question. I wouldn't want you to put yourself in a bad position over me," Amber said, clarifying.

"With all due respect, I can decide the risks I'm willing to take." The man's loyalty would never be in question, and Rylan couldn't help thinking that Isaac would've made a good soldier. He had all the right qualities: honesty, loyalty and bravery. Everything else could be taught.

Amber pursed her lips, no doubt wanting Isaac to think of himself first but obviously realizing he wouldn't. When she finally spoke, she said, "Thank you, Isaac. You're a good man, and you can't know how much I appreciate everything you do for my family."

Isaac allowed himself a small smile before nodding.

Rylan pulled away and navigated around the house toward the barn. Between family members and ranch hands, there were enough vehicles at the Kent main house parking lot to slip into a spot and have a reasonable expectation no one would be the wiser.

"There are sleeping quarters in the barn if you'd rather go with the men—"

"I know." He'd worked three summers in that barn alongside his best friend, Will. Damn. Everything good about Rylan's childhood always came back to the Kent family—a family that had always made him feel like one of their own despite him being from the wrong side of the tracks, coming from a no-good father and having a decent hardworking mother who had no gas left in the tank to spend time with him on the rare occasions she wasn't at work. "I don't want to be separated from you, Amber. Not right now."

Amber gave a small smile before fishing out her key ring and fanning out the keys. After sliding a couple around the ring, she selected one. "I'll grab a few things from the main house and meet you in the bunkhouse."

The thought of being alone with Brooklyn set his stress levels on high alert. This was his daughter, and he had to learn how to be alone with her. Rylan had been to a hostile country. He'd encountered enemies with every kind of face-to-face weaponry. He'd endured hostile, unforgiving terrain.

But he'd never imagined something that weighed next to nothing would be the thing to take him down.

Rylan brought the whole car seat inside with him. The bunkhouse was actually an apartment over the Kent Ranch offices.

In a few hours, Lonnie would be awake and ready to start the day. It wasn't uncommon for one of the Kents to sleep over in the second-story apartment, so Lonnie most likely wouldn't be the wiser as to who was actually there. He wouldn't bother the occupants.

It didn't seem right to sneak around the same ranch he could practically call home. Being here brought back so many memories, most of them were good. His last year in Jacobstown had been hell after his mother had passed away.

The offices smelled the same, hay and horses. With a diaper bag over his shoulder and a baby carrier in his left hand, he would be a sight. No one from his past would believe this to be possible. Hell, he was still trying to digest this one.

He shuffled up the wooden stairs, looking over the offices where he'd spent so much of his childhood.

The apartment was small but cozy. The furniture was arranged just like he remembered. There was an open-concept living room with a kitchenette. A flat screen was mounted on one wall, with the most comfortable couch Rylan had ever slept on across from it.

The kitchenette was in the corner. This close to the offices and barn it only had a sink, a fridge and a microwave, but that was good enough to get by in a pinch.

The apartment was never meant to be a permanent residence. The rectangular dining table had one of its long sides pushed up against the wall. Two chairs were at opposite ends, and two were tucked into the same side. It was comfortable for two, maybe three people to eat there. Four was a stretch even though there were four place settings.

And Rylan had crammed at the table with Will and a couple of ranch hands more than once. Being here reminded him of everything he'd lost, his mother and then his friends, and anger welled up inside him at his past weakness.

He couldn't help but glance down at his daughter and feel nothing but pain at the fact she would never meet her grandmother. Had his mother been around for him? No. But she'd worked hard to keep food on the table and never asked for anything in return. As far as Rylan was concerned, the woman was a saint. It mattered little that he didn't really know her. He loved her the same. Losing her had sent him into a downward spiral that had cost him everything he cared about, and most of his self-confidence.

The door opened and Amber slipped inside carrying a full armload of baby items.

"That was quick," he said, ignoring the way his heart fisted when he saw her again, and how much he didn't want to think about her but did while she was gone.

The kiss they'd shared on that couch had been out of nowhere and one he'd never forget as long as he lived. She'd turned to him, locked gazes and then pressed her lips to his. He should've stopped her and eventually he did. But not before a bone-searing kiss that left him wanting more than he could allow.

"I knew where everything was." Before she could finish her sentence, he was by her side, helping her unload the supplies. She had a smaller and softer version of the baby carrier. She set it up next to the couch. "When she wakes and has a feeding, which should be any minute now, we'll change her and move her to where she'll be more comfortable."

Rylan stood by helpless as she unfolded the cloth seat and opened the straps, so it would be ready for Brooklyn.

"Dinner's in that bag," she continued. "I grabbed a pan of Joyce's lasagna from the fridge."

"I miss her cooking," he said.

"Heat it up and I'll get everything ready over here." This wasn't the time for old memories. Rylan knew better than to allow Amber's voice to roll over him like it was. He knew better than to think about the kiss they'd shared. And he especially knew better than to compare it to all the others since, because they came nowhere close to matching until she'd kissed him again the other day.

Amber Kent proved to be trouble he didn't need in his already overcomplicated life. Damn that life could change with the snap of a finger. It had been like that when he'd lost his mother and had caught him completely off guard.

Being here on the Kent property, Rylan couldn't help but remember the past—a part of his past that he wasn't exactly proud of. He wouldn't go back and change it if he could, mistakes and all. It had made him a better person. It had made him the man he was today. The kind of man who would step up and take care of his responsibilities no matter what else it cost him. A man who wouldn't think twice about offering a helping hand to anyone in need.

Amber's words from earlier started to take root. Maybe he hadn't taken that first drink. Rylan hoped like hell that was true because if he had, that said there'd been no change in him, no growth, and after everything he'd been through to earn his sobriety, he didn't want that to be true.

Brooklyn started to cry, and Amber went right to her while he fixed a bottle. They were getting pretty damn good at parenting together, and he couldn't imagine doing any of this without her. Reality was a gut punch. Because once this ordeal was over, she'd go back to her life here on the ranch and he'd go back to his. For the first time, he felt unsettled about his decision to come back to Jacobstown. But where else would he go?

He chalked his feelings up to not facing the Willow family yet. It was part of his commitment to his sobriety to apologize to those he'd hurt in the past. He'd saved the Willows for last along with Will. Facing those two was going to be the most difficult, and he'd wanted to be strong.

Amber fed his daughter while he set the table.

Rylan's cell buzzed, and he stopped long enough to answer. "What's going on, Zach?"

"I did some digging around into Mr. Robinson's business—"

"Hold on a sec while I put you on speaker," Rylan interrupted. He moved to the couch and sat on the arm while holding out the cell between him and Amber while she burped the baby. "Amber's here. You were saying that you poked around in Mr. Robinson's business?"

"That's right. It turns out that Alicia Ward was one of his employees. She left almost a year ago," Zach informed them.

"That would be around the time Alicia got pregnant." Amber looked up at Rylan, and his fingers flexed and released from wanting to touch her.

"There've been domestic violence and assault claims against Mr. Robinson by his wife and a woman by the name of Charlotte Pemberton. I traced her to an escort service out of Dallas. Most of the claims came from his wife, but she dropped each one. It's the same story for Ms. Pemberton," Zach said.

A picture emerged that made Rylan's gut twist into a knot.

"Would those cases be enough to stop the Robinsons from being able to adopt a child since they didn't stick?" Amber asked.

"A legitimate adoption agency would have a difficult time getting over physical violence charges. A good interviewer would be able to see right through the Robinsons." Zach paused a beat. "Mr. Robinson also chairs a reelection campaign for the judge who resides over his county. George is influential in Texas."

Several thoughts raced through Rylan's mind. Had Robinson paid Alicia to get pregnant when he and his wife couldn't have a child? And then had Alicia decided not to go through with it? That she couldn't do that to a child? To the man she'd targeted to be the child's father?

"I also found out that Alicia has a sister who lives in Austin. Her name is Adeline. The two were reportedly close until last year. Adeline claims not to have seen or heard from her sister in the past six months," Zach stated.

"We know she's alive," Rylan stated. "Or she was. Otherwise, Brooklyn wouldn't be in the world. We know Alicia was alive a few days ago because she fits the description given by Chess."

"That's what I've found out for now. Technically, I can hold Mr. Robinson for seventy-two hours, but that's a risky move. For now, the Robinsons are in my office. I'm treating them like victims rather than suspects. I thought you should know where we stood," Zach said.

"I appreciate it," Rylan offered.

"Zach, before you go. Can I ask a question on a different subject?" Amber asked.

"Go ahead."

"It's about Breanna. With everything that's going on, have you been able to locate her parents?" Amber's voice was low and reverent. Rylan could see the sadness in her eyes when she spoke about the victim.

"No, I haven't. I have a deputy dedicated to searching for them, though," he said.

"Word was that they moved to San Antonio a few years ago." Amber paused a beat. "I'd heard Breanna was back and that she was still using. I know that won't affect how vigorously you work to bring justice to her killer, Zach. I'm just saying we might want to look into that community to see where she's been and who she's been hanging around with lately."

"I'll make a list and start there, Amber. Thanks for the information." Zach's voice was somber.

"You're welcome, Zach. Are we back to the same suspects?"

"Reggie Barstock still tops the list. I'll look for any connection between him and Breanna. There were no signs of a struggle, which leads me to believe she was familiar with her killer." Amber visibly shivered, and Rylan figured it was the thought someone she knew could do something so unimaginable.

"There's one more thing," Zach said. "I had Deputy Perry poke around in Teague Thompson's practice, and he's been associated with illegal adoption rings in the past. The guy is dirty but he's also connected. His uncle is a senator, and their connections in Texas run deep."

"Sounds like one hell of a web," Rylan stated.

"It is, which means we have to build a solid case for you and Brooklyn in order to keep the two of you together. Perry is on his way over to Alicia's sister's house in Austin. Turns out Alicia's laptop is at her sister's place." Zach was a miracle worker and a damn fine investigator once he had a trail to follow. "Hang in there a little longer. I'm tying up the Robinsons here, but I don't have enough evidence to hold them if they decide to walk out the door. If I can support the emerging picture, I'll have enough evidence to make an arrest."

"Any sign of Alicia?" Rylan asked. The unspoken possibility was that Mr. Robinson had already gotten to her and she was already dead.

"Nothing yet but her laptop might give us a few leads," Zach said.

Rylan ended the call after thanking the sheriff for the update.

"I vaguely remember Reggie Barstock growing up. What's the deal with him?" he asked Amber.

"He was Maddie's boy," Amber told him.

"I remember her. Sweet lady." Rylan didn't know the family very well, and he had no memories of Reggie. "She had that business downtown for the longest time."

"That's right," Amber agreed. "All I remember about

Reggie is that he stuck to himself in school. He didn't play any sports, and I don't remember him being much of a student. I think Deacon was a little surprised he graduated from high school. My brother said there'd been some talk of Reggie being held back for grades or absences. Maddie Barstock was a saint. No one could figure out how Reggie had turned out so opposite except that he'd had a no-good father. You know how the town can be once they lock on to something. Anyway, his mom's reputation was golden, and she'd been a kind employer to everyone who'd worked for her. She passed away last year and left Reggie out of the will. Ms. Barstock left everything to her grandniece, Chelsea."

Rylan perked up at hearing the name. "The same one I met at your home the other day?" he asked.

"That's her. She's an amazing person, and she owns the craft pizza restaurant on the town square." Amber practically beamed with pride. She'd always been all about family. But then the Kents were a tight-knit bunch. Rylan had seen it firsthand even though he'd learned to appreciate so much more now that he was a grown man.

"I'm sure Reggie didn't take too kindly to what he would view as his inheritance going to someone he didn't know," Rylan concluded.

"It was strange knowing he'd been slipping in and out of town without anyone seeing him. Zach found out last year and since Reggie has a limp on his left side—"

"Those are easy dots to connect, considering you said it was always the left paw or hoof. And now Breanna's left foot was—"

She flashed her eyes at him like she could hear the

details even though they both knew what had happened because of the crime scene photos.

"So, yeah, the guy disappeared after high school and most had believed him to be gone for good. He resurfaced last year full of bitterness, and not the least bit sad about his mother's passing. All he seemed to care about was his inheritance. He tried to scare Chelsea into leaving town, which was awful. Apparently, he's been living in Louisiana all this time getting in and out of trouble," she said.

"What kind of crimes was he committing?" Rylan asked.

"Zach said it was small-time stuff. But everyone agrees that he needs to be watched. I mean, he knows Jacobstown, having grown up here. And, sure, a picture has been emerging that he's the one, but Zach isn't convinced yet. No one can reconcile the fact that he didn't come across as the smartest guy, and the profile of the Jacobstown Hacker indicates someone with a higher IQ." She blew out a breath in frustration, and he realized how taxing it was for her to talk about this.

Brooklyn started fussing, and before he could react Amber was at the little girl's side. It was a good time for him to think about getting a meal into Amber and making sure she got rest. He could see that she took care of everyone around her. But who took care of her?

"The baby's settled," Amber announced with pride that stirred places in his heart he thought long since dead. He'd been dead inside far too long.

"Come eat." He'd set the table, and the lasagna smelled damn near out of this world.

Amber joined him and took her seat. Tired and frazzled, she was still beautiful. She must've been starved because she didn't say a word until she'd cleared half her plate. Rylan liked watching her enjoy a good meal. There were other things he liked about her that he didn't want to focus on.

"I know Joyce is an amazing cook but this food is beyond good," Amber said. The sound of appreciation in her voice stirred his heart.

Rylan glanced down at his empty plate with a forced smile. "Like I said, I haven't had this good of a meal in longer than I can remember."

"I'm going to finish eating, take a shower and then I want to talk about why that is, Rylan."

Chapter Sixteen

Rylan made a pot of coffee. He'd been successfully avoiding the topic of his and Will's blowout up until now, but he figured he owed Amber an explanation. She deserved to know the reason because he could see an emotion stir behind her eyes that he hadn't been able to pinpoint until now. It finally dawned on him that she blamed herself, that kiss, for him running off to join the military. So, she most likely blamed herself for the fight between him and Will.

He'd showered in the spare bathroom downstairs while Amber used the one in the apartment. He knew his way around the Kent Ranch, so it was easy to navigate even with little lighting. He also knew where all the supplies were stocked. He'd found an extra set of clothes that roughly fit, brushed his teeth and had settled at the table with his first cup when Amber emerged from the bathroom.

Her hair was down. It fell well past her shoulders. She had on a Grateful Dead T-shirt and shorts that were almost hidden by the oversize tee. Her long legs looked silky and smooth. He clenched and released his hands. Then, he picked up his coffee mug and forced his gaze away from her attributes. After taking a sip, he stood up. "You want a cup?"

"Stay right where you are, Rylan. I'll get it." She shot a smile that was a dagger to his heart. It was difficult to maintain objectivity when she was in the room and everything about her was temptation.

After pouring her cup and doctoring it up, she joined him at the table.

"You should probably get some rest," he said to her.

"I highly doubt if I could. I keep thinking about Breanna and what happened. And then this situation, the uncertainty... Besides, if I'm really that tired, I could drink a cup of coffee on my way to bed and still sleep," she said with a half smile. It didn't reach her eyes and he knew why.

"You want to talk about it?" He liked talking to Amber even though he was normally the silent type.

"I know you and my brother got into a fight but you left and never looked back. I didn't think I'd see you again." Her voice hitched and her cheeks flushed as though the admission, the sadness, embarrassed her.

When she looked up at him with a mix of hurt and defeat in her eyes, his heart fisted in his chest.

"I'm sorry I disappeared on you," he admitted. "My life had spiraled down a bad path and..."

"Was it because you kissed me? Because I've been thinking about that night here in the apartment a lot lately and it was my fault, Rylan. You didn't kiss me. I distinctly remember that I kissed you." Suddenly, the rim of her coffee mug became very interesting to her. Her cheeks flushed with what looked like embarrassment, and he'd be damned if it didn't make her look even more beautiful.

"There was so much more to it than that," he said, hating that she'd carried a sense of shame with her all these years. "My life became a mess. That's why I kissed you back and—"

"Oh. You don't have to explain—"

"Hang on. I didn't mean it to come out like that," he said, backpedaling. "What I'm trying to say is that there are lines that shouldn't be crossed. Kissing your best friend's little sister behind his back is not exactly a stand-up thing to do. Mine and your brother's relationship was already strained. I had no right to do that."

Amber stood, picked up her dish and silverware from earlier, and said, "You don't need to defend yourself."

"Is that what you think I'm doing?" He stood and followed her into the kitchenette where there was barely room for one.

She turned on the faucet and rinsed her plate, keeping her back to him. The only time she ever did something like that was when she was too angry or too embarrassed to talk, and his heart took a hit thinking he'd caused her reaction.

He'd gone and made a mess of the situation.

"Amber—"

"Don't, Rylan. I'm not in the mood to be insulted by the person I'm in the middle of helping. A person who won't tell me why he won't sleep inside the main house. A person who disappeared into the military after a blowout with my brother and never looked back and won't tell me what happened in the first place." She kept her back to him as she stood in front of the sink.

"You think I walked away and never looked back?" He was so close behind her that her flowery scent filled his senses. He could reach out and touch her, so he did.

He put his hands on her shoulders and felt her skin heat a little under his touch. Her body's reaction to him stirred an already awake part of his anatomy that was difficult to hide underneath jogging shorts.

"Isn't that what you did, Rylan? Isn't that what you're going to do as soon as the dust settles again and you get bored or whatever it was that caused you to go to Collinsville in the first place? Isn't that exactly how you got into trouble before?" Her words rushed out like they did when she was stressed.

He took a step closer and was almost body to body. It was taking all his self-control not to reach out and touch her. It would be so easy to move her hair away from her neck and start kissing her there.

Before he could drum up the willpower to turn away, she took a step back and leaned against him.

Rylan had to admit his feelings for Amber were always brimming underneath the surface. Seeing her with his child did things to his heart that he knew better than to allow. He had no business falling for a Kent.

Honestly, she was too good for him but she'd never see it that way.

"Are you going to answer me?" Her pulse drummed underneath his fingertips.

"What can I tell you, Amber? Do you want to hear that I think you're beautiful? That you make me want things that I don't deserve? That I will never deserve and, by the way, your brother agreed with me? Because I'll say it. And then what? You'll feel sorry for me—"

Amber spun around with all that ire in her eyes that was so damn sexy. "I couldn't possibly feel sorry for you, Rylan. As far as my brother goes, he has no idea what's best for me."

This close, her body was flush with his, and he could feel her breasts rising and falling when she spoke. He dropped his hands, looping his arms around her waist. All he could feel right then was the desire sweeping through him, consuming him with need.

"All I can feel is the same thing you do." Looking into her glittery eyes wasn't helping his situation any.

"This is a bad idea," he said.

AMBER BROUGHT HER hands up to Rylan's chest and smoothed her fingers over the ridges beneath his T-shirt. She blinked up at him. "Is this a bad idea, Rylan? Because I can't think of one good reason why this shouldn't happen. We're adults now. Adults who are capable of making the decision to have one night of amazing sex together."

She pushed up on her tiptoes and kissed him. His body went rigid at first, but then he pulled her tighter against him.

"I won't deny that you've grown up, Amber. You're incredible. You're smart. Beautiful," he said.

Pulling back, she looked directly into his eyes and realized just how much trouble she was in. The more time she spent with Rylan, Amber could sense herself falling further down that slippery slope of feelings. The heat that had been burning between them was like nothing she'd ever felt in her past relationships. Their chemistry sizzled, and she assumed the sex would be beyond anything she'd ever experienced.

It would be so easy to get lost with this man in this moment and forget about the past, about their history.

And that's exactly what she planned to do for at least one night.

She dropped her hands to the hem of Rylan's T-shirt while locking gazes with him. His hands joined hers, and a few seconds later his shirt was on the floor.

His hands went to the hem of hers, and her fingers trembled with anticipation as she fumbled with the fabric, trying to help. He captured one of her hands in his and brought it up to his lips. He pressed a kiss on the tip of her fingers and then on her palm. He peppered kisses on her exposed wrist. Sensual shivers skittered across her skin and her stomach went into free fall.

"I said it before and I'll say it again—you're beautiful, Amber Kent." His voice was low, raspy and sexy as hell. "You're even more beautiful than I remembered, and that's saying a hell of a lot."

He pulled her T-shirt up and over her head, and it joined his shirt on the floor. He palmed her breasts and she released a moan as she unhooked her lacy bra. His hands were rough from working on his house. She liked the feel of them against her skin as they roamed.

He toed off his boots and she followed suit.

"Why did you disappear after you kissed me?" She couldn't help but ask the question that had been on her mind far too long.

"You really want to talk about this now?" He ran his finger along the waistband of her shorts. "Because I have something else entirely on my mind, and it's a hell of a lot better than dredging up the past. It's the here and now, you and me. And I've been waiting a long time for the chance to do this."

He sure knew the right things to say as he dipped his head and ran his lips across her collarbone and then along the base of her neck. Warmth coiled low in her belly.

"It can wait." She wanted this to happen, this thing that was happening between them. She wanted it more than she wanted air.

Maybe she was caught up in the moment, but she didn't care. She'd denied herself too long. She moved her hands to the waistband of his shorts, and a few seconds later those were on the floor in a pile with their clothes. Her shorts joined his.

He hooked his thumbs on either side of her panties, and those went on top of the pile along with his boxers.

Rylan Anderson stood there, naked, and in front of her. His glorious body glistening in the moonlight streaming in from the top of the window. Shadows highlighted a strong male body. His erection pressed against the soft skin of her belly when he pulled her close to him. Again, their bodies were flush and she could feel every time he took a breath.

How many times had she wished for this when she was still naive enough to believe in wishes? One of the biggest problems with her relationship with Red was that he wasn't Rylan, would never be Rylan. She'd told herself to get over her crush and move on. And she believed she had until now. Now she realized she'd just stuffed her feelings down so deep that she'd become numb.

She brought her hands up and dug her fingers into his thick hair and breathed. Her breasts pressed against him as his hands roamed around her back and then cradled her bottom. A thunderclap of need exploded inside her and all she could think about was this man, his weight on top of her, pressing her deeper into the mattress.

Amber had no idea the air could heat up so quickly or the chemistry between two people could be so explosive until Rylan. She'd call it attraction or chemistry, but there was so much more to it than physical. Although, he was one damn hot man. With Rylan, there was a deeper connection.

He lifted her up and she wrapped her legs around his toned midsection. She could feel his erection pulsing against her heat. With her arms around him and his hands cupping her bottom, he walked her into the bedroom and set her down on top of the covers.

It took less than a minute to retrieve a condom and sheath his stiff length before Amber wrapped her arms around his neck and kissed him. His response? He kissed her so thoroughly that if she wasn't already on the bed, her legs might have given out from underneath her. He cupped her breasts with his right palm as he balanced most of his weight on his left hand. Her nipple beaded as he rolled it between this thumb and finger, teasing her. Her back arched and she let out a mewl.

He captured it with his mouth.

"I want to feel you moving inside me, Rylan," Amber coaxed.

It didn't take much encouragement.

He pinned her to the mattress with his heft, careful not to overwhelm her with his weight. She wrapped her legs around his midsection and he drove his tip inside her heat. For the first few seconds he just teased her, driving her to the brink of craziness.

Amber bucked her hips as she dug her fingers into Rylan's shoulders. He drove himself deeper inside her as he lowered his head and captured her mouth. He tasted like a mix of coffee and peppermint toothpaste.

Bare skin to bare skin, he groaned as he thrust harder

and faster. She matched his pitch as they practically gasped for air.

His stiff erection drove to her core, and she rode the feeling to the brink. Faster. Harder. More.

"Rylan," she rasped.

He pulled his head back far enough to really look at her. "You're incredible, Amber."

She loved the sound of her name as it rolled off his tongue. She heard something else that sounded a lot like, "I love you." But she was probably just hearing what she wanted as he pushed her over the edge and rocketed her toward climax.

It was then he drove himself faster and harder until his entire body tensed…and then sweet release seemed to wash over him as he let out a guttural groan.

Rylan collapsed alongside her. She rolled onto her side to face him, and he pulled her into the crook of his arm. He kissed her again and she memorized the look on his face. It was the first time she could remember seeing him with a smile that lit his eyes. It was addicting and dangerous, making the pull to him even stronger.

"Amber Kent, I hope you're not tired because one time is not nearly enough with you."

Chapter Seventeen

Making love with Amber changed things for Rylan. Now that he'd cracked the lid on that pot, he could only hope she felt the same. Lying there, skin to skin with her, he knew he was only beginning to scratch the surface of his feelings for her.

Amber's steady, even breathing said she was asleep, and he didn't want to disturb her. Brooklyn would be awake soon, needing another bottle. He peeled himself away from Amber and out from under the covers, moving slowly and quietly so as not to disturb her. She needed rest. If she heard the baby, she'd hop up before he could throw his shorts on.

Rylan walked into the kitchenette area and put on a pot of coffee. There was no way he could sleep thinking that Brooklyn's mother might already be dead. His mother had passed away while he was in high school, but looking back as a man he was nothing but grateful for the time he got with her.

It was taking all of Rylan's self-control to stop himself from going down to Zach's office and forcing the smug Mr. Robinson to talk. The sheriff had laws to follow whereas Rylan had better ways to make the man talk. And if the Robinsons weren't still there, he'd hunt them down. But then, he hadn't let his temper rule him since those bad decisions he'd made in high school. He'd finally realized letting his temper control his actions hurt him and the people he cared most about in the long run. But times like these tried his patience, and a woman's life could hang in the balance.

Patience had never been his strong suit.

He was deep into his second cup of coffee when Brooklyn stirred. Staring down a baby alone was enough to make this strong man crumble.

But he was nothing but proud when he made her bottle, fed her and burped her, before changing her diaper. Since he'd acted fast the little girl had never properly woken up and that made changing her diaper a hell of a lot easier. He had Amber to thank for helping him get the hang of things.

Pride filled his chest when he placed her back inside her infant bouncer and successfully strapped her in. For the first time since having her handed to him out of the blue, he was starting to think he might not be awful at caring for her.

It was even better that Amber was still sleeping. The thought of being her shelter and taking care of her stirred his heart. Not that Amber Kent couldn't take care of herself. It was sexy as hell when a strong woman could open herself up and allow herself to be vulnerable. And he liked the feeling of taking care of someone who did so much for others.

Rylan thought about Mr. Robinson. A picture emerged that made him sick to his stomach. Had Alicia been forced—or pressured might be a better word—into having a child for her boss? A man with his temperament and dominant tendencies would see no problem in forcing one of his employees to do something she didn't want to. If the man didn't treat the woman he was supposed to love above all else with respect, how was he supposed to treat people he would see as pawns?

There were other thoughts that popped into Rylan's mind. Why did Alicia have a change of heart? Although, looking at the way Amber had almost instantly bonded with Brooklyn, he figured there was a built-in protection hormone for mothers. Had Alicia bonded with the baby during the pregnancy? He'd heard about rogue hormones in pregnant women. They served a purpose, and he figured most of them were to ensure survival of the child.

Thinking about Zach's phone call earlier got Rylan's mind spinning. He wasn't quite ready to let himself off the hook about the slip last year in his sobriety. Evidence was mounting that Alicia might've been desperate to get pregnant. She could've locked on to him after seeing him at the party. And she could've slipped something into his coffee.

Until he had proof, Rylan couldn't afford to let himself off.

He grabbed a small notebook and pen from the junk drawer in the kitchenette, and then started jotting down notes.

By the time he looked up fifteen minutes later, Amber stood in the doorway to the bedroom staring at him.

"Hello, beautiful," he said, and she broke into a smile.

"Rylan." Her voice had a tentative quality to it, and he figured he knew why.

"You're important to me, Amber. Last night changed

things for me. I just don't know what that means yet,"
he offered, and thought he saw a flicker of disappointment behind her eyes as she approached.

He grabbed her hand and tugged her down onto his
lap. He kissed her, wishing he could say what was really
on his mind, that he'd had a hell of a time going all-in
with anyone. But the thought of losing Amber was a
knife stab to the center of his chest.

The sound of boots shuffling up wooden stairs had
Rylan reaching for his weapon. Amber immediately
went toward the baby.

"Will you take her into the bedroom?" She had her
SIG and could protect them both given the time.

"Be careful, Rylan."

"Close the door but wait to see who opens it before
you shoot." He fired a wink and it was meant to break
the tension.

She frowned.

"Don't count me out yet, Kent. I'm actually damn
good in these situations."

Amber smiled but it didn't reach her eyes. Worry
lines creased her forehead as she picked up the baby
in her bouncer and glanced back one more time before
closing the door. He could've sworn she whispered that
she loved him, but it could've been his imagination.

A knock sounded.

"It's Will. Open up."

The bedroom door cracked open. "I'll let the two of
you talk while I hang out with this sweet girl."

Amber stood there holding Brooklyn in her arms.
The baby smiled up at Amber. And a fire bolt struck
Rylan square in the chest.

He walked to the door and answered. "How'd you know I was here?"

"Where's my sister? Is she safe?" Will's concern touched Rylan. Although, he shouldn't be surprised a Kent would look out for another Kent.

"She's here." Rylan opened the door all the way. "You want to come inside?"

Will glanced at him before nodding.

"A lot has happened since we last spoke." Rylan motioned toward the table. "You want a cup of coffee?"

The sun wasn't up yet, but days started on the ranch at 4:00 a.m. Rylan should've known they couldn't fool her family, thinking they could go unnoticed on the property.

"I'll take a cup if you've got it. Black." Will took a seat.

Rylan poured two and joined Will. He set down one of the mugs in front of his former best friend.

"Before you say anything, I'd like to apologize to you," Rylan began.

"There's no reason to rehash the—"

"I believe there is. And it's an important step in my sobriety."

Will's eyes widened in surprise.

"That's right. I've been sober for many years now, but facing you has been the most difficult part of the journey," Rylan admitted.

"Why is that?" Will took a sip and studied Rylan's face.

"I needed to be ready to forgive myself if you accepted my apology. And I'm not there yet but—"

"Losing a friendship, hell, a brotherhood has been

punishment enough. Don't you think?" The sincerity in Will's words struck like a physical blow.

Had he missed the friendship as much as Rylan?

"You covered for me that night. What I did was wrong, and you stuck up for me even though I didn't deserve it. I was a stupid kid—"

"You lost your mother, and I couldn't seem to help pick you back up or get you on the right path again," Will said.

"I let you down, not the other way around. And I let the Willow family down by catching their crops on fire." Saying those words still hurt. "I had no business—"

"Hold on a second. You think it was *you* who lit that fire?" Will's voice was steady.

"I was the one there. You said it yourself. That's where you found me. You took the blame so I wouldn't end up in juvenile detention." That's how Rylan remembered it.

"The McFarland boys set that fire, and they did it on purpose. I just couldn't prove it. They were drunk and seemed to think it would be real funny to destroy the field. You were passed out. I found you before the flames got to you, or they would've let you die. I was angry with you at the time for choosing those jerks over our friendship. You never had anything to do with the fire. My parents helped the Willows get back on their feet. But you almost lost your life." Will smacked his palm on the table. "I was almost too late that night, but it never should've gone that far. I should've been a better friend."

Rylan let those words sink in. All the guilt he'd been feeling these years for the fire had been wasted? Damn, those were a lot of years to be carrying around shame for something he didn't do. Looking back, they'd been for nothing.

He didn't regret his time in the military. He'd gotten his act together there. His service had been good for him. "Thank you for telling me, Will."

"I tried to talk to you before you left, but you said you didn't want to look back."

If only he'd known. "Being stubborn isn't my best trait."

Will chuckled and it broke the tension. "You think?"

"I'm sorry for the pain I caused, man. I missed our friendship. It's one of the main reasons I decided to straighten up my act."

"That means a lot to hear." Will offered a handshake. "How about we pick up where we left off, but from the good times?"

"Now that's a deal." Rylan took the hand being offered. "For the record, I had no idea I was getting your sister into a mess when I called her the other day for help." Those words couldn't be truer.

Will didn't respond right away. He seemed to take a minute to think. "I realize you would never put my sister in harm's way."

"She means a lot to me, Will."

"I saw that the other day. That's why I walked outside to clear my head. I'd imagined a different scenario happening if you and me were ever in the same room again." Will's face brightened. "It involved fists."

"Yeah, I deserve it after the way I messed things up in our friendship," Rylan said.

"Well, I thought you'd be throwing the first punch," Will admitted.

"I guess I had a lot of pent-up aggression in high school." Rylan took a sip of coffee. "The only punch I want to throw now is at the person who's trying to take my daughter away."

He updated Will on the situation with Alicia and the Robinsons.

"Zach promised to call when he got further into the investigation." Rylan set his mug down. He looked up at Will. "Your sister's in the other room if you want to talk to her."

"I don't have anything to say, except take it easy on her. She went through a lot and, strong as she is, none of us want to see her hurting like that again. It nearly cracked us in half when we saw her after she lost the baby. Her son-of-a-bitch ex took off, not that she ever cared about him the way she does about you." Will lasered a look at Rylan. "You do realize my sister has feelings for you, right?"

"I hope so." Rylan sure as hell had feelings for her. What that meant in the long run, he had no idea. Right now, all he could think about was putting Mr. Robinson behind bars and making sure that both Amber and Brooklyn were safe. For his daughter's sake, he needed to find her mother.

"Good. Because even when she was married I never saw her look at him like she does you." Those words broke through the walls he'd carefully constructed.

"The truth is, Will, I'm not nearly good enough for your sister." He kept his tone church-quiet because he knew she'd argue if she heard.

"You know what, buddy? There was a time when I would've blindly agreed with that statement. Not anymore. For what it's worth, I think you're exactly who she needs." Will set his mug down and stood up. He turned toward the cracked bedroom door. "Did you hear that, Amber?"

"I sure did," she said with all that stubbornness and ire he loved about her.

Will left and Amber walked into the room.

"We need to talk," she said. "Later."

Rylan wasn't sure he liked the uncertainty in her tone. Was she shutting down on him? Was this—whatever *this* meant—moving too fast? He felt caught up in a rogue wave. For now, he was riding on top but how long before it sucked him under and tossed him out to sea?

AMBER HELD BROOKLYN to her chest. She couldn't allow this angel to cloud her judgment and yet how could she not? Holding this baby felt so right. Being with Rylan felt so right. But what didn't feel so right was the fact that Amber wasn't Brooklyn's mother.

Boots shuffled up the stairs and Amber's gaze went to the table, searching for whatever it was that Will forgot. She made a move toward the door, but it swung open and Mr. Robinson stood at the entrance.

Amber stared at the barrel of a gun.

"Hold on there, buddy," Rylan said. His cell buzzed on the table.

"Come over here," Mr. Robinson ordered. His eyes wild and angry, he looked like a hungry predator closing in on prey.

Amber was paralyzed with fear. All she could do was hold the baby tighter to her chest. If danger involved only her, she wouldn't hesitate to fight back or try to duck for cover. But holding the baby ensured Amber would move slower. A half-second hesitation could give

Mr. Robinson the upper hand. Damned if he didn't already have it, and that just burned Amber up inside. She'd never played the victim role and had no plans to start now. She would, however, do whatever was necessary in order to ensure Brooklyn's safety.

Rylan was near the table on the opposite side of the sofa. His cell was buzzing madly on the table. Even a skilled soldier like him couldn't make that leap before Mr. Robinson got off a shot.

"You don't want her," Rylan interrupted. "I'm the one you want."

Mr. Robinson's hand trembled, and she could almost visibly see his blood pressure rise. "I'll decide who's going with me."

"Where's the baby's mother?" Rylan asked.

"She's not coming back." Robinson's face twisted when he said the words. "I killed her with my own hands. Stupid bitch couldn't follow simple directions. All she had to do was have the baby and hand her over. I would've preferred a son. Women are so weak. But my wife wanted her anyway."

Amber glanced at Rylan, half expecting him to make a move but knowing he couldn't. Her heart ached for how calloused this man sounded about taking Brooklyn's mother's life. No matter how bad of a mother Alicia might've been or undeserving of this angel, the woman didn't deserve to have her life cut short.

Amber was close to the door. The gun was pointed at *her*.

There was no way she'd allow this man to shoot the baby. Amber turned to block Brooklyn and give Mr. Robinson a clear shot at her instead.

"It's okay, Rylan," Amber said in as calm a voice as

she could muster. If anyone made a wrong move, Mr. Robinson could get spooked and pull the trigger.

"No one told you to speak," Mr. Robinson seethed.

Didn't those words grate on Amber. This man needed to wake up. It wasn't 1950 anymore. Women could vote. They could run ranches and have a variety of careers. And, at least in her case, could shoot a gun. So, he'd better watch his mouth.

"If anything happens to me, you won't get what you came for." Amber motioned toward the baby. "I go down and I take her with me. You lose. You'll be arrested. My cousin, Zach McWilliams, won't sleep or stop until he hunts you down. So, it seems we're in a bit of a stalemate."

"Her cousin might go after you legally, but I'll go after your family. Your wife. Your mother. Any living relative you hold dear. And then I'll come after you. You'll know it's coming. It's going to happen but you won't know when and you sure as hell won't be able to stop me." Rylan's voice was a study in calm composure.

"You'll come with me and bring the baby with you." Mr. Robinson practically spat the words. His voice was filled with the tension of a man on the edge.

And then he shifted the barrel of the gun toward Rylan and fired.

Chapter Eighteen

Rylan was hit. He made a show of flying backward and landing hard against the back wall. He dropped onto the dining table and then rolled off of it. The bastard had to pay. No matter what Alicia had done, she didn't deserve to lose her life. He, of all people, knew what it was like to make mistakes. There should be second chances and not the finality of death.

Amber gasped. The horrific look on her face slammed guilt into him. Yes, he'd taken a bullet, but he'd been in worse tactical situations. A good soldier could detach emotionally and stay logical. So, he'd gone back to his training the minute he realized Robinson was going to walk out the door with Amber and Brooklyn.

Playing up his injury gave him an advantage when there weren't many to be had.

Robinson pushed Amber out the door, and the look of horror on her face would keep Rylan awake at night if his plan failed. It would be the last time he saw her if he didn't play his cards right.

The minute Robinson got Amber into the stairwell, Rylan jumped into action. He moved stealth-like toward the window behind the kitchen sink. He opened it, climbed on top of the counter and slipped out.

Hanging on to the outside of the window, he was able to cut some of the distance to the ground. He'd landed behind the offices. Damn, the sun was coming up, and that meant Lonnie and the ranch hands would be out on the property.

Where was Will?

Fire shot through him at the possibility that anything had happened to his friend. No, that wasn't possible. Rylan and Amber would've heard something. Robinson must've hid in the shadows and waited.

Blood dripped from his left wrist where the bullet had grazed him. Even one-handed he could take down Robinson.

Rylan moved along the shrubbery line at a healthy clip until he saw movement. Robinson had Amber's elbow in his grip. Seeing that shot more fire through Rylan.

He dropped and crouched low so he'd stay below Robinson's line of sight through the brush. He caught his first break when he saw that Robinson was walking Amber toward Rylan's position. The man was a hothead and not a career criminal. All Rylan had to do was exercise patience and wait for the man to slip up.

With a useless left hand, Rylan would have to rely on his right. It wasn't his dominant hand anyway, but one hand down wasn't ideal in any fight. He didn't doubt his skills. Emotions had gotten the best of him in the apartment. How could they not? It was Amber and his child, a child he didn't know about last week and now couldn't imagine living without. The little bean had wiggled her way into his heart.

Steady, Rylan controlled his burst of adrenaline. Part of it came from the pain in his left wrist and the other part was due to the circumstance unfolding. He couldn't allow himself to consider any other outcome than a successful mission. And yet his heart was engaged. It was too late for going all-logic and no-emotion. Which was funny because Rylan had never been one to get caught up in emotion.

Guess he was a changed man now that he could see a future. And his future involved Amber and the baby in her arms, if Amber would have him.

He'd work double time to make up for the loss of Alicia in Brooklyn's life.

Robinson drew near and Rylan caught his second break. The man's nerves were getting to him. It was possible he'd never shot anyone before. Although, he'd admitted to killing Alicia. Was that big talk for a small man?

Rylan had no doubt that Alicia was gone, but one of Robinson's henchmen might've done it. Most people who'd actually taken another life found no need to brag about it.

As the increasingly nervous man looked from side to side, he let the gun barrel point away from Amber.

In a split second, Rylan leaped out of the brush and tackled Robinson before the man's brain could send a message to his finger to pull the trigger.

Rylan disarmed Robinson with ease, knocking the gun loose and causing it to tumble a few feet away onto the grass. It fired and he heard Amber scream.

"Take Brooklyn away from here," Rylan said to Amber. He wanted both of them as far away as possible.

Engaging in death rolls to disorient Robinson, Rylan stopped when he was on top of the older man and squeezed his arms to his sides with the force of his thighs. He might've been one wrist down, but his legs were far more powerful.

Robinson tried to buck, but Rylan just smiled down at the man.

Amber was already shouting for help.

"You're going to spend the rest of your pitiful life behind bars. You're going to make new friends with that winning personality of yours. And if one of your henchmen so much as drives through this county, he won't drive back out alive. Are we clear?" Rylan reared a fist back and punched the jerk who'd killed the mother of Rylan's child and had almost killed the love of his life.

When he looked up at Amber, he saw her handing over the baby to her cousin Amy. And then he saw a red dot flowering on Amber's shirt. What? When?

The next few moments moved as though in slow motion. A security team descended on the scene in less than a minute. Isaac pressed his knee into Robinson's back as he zip-cuffed him.

Rylan flew to Amber the second Robinson had been secured.

Nothing in Rylan's life made sense without Amber. He dropped to her side on the green turf.

"Don't you leave me," he said to her. "I love you, Amber. I *need* you." Rogue tears broke free and fell from his eyes. "Please, stay with me."

Her eyes fluttered and a ghost of a smile crossed her purple lips. She was losing a lot of blood. He pulled up her T-shirt and saw a bullet wound the size of his fist where the bullet exited. Rylan wasn't a religious man, but he cupped her face in his hands and said a protection prayer that he'd learned as a kid.

He vaguely heard crying in the background along with shouting.

"Come on, Amber."

When she didn't respond, he took off his own shirt, balled it up using his good hand and gently pressed it into her wound to try to stem the bleeding.

"I need an ambulance," he shouted as the shirt was almost immediately soaked.

Rylan couldn't be sure how long it took for the EMTs to arrive on the scene. Time slowed to a standstill as Amber lay on the grass. She had a pulse, but her breathing was shallow.

And his heart nearly stopped beating in his chest.

The EMTs went to work immediately, giving Amber oxygen. They put pressure on the wound and stabilized her enough for her to be transported to County General, which was a twenty-minute drive.

On the way, Will instructed Rylan to pull a shirt out of the gym bag in the back seat. Rylan did as instructed. Pulling it over his head with one hand was tricky, but he managed.

The ambulance driver made it in half that time as Rylan followed. Will had practically dragged him to his vehicle. And then he'd chased that ambulance all the way to the hospital.

Will offered reassurances along the way, but the words were as hollow as the space in Rylan's chest. He pulled into the ambulance bay at the ER. "Go. I'll park and be right up."

"Thank you." Rylan tore out of the passenger seat and was next to the EMT as he brought Amber's gurney out the back of the ambulance.

Lights blared, twisting together as Rylan followed

Amber inside. A team waited for her, and he figured that wasn't a good sign under the circumstances.

"Sir, are you hurt?" The intake nurse seemed to notice the blood all over his arm and wrist. Some belonged to Amber and some was his own. The nurse's gaze landed on his wrist as he favored it. No amount of pain could distract him from why he was really there.

"I'm fine. This isn't my blood."

The nurse cocked a concerned eyebrow.

"I'm Ophelia and I'd like to take a look at that wrist if you'll allow it," the nurse said.

"The only person who needs treatment is behind those doors. When can I get an update about her condition?" he asked. He was locked on to a target and nothing else mattered.

Will burst through the ER doors. "I'm with him."

"Any chance you can convince him to accept treatment on his wrist?" Ophelia asked.

"Not until he hears a positive report on my sister, Amber Kent," Will told her.

The last name seemed to register because Ophelia's eyes lit up. "Your family has been so generous to this hospital. Please, follow me."

For once in Rylan's life, he was grateful the Kents had money. He'd sign over his own life savings if it meant getting information about Amber's condition.

"She's brave, Rylan," Will said as Ophelia led them into a private lounge. There were leather chairs instead of hard wooden ones. There was a nice coffee bar off to one side and a fridge with a glass door next to it. Every popular soda was in there along with all the sparkling waters a person could drink.

"Help yourself to a drink or a snack," Ophelia said.

"I'll check with the nurse on duty and see if I can get an update for you gentlemen."

Every half hour from that point on, a nurse showed up in the waiting room to talk to Will and Rylan. After two visits, the room was filled with Kents and their spouses. Rylan learned that Brooklyn was safe on the ranch with Joyce, who couldn't stop doting on the little girl. Brooklyn seemed happy as a lark in Joyce's care. She'd been there from day one for Mitch's twins and the other babies as the Kent brood grew.

Zach was the only family member missing, and he was busy arresting Mrs. Robinson for being an accomplice in Alicia's death, a death Zach had confirmed by the coroner's office. He phoned with an update that Alicia's laptop browser had searches for date-rape-type drugs like ketamine. She'd also done research on fentanyl.

Knowing that Rylan had maintained his sobriety felt hollow without Amber to talk to. He missed the sound of her voice, the feel of her skin. He missed her quick wit and even faster smile.

The light that had always been Amber might've dimmed, but in the past twenty-four hours he'd seen it return full force.

After Amber's loved ones waited an agonizing twenty-four hours and she had had three blood transfusions, a nurse walked into the waiting room. Chatter stopped and the room fell silent.

"She's in recovery and she's asking for Rylan Anderson and her brother Will," the nurse announced.

The pair had been hovering over the coffee machine, waiting for news. Rylan had allowed his wrist to be tended to an hour ago once he'd learned that Amber was out of surgery to remove bullet fragments from her hip.

Rylan took the lead and Will followed the nurse down the hall.

"The doctor will be in to speak to the family soon, but he was pleased with how the surgery went," the nurse stated. "She'll be moved into a room soon. He wants to keep her here for a few days to make sure her recovery is smooth."

The middle-aged, short redhead stopped in front of a door. "She's right in here."

Rylan wasted no time walking in, and Will was on his heels.

Amber's eyes were closed. Seeing her in that room with all the machines beeping and tubes hanging out of her gutted him.

He and Will flanked the bed, and Rylan took her hand in his.

She blinked her eyes open, locked on to Rylan and smiled.

It took another fifteen minutes for her to open her eyes again. This time, she kept them open a little longer.

"Did you mean what you said, Rylan Anderson?" she finally said. She coughed. "My throat is dry as a cactus."

Rylan couldn't help but crack a smile. He picked up a water container and helped her get the straw to her lips.

"Thank you. That's better," she said after taking a drink. "Where's the baby?"

"You gave us a scare," Will said.

"Believe me, I wasn't trying to." The smile faded too soon. "Is everyone else okay? Brooklyn is good, right?"

"Yes. The Robinsons are going to separate prisons

where at least Mr. Robinson will spend the rest of his life. Brooklyn is with Joyce, waiting for you to get better so you can hold her again," Rylan said. "And I meant what I said. I love you, Amber. I can't imagine my life without you."

Amber's eyes lit up.

"You heard that, right, Will?" she asked.

Will couldn't help but laugh. "I did."

"Then you can go," she teased.

"I'd like him to stick around if you don't mind," Rylan said, and the room fell quiet from the seriousness of his tone. "Your father was a good man. He was kind to me. I wish he was here all the time, especially now because I'd like to ask him for your hand in marriage. But if Will can step into his father's shoes for a minute, I'll ask him instead."

Will practically beamed as he looked at his sister. Her smile displayed a row of perfectly straight, perfectly white teeth. Not everything was so perfect about Amber, except that she was perfect for Rylan. "Permission granted."

Rylan bent down on one knee. He was still holding on to Amber's hand when he said, "You're my best friend and the first person I want to speak to no matter what kind of day I've had. My heart is yours, Amber. I can't imagine loving anyone more or finding a better partner to spend my life with. So, if you'll do me the honor, I'm asking you to marry me."

"It ALWAYS BEEN YOU, Rylan. Ever since that first kiss at sixteen years old I knew there was something special, something that I'd never find with another man." Tears streamed down her cheeks. "So, yes, I'll be your partner, your wife. And I promise to love you with every breath until my last."

Rylan stood up and leaned over the bed to kiss the woman he loved. He finally found where he belonged.

"What do you think about a Valentine's wedding?" Amber asked.

"That's not far off. You sure you don't want time to plan a wedding?"

"I don't want a big wedding. I want a marriage. And I can't think of a better Valentine's present than to make our family official," she said.

Those were all the words he needed to hear. "Valentine's it is."

Will moved around the side of the bed and gripped Rylan in a man hug. "You've always felt like a brother to me. Welcome to the family."

Rylan couldn't think of a better way to spend the rest of his life than with a real family, his daughter and the woman he loved.

* * * * *

IF YOU ENJOYED THIS BOOK
WE THINK YOU WILL ALSO LOVE

⬧ HARLEQUIN

INTRIGUE

Seek thrills. Solve crimes. Justice served.

Dive into action-packed stories that will keep you
on the edge of your seat. Solve the crime
and deliver justice at all costs.

6 NEW BOOKS AVAILABLE EVERY MONTH!

*Still haunted by the serial killer she couldn't catch, police
detective Bree Clark doesn't hesitate to accept
PI Ryland Beck's offer of redemption. The Smoky Mountain
Slayer cold case has gone hot again and working together
could bring the murderer to justice. But is the culprit the
original slayer—or a dangerous copycat?*

*Read on for a sneak preview of
Serial Slayer Cold Case,
part of A Tennessee Cold Case Story series,
from Lena Diaz.*

Chapter One

Maintaining a white-knuckle grip on the steering wheel while
negotiating the treacherous curves up Prescott Mountain on his
daily commute was typical for Ryland Beck. *Smiling* while he
resolutely refused to look toward the steep drop on the other
side of the road *wasn't* typical. Nothing, not even his phobia
of heights, could dampen his enthusiasm this chilly October
morning. Today he'd begin his investigation into a serial killer
case that had gone cold over four years ago.

Bringing down the Smoky Mountain Slayer was the challenge
of a lifetime. No suspects. No DNA. No viable behavioral
profile. In spite of the lack of evidence, Ryland was determined
to put the killer behind bars. He wanted to give the families of
the five victims the answers and justice they deserved.

Unfortunately, what he couldn't give them was closure.
Closure, as he well knew, was a fictional construct. The death of

a loved one would always leave a gaping hole in the hearts and lives of those left behind. But knowing the victim's murderer had been caught and punished would go a long way toward making the excruciating grief more bearable.

He continued winding his way up the mountain toward UB headquarters as he considered the limited information he'd found on the internet about the killings. The Slayer's modus operandi was consistent: all of his victims were strangled, their bodies dumped in the woods in Monroe County. But aside from them being young women, the victimology was all over the place. Their educational and economic backgrounds varied, as did their ethnicity. Some were married, some weren't. Some had children, some didn't. All of that made it nearly impossible to build a useful profile to help figure out who'd murdered them.

The detectives from the Monroe County Sheriff's Office had deemed the case unsolvable. But here in Gatlinburg, Ryland had a unique advantage: an über-wealthy boss who knew firsthand the suffering a victim's family endured when a murder case went cold.

Seven years after his wife was killed and his infant daughter went missing, Grayson Prescott had given up on the stagnant police investigation. He decided to create a cold case company called Unfinished Business. Just a few months later, UB had solved the case. Now, the thirty-three counties of the East Tennessee region had formed a partnership with UB and were clamoring for them to work their cold cases.

Don't miss
Serial Slayer Cold Case *by Lena Diaz,*
available March 2022 wherever
Harlequin books and ebooks are sold.

Harlequin.com

Love Harlequin romance?

DISCOVER.

Be the first to find out about promotions, news and exclusive content!

Facebook.com/HarlequinBooks

Twitter.com/HarlequinBooks

Instagram.com/HarlequinBooks

Pinterest.com/HarlequinBooks

YouTube.com/HarlequinBooks

ReaderService.com

EXPLORE.

Sign up for the Harlequin e-newsletter and download a free book from any series at **TryHarlequin.com**

CONNECT.

Join our Harlequin community to share your thoughts and connect with other romance readers!
Facebook.com/groups/HarlequinConnection

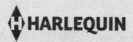

HARLEQUIN

Heartfelt or thrilling, passionate or uplifting—Harlequin is more than just happily-ever-after.

With twelve different series to choose from and new books available every month, you are sure to find stories that will move you, uplift you, inspire and delight you.